# Drawing on the Past

by

Cynthia Raleigh

Copyright © 2017 by Cynthia Raleigh. All Rights Reserved

No part of this publication may be reproduced, distributed, or transmitted in any form or by any means, including photocopying, recording, or other electronic or mechanical methods, without the prior written permission of the publisher, except in the case of brief quotations embodied in critical reviews and certain other noncommercial uses permitted by copyright law. For permission requests, write to craleigh@cynthiaraleigh.com.

This is a work of fiction. Historical figures and events are mentioned throughout the book, but the characters particular to this series are wholly imaginary and do not represent real persons, living or dead.

Cover art by Colin Lawson
Cover photography © Cynthia Raleigh

Drawing on the Past / Cynthia Raleigh: First Edition
Also available on Kindle and other devices
Paperback: ISBN-13: 978-1548773380, ISBN-10: 1548773387

## Chapter 1

May 29, 1819, 9:20 a.m.

Samuel had been sitting on top of the small outcropping of rock for at least a couple of hours. It was late morning and the May sunshine was finally warming the air enough to encourage small flying insects to buzz and hum around his head. The broad river flowed majestically through the countryside. From his elevated position, he could see it forming silty arcs in one direction and then another as it progressed into the distance like a brown sidewinder. For as far as Samuel's eyes could see, the trees of the dense forest fought for position at the bank, clinging to the rich bottom land right up to the water lapping at the shore, with only a few gaps where swaths of cane grass grew from the marshy ground. Here and there along the river, a sand bar or small island broke the current of the water as it parted momentarily then rejoined as it passed the obstruction.

He felt himself being lulled into slumber by the peacefulness and the golden light glinting off the tall grasses around him. A spider's web, stretched between two stalks, still clung to a few beads of dew. The soaring screams from a pair of red-shouldered hawks above him broke the silence. He shook his head to wake himself and refocused on the scene. After passing the previous night in the cave, or "the House of Nature" as Major Long called it, the party was planning to set out again before noon. Two pencil drawings of the cave entrance, outlines he would flesh out with watercolor later, were completed and safely tucked away in his portfolio with the other landscapes and drawings he had done so far, but he needed to finish this drawing of the river and its course before it was time to board. He had allowed himself to be distracted by the lilting music of the birds, the darting dragonflies, rabbits stealthily hopping through the brush, and other sights of the small cliff-top meadow.

The crew of the steam-powered boat spent the early morning hours adjusting the stern paddle and rechecking the engine to make sure it was in working order. The day before it had stalled as they passed the mouth of the Wabash and they were forced to drift down river until they could find a place to land for repairs. The engine had been repaired at Shawneetown and, after loading up with a couple barrels of salt from the nearby salt works, they had relaunched and continued their trek.

As Samuel added a few more peripheral details to the drawing, he heard shouts rising from below the cliff. He pocketed his pencils and pulled a thick piece of parchment over the drawing fastened to his portable drawing board. He set it atop the stone and walked gingerly toward the edge to see what was happening. He ventured no closer than a couple of feet from the edge and carefully leant forward to peer to the shore below. On the narrow, rocky beachline in front of the cave, he saw Edwin waving his arms and shouting. When he saw Samuel peering over the edge, he motioned excitedly for him to come down. He couldn't understand most of what Edwin was yelling, but he did make out, *"Hurry!"* being repeated multiple times.

Samuel turned and ran, scooping up his drawing board as he sped by the rock where it lay. He didn't know what the problem was, but in this still largely untamed territory, he did know you didn't stop to find out first. Even though he was just above the site where the boat was docked, the terrain back to the bank was mostly steep and rocky ground. In his haste, he overshot where he had ascended to the meadow and had to back track. He started downward and his feet flew out from beneath him almost immediately, sending him bouncing and scuffling down a yard or more on the stones sticking out of the ground. He momentarily panicked that he would go tumbling head first so he tucked his board under his left arm and resumed his descent facing the hillside, grabbing onto roots and rocks to steady himself.

When he finally skidded out onto the tiny landing area, moist dirt was smeared into the knees of his trousers and scuffs raked down the sides of his shoes. Mr. James was impatiently waiting near the gangplank. "Come. Now, Samuel! We must leave instantly."

"Of course, Edwin, I'll quickly retrieve my portfolio from the cave."

"No, no time, now!" Edwin seized Samuel's arm and tugged him toward the boat. Samuel saw the other party members and crew on deck, nervously watching. Some were hissing to him to get a move on and get aboard.

Samuel pointed toward the cave and attempted to turn, "But I can't leave my drawings, I have my…"

Edwin yanked, hard, on Samuel's arm. He hadn't been ready for it so had offered no resistance. His head snapped back and he stumbled as he was dragged up the ramp. Samuel's other arm was firmly gripped by the outstretched hand of a crew member as he neared the edge of the boat. The outward movement of his arm loosened his hold on his drawing board. It fell, landing on its corner, the fine wood made a soft crunching noise. It seemed to hover for a split second, suspended, balanced on one corner on the ramp, before it toppled into the gurgling waves of the river as they slapped the stones of the shoreline. "No, wait!" He struggled, looking over his shoulder as the case sank to the bottom of the shallows but still in view, resting on the smooth pebbles of the river bed. The two men lifted Samuel off his feet and almost tossed him onto the deck as the boat was already pulling away from the bank. The ramp was immediately withdrawn by two other crew members, their well-muscled arms expertly heaving against the ropes.

Samuel plunged halfway across the width of the deck flailing his arms and stumbling, bent-kneed, trying to keep his balance. Regaining his composure, he tugged his rumpled vest and coat, his face warm with embarrassment, then turned around with a retort ready on his lips. But no one was looking at Samuel.

Edwin was leaning forward, his hands on his knees, breathing hard. His face was flushed. From his bent position, he squinted his eyes, the skin around them crinkling into furrows, and ran his gaze over the shadowed landscape as it retreated, the gloomy darkness of the cavemouth gaped in silent entreaty at their exit. He turned to Samuel, still breathing heavier than normal and shaking his head in apology, "We were about to be ambushed and you had no time to go back into the cave. I'm sorry. It was leave the portfolio or leave you there." He paused for another couple of deep breaths. "Or risk some of us being killed to save you."

Samuel sat down on one of the wooden benches bolted to the deck. "Save me? Save me from what?"

Several crew members, armed with rifles, stood at the railing nearest the shore, watching. Edwin jerked his thumb toward a man sitting in the stern. "Barrett was out scouting around for any animals in the area." Samuel looked over at Barrett who was resting against the rail while watching the shoreline. The tall, rangy man, obviously still a little winded, was included in the company to document the wildlife along the river.

Edwin continued, "He'd been sitting in a copse of trees with a view of a stream. He'd seen a herd of deer, some small animals, I don't know. He was just about ready to stand up and move a little further inland when he heard movement. A lot of movement."

Samuel felt a flush of warmth travel over his face with the suspicion that they had, indeed, just escaped real trouble.

"Barrett kept still and watched. Seven men on horseback ambled out of the woods, they all had rifles. They dismounted and let their horses drink. Barrett says they were passing around a flask, drinking, and talking."

Samuel swallowed. He had been prepared for the news that a couple of bears had issued forth from the depths of the woods, not men on horseback. With dreadful curiosity, Samuel asked, "What were they talking about?"

Edwin replied, "Us."

"Us?"

"They're nothing but a band of cutthroats, a gang of thieves. They keep lookouts along the shoreline above and below the cave. It's a natural place to tie up on a journey, and when someone does, the lookout sends word to the others. If they miss you here, they get you downriver. We'll need to stay away from the islands or the banks for a while."

Edwin reached inside his coarse linen vest for his flask and took a swallow. "This area's been thick with robbers and murderers in the past, but I thought it was cleared up now. Evidently, there's a new group of criminals in the cave area.

This'll need to be reported when we land at a larger town where we can send word to … someone in authority." He shook his head as if to dismiss the thought, "Well, that's Major Long's job, not ours." Edwin looked over to the cabin where Major Long and the captain bent their heads together in discussion.

Samuel's face fell as he recalled that the portfolio and drawing supplies he had taken ashore with him were gone, and along with it the five completed drawings he had left in the rear chamber of the cave while he was out in the meadow. He was relieved, though, that all the other drawings done previously, and the bulk of his artist supplies, were stowed in his locker, safely on board. "Thank the powers that be that I didn't take my entire pack with me into that cave last night, or I'd have nothing to show for the trip so far."

Edwin nodded in understanding and added, "I'm fortunate I only took my pocket sketchbook with me and I had it on me at the time the warning came." Edwin was included on the trip to document the flora of the Ohio and Mississippi rivers.

As the tip of Hurricane Island came into view, the captain called out to the crew, "Keep to the north side of the channel." He pointed at two men, "You two watch the bank of the island," then pointed at three others, "and you keep your eyes on the shoreline. They can't keep up with us, but we don't want them taking shots at us. Make sure fire power is at the ready on both sides and the front." He strode back into the pilothouse

Samuel pivoted on his bench and squinted at the retreating shoreline at the mouth of the cave. He saw several men ride their horses into the shallows from where they had just departed. He continued watching them watch the boat as it deftly skimmed along the water, maneuvering around sandbars and keeping well to the channel, away from Hurricane Island.

## Chapter 2

October 7, 2016, 8:45 p.m.

    The sagging field gate swung open, hovered while the wind buffeted it back and forth by fractions of an inch, then slammed back against the post. The sound carried across the hilltop in the otherwise peaceful night air. The aging, weathered gate no longer latched automatically, so the gate opened again with the next gust of wind.
    Every light in the Duncan house was off. It was dark except for the beam of a flashlight, dimmed by a t-shirt slipped over the end and held on with a rubber band. It lent an eerie red cast to the light, like a bloody orb sweeping across the floor and hovering around the baseboards. Floorboards creaked under slowly advancing footfalls along the upstairs hallway then turning into a bedroom.
    The circle of light, dipping below the sill when it came to a window, raked steadily back and forth. The closet door was opened and all the contents examined. Lids were tossed from shoeboxes and storage containers on a shelf into a pile on the floor. Hangers were emptied of their garments and the shoes and slippers neatly lined up in rows on the closet floor were kicked into the room and the interior walls and ceiling examined. The light brushed along each side of the bedroom, locating another doorway to a connecting bedroom. The same procedure was repeated and eventually the light moved back to the hallway.
    At the end of the hall, it stopped outside a narrow door with an oval brass doorknob, the surrounding plate decorated with a tarnished art deco design. The hardware rattled in its setting as the

knob turned loosely and the door was pulled open. Stairs to the attic rose abruptly and steeply inside the doorway. The reddish oval bobbed upward during the slow and careful ascent.

The windows in the attic were small and covered with tired, ragged lace curtains hanging limply from dingy white café rods that sagged in the middle in spite of their short length. Probably moved to the attic after life elsewhere in the house. A muffled cry from the second floor of the house reached the attic but was not repeated.

The attic space was full of the typical detritus: boxes, chests, old furniture, and miscellaneous junk. The bare wood slat floor was rubbed smooth and the supporting beams were darkened with age. Motes of dust disturbed by footsteps rose in clouds, suspended in the beam of light. A rapid intake of breath broke the silence when the flashlight momentarily cut across a torso only a few feet away and was quickly jerked back to illuminate a dressmaker's form wearing a muslin, sleeves pinned at the shoulders, awaiting the finishing it would never see. The beam moved back to a slow sweep of the room. After a hesitation, the methodical search began, beginning with a humpbacked trunk in a far corner. A large drawstring bag was deposited on the floor near the trunk, waiting.

At least two hours later, all the boxes had been opened, trunks searched, furniture shoved aside, and the floor and walls scrutinized. The brown velvet upholstery of a 1920s-era chair, rubbed bare in patches, had been slashed open, the antimacassar hung askew. An old iron umbrella stand containing an assortment of wallpaper remnants was knocked over, each of the rolls unwound a few feet, then tossed aside. Other types of papers were scattered about the floor: old sheet music, photo albums, bound journals, school assignments with good marks, and bundles of long forgotten business records, the last couple inches of the black silk ribbons frayed and decaying into shreds

The attic now abandoned, the door gaped open as it had been left. The light currently turned its attention to the dry, crumbly cellar walls. Boxes, some mildewed on the bottom and up the sides, had been opened and the contents shuffled about, then either left where they sat or pushed aside to get at the boxes below them.

Removal of a stack of soft drink crates revealed a crude, home-made plank door about four feet in height situated just off center in an otherwise unremarkable wall. The boards displayed at least four different layers of chipped paint. The door was tugged open, revealing the old coal room. Every inch of the floor and walls was covered in black coal residue, greasy looking from many years' worth of loads of coal being shoveled in through an opening covered by an iron plate and latched on the inside with a rusty hook. The light slid over the glistening remains of its former content, finding nothing of interest. A cross-trainer-shod foot savagely kicked a lump of coal which shattered against the outer stone wall, the falling pieces imitated the tinkling sound of broken glass. A black smudge remained on the toe of the shoe.

Back in the main room of the cellar, the beam of light hesitated in response to a loud thump from upstairs before continuing to peer into and investigate boxes, barrels, cans, jars, and every possible hidey-hole. A hubcap for a 1950's Bel Air went skittering and banging along the packed dirt floor of the cellar, having been drop-kicked in frustration. The shelves over the work bench were lined with work boot boxes, but they were filled with oddball auto parts, fuses, wax pencils, and hundreds of nails, bolts, screws, washers, and one that was jammed with unidentifiable metal contraptions, all coated with a layer of gritty oil. The lower walls of the basement were stone which gave way to brick just below the level of the first floor. A hulking oil-burner occupied one entire quarter of the cellar. There were no other discernable openings other than the coal room.

A final round of the cellar didn't turn up any undiscovered compartments or loose bricks hiding a niche in the wall. Coal-smudged trainers climbed the stairway back to the main floor. All the blinds were pulled and the doors closed. Hesitation, the rasping sound of breathing through an open mouth, listening, the light forming an oblong beige puddle on the area rug in the living room. The bearer of the flashlight arrived at a decision and moved purposefully down the hallway to the laundry room.

\*\*\*

Friday, October 7, 11:45 p.m.

"For Pete's sake, Lou, I've been listening to the Duncan's gate bang around for three hours. Get up and go close it since they obviously don't hear it."

"Go back to sleep, Millie."

Millie sat up in bed. Her salon-assisted ash blonde hair pressed flat against the side of her head. "I can't sleep with that racket going on! I can't imagine why they don't go out and close that thing." She waited, watching Lou, who had drifted back to sleep. She shoved two fingers into his ribcage, "Go shut it! I can't sleep."

Lou grunted and threw back the covers. He lumbered out of bed, sighing heavily, knowing the only way to get back to sleep was to go close the gate. "Alright, alright," he mumbled as he pulled his grass-stained Carhartt work pants on over his pajama bottoms. Stopping at the back door, Lou lifted his jacket with a Cargill agricultural co-op patch over the pocket from a hook, sleepily rammed his feet into a pair of old shoes, and tugged his Naab Seeds hat on over his mostly bald head. The back edge of the shoes crumpled under his heels so he had to sit down at the kitchen table to pull them on since they would probably fall off halfway across the field. He blinked a few times and was tempted to keep his eyes closed, but slapped his palms on his knees and grunted again.

A small pasture separated the backyards of the two neighbors. The offending gate was just on the other side of the one-acre field that was sometimes used for a garden, sometimes left fallow, sometimes used to contain livestock temporarily. The Duncans and the Vincents shared the ground, depending on who needed it, and had done for so many years that neither neighbor remembered the actual location of the property line. The land had all belonged to one owner in the past but was divided when the Vincent's house was built in 1952. The unlatched gate opened from the shared field into the back yard of the Duncan house, the original house to the property.

It wasn't like Ruby or George to leave it unlatched, or to let it slam away during the night. Maybe they weren't home, Lou mused as he trudged across the stubbly terrain, the wind coming off the river whipping the corners of his jacket open. He grabbed the gate just as it was fixing to slam shut again. Reaching over the top, he looped the piece of baling wire around the post to secure it. Lou acted unconcerned to Millie, but it did seem strange for the Duncans to be oblivious to the gate and for there to be no lights on in the house all the previous evening even though their car was still in the carport at the side of the house. It was there because he could see the glint of moonlight off the chrome bumper.

He considered knocking on the back door to make sure everything was ok, but after casting another glance at the house, he turned back toward home and his bed. As he latched the gate of his own backyard, he thought he saw the briefest flash of headlights in the road in front of the Duncan house, but they moved on down the street, out of sight.

Chapter 3

October 8, 2016, 9:12 a.m.

"It should be that way." Reuben squinted into the morning sun toward the heavily wooded area that ran along the south bank of the Saline River southeast of Equality. "That may be the path." He pointed to the faintly discernable trail which began just a few feet off Salt Well Road and progressed through the scrubby grass, plantain, and weeds until it disappeared into the trees about one hundred feet off the road.

Carmen leaned over the creased map Reuben held in his other hand, scrutinized it, then assessed the lightly-worn track. "Yeah. I think so too. This would be about the right spot for the old salt well. Let's try it." She hefted her backpack into place and plunged ahead onto the path.

Her rapid exit startled Reuben from his reverie. "Hang on." He gathered his pack and hustled to follow Carmen, who was already halfway to the tree line. "Wait up. It's been there for over two hundred years, it isn't going anywhere in the next half hour."

"No, I know that, but I've wanted to see this for a long time." Carmen's boots snapped dry twigs and rustled last season's brittle leaves as she entered the woods. "Keep up, old boy, keep up."

"Hey!" Reuben jogged over the scraggy grass to catch up with her, smiling good-naturedly. "If I didn't know your sense of humor, I'd be upset by that remark."

Carmen called over her shoulder, "But you do, so you aren't." After skirting a group of huge old hickory trees, she asked, "When did you say this place started salt production?"

Reuben ducked under a hanging grapevine as thick as his wrist hanging across the path. "Well, the French settlers were obtaining salt from this area back as far as 1735 and the Native Americans had been getting it long before that. It was in 1803 that the local tribe ceded the salt spring to the US government via a treaty. Extracting salt from the underground salt water here continued for decades."

"And you say that one of the wells is still here, with salt water still in it?" Carmen swatted small branches out of her face as she walked the path.

"Yes, there is supposed to be anyway. I'm hoping it is clear enough to see a few feet down into it, but with the rain we've had, it may have gotten stirred up. I see there are some leaves down and that might make it murky too if the tannin is leaching into the water."

"How far down does it go?"

"I'm not sure. Various people have lowered cameras into the well, but even when the water is clear, there are a lot of obstructions the farther down you go. Limbs, structural beams that have come loose, old tools, even trash people have tossed into the well over the years."

"Why do people do that? Makes me mad. They can't throw their garbage away where it should go but don't mind coming all the way out here to dump it?"

"I don't understand it either. They probably wouldn't like it if someone dumped trash in their yard."

"No, they'd squeal like stuck pigs." Carmen laughed. "It should be right … there it is!"

Carmen and Reuben came into a small clearing. Smack in the middle was a rectangular wooden-framed well. The ghostly gray planks and beams of wood were worn and lined with deep tracks of erosion from the elements. No other remnant of the huge salt works and its production was visible here.

About six feet of a lichen-covered tree branch jutted up from the water, extending over the edge at a forty-five-degree angle. Reuben placed his pack and Nikon camera on the ground and stepped over to the edge of the well. "I'll get this branch out and then we can clear the leaves from the surface. I'm hoping I can get some decent photographs."

He grasped the end of the fallen branch and tugged, expecting it to easily come out of the well, but it didn't budge. Reuben's hands slipped over the bark, breaking off pieces which fell like confetti onto the framework and ground. "Ouch! Well, there's my first splinter. This is why I pack gloves. Should have had them on." He unzipped the largest outer pocket on his pack and retrieved a pair of Kevlar gloves. After slipping them on and fastening the Velcro, he grabbed the branch with both hands and pulled harder. The exposed narrow end of the branch, which had been long dead by the time it fell, was so dry and brittle that it snapped off in his hands.

Carmen spoke up. "It must be stuck on something inside. Why don't we go ahead and get these leaves off and see if we can find out what it's hanging on?"

Reuben nodded, and as Carmen began scooping leaves off the surface of the salty water, he said, "Aren't there a lot of leaves in the well compared with what's on the ground. It's early October and not that many leaves have fallen, except what came down with the rain a couple days ago."

Carmen looked around at the surrounding woods and nodded slowly. "And the top layer of leaves in the well are brown and crumbling, not newly fallen."

"Right, these look like last year's leaves," Reuben glanced around the tiny clearing. "like someone piled them in the well."

"Maybe someone dumped trash in here and wanted to cover it up?"

"It's possible but I don't know why they'd do that." Reuben continued pulling out leaves. "Let's have a look."

Carmen and Reuben worked to clear the top of the well. After removing the top layer of dry leaves, they used small branches to skim the sodden bottom layer of leaves from the center to the edge then lifted the dripping mass out and plopped it on the ground.

Once the surface was relatively free of leaves, Carmen leaned over the edge and looked down into the water. "Yep. It's pretty murky. I can only see a few inches down." Craning her neck, she looked up at the small break in the canopy. "If the sun were overhead it might illuminate the depth a little more. Or it might just create a glare off the surface. There are a lot of particles floating around. It'll be a while before the sun is directly overhead." Glancing at her watch, she said, "It's only 9:30 now."

Reuben nodded in silent agreement, thinking. Carmen watched him rummage through his knapsack. The contents surrendered a headlamp that he situated on his head and secured by tightening the elasticized band. He flicked on an intense white light and peered into the well. "That reflects. Too much glare. Let's try a couple of filters and see if it helps." Reuben reached up to the headlamp and pressed a button twice, changing the white light to green. "Hmm, still no good."

He used both hands to hold one button and press another. Carmen chuckled and remarked, "That a secret decoder headlamp?"

"Uh huh." The magenta filter activated. "A bit bright." Reuben reached up again and held a button on the side to dim the light to the level he wanted. "Now let's see."

"Where did you get that?" Carmen asked, impressed.

Reuben tilted his head back to keep the light out of Carmen's eyes. "Bought it online. I do a lot of walking around in ruins and rubble, sometimes at night…"

"Why would you do that at night? It isn't tough enough during the day?" Carmen interjected, shaking her head.

Reuben stared at her, considering his answer, then said, "Let's just say sometimes it is more advantageous to engage in my wanderings under cover of night." He gave her a devilish grin.

"Ah. I see. Big change from a stuffy classroom. Quite the cloak-and-dagger explorer now, aren't you?"

"That's me alright. And this is waterproof, so if, or rather when, I drop it into a puddle or fall in a pond, it won't be ruined." As Reuben spoke, he shone the light into the sienna-tinged water, tilting his head to angle the beam in different directions.

"Ok, I can see a few feet down. Lots of suspended particles in the water from us disturbing it." He rounded the corner of the old salt well to the side where Carmen stood.

Carmen squinted through water illuminated by the red light and pointed, "Looks like the end of the branch is jammed in between a couple of the wooden beams used to line the well."

"It hit just right with enough force to lodge between the decaying beams." Reuben's head bobbed up and down as he trained the light on different areas. "There's something light-colored, looks like yellow, pinned down under the limb, probably trash, but I can't tell because there is a cluster of dead leaves still clinging to one of the smaller branches coming off the limb and it's covering it."

"What do you want me to do to help?" Carmen asked as she walked around to the opposite side of the well and leaned on the edge, her forearms pressing against the rough channels in the wood, fingers trailing in the water. Her arms and face were deeply tanned, her hair sun-lightened, and freckles were casually sprinkled across her cheeks and nose."

"Let's try to dislodge it. Maybe you can move it around a bit, gently. Or we can use something to break it off close to the wall of the well."

"Ok."

Reuben said, "Take hold of it as far down as you can without leaning too far over the edge."

Carmen braced her knees against the ages-old wood and reached into the well. "Here g…ahhhh!"

Reuben threw his head back in alarm. Carmen had leapt away from the well, her hands flying around and swatting at the air as though shooing off a swarm of bees. "What? What's wrong? What's happening?" He ran clumsily around the well, his arms outstretched, head tipped back. He slipped on the blobs of saturated leaves where they had been dumping them as he rounded the corner. Once he regained his balance and reached Carmen, she was bent forward at the waist, hands on bent knees, her head tucked against her thighs. "What's wrong? Are you okay?" He could see her shoulders and back shaking and could hear a faint keening sound.

"Oh my gosh…are you hurt? What should I do?" Reuben wildly looked around on the ground in a panic, expecting to see a copperhead or some other venomous creature that he needed to identify when he heard laughter. Bewildered, he turned back to her.

Carmen straightened up. "I'm not jumpy at all, am I?" She continued laughing as a tear ran down her cheek.

"What happened?" Reuben felt the warmth of relief weakening his arms and legs.

"It was a toad."

"A toad?"

"Yeah, just a little toad. It startled me. It came out of nowhere, was probably hiding in the leaf cover on the ground and I disturbed it. It smacked right into my cheek and I totally lost it."

Reuben slumped out of his fighting posture, "Well, you unnerved me, that's for sure."

"Oh, Reuben. The look on your face was worth the toad collision." He turned and headed back around the well. "I'm sorry, I'm sorry, but oh, that light on your head and you were sliding around in the leaves…" She could see that Reuben was not as amused as she was. "Think how funny this will be later."

"Mmm."

"Alright, serious again. Promise." She couldn't keep a few small noises from escaping her throat as she tried not to laugh. Carmen gently raised and lowered the branch a couple of inches. "It feels pretty brittle. It's dried completely through where it's jutting out of the water but maybe the part under the water has absorbed enough water to be a little more pliable."

Reuben tipped his head down and looked at her over the top of his glasses, the light nearly shining in her eyes. "Am I correct in assuming you are not hampered by a concern of more toad attacks?"

Carmen assumed a contrite tone to assuage Reuben's hurt pride. "Not in the well. It's salt water. But there are probably a lot of frogs and toads around with the river so close, and plenty of streams."

She stretched her torso out further over the edge, this time balancing her weight on her abdomen. Reaching down into the water as far as she could, she took hold of the submerged limb. "Let's see how this feels." She repeated the motion. "A little more stable." She rocked the limb up and down trying to free it.

"Ok, keep it up, I can see some pieces of moss floating up through the water where they are being scraped off, so it's moving. There are some bubbles rising up too. You must've dislodged whatever's beneath it. Probably trapped air from whatever was hoisted in here."

On a downward motion, Carmen felt the resistance suddenly disappear and her arms plunged under the water. She caught herself before falling in, but not until her shoulders, neck, the lower half of her face were submerged. She scrambled back out, spewing salty water from her mouth. Rivulets streamed from her fingertips as she held her arms away from her body. "Don't even!"

Carmen watched Reuben struggle to keep from laughing. He let out a loud guffaw and said, "Well, it's free now!"

Carmen spit into the leaves. "I have grit in my mouth. Yuck! There's no telling what's in there. Blechhh."

Reuben's mirth subsided. "Ok, I'm sorry. That had to be unpleasant. If you are cold, we can go back to the car."

"No, I'm good. Let's get this out of here."

The stubborn limb scraped its way up the side as they both pulled on it. The smaller branches caught at the sides of the well and flicked the briny water in their faces as they broke the surface. The stump of the branch finally dragged over the edge and fell to the ground with a sodden thump.

"Glad that's out." Reuben nodded to the trees, "Let's drag it into the trees so we don't trip on it."

As they carried the limb into the underbrush, Carmen commented, "I guess we freed up whatever is in there. I just heard something in the water."

Depositing the branch in the leafy undergrowth, Reuben said, "Let's see." They turned and waked back to the well but stopped a few feet away from the edge.

It took several seconds for the image to register with either of them. They stood, stock still, eyes locked on what they'd brought up from within the old salt water well.

Carmen's head was shaking back and forth, the word 'no' forming on her lips but not escaping. She reached for Reuben's arm and squeezed it painfully with both hands. He loosened her grip and said, "Stay right there."

Carmen couldn't look away. She couldn't see all the way over the edge of the well, and was glad of it. It was enough to know that it was a pair of human hands bobbing up and down at the surface.

Reuben looked down into the well and caught his breath. He glanced back at Carmen's stricken face. Her freckles stood out like they were made by a felt tip marker on a white sheet. She edged up to stand beside him.

"Oh. Oh god."

"Hold on, ok? I'll, uh, check…"

"Check what? I'm thinkin' they're dead, Reuben."

"Yes, I know that," Reuben hissed. "I mean, I want to have a look."

"A look at…?" Carmen let the question hang.

"I don't know, I just want to make sure there aren't more than two, or if it is two men, a man and a woman. You know, so I have something to tell when I call the police."

"This isn't enough for you to tell?" Carmen clutched at Reuben's jacket sleeve as they slowly advanced the rest of the way to the edge of the well and looked down.

"Uhhh." Carmen tightened her grip on Reuben's arm.

Reuben gently loosened her fingers. "Before you cut off my circulation."

"Sorry. They didn't gag and tie themselves up and climb in there, that's for sure."

Reuben nodded toward his pack which sat against the well at the far corner. "We need to go. I have to get my stuff. Stay right here."

Carmen stood, strangely fascinated by the bloated face of a woman, a few strands of long gray hair plastered across her face where it was exposed to the air. Other wisps moved through the water around her head. The milky corneas nearly concealed the blue of her eyes which sightlessly gazed at the brilliant autumn sky. There was another body, mostly still submerged, the rope binding them together, back to back. The rope wrapped across the woman's neck, chest, and abdomen. She wore a yellow apron with white piping, the style that went over her head and tied at the waist. Beneath it, the rolled-up sleeves of her dress exposed her ample arms. The bluish-white flesh would have looked like marble had it not been for the bruises, both on her face and neck, and on her arms. Her teeth were bared over the tight red and black material used for a gag, like she had been trying to chew her way through it. Carmen shivered, both from horror and the chill of standing wet in the shade in October.

Carmen was pretty sure the other body was that of a man, it seemed most likely they were a couple. A torn strip of the plaid flannel from his sleeve floated atop the water near the woman's elbow. Carmen realized with a shudder that this was the material used for the woman's gag. The man's hand jutted out at an awkward angle, all the fingers extended and frozen in a clutching position.

She felt a little unsteady and turned her head away from the bodies which now slowly rotated in the tannin-tinted brine, no longer pinned beneath the water. She realized that, even though the well water was saline, which would interfere with decomposition somewhat, the bodies couldn't have been there very long. The forest suddenly took on a more ominous atmosphere, even though nothing else had changed. She and Reuben had been here over an hour and everything was quiet. It was still the sunny, crisp day it had been, but finding two newly murdered bodies trussed up and stuffed in an abandoned well did tend to spoil the idyllic woodland peace.

Reuben hastily retraced his steps across the clearing with his camera around his neck and the pack on his back. His phone was in his hand. He took Carmen's elbow, "Let's go back to the car. You need to get warm. I have a blanket in the trunk. I'll call 911 from there. I certainly don't want to stand out here like this."

"Sounds like a good idea. Surely the person who did this isn't still hanging around, but…"

"Yeah, it's that 'but' that worries me."

They hustled back up the path to the road. As they reached the safety of Reuben's car, Carmen realized she'd been holding her breath and now it came in short gulps. She hopped into her seat as Reuben slung his pack and camera in the back, then got in the driver's seat. The door locks clicked and Carmen laid her head back on the headrest, breathing in through her nose and out through her mouth, still clutching her bag. She cracked one eyelid open and peeked at Reuben. "Did I hear your camera back at the well? Did you take a photo?"

"It was already out of the case. I was putting it back in the case when I figured one photo might be a good idea. I don't know why."

Carmen didn't respond to that. "You gonna call?"

Reuben took a deep breath and sighed, "Yeah." He dialed 911.

*\*\**

Saturday, October 8, 4:50 p.m.

"I know this is very upsetting, Mrs. Vincent, Mr. Vincent," the detective nodded to each in turn, "but we're nearly done here and I'll ask you to bear with me just a while longer." An officer clomped through the front door into the living room, mouth open ready to speak. The detective held his hand up and said, "In a moment. Wait for me outside." The officer hesitated. "Outside, Officer. Now." The policeman hastily retreated, closing the door without a sound.

Mickey Knox shifted his bony rear end on the low, soft ottoman placed in front of the Vincents who occupied the center of the sofa and leaned on each other in mutual support, Mr. Vincent's arm around his wife.

The detective sank farther down into the cushion than he expected and found himself looking slightly upward toward the couple. Rather than project a sympathetic yet professional manner, he felt like an adult sitting in a child's chair with his knobbly knees jutting out awkwardly, his pocket notebook balanced on one of them. But, he didn't want to risk a possibly embarrassing struggle to climb out of the giant footrest and shift to another seat.

Millie Vincent had thoroughly destroyed her tissue and without blinking or breaking her stare at the floor in front of her feet, she absently dragged another from the plastic canvas-covered box Lou had brought to her from the bathroom.

"I just need to verify that I have the times correct, or as accurate as we can get them." Lou Vincent's lips formed a tight, straight line as he bobbed his head to acknowledge forbearance and cooperation. "Ok. Mrs. Vincent, you said you were woken during the night, that was Friday night, by the Duncan's gate which was banging open and shut. You didn't look at the clock, not having your glasses on, but you woke Mr. Vincent who went outside to secure the gate." Millie's head automatically nodded up and down several times.

"Mr. Vincent, you went downstairs and put your shoes and jacket on and left your…"

"And my hat." Lou added in a lackluster tone.

"Yes…and your hat. You left your house by the back door, crossed your back yard and the shared field between the Duncan house and yours. When you got to the gate, you saw no lights or movement anywhere in or around the house. As you were leaving to return home, you thought you saw headlights briefly between the house and carport as a vehicle moved south down the road. When you came back in the house, you did glance at the clock on the stove and at that time it was 11:58 p.m."

Lou responded, "Yes sir. That's right."

"Have you noticed any vehicles at the Duncan house lately that you hadn't seen before? Anything out of the ordinary?"

"No. If there'd been something going on, George would've told me, I think. We spoke nearly every day, maybe just to say hi, but he would have told me if there was someone giving him grief."

"You stated that you didn't clearly see the vehicle at the Duncan's last night and couldn't determine if it was a car, truck, or an SUV and you would not be able to identify it?"

"Right. The Duncan's car was in their carport, I could see that. There's a few feet of road visible between the house and the side of the car when it's parked there, but it's only enough to get a flash of the headlights in the dark from that distance."

"You were able to determine the vehicle was traveling south, but couldn't follow it?"

Lou gave Mickey Knox a disgruntled look. "No, I couldn't follow it. The barn is in the way of the road once it gets past the carport and then you got the woods. I didn't stick around watching for it neither because I didn't have no reason to think it wasn't just somebody goin' home, did I? Friday night, people come and go, even here in Old Shawneetown, you know? Ain't my business. Or, it wasn't my business, but it'll be my business now, won't it?" Lou Vincent answered with a flash of defiance in his eyes.

"Vigilance may be a good idea, Mr. Vincent, at least until we know who is responsible for the death of your neighbors?"

Lou growled a response, nothing more. Millie gasped out a sob and stifled it with a tissue pressed across her mouth.

Detective Knox turned in agitation when he again heard the front door open. Through gritted teeth, he asked, "What is it, Officer?"

"Sir, I'm sorry to interrupt again, but there's a family member, of the Duncans I mean, at their house demanding to be let inside. We've explained to her that she can't go inside the house yet, but she's belligerent. I thought you would want to talk to her.

She's in the back of my car." The officer gave Detective Knox a hangdog look. "She wouldn't settle down."

"Ok, Simzyk, I'll be right there." He turned back to the Vincents. "And you have no idea who might have been an enemy to the Duncans? No one they'd had trouble with lately?"

"No. I don't." Lou glanced at Millie, in case she had something to add, but she had her eyes covered with her hand and didn't look up. He shook his head. "No."

Mickey rose from the ottoman with some difficulty but, to his relief, managed to not require a second attempt. Mr. Vincent rose and they shook hands. "I appreciate you talking with me. It'll help with the timeline. If I need to talk to you again, I'll be in touch." He nodded to Millie. "Ma'am."

He walked from the living room to the entry foyer. As he reached for the front doorknob, Mr. Vincent came up close behind the detective and nodded outside. They stepped out to stairs covered with green indoor/outdoor carpet made to look like turf but really didn't. Mr. Vincent closed the door behind him. "You'll let me know if you think we have anything to worry about, won't you?"

"I will. Right now, we have no reason to think you are in any danger."

Lou nodded. "Ok then."

Their attention was drawn toward the Duncan house, the driveway filled by two police cruisers and an unmarked car. A piercing female voice carried across the field. Detective Knox frowned.

Lou Vincent gave a salute-like gesture and turned to go back in his house, saying, "You've got your hands full, Detective."

## Chapter 4

October 8, 2016, 10:00 a.m.

"Is that something you want to do?" Nina asked Perri, with more than a small helping of doubt.

Perri shifted her cell phone to her other ear while she folded several sets of scrubs and placed them in her suitcase. "Well, it isn't my first choice, but I'm not going to continue at twenty percent less pay. If I do that, I'll never get it back, even if I get another contract with that agency. You know how that stuff goes, any calls made to ask about it later fall on deaf ears."

"Yeah." Nina was quiet for a moment, then said, "If you just tell them you won't accept the pay decrease, what grounds would the agency use to terminate your contract? They have obligations too."

"That good old phrase that always pops up in the fine print on contracts. 'Circumstances beyond our control which render completion of the contract infeasible,' or something like that. Not being able to pay me at the agreed upon rate makes it impossible for them to complete the contract alright. Why don't they just say, 'if we decide we want to terminate the contract, we can, but nothing short of death will excuse the nurse?'"

"Yep, that's basically what they do."

"I don't want to switch from travel nursing to stationary, but I'm getting tired of these agencies and their games. Remember the one that lowered everyone's pay by 8% and said it was 'to help us pay less taxes'? What a crock!"

"Yeah, I do remember that. They even had their CFO make an online video explaining how it would benefit everyone. Anyone with an ounce of sense could see it only benefited them."

"Right. It's my business how I handle putting money back for taxes. They took away their contractors' ability to invest their money and then pay taxes out of it when they're due. All so they could pay less and keep more money from the contractors to pay their own portion of the taxes." Perri sighed. "But…some people believed it and are still working for them for less money."

Have you called them back yet with your decision about whether or not you'll accept the pay decrease?" Nina was on her break at the same hospital where Perri had been working two days before when Angela, her contact at the nursing staff agency, had called her to notify her of the change. Nina was a full-time hospital employee as a scrub nurse in surgery. Perri worked as a travel nurse, normally taking thirteen-week assignments. Sometimes she worked in her hometown hospital when they were short-staffed, which was always, but often traveled to other cities. The changing assignments were something she liked about the job; travel with accommodations paid along with her salary, but it had its downside too.

"No. I wanted to make sure I had something else lined up first. I called the other agency I work for sometimes first thing the next morning, that was yesterday. I haven't worked for them as often. The assignments I have had with them were over a year ago." Perri poured another cup of coffee and dumped creamer and sugar into it. "I'm all grumbly now because my routine has been upset. I have to shift my mind-set to the other agency and their policies, not to mention a completely different kind of assignment than I'm used to working. You know me, I like variety but don't like sudden changes."

"Me either. We're in the wrong field then, aren't we?" Perri had to strain to hear Nina over a Code Blue being called on the PA system of the hospital. Nina spoke louder, "Have you ever worked Home Health before, I can't remember? The A/C wasn't working in OR 4 and I think my brain is cooked. It may be cool outside, but it's hotter 'n Hades under the gown, gloves, masks, goggles, and caps with all the equipment running."

"Once, way back when I first started as a nurse. Remember that place that had day-to-day shifts you could pick up?"

Nina answered through a mouthful of whatever she was eating for lunch, "Yhrh, ah boo."

"I was working full time on a Med/Surg unit, back when Alan and I were just married, and then I'd work a couple shifts for the home health agency on the weekends to pick up some extra money."

Nina swallowed, her voice now loud and clear. "You bet I remember when you were the only one working. Lazybones was too delicate to find a job...sorry. Still scorches my butt that he let you do all the working for several years while his majesty played the role of professional student. Then as soon as he graduates and gets a job, and a great job at that, he starts dating around like he was single."

"It didn't make me any happier than you, believe me." Perri didn't like remembering those times except that it reminded her how much better off she was now and that she was grateful for the present. With Alan and all his problems finally settled and gone, she had her own home and bills to worry about, and none of the drama and surprises he so regularly presented her with.

Nina continued. "I see that piece of crud every now and then on one of his nauseating commercials. She mimicked Alan's voice, 'Have you been hurt in an accident?' Standing there in his tailored suit, acting all serious and concerned." Nina made a gagging noise. "I do have to laugh how the wind in that commercial keeps blowing his thinning hair around though. And don't you just nut up over that jingle, the one with the meandering melody that sounds like someone making the notes up as they go along?"

"Oh, I know, it's cringe-worthy. I think one of his new girlfriends works for a marketing and public relations firm. Nice work, huh? Anyway, I took the Home Health assignment."

"Where will you be working?"

"It's a half-length assignment, six weeks, or longer if they haven't found a permanent replacement and I want to stay with it. I'll be working with patients in a southern Illinois region. It includes several towns: Eldorado, Harrisburg, Equality..."

"Oh. Okay."

Perri laughed. "I don't know if you remember, my Dad's family was from that part of the state and I spent time there every summer. I'm looking forward to it. I haven't been over there for ages."

"Oh sure, I remember that time I went camping with you and your family. That was near there, right?"

"Yeah, at Pounds Hollow. I'm glad to be going there because I have wanted to do a little more research on my family who moved there from Kentucky back in the 1830s. A local genealogical society has a great reference library in Harrisburg and I'll only be about twenty minutes away."

"Where are they putting you up while you are there?"

Perri answered, "I'm staying in Eldorado. It isn't that far to any of the other towns so it is as centrally located as it gets. It's like a big triangle. The agency rented a furnished apartment. Apparently, the previous nurse had an accident and can't work for a while, so she left in the middle of her contract."

"Know anything about it, the apartment I mean?" Nina asked between slurping whatever she was drinking.

"I looked it up online. I thought I recognized the building in the website photo, but couldn't be sure because it looks so different. After checking the address on Google Earth and reading about it on the rental page, it is where I thought. It's right on highway 45 and used to be some business or other a very long time ago. That place was already empty and gutted with all the windows knocked out when I was a kid. Someone fixed it up, and it would have taken a whole lot of fixing up, but they made it into four apartments. It isn't huge, but I don't need huge. It's fairly new and looks clean. I'll know soon enough, I'm leaving this afternoon."

"Great! Maybe I can come over on a weekend."

"That would be great! We could get in a hike. The trees should be beautiful in a couple of weeks. Or we could risk something really strenuous like sitting around, drinking some wine, and yakking. Another thing I'm going to do on this trip is write that article I promised Gloria I would do for her genealogy e-zine."

"Oh yeah, I forgot about that. Do you know what you're going to write about yet? Genealogy, I guess, huh?"

"Smartass. I'm not sure yet, but I need to think of something soon so I have time to research and write it. Will you proof it for me?"

"Sure, no problem."

"Thanks, sometimes I can read right over my own mistakes, more than once." Perri climbed off the couch and paced around the living room as she talked, a subconscious nervous response to her next topic. "I'm going to call Nick and ask him to come over to visit with me, at least for a few days, if he can."

"Yes, good for you! You absolutely must call me tonight and tell me what he says."

"Nosy Parker." Perri smiled.

"Darn tootin' I'm nosy. I wanna know all about it." Nina heaved a huge sigh, "Dang it, I gotta go. My time is up and I must return to the hamster wheel." Perri could hear Nina's chair scoot across the floor, the PA system paging a physician to the OR.

"Alright. I won't say it, don't want to jinx you, but you know." Perri said, honoring the taboo of speaking aloud the wish for a quiet shift since saying the 'Q' word seemed to open the floodgates just as surely as a full moon or the 4th of July.

"I do, thanks a bunch. Talk to you later." Nina hung up.

Perri scrolled her phone to her Favorites screen and tapped Nick's icon to call his cell phone. Although he was probably at work by now, tending to the lunch crowd, she figured she'd leave him a message. Nick still worked his job as bartender at the Arrogant Rogue tavern in Russellville, Kentucky while trying to get his sound equipment service company off the ground. He had just started the business when Perri met him the previous summer when she had been in Russellville for one of her research trips.

Nick had several years of experience working as a sound technician in the Nashville music world but after being worn down by the grasping and underlying politics, he decided to return to his hometown. Business had improved over the last year, but the regional market was small so it was slow going. He had picked up a decent amount of jobs providing sound for receptions, outdoor summer festivals, and parties, but his goal was to expand to some of the larger cities.

As the phone rang, Perri rinsed out her coffee cup then dumped the grounds out of the percolator into the old plastic mixing bowl she used to collect them. She bought a composter two years ago for recycling grounds, peelings, and other kitchen debris for use on her flower beds, if she ever stayed home long enough to plant them. For now, she composted and when the barrel was two-thirds full, she tilled it into the soil of the beds. At least they'd be ready when she was.

She expected to get Nick's voice mail message but was startled by his quick, "Hey-a! What's up, you?" The background noise increased in volume when he stopped talking: the clinking of glass, the scrape of a metal scoop against ice, bottle caps popping, and a din of chatter from the customers.

"I didn't intend to interrupt you at work. I figured I'd get your voice mail."

"Not a problem, hang on, let me go to the back." Perri could hear his muffled voice say, "Tracy, I'll be back in a few minutes." There was a rustling sound for several seconds before the low roar diminished. "Ok, this is better. I'm glad to hear from you, as always. How's it going today?"

"Thanks, I won't keep you long, I know this is a busy time of day."

"There is never a time that I don't want to get a call from you, you know that. Anything wrong or did you just need to hear my amazingly sultry voice?"

"I always want to hear that." She smiled and was irritated at herself to realize she was blushing a little. "What I called you about, well, I'll have to explain the whole thing to you later, but we've been talking about you coming up to see me sometime soon."

"Yes?" Perri could hear the tightness of anticipated disappointment in Nick's voice. She was glad she didn't have to deliver that disappointment.

"Instead of coming here on your time off, I wanted to know if you thought you could visit me while I'm at my new assignment?"

Nick hesitated, thinking, then said, "New assignment? I thought you had another month and more left there in Vailsburg?"

"That's the part I'll have to explain to you later. It would take too long to tell you now and I know you have to get back to work and I need to finish packing. I'm going to be in the southern Illinois area. I'm leaving today and will be starting the job Monday. It really wouldn't be much farther for you to visit me there than it would here, so I thought we could just shift our plans."

"Oooh, working in Little Egypt, huh?" Nick sounded amused and relieved. "Good, I was afraid you were going to tell me you were jetting off to the west coast again."

"Not this time. Think about it and call me when you get off work tonight."

"You got it. Talk to you later."

After she hung up, Perri felt better about the new assignment. Not that Nick would be there the whole time, but just having someone to share even a few days with helped smooth over the uneasiness she felt about being unfamiliar with the job. She had a habit of getting a little too routinized and it was probably going to be good for her to disrupt that a bit.

Her outlook brightened at the thought of the chance to go back to the towns she visited during her childhood. Those relatives weren't there anymore, all of them had passed on, but just driving around would be nostalgic and there would be enough time to pay respects at the graves of family members she hadn't journeyed to in a long time. She made a mental note to get together a few items to take with her to decorate the graves, nothing big, just something to signify her presence and that they weren't forgotten.

In the little time before she needed to leave, she'd make a quick review of her family tree and printed a list of documents she needed from the counties in Illinois and put it with her research materials. She much preferred getting documents in person when possible if only because she enjoyed the process. Some courthouses were very new and modern, but she particularly savored visiting the oldest ones with their creaking floors and stairways. Perri flipped open her laptop and switched it on.

The internet had certainly made it easier to search for documentation and obtain some of those items without having to travel, but there were still locations where only an in-person appearance would suffice. Her home county in Indiana would not release a birth or death certificate by mail, no matter how long ago the person had lived. The only way to get it was to physically go to the health department, fill out their request form, show ID, and pay the fee. Even then, the person making the request had to be within an acceptable degree of relation or they still wouldn't release the certificate. And you had to be willing to wait. There could be no one in the office but her and somehow it still took an interminable time even though the certificates were called up from a database and printed in a matter of seconds.

Perri's immediate family was only superficially interested in genealogy and had told her what they knew, or were willing to take the time to think about. She'd spent several years putting together pieces of her family history and had, so far, tentatively traced her maternal line back to the latter part of the 1700s in Scotland.

Many times it was possible to order documents by mail but, just like the birth certificates in her own county, some things just couldn't be found online or obtained without physically visiting a records repository. That was fine with Perri, because for her, those visits were part of the pleasure and satisfaction of genealogy. Internet research was fantastic with the availability of so much information, but replacing a few happy hours of poring over dusty files, some you didn't even need, with online ordering took the personality out of it for her.

Perri thoroughly enjoyed viewing extant paperwork and appreciating the old documents with their scrawling pages of difficult-to-read handwriting. She imagined the clerks, assistants, and scribes who toiled away with pen and ink a century and a half ago, day in and day out, laboriously copying out pages of detail from court proceedings, land purchases, and wills. Holding in her hand the same piece of paper that someone had covered with elegant penmanship and flourishes, or sometimes with crabbed, unreadable squiggles, made that person real again, just for a few moments. The names of people who may not be remembered for anything else could once again be read, spoken aloud, and enjoy a little life breathed into their memory for an instant by someone nearly two centuries in their future.

She and Nina often took advantage of one of her information gathering trips by turning it into a girls' weekend away. They had known each other since kindergarten, but life was hectic at times and they both enjoyed spending time together to catch up on life.

For Perri, while being very useful for locating burials or cemeteries, the internet could never replace the satisfaction of finding an ancestor's marker in person, whether it was after walking the rows of a manicured cemetery or struggling through the underbrush of a burial ground overtaken by vines and thorny brambles. There was no substitute for it in Perri's mind. Technology was great, but she liked hands-on experience.

A few of the grave sites Perri wanted to visit in Illinois weren't readily accessible since the crumbling cemeteries they were in had been reclaimed by woodlands or were located on what was now someone else's private property. Many states had laws requiring landowners to provide access to these cemeteries, but Illinois was not one of them. Unless there was an existing easement for access, permission would need to be obtained first, but Perri knew there were no easements for the ones she wanted to visit. She'd have to contact a couple of property owners before she made the trip to get permission to traipse across their land. The names of the current owners would be available in the county deed office. She decided there were going to be too many mental notes to remember, so she fished her agenda bag out of her satchel and scribbled a list of things to do.

## Chapter 5

October 9, 2016, 12:05 p.m.

    By just after noon on Saturday, Perri was ready to hit the road. She had placed holds on mail and newspaper delivery and let her neighbor, the Parkers, know she would be gone since they were kind enough to keep an eye on her house when she was away.

    Being accustomed to traveling frequently for work, it didn't take her long to get packed. She always kept a bag with toiletries, a hair dryer, and other generic items ready to go so that was already done. She had packed up her genealogy materials. At any given time, she had several different family lines going so she sorted through for the line that had lived in the southern Illinois area. She printed profiles for the ancestors she was trying to document, maps on which she marked the cemeteries she wanted to go to, and the address and phone numbers of the county offices she might need to contact. She also took a copy of an old plat map along with a new map, hoping to locate the original land purchase of her 3x Great Grandfather.

    After contacting the farmers who owned the land she needed to cross, Perri had received permission from them. One cemetery was in a wooded area and the other was on a tree-covered hillock out in the middle of a field. She had written down their names, phone numbers, and the dates she talked with them, then tucked the paper inside the zip-up binder she took everywhere with her.

    The sky was huge and the air smelled fresh and clean. Perri gratefully inhaled deeply as she took her bags out to her red Mini Cooper. It was a day of crisp blue skies without a single cloud. The leaves on the maple in her front yard were just turning yellow and they waved gently with every breath of air. For once, the sunshine was pleasant without detectable humidity, unlike during the summer when it felt like being in an oven. The heavy, viscous air of summer had been whisked away by northern breezes.

This was the kind of weather that energized Perri. After a summer of avoiding the baking outdoors as much as possible, she was looking forward to going hiking in several places she had good memories of with her parents. She had poured over a map of southern Illinois to rediscover them: Garden of the Gods, Pounds Hollow, and Rim Rock Trail in the Shawnee National Forest. All the locations were fairly close to where she would be staying. She'd made sure to include her trail boots and the few hiking-related items she had.

Feeling more upbeat than before, the idea of these side trips gave a new perspective on her change of work plans. She found that she was excited about going rather than feeling dread at the newness of the assignment. Plus, Nick would be there at least for a few days. He was eager to try out some of the trails with her and see the view overlooking Camel Rock; a place he'd never been.

A couple of times, when she had time between jobs, Perri had visited Nick in Kentucky and they'd done some hiking, as well as paid a visit to Mammoth Cave. Both Perri and Nick had been through the cave, considered the world's longest cave system, multiple times as children and enjoyed seeing it again through adult eyes. After taking the four-hour tour, they agreed the cave was still as beautiful and astonishing as it had seemed to them when they were small, unlike some fixtures of childhood memories which can seem diminished in grandeur when revisited as an adult.

The cave had quite a history. Ancient Native American remains had been found from many eras. The cave had been used for experimental archaeology to learn about living with prehistoric technology. It had even, appallingly, served as a hospital for tuberculosis patients in 1839 when tuberculosis was at epidemic levels. John Croghan had believed the cold, subterranean air, or vapors, would cure sufferers of the disease. It did not, and John Croghan eventually succumbed to the same disease as his patients. On the ceiling of the Gothic Avenue chamber, thousands of names are scrawled, chipped, and engraved; a few are from 1812. Some of the names were written by using the soot from a burning candle on a pole held close to the ceiling to form the letters.

The waterfalls of solid rock formed over millennia, vast echoing chambers as large as an arena, and the dizzying heights and depths were much as Perri remembered them. She had been pleased to see that the Snowball Dining Room, a café in a wide, low-ceilinged chamber, was still operating. Sharing their memories of the cave, she and Nick both remembered floating through the eerie chambers in a boat on the Echo River, an underground waterway that wound through the cave in places. A very young Perri had listened in fascination as the guide described the different creatures that made the cave their home, including the eyeless fish that lived in the water. They had evolved without eyes, since deep in the cave, far underground, there was absolute darkness. To protect the habitat for the species that lived there, the river tour was no longer offered. Perri would rather the environment be protected and was happy enough with the glimpses of the river that could be seen from a spot on their tour.

She smiled in anticipation of the weeks ahead as she did a final walk-through of her house to make sure everything was unplugged, put away, or otherwise ready for her absence. She'd be close enough to home to come back if she wanted to, but didn't want to feel she needed to return every weekend. Perri climbed into her car, rolled down both front windows, turned the music on full blast, and rolled out of the driveway.

***

Air whipped through the car, blowing strands of Perri's reddish-brown hair across her face, sometimes catching in the corner of her mouth. The passing fields had been harvested of their corn, soybeans, and melons. Farmers were plowing under the chaff, breaking apart the scattered angular shapes formed by the remaining brittle corn stalks. At a tractor's approach, a murmuration of starlings lifted from a field and shifted directions in the air like a scarf being blown in the wind before gradually landing on a power line, stretching from one pole to another and on to yet another. A turbulent cloud of dust rose just behind the tractor, streaked out and away on the coattails of the wind before it finally faded, settling back to earth and coating fenceposts in light tan layers.

Crossing the Wabash River into Illinois, Perri could see the water was up somewhat from its previous low level following a couple of months of nearly no rain during the summer. The old train bridge was still only partially demolished. Three rusted sections remained on their pylons, futilely reaching out from the Indiana side, but the opposite bank would never again be within its reach. There was now only a startling void where a couple of sections had been knocked out, presumably to allow river traffic through. Of the five surviving pylons, no two were alike; the remaining dusky iron girders sat quietly corroding.

The rest of the trip went by quickly. Perri enjoyed the scenes of rural Illinois: farms getting ready for winter, horses ambling through their corrals, a group of people collecting walnuts from the trees growing along a stretch of highway.

After a relatively straight shot on Highway 45, Perri could see the S-curve of the road ahead as it entered Eldorado. It was a familiar scene, but she felt some anxiety form in her gut. "Just the new job jitters," she told herself.

She passed by the apartment where she would be living on her way into the downtown area where she needed to meet with the rental agent to sign for the key. Most of the buildings she remembered were still there, although she noted with more than a little sadness the loss of a couple of the older ones which had been razed to make room for bank buildings.

Perri felt slightly guilty that the agent had to meet her on a Sunday afternoon, but knew it shouldn't take long. She parked in front of the row of buildings that housed various offices and stores where the agency was located on the second floor. A sign hung from an iron pole projecting out of the brickwork next to a doorway, "Fuller Properties." The thick paneled door was painted a nondescript brown, the paint was uniformly peeling off in small flecks over the surface of the old wood. There were no windows in the door or on either side. Perri pushed the door open to find a steep staircase rising immediately from a very short entryway.

After climbing to the second story, she reached a small foyer occupied by an area rug and a short table with a lamp. The lamp was on, illuminating the area, which otherwise would have been quite dark since the only light was what managed to filter up through the stairway. The one door leading from the foyer said Fuller Properties, painted right on the frosted glass. Perri turned the wobbly, battered metal knob and walked into the office.

The inner office was a definite contrast to the foyer. The huge single-hung windows let in the golden autumn light. Every mote of dust in the beam wavered and flashed as it tumbled through the air. The large room contained three desks that were arranged in their own areas, each with a chair for a visitor, a potted plant or two, and photos of family members. All the detritus of daily business had been put away for the weekend.

Perri heard footsteps on the wooden slat floors and turned toward the rear of the room where there was a hallway extending toward the back of the building. A woman appeared out of the gloom. She looked to be in her mid-twenties, her pixie-cut blond hair was dyed black at the tips and swept forward against her forehead and cheeks. She was dressed in a pair of jeans and sweater. She smiled with her hand extended as she walked toward Perri. "Hi there. Perri, right? I'm Bethany Trammel. Glad to meet you!"

"Nice to meet you, Bethany." Bethany was a couple of inches shorter than Perri, she guessed around five-foot-five, even in her thick-soled shoes.

"Call me Beth. Bethany was popular when I was born and I went to school with half a dozen of them, but Beth is what everyone calls me now."

Perri nodded. "I'm sorry you had to come in on a Sunday. I needed a little time to get things in order before leaving home. My assignment was on short notice. Otherwise, I would have come tomorrow, but I have to start work in the morning."

"Don't mention it. I was going to be down here anyway sometime today. We manage a lot of apartments and duplexes and sell some property too. I usually come in one day during a weekend for showings. People can't always get away during the week."

Relieved of total responsibility for Beth being in the office on Sunday, Perri said, "I'm glad you didn't have to come in just for me."

"Have a seat. You want some coffee or a soft drink? I just started the pot of coffee right before you got here."

"That sounds great, thanks." Perri sat in the visitor's chair next to the desk by the windows overlooking the street.

Beth turned to walk away but pivoted back, her eye settling on something on her desk. She reached across the desk from the front, retrieving a fat manila folder next to the green-shaded banker's lamp. After tucking the file under her arm, she pulled a couple of sheets of paper from another folder on the center of her desk and placed them in front of Perri. "Have a look over the contract agreement while I get the coffee. Any questions, just ask." As she left the room, she called back over her shoulder, "Cream, sugar, both?"

"Both, heavy on the cream." Perri replied.

Beth nodded, "Be right back."

Perri read the first couple of paragraphs and frowned a little at the document. She had always signed for the key when her housing was provided by an agency, but she hadn't had to sign a contract of this type before. The agreement had always been exclusively between staffing agency and the rental agent, but then she had never needed housing before when working for this agency. Her previous jobs with them had always been local. Every company operated differently. She sighed as she picked up the papers and continued reading the legal jargon.

Beth returned with two large mugs of coffee and set them on the desk as she settled into her chair. "Hope you like it on the strong side. I'd just as soon not drink coffee if I can see through it."

"Me either! The stronger the better." Perri agreed.

"Now, any questions about the agreement? Did I give you enough time to read through it?"

"Yes, it pretty much says I won't have pets and I won't destroy the place, right?"

"That's about it. I know you are probably used to your recruiter signing these contracts, and they did as well, but the owner of this particular building wants a secondary contract with the actual tenant. I'm sorry."

"Don't apologize, I know it isn't your fault. Renting property to people is a crap-shoot. The only thing I am concerned about is that I'm not held responsible for payment if, for some reason, the staffing agency doesn't pay." She scanned through the document again. "I don't see anything in here saying I would have to take over the payments."

"No, that's not part of your contract. The owner is more concerned about the property being maintained. The owners are a local couple and they put a lot of work themselves into renovating the old building."

"I remember how it looked, at least several years ago. It sat empty the entire time I had family living here. It was pretty much gutted, so I can imagine it took quite a bit of work." Perri took a drink of her coffee. It tasted good, but it was drip coffee and drip coffee was never as hot as percolator coffee.

"Definitely, and plenty folks are glad they restored it rather than had it demolished." Beth answered. "I'm an adherent of restoring older structures any time it can be done. I think too often it's overwhelming and owners just don't want to face it. I want to invest in some of the older property myself, but I'm still trying to work up enough capital to buy my first one."

"I noticed that a couple of the downtown buildings have gone though. I hate to see that."

"Me too. There was a movement to try to save them, but it didn't happen." Beth shook her head. "One of them looked like it might be up for restoration when someone wanted to buy it, but the owners held out for *way* too much money for a building that was condemned. Before the potential buyer responded, the building burned and was unsalvageable."

"Sorry to hear that." Perri made a face and said, "Sounds a little…unlikely, don't you think?"

"Unlikely?"

"Well, I mean, maybe it's me, but anytime a building that's been around for over a hundred years suddenly burns down right in the middle of litigation or conflict, I always wonder about it."

"You think maybe the owner burned it to get the insurance money?"

Perri shrugged. "I don't know. I guess that would depend on how much coverage they had versus what they could get for it on the market." Bethany stared at her, wide-eyed. "Heck, I don't know, just guessing." Feeling a little self-conscious, Perri put down her mug and slid the contract a bit closer to herself. "I can sign this if you have a pen handy."

"Sure thing." Beth took a pen from a decorated canister that looked like a coffee can wrapped with craft paper covered with crayon butterflies and big, loopy flowers. Beth noticed her gaze and said, "My niece. She loves artsy stuff and made everyone in the family a pen holder. It has come in pretty handy."

Perri grinned, "I love homemade stuff. I'm sure your niece is proud that you are using it." She signed the contract and turned it back toward Beth, laying the pen down on the desk.

Beth took the contract and slipped it into a manila folder, then slid a key ring with two keys across the desk. She tapped the keys, "The largest key is to the apartment and the smaller key is for the storage area. Each tenant has a storage closet at the back of the building on the first floor, accessed off the main hallway. It isn't huge, but it works fine for things you don't use often, like decorations. You may not even need it since you won't be here too long, but you have it just in case."

"Ok, thank you." Perri gulped down most of the rest of her coffee and stood up. "And thanks for the coffee."

"Here's one of my cards," Beth handed her a business card, "just call me if you have any issues or questions."

Perri looked at the card. *Bethany Trammel, Real Estate Agent, CRS, ABR.* "CRS and ABR?" She laughed. "I'm not fluent in realtor-speak."

Bethany answered. "Certified Residential Specialist and Accredited Buyer's Representative. It means I have extra training in housing real estate and as a buyer's representative."

"I see. It's been a while since I bought my house. I'm sure the realty world changes rapidly like a lot of other professions."

"True. I also want to start my own realty company, someday. Still getting experience and the ever-elusive capital. I was one of the bidders on the old building down town. I didn't have enough to buy a property in decent shape, but I could have swung that one had it not burned."

"Oh, I'm sorry, I didn't mean to…"

"No, no, you didn't."

"Well, good luck with your showing today." Perri tucked the card into her purse and crossed the creaky floorboards to the door. Beth gave her a thumbs-up and waved.

Even with the lamp, the stairwell seemed very dark after the blazingly sunlit room and Perri needed a couple of moments to adjust. Just as she was able to clearly see the top step in front of her, she heard the old wood of the staircase squeaking, loud in the enclosed space, like someone wearing a pair of wet galoshes on a tile floor. She backed away from the top of the staircase to let the newcomers, a man and woman, pass before she began her descent. The man nodded to Perri and the two entered the office.

Back outside, the sun had settled below the roofline of the opposing building. There was a comfortable feeling of quiet dusk, peaceful, not cold, not hot. She decided to take a short walk, just around a couple of blocks, before going to check out her new digs for the next few weeks. There were a couple of people walking toward Perri on the sidewalk further down the street, one of whom dropped an envelope into a mailbox, then they turned and retreated in the opposite direction.

Perri oriented herself to the street since some of the landmark buildings she remembered were gone. As she strolled slowly down the block, she saw there were still some active businesses, but many buildings were empty: the old cinema, the once busy box office now crammed with boxes; glass display cases empty for so long the wood was bleached from sunlight and stained from water leaks; storefronts with the large glass tiles falling away or being pulled off, the black empty spaces with white glue marks remaining looked like dominos, or dice. It didn't look like the same place, but her memories of this downtown area lived on, as well as in photos of her family, all the way back to the 1920's. She remembered a picture of her great-grandmother standing by a car parked in front of the Eldorado Hotel. It still had a second-floor balcony with a railing built over the sidewalk, other cars lined the street, and her great-grandmother was sporting a jaunty 1920's haircut and a nautical-themed dress with a big bow tied in front.

She wished she could step back in time. 'How many people have wished that,' she wondered to her herself. Many. As she continued along the now-deserted street and turned the corner, she reflected on the painful paradox that as children, when our relatives are still all around us, we haven't developed an interest in family history or who Grandma's grandma was. Once we are old enough to want to know and appreciate the value family history can have for us, those people are mostly gone and the information with them, or it we have to find out through research, if it can be found at all. Stories told and re-told at gatherings and holidays recounting the antics of family members can be sketchily remembered and usually aren't documented. After the passage of a decade or two, at least for Perri, there was no one left to ask or verify details. Her parents were still living, not even considered old, but they didn't know much more than she did. Her remaining grandparent had been afflicted with Alzheimer's for many years. While Alzheimer's patients frequently could better recall the distant past than the present, her grandmother had passed the point of being able to communicate on more than a very short term, immediate basis.

Rounding another corner, Perri arrived back on the street where her car was parked. It was getting darker outside, the street lamps were on and the lights from the rental office were now off. She unlocked her car door and slid into the seat. It took only a couple of minutes to reach the apartment building. Her unit was on the second floor, to the left of the staircase. She decided to go in and open the door before lugging her suitcase and bags up the stairs.

She was met with the smell of fresh paint and newly sawn wood as she entered the common area on the first floor. It was covered with short, dense, gray carpet. A black rain mat was placed just inside the door. There were metal-fronted, recessed mailboxes along the short wall beneath the stairs. Perri glanced at her keyring. Unless one of these keys also fit the mailbox, which she doubted, she hadn't been given a key to her mailbox. She'd have to check with Beth about that. Not that she expected much mail, but she would need to check it regularly.

The stairs were divided into two sections. The landing on the second floor opened toward the front of the building. A window was situated on the front wall and gave a view of the curve of Highway 45, so Perri could see down the road a little in each direction. Her front door was located at the back of the landing, for which she was grateful. She'd lived in apartments before where her front door was right at the top of a flight of stairs. Not that there would be as much activity here with only one other apartment on the second floor, but she was still happy about it. Noise didn't have to come from traffic up to a second floor, it could funnel up through a stairwell from the floors below too.

The key fit both the handle and the dead bolt on the front door. The furnished rooms were open and airy; the living room faced the front of the building, as did the kitchen which was located just to the left inside the door. They were arranged in the currently popular open concept, with only a bar between the kitchen and living room. The bed and bathroom were across the back of the building. The bedroom had a large closet, a dresser, and chest of drawers, so she'd have no problem storing the clothes and gear she had brought.

Having brought her luggage up to the apartment, Perri was just closing the door when the door of the apartment across from hers opened. She stopped short and pulled the door open a bit more. A man exited the apartment facing her, and stopped when he saw her looking out at him. He looked to be about in his mid-sixties, dark gray hair which was a little white at the temples, not exactly long but it was hard to tell since it looked like it was combed back. He wore black jeans and a gray long-sleeved jersey, the sleeves bunched up to his elbows. "Oh. Hello. Are you the new tenant, I guess?"

"Yes, sorry." Perri walked out onto the landing. "I'm Perri Seamore."

The man stepped forward and reached out a hand to shake, "I'm Webb, Reuben Webb. Very nice to meet you, uh, Perri, you say?" His handshake was firm.

"Yes, Perri, it's short for Perlina. My great aunt several times over was named Perlina and I was named for her."

"It's a respectable mid-19th century name. It was popular for a time."

Perri's expression betrayed the fact that she was startled. "You've heard it before?"

Reuben laughed, "Oh yes. I was a school teacher for thirty years and now I'm a research historian, so yes, I have come across the name once or twice in my time. Well, not to say that I came across it while I was a teacher, no, of course not, but I have in doing research."

"I see. What type of research do you do?"

"Various types, depending on what the person who hires me needs done. I generally do local and regional research for authors who are writing books but can't make the trip or stay somewhere long enough to do their research on site. I have done some deed and title search work while I've been here, but that tends to be geared toward land acquisition in which I'm not interested. I'm here to do some snooping around for my own project though. I'm writing a history of lost villages and towns in Southern Illinois, including photographs."

"That sounds like a great job! I'd love to be able to do that for a living."

"Uh, it can be very rewarding, also very…surprising at times."

"Surprising? You mean when you find a lost settlement?" Perri asked.

"Well, yes, that too." Reuben stopped talking and fidgeted. Perri, sensing a juicy story here, let the silence stretch out until he continued. "I went out yesterday to photograph the old salt works well, off Salt Well Road."

"Uh-huh?" Perri had taken a step closer to Reuben, listening attentively.

Reuben's uncertainty resolved. "I guess it doesn't matter me telling you, it isn't like it isn't all over the news." He related the events of the day before and described finding the bodies in the well."

"I haven't listened to any news yet today. What happened?" After listening with a mixture of horror and rapt curiosity, Perri said, "Oh wow! I can't imagine having two bodies pop up at me out of a well. Do you know who they were? Do they know who did it?"

Reuben shook his head in the negative. "No, not that I know of anyway. Of course, they didn't tell me any details, just asked questions for what seemed like forever. Finding murdered bodies is not something I'd recommend. From the news, I know they were a married couple from Old Shawneetown, but no word yet on the motive or if they have any suspects."

Perri nodded as Reuben spoke, then said, "I'll have to catch up on the news after I get settled in. I had planned on a few hiking trips while I am here, but I don't want to be wandering around if there's a murderer out there."

"No, definitely not. What is your profession, if you don't mind me asking?" Reuben asked.

"I'm a nurse. I'm here temporarily, filling in for someone. If I'm not being pushy, I'd love to hear more about your lost village research sometime."

"Sure, we'll have coffee or lunch one day. Right now, I'm working on a history of the smaller towns along the Ohio and surrounding areas mentioned in old records but are now either gone or of which very little remains. A lot of towns vanished when their industry dried up or left for other places. In some cases, I'm photographing nothing more than land where a town used to be." He laughed. "But, that's part of it."

"That's a book I'd be interested in reading. It sounds right up my alley. I like exploring ruins, old cemeteries — maybe not the safest thing to do though, considering. You're also in this apartment temporarily?"

"Yes. I've been here about a week and a half and will be here at least another two to four weeks."

Not wanting to hold him up any longer, Perri said "I'd better get back to unpacking. Have a nice evening and I'll look forward to talking to you again."

Reuben nodded and said, "Same here." He energetically trotted down the stairs, using the handrail to propel himself around to the second flight.

Perri heard the outer door open and whoosh closed as she shut her door, said aloud, "He has more energy than I do sometimes." She stood with hands on her hips, thinking about the murdered couple floating around in the salt well. "I wonder what the story is behind that? Let's see what I can find out." She set about unpacking her bags.

## Chapter 6

May 29, 1819, 9:35 a.m.

"What in tarnation is that?" Alexander Mason sat comfortably on his horse, one arm resting on the horn of his saddle, the other holding the loosely draped reins. Leaning his weight on his left arm and squinting into the sun, with an amazed smile he watched the departing flatboat for as long as he could see it clearly. The shimmering reflection of light off the water surrounded the craft in a haze that blurred the detail. The rotating paddle churned the river water into a froth around the boat, further interfering with his view.

"I don't know, Alexander. I've never seen a boat like that." The other man, also astride his horse at the river's edge, watched the boat disappear. The other five men also watched in amazed silence.

When the boat finally cut northwest to follow the channel around Hurricane Island and disappeared behind the gentle curve of the shore line, Alexander turned his horse away from the river and rode several yards back into the woods, slowly shaking his head from one side to the other. He stopped and the men formed a rough semicircle in front of Alexander and waited.

Alexander ran a long-fingered hand through his curly black hair. His green eyes shone bright even in the shade of the cypress trees overhanging the river. "Gentlemen, we've just seen something very unusual."

Joshua Rutledge spoke up first, incredulously, "It had smoke coming out of the figurehead."

"And it was a serpent's mouth." Abrahm Stegall replied.

"Yes, very…unique. I am sorely regretful that we didn't get to board her." With one fluid motion, Alexander expertly slung his rifle back into the leather scabbard fastened to his saddle. He rubbed the side of his cheek, thinking. "Well, nothing to do for it now. Maybe we'll get another chance at it. Let's go to the cave, maybe they left something of value behind." He grinned, "Seemed like they scurried off in a hurry, didn't it fellas?"

The seven men threaded their way out of the thick growth of trees and brush onto the rocky beach, tethering their horses to trees. As the group crossed the limited clear space at the base of the cave, Luke Potts pointed to the water's edge, "What's that?" He stepped a couple paces into the shallows then knelt and reached in, retrieving a dripping rectangle of wood. Alexander, who had clambered up onto the terrace of limestone that faced the cave and was watching, called down, "Bring it up," then turned and disappeared inside.

The mouth of the cave looked like it had been purposefully carved in the shape of a keyhole. The group passed through the narrow portion beneath an almost perfectly arched opening. The path into the cave remained slim and straight, with layers of flat limestone on either side, perfect for keeping a vigilant eye on the river and the banks. At the back, the cave opened into a roughly circular area where the floor was lower than the entrance. It tended to be dank since the river entered the cave during floods and the water pooled in the bowl-like area and remained for some time after the river had receded.

There was a natural opening on the eastern wall of the cave, not much wider than a barn door. A passageway ran to either side of the opening, but didn't go very far in either direction, only a few feet toward the north and about two or three yards toward the south. Alexander Mason had discovered this to be a very effective hiding place when unsuspecting, curious travelers entered the cave. By the time they realized they weren't alone, it was far too late to escape and Alexander could relieve them of their money and valuable items with ease. There was a small opening in the roof of the cave which let in a minor amount of diffuse natural light, and some rain as well, but the cavern was large enough to avoid the puddles. Silt had built up against the rear surrounding wall in a crescent-shaped area that gently sloped from the wall to the center. This contained the rainwater until it filtered down through the floor of the cave into whatever waterway survived that had originally channeled the water through the limestone and formed the cavern in the past millennia.

Once they were a few steps inside the cave, Luke held out the item. Alexander exclaimed, "What have we here?" He took it from Luke. "It looks like someone ran away without their property. That's such a shame, and we have no chance of returning it to him since he hastily sailed away on that spectacular boat."

It was a solid piece of hardwood with two clamps screwed into the top. They could be opened and closed with mild pressure. The clamps were holding a piece of parchment to the wood. Alexander lifted the sodden square by the bottom corner. There was another paper beneath it, but it stuck to the piece of parchment. He carefully pulled at the corner of the bottom sheet. It came away without tearing; the paper was thick and of high quality. He glanced at it, then laid it on a flat section of stone. He'd take it with him and allow it to dry then see if it had any value.

Alexander walked to the rear of the cave and looked around the interior. He threw a glance at Joshua and jutted his chin toward the wall near the back. Joshua followed Alexander's gaze and spied the shape on the floor, picked it up, and brought it to him.

Alexander flipped back the hem of his nankeen coat as he settled on the edge of one of the limestone terraces, depositing the haversack between his feet. He looked it over, pulled the long, supple leather strap through his fingers, and took his time unfastening the rolled leather ties, "Looks like our fleeing visitor is accustomed to quality goods." He flipped open the top and peered inside. After reaching in, he pulled out a handful of pencils of various sizes and lengths. Alexander's forehead wrinkled in consternation. He reached back in and tugged several times before freeing a packet of paper rolled and tied with twine. His face darkened. "What the devil is this? Papers?"

Stewart Pike suggested hopefully, "Maybe it's money!"

Alexander shifted his unsatisfied gaze to Stewart. "Does this wad of papers look like money to you, Stewart?"

Stewart instantly backed away shaking his head.

"Why don't you search the rest of the cave, Stewart?" Alexander Mason untied the twine and allowed the bundle to loosen. He turned to the side and laid it on the rock shelf next to him, smoothing it out with both hands. After sorting through the stack, "Pictures. This is just a collection of drawings. Some are pencil and some are colored in."

Joshua asked, "What are they pictures of?"

Alexander curled his upper lip toward his nose. "Places." He held up two of them. The other men drew closer to get a better look at them. "This one here's a town on a river, this river I s'pect." He took a second look at it, "I don't know for sure but I think it might be Red Banks."

"Ain't that in Kentucky?" Abrahm asked.

"Yeah, upriver from here." Alexander hesitated, then said, almost under his breath, "I been there before." He shifted and said in a louder tone, "This other one…" he turned it back toward himself to scrutinize it closer, then showed it to the men again. "Any of you men recognize this place?"

Joshua stepped forward and, with his hand extended, looked questioningly at Alexander, silently asking permission to take the drawing. Alexander handed it to him. Joshua turned his back to the cave entrance and angled the sheet of paper to get better light. "I think…I think this might be around Louisville."

"Oh yeah?" Alexander thumbed through the stack of drawings while listening.

"Yeah. I'm from Pittsburgh, and I got here to Illinois by coming all the way down this river. I remember going over these rapids just after Louisville. They aren't too bad, but you have to be careful. I remember these islands over here at the side too." He held the drawing toward Alexander. "I think that's where it is."

"Mmm." Alexander took the watercolor from Joshua and replaced it on the stack. Rerolling and tying the bundle, he placed it back in the haversack and secured the ties. He slung the bag over his shoulder and brushed the dust off his blue trousers. "Well, gentlemen, let's make the trip back to the Inn and see what other prospects we might have."

## Chapter 7

October 10, 2016, 7:15 a.m.

Perri had inadvertently hung up on Nick twice already trying to talk to him while she got her work bag together, poured her travel mug full of coffee, and put her shoes on. "I'm sorry."

Nick's soft chuckle came over the line. He yawned and said, "Don't worry about it, I know you're trying to get ready to go. I need to let you get started and then I'm going back to sleep."

"You creep! That's mean." But Perri couldn't help laughing too. Nick worked split shifts at the tavern and he had worked until the wee hours of that morning at one of his jobs providing sound for a family reunion in Hopkinsville which had run pretty late. "I'd better get my butt in gear. I want to run by Fuller Properties again first thing to get the mailbox key. I didn't get it yesterday."

Nick made luxurious stretching noises and Perri pictured his tall, muscular form languorously tangled in the sheets of his antique mahogany sleigh bed his grandfather had made. "You are doing that on purpose. It is not appreciated."

"Come on now. You do that to me all the time when I call you during a late shift," Nick humorously responded.

"I know, but that's different."

"How exactly is that different?"

"Because."

"Ok. Sorry. Probably wasn't the best time to repay the favor. But hey, you sound *so* motivated," Nick teased.

"I always get nervous on the first day, until I get my bearings anyway. Makes me snippy."

"Is *that* what makes you snippy?"

"Watch it."

"I'm kidding. Have a great first day and call me tonight, ok? And be careful, please."

"Will do." At that moment, Perri would have much preferred to be setting out on a drive to Russellville than starting a new job. She hated the stomach-churning anxiety she always went through at the outset of a new assignment, and today was no different. "I appreciate your effort to loosen me up a bit. Well, I'll definitely call you, but I've gotta get this show on the road. Thanks."

After they said their goodbyes and hung up, Perri locked her door behind her and rushed down the stairs, her work bag thumping against the railing as she juggled it, her coffee, keys, purse, and phone. She had queued up the first address on the map application on her phone. Once in the car, she clamped the phone into the holder on the windshield where she could see it. She wasn't as familiar with Harrisburg as Eldorado.

That morning, her dispatcher had confirmed the email she received the night before detailing her assignments for the day. She had five patients to see, spread out over Eldorado, Harrisburg, and Muddy, beginning with a diabetic who needed a blood sugar check with insulin coverage, a couple of dressing changes with assessment and wound care education, a follow-up on a former home-hemodialysis patient who had an infection in his access site, and finally a check-up for an elderly man recovering from a sprain.

She drove downtown to the rental agency first, parked the Cooper right in front and quickly ran up the stairs. The office was bustling this morning.

"Hi there," Perri said brightly to a young man working at the desk nearest the door. "I'm Perri Seamore, I'm renting one of the furnished apartments on highway 45."

"Yes?" He pushed his glasses up on his nose and listened. He looked like he couldn't have been out of high school very long, but Perri knew the older she got, the less accurate her estimates of younger people's age became.

"I didn't get a key to my mailbox when I picked up my door key yesterday and was wondering if I could get that?"

"Oh, ok. I'll have to ask Beth about it. Hang on." His voice was helpful but his expression looked distinctly like someone who didn't want to be pulled away from whatever he was working on.

Perri smiled at him and resisted the temptation to tap her foot. "That would be great."

He rolled up the sleeves of his blue and white plaid button-up shirt as he crossed the room. Perri stood near his desk while waiting. A woman who looked to be around fifty or so was on the phone at another desk. She glanced at Perri, gave a distracted smile, and went back to her conversation.

The young man returned. "She'll be out in just a second." He started to take his seat again, paused with his back to Perri, then turned and introduced himself. "I'm Timothy Farris."

"Hi, Timothy. Perri."

Timothy sat down and, with a brief smile, rolled his chair back up to his desk and resumed working. Sharp little daggers of worry about being late began to stab their way into Perri's mind. She had left the apartment fifteen minutes early which she thought would be ample time, but now she wasn't sure.

The room was too quiet. The only noise was the occasional sound of a piece of paper being turned over, or a comment by the woman on the phone, the volume of which was intensified by the silence. Perri could hear another woman's voice emanating from the rear of the office, either talking to someone in the room with her or on the phone, although only one voice was audible. The discussion was an unintelligible muddle at first, but the tone escalated and the words became clearer as the conversation evidently became more heated. The woman's voice became louder and more agitated, turning into a raucous debate.

"And why *not*?" Perri heard the voice say, accompanied by a stamp on the floor, followed by silence, so it was a phone conversation. The silence in the office became even more awkward.

The woman on the phone deftly swiveled her chair so she faced the windows. Timothy became thoroughly engrossed in the paperwork he had previously appeared to only be skimming and bent his head close to the document, his left shoulder shielding his face. Perri decided he might be able to discern individual paper particles as close as he was. She sincerely wished she had waited until another time to pick up the key.

The angry voice persevered, spitting the words out like individual nails. "That's ridiculous. What on earth do they *expect*? What do they *want*?" A pause, then something being slammed down, either on the floor or the desk. Perri jumped, making her keys jangle in her hand and a little sound escaped her throat in surprise. No one moved. Perri felt her ears get hot and she just knew they were flaming red.

"Oh, alright! That's just *fine*." The phone was then savagely crushed back into the cradle and a very uncertain peace wrestled with the discomfort in the office.

Perri had arrived at the decision to nonchalantly leave, maybe act as though she suddenly remembered something pressing, which wasn't untrue. She had already subconsciously shuffled backward toward the door, figuring she'd come back some other time after calling ahead first to make sure there weren't any ongoing battles.

Before she could catch Timothy's eye to indicate her intention to escape, something she bet Timothy and Swivel Lady both wished they could do, Beth emerged from the hallway, having been preceded by the rapid sound of her clattering heels. Her face was flushed and tense, her jaw clenched. Probably more brusquely than she intended, she said, "I don't know how I forgot to give you the mailbox key." She hurriedly zig-zagged between the desks and noisily jerked open the second drawer of an old metal filing cabinet. The hanging files swung backward and then forward on the framework in the half empty drawer and collapsed against the front panel.

"It isn't a big deal, Beth, I may not even get any mail here, but I want to be able to check. I didn't mean to interrupt you, I was just on my way to…" Perri let the explanation taper off.

Standing on tip toe with her head bent over the open drawer, Beth said, "Of course, of course." She fished something out of one of the folders and gave the drawer a sturdy push shut. While she threaded her way through the desks toward Perri with the key, she nearly barked to Timothy, "You get an assessment on that property yet?"

Timothy's hand shot out across his desk to a brown folder which he snatched up with one hand while rescuing his teetering coffee cup with the other. "Yes, right here."

Beth handed the small key to Perri. "I'm sorry you had to come down here to get the key. I've been so caught up in a couple of projects here that my mind is just scattered. I hope it didn't put you out too much. Is the apartment working out for you ok?"

"Yes, it's working out very well, it has everything I need, much better than a hotel room." Perri conspicuously glanced at her watch. "Thanks for the key. I gotta get to work."

"Let me know if you need anything else." Beth had already turned her back, gestured to Timothy to follow her, presumably with the file, and was scurrying back to her office. Swivel Lady was still on the phone, or at least still held the phone to her ear but wasn't talking. Perri thought, 'I've seen that trick. I've pulled that trick,' and formed a little corner-of-the-mouth smile. Thinking she was smiling at him, Timothy gave Perri a sheepish grin as she made tracks for the door and rapidly descended the stairs, eager to get on with her day.

## Chapter 8

October 10, 2016, 7:33 a.m.

There was no traffic, and she only had one stoplight to get through until she reached Harrisburg. The lonesome fields clung to their damp blanket of morning mist, the dark tree line across the field was barely discernible through the brume. She noted a cemetery on her left just outside of town. The stones nearest the road were clearly visible but each successive row progressively dissolved into the hazy fog until they disappeared altogether. She hadn't been to this one; all her family was buried at Wolf Creek on the other side of town. She decided she should drive through this one some afternoon and give it a look.

The red Cooper flashed past the tiny village of Muddy in a matter of seconds and in another couple of minutes Perri entered the city limits of Harrisburg. She stopped at the first light, and every light after that one until she came to Sloan Street, where she turned right. She drove several blocks west and found the address she needed. She could see the sign for Sunset Hill Cemetery ahead. She parked and switched off the ignition, resting her hands on the top of the steering wheel, 'Your life is beginning to be measured by cemeteries. You have got to get out more.'

Perri took another deep breath as she got out of the car and put her purse in the trunk. A tip she had from a fellow nurse who had worked home health was to not take anything in with you that you didn't need and don't sit your bag on the floor. Most homes probably would be fine, but there were going to be some where you wouldn't want to take anything home that you didn't bring with you.

Shouldering her work bag, she walked up the concrete path. The years had separated the sections by a few eighths of an inch and grass grew between them, making the sidewalk look like a row of large, rectangular stepping stones. Tree roots had grown under the pavement to the house and broken it about halfway between the house and sidewalk. One of the trees responsible for the damage was gone, the three-foot diameter stump was gray and cracked from multiple winters and summers since its branches had last reached up to the sky. On the other side of the walk, a giant silver maple rose far above the house. The silvery undersides of its leaves made a shimmering sound as they rustled in the breeze.

The house was a type commonly built in the early 1900s, basically square with a hipped roof and a screened-in porch on the front. She could see a swing suspended from the porch ceiling by thick-linked chains. An L-shaped extension was visible on the right side of the house as Perri walked toward it.

She climbed the six shallow steps up to the door of the porch and knocked, the door rattling loudly with each rap of her knuckles. She waited, but no one came to the door. She clamped her top lip between her teeth. Knowing the patient was diabetic, she hoped nothing was wrong, and knocked again, louder this time. She listened. Just as she was about to go around and peer through a window on the side of the house, she heard a woman call out, "Come on in."

Despite its loose rattling, the top of the door caught against the jamb when she pulled on it and she nearly lost her balance when it opened suddenly. She had to back down a couple of stairs to get the door open enough to allow her and her supply bag into the porch area. The swing was to her right, as well as several potted plants arranged along a projecting ledge built right along the base of the windows. On the left, against the wall and just beneath a window into the house was a twin bed. It was covered with a bedspread of heavy striped fabric in red, green, blue, and yellow. The colors had dulled and the spread was very dusty. A tiny square bookcase in the front corner was crammed with old books, mail, and slips of paper squeezed in at all angles. A calendar that was out of date, not by years, but by decades, was hanging stiffly from a nail hammered into the wood between the two end windows. A robust, cheerful woman pouring a Rheingold beer into a tall pilsner glass beamed out at Perri through the grime.

The door into the house was ajar, so Perri pushed the door slowly inward and called out softly, "Hello?"

"In here, honey. Just come on in, no need to loiter around on the porch."

Perri entered the living room, pushing the door shut behind her. The room was wallpapered, including the ceiling, and was stuffed full of furniture of all designs and fabrics of numerous prints so she didn't instantly locate the woman sitting in a chair with her feet up on an ottoman. She had a cross-stitch project on her lap but laid the hoop aside as Perri crossed the room, stepping carefully across numerous small rugs scattered over the carpet. "You're the new girl, aren't you? They told me there'd be someone new today after Lana retired so suddenly."

"Yes, hi, I'm Perri Seamore. I'm glad to meet you." Perri noticed the woman's eyes were reddened. She looked tired.

"I'm Pearl. Pearl Gentry." Pearl took Perri's hand and squeezed it in both of her soft, full hands, then patted it before releasing it. "Yeah, that Lana was a good nurse, I really liked her. But she fell, you know? Fell smack down her basement stairs at home. Laid there for a good part of the morning before somebody finally wised up and realized she wasn't at work."

"That's awful, I'm sorry to hear that. I knew the previous nurse left rather quickly, but I didn't know why." Perri reached behind her to set her bag down on another footstool in front of the massive couch as she made a quick visual assessment of her patient. Pearl had been crying, her eyes were red and puffy and she had stuffed numerous used tissues into a plastic grocery sack on the floor next to her chair. Her complexion was pallid and she looked exhausted.

Pearl smoothed her robe and pulled at her sleeves, her countenance changing from tired and sad to indignation. "I tell you what, had it been her day to be here, I would have known right away and I would have called right away too. Old Mr. Tollander was her first one that day and that old fool didn't call anybody when Lana didn't show up. Silly codger, always fluttering over his hinky, old leg. If he'd leave it alone, it'd be fine."

Perri switched on the glucometer so the calibration process could begin, since this was its first use of the day. At the same time, she mentally ran through her list of patients for the day, hoping Mr. Tollander of the hinky leg wasn't on it.

"Well, I'm sorry about Lana, but I hope she'll enjoy her retirement once she heals." The quick self-test was complete and the meter beeped. "Let's get your blood sugar checked, shall we? Now you take daily oral medication for your diabetes as well, is that right?"

"Oh yes, I take that."

Perri pulled on a pair of latex gloves, "And your insulin is only for coverage if your oral meds are not doing the job?"

"Yes. I usually need a shot a couple times a week though." She pursed her lips, then said, "I confess I don't stick to my diet very well."

"I'm scheduled to see you each morning during the week. Do you check your own sugar on the weekends?"

While Perri was prepping Pearl's finger, she noticed the slight change in her demeanor when she talked about her daughter. She had looked away from Perri when she said, "Yes, I have my daughter give me the shot if she's here. Otherwise, I do it myself. But, my eyesight isn't what it used to be and I'm a mite clumsy with the needle, so I'm glad to have someone here on the other days."

"Can you tell me everything you've had to eat today?" Perri had learned not to ask what the patient had for breakfast. There were those who might be completely truthful about what they had for their official breakfast, but they wouldn't tell you about the extras unless you asked the right question.

"Oh lawsy-mercy, yes." Pearl proceeded to tell Perri about her breakfast which fit nicely into the recommended diet, but the extra piece of microwaved frozen French toast with syrup did not.

"Well, your blood sugar is 274, Pearl. I'm going to need to give you three units of insulin, ok?" Perri recorded the value and the time on her organizational sheet.

"I figured, honey." Pearl pulled one arm out of her robe and lifted the short sleeve of her gown for Perri.

After depositing the syringe and needle in the sharps container, Perri turned back to Pearl. "I'll understand if you don't want to talk about it, but you are upset about something, enough to have been crying. Anything you want to talk about?"

Pearl crumpled. "You don't know, since you don't live here."

"What is it, Pearl?"

"My sister, Ruby." Pearl snuffled a huge breath and blew her nose into a fresh tissue. "She and her husband were killed over the weekend."

"Killed? They…" Perri hesitated, not wanting to sound harsh.

"Someone went in their house on Friday night and took them away and killed them. Hid them in that stupid old well! Can you believe that?" Pearl straightened up, angry now, and fiercely looked around her living room. "Who does something like that? Why? And they went through the entire house!"

"I heard a little about this on the news last night, but they really didn't have much information. You have no idea who might have done it?" Perri asked cautiously, resisting the urge to pepper her patient with questions for more detail.

Pearl sighed. "No, I wish I did though."

As delicately as she could manage while still wheedling for information, Perri asked, "You said they went through the whole house. Do you know what they might have been searching for? Something specific of value your sister and her husband may have had?" She winced a little, afraid she might have seemed overeager.

Pearl considered before answering. "Well, the house itself is considered historic, so I guess you could say it is valuable, but they weren't going to steal the house, were they? It's been in my family for a very long time, back to the early 1800s." Pearl's face radiated pride. "I lived there until Charlie and I married and bought this house here in Harrisburg. But Ruby and her husband still lived in the old place."

After taking Pearl's blood pressure, Perri wrapped her Littmann stethoscope around her neck and put the sphygmomanometer back in the bag. "It sounds like your family home has quite a history, I bet there are some great stories about it. Where is the house?"

"It's in Old Shawneetown, overlooking the river. My ancestor, Francis McCade built that house for his wife during Shawneetown's heyday. It was one of the first brick houses there, heck maybe even the first, and now it's the last. All the others are gone. And I guess now that Ruby is gone, I'm one of the last of the McCades too."

"Was your maiden name also McCade?"

"Sure was." Pearl lapsed into momentary silence, gazing into the past. "I don't know what will happen to the house now. I hadn't even thought about that yet."

Perri felt she had asked all the questions she politely could ask and she needed to get to her next assignment. She picked up her bag. "I'd love to hear more about the house sometime, Pearl. I have a special interest in history and old houses and I'll bet yours has a lot of history. Is there anything I can do for you before I go? Do you need help with anything?"

"No, no, I'm fine, honey."

"Ok, if you're sure, because I don't mind. Do you have any other family close by who can come over?"

"My daughter will be coming by in a little while." Pearl reassured her and waved her away listlessly.

As Perri picked her way across the throw rug gauntlet to the front door, she wondered how Pearl kept from tripping and dashing her brains out on the corner of any one of the multiple coffee and end tables. Being diabetic, any neuropathy in her feet would make it even harder to navigate the landmines on the floor. She half turned back to ask Pearl about it, but seeing her patient's downcast and sad demeanor strongly felt it wasn't the best time to ask to make a wholescale change to her living room. Instead, she said, "Oh my gosh! I'm so silly and I almost tripped on this rug here. Would you mind if I moved it over a bit Pearl? I think it must have gotten moved into the walkway."

"Yes, that's fine." Pearl watched her as she moved the rough textured brown rug out of the traffic area. At least it was one less hazard. Perri would try again on her next visit for permission to remove some of the others. And since Pearl's daughter was supposed to arrive soon, she wouldn't be alone for very long. Maybe tomorrow Pearl would allow her to at least round up some of the throw rugs and get them out of the way.

"Alright, then. I'll see you tomorrow morning."

Feeling sympathetic for Pearl, yet still having a sense of accomplishment, Perri got back in her car and checked the list for her next patient. She jotted down the name Francis McCade and decided to try to find out more about Pearl's family and home in Old Shawneetown. She didn't want to be morbid, but she did still need a topic to write about for the genealogy e-zine and a home like Pearl described, with a long family history, might be it, provided the family didn't object. The tires crunched on the scattered gravel as she pulled away from the low curb.

The next three patients were quick, one in Muddy and two in Eldorado, each needing only a dressing change and to check for signs of infection in a healing abdominal surgical wound.

For the last patient, Perri traveled due east along highway 13 to Equality to see a 76-year-old man who had sprained his ankle. He wasn't at all feeble or infirm, but had twisted the ankle and fallen during an attempt to avoid an impromptu phalanx of his neighbor's escaping goats. Perri was sure Mr. Gilbert Sherman had told the story many times, and thoroughly enjoyed retelling it in what she figured were rapidly lengthening versions. As she checked his pedal pulse, swelling, and range of motion, she had laughed along with him as he described the 'great goat stampede' as they ate the neighbor lady's mums from her flower beds then tore through his yard to get to the remains of his vegetable garden. It had induced quite a commotion and sightings of the gang of eight goats had been reported all over town as they gobbled produce and landscaping. They remained at large for two days before being captured and escorted by local animal control officers to their newly reinforced barnyard. The goats' owner had allegedly gotten a good belly laugh out of the havoc his livestock had wreaked on the community, except of course for Mr. Sherman's injury. The recalcitrant goat owner was paying for Gilbert's medical expenses.

After finishing up with Mr. Sherman, Perri was done for the day and returned to the apartment feeling pleased with her day's work.

*** 

"You survived your first day!" Nick exclaimed in feigned surprise. He couldn't help poking a little fun at Perri. "You almost always think you will fail miserably somehow, yet that never happens."

"Oh, stop it." Perri tied the belt of her robe and slouched into the recliner, her damp hair was cold against the back of her neck. The warmth of the thick terry felt good, forming a toasty barrier of warmth against her skin in the chilly apartment. She drew her knees up in the chair.

"I'm kidding. But you do always think the worst and it always turns out just fine."

"Until it doesn't."

"Negativity, I'm tellin' ya." Nick laughed.

"I know. I'd rather expect the worst and have it turn out fine than the other way around. I think it's normal to be anxious or a little stressed at the start of a new job. Don't you get a little antsy before one of your sound jobs? It's usually in a place you haven't been before. What about that time you got to the job for a big family reunion picnic and discovered the people who hired you didn't tell you it was in a shelter house out in the middle of the woods and there was no electricity? You weren't prepared for that, were you?"

"That's different." Nick protested but Perri was laughing now. "And...hey, stop laughing, I learned from that. Now I know to ask. You'd think it would be obvious, wouldn't you? But people can surprise you."

"Just say'n."

"Ok. Truce?"

"Truce." Perri laughed.

Nick changed the subject. "I've got several options for when I can come over to Illinois to visit you. Is there a time that is better for you, or do you even know yet?"

"I don't think one time will be much different than another as far as I can tell right now. When is the soonest you can come?"

"I like your enthusiasm." Nick cleared his throat. "Alright, this is Monday. I could work through Thursday night and head over there Friday morning. I'd make it sooner, but I'm helping set up the Fall Harvest Festival stage area here in town on Thursday afternoon. That work for you?"

"You bet! That's awesome." Perri switched the phone to her other ear so she could grab her laptop. "Hey, on a more serious note..."

"Yeah?"

She flipped up the foot rest, settled back into the recliner, and switched on her laptop. "Do you have another couple of minutes?"

"Sure, what's up?"

"We planned on going hiking, right? Well, I've been looking at the map of the places we planned on going. We may want to adjust our plans a little. There was a murder here, a double murder actually."

Nick's concerned voice quickly interjected, "What happened? And why does that affect our hiking?"

"Remember when I was telling you about the places I wanted to visit again, and I mentioned the old salt works?"

"Yes."

"The guy in the apartment across the hall from me, Reuben Webb is his name, is writing a book about lost villages in southern Illinois and he and a friend went out to the salt well Saturday morning so he could document it and get photos."

"Ok. And?"

"There were two bodies, an older couple, tied together and shoved in the well. They were held down with a big limb and the water was covered by piles of leaves."

"Holy crap! Do they know who did it?"

"They have no idea who is responsible, or why. They haven't released the cause of death either. What makes this even more interesting is that the couple's house is an historic building over in Old Shawneetown. It was searched, from top to bottom. I talked to…" Perri stopped mid-sentence before she spouted off about talking to her patient, which was against the privacy laws.

"You talked to who?" Nick asked.

"I, um, talked to the guy across the hall and he told me about finding the bodies, and I heard the rest on the news. The reports say that the neighbors noticed an unlatched gate late Friday night. The neighbor went out to fasten the gate and saw some headlights go past, but they aren't sure if it was related to the murders or not."

"I have to agree we should probably avoid that area and not go blundering around in the woods if some crazy is still out there."

"Yeah, the thing is, unless the person is just loitering around the woods for some reason, they probably don't live there. Sounds like a body dump, or, well, maybe that's how they died, by drowning." Perri mused over that thought for a few seconds, then continued. "They haven't said what the cause of death is yet, so we'll see about that. But what I'm saying is that the Salt Well is located inside the Shawnee National Forest, although right at the edge of it. There are some farms nearby, but it definitely isn't a residential neighborhood. It's remote."

Nick's voice was stern, "Even more reason to not go blundering around there right now. If I'm floating in salt water, I want it to be ocean side."

"I can't help but wonder why someone would kill two people in Old Shawneetown, or at least take them from there, and transport the bodies to the salt well when their house is right on the Ohio River. You'd think the killer would have dumped the bodies off the bank or just left them in the house." She thought to herself a moment, then said, "Unless they weren't dead when they left the house. But in that case, it would be even harder to take them ten or fifteen miles away. They must have been afraid they'd be spotted too quickly at the river's edge."

There was dead silence until Nick said, "You have that tone in your voice."

"What tone?"

"The I'm-going-to-check-into-this-myself tone. Perri, seriously, please don't go poking around in this."

"Nick, come on, I just want to research the house. It has been in the same family since the original owner built it way back in the early 1800s. You know I need something to write about for my article."

"Do you think you should write about a house where people were just murdered?"

Perri paused. Nick waited while Perri conjured up a way to get around the obvious issue. She said, "I'll allow that I would need to handle it delicately and not be insensitive, but I think I could present the information in a way that was more of a memorial to the family that lived there than taking advantage of the situation. Anyway, aren't you curious about what they may have been looking for? This area has a lot of rumors and legends, some of them are bound to be true."

Perri knew from the audible cues coming through the phone that Nick had his head tipped back, mouth open, eyes closed, exhaling steadily as he struggled not to demand she not get involved for her own safety. She beat him to the punch, "I know! I know. I need to be careful, and I will. I am going to go to a local genealogy research library to see what I can find. Unless the murderous thug volunteers there, I'll be fine."

"Well, you never know, do you?" Nick knew Perri would start looking into it no matter what he said, so he decided to bolster the safety idea and doing her research only in well-lit, populated buildings. "Just be careful, will you? Promise me you won't go galivanting off through those woods or skulking around the murder house by yourself."

"I promise. I'll wait until you are here."

"I have to pick my battles, so we'll leave it there for now. I'd better get back into the bar. Business is already picking up for the start of the festival this weekend. Place is jam-packed. I'll turn in my vacation request to Howard tomorrow. I hope it flies with him because next week will be busy, but I haven't had a full week off for over two years. I'm really looking forward to it."

"Me too." Perri hesitated, then said, "I'm really looking forward to seeing you, Nick. I've missed you."

There were a few moments of quiet while the tension of the previous conversation drained away. Nick said, "I'm glad to hear you say that. I've missed you too." In a lighter tone, he said, "Welp, I've got drinks to mix and done-me-wrong stories to listen to, so I'll catch you tomorrow."

"Until tomorrow, have a good night."

"My pleasure. Good night."

"And…thanks, Nick."

Perri turned the television to a local news station. Resting her legs on top of an extra pillow from the couch, she signed in to Find-a-Grave to look over the burials in the cemetery along highway 45. She clicked on Search for a Cemetery and typed in Lindale Cemetery. She had noted the name of it as she drove past that morning. Filling in the blanks: the state as Illinois and the county as Saline, she hit enter. *No matching records*. "What?" The brick columned sign had clearly said Lindale Cemetery. She backed out to the search page and removed the word 'Cemetery.' This time there was one result, Lindale Memorial Gardens. "There it is." She clicked the Map tab to check the location and verified that it was the one.

The listing showed the cemetery had 1,288 internments. With interest, she noted there were twenty-three photo requests. Anyone could request a photo of a memorial for someone buried in any cemetery on Find-a-Grave. Volunteers could search for and photograph memorials, then upload the photo to the site to fulfill the request. The photograph would post on the memorial page for that person. For many people who lived a long way from where their family was buried, or for those who simply couldn't make the trip, these photos provided an image of the grave marker of their ancestor or relative they might not otherwise be able to get. The headstones often were a source of, or at least verification of, information regarding birth and death dates, as well as spouse and middle names. The volunteer may also photograph nearby stones of the same family name which sometimes turned out to be yet unknown family members.

Some requests were never filled for various reasons. Sadly, many of the graves were so old the marker had vanished or disintegrated to the point of being unidentifiable. Even more dismally, some were never placed because the family couldn't afford it or there was no family. In other cases, the location was no longer accessible to the public. Perri had come across that once near Harco, Illinois. Several years before, she and Nina had tried to go to a cemetery to take a volunteer photo but the road leading to the site was blocked by a metal fence with the name of a mining company and No Trespassing emblazoned ominously in large red and black letters.

Perri was perusing the seven results in Lindale from her search on the Seamore name when the news story being broadcast finally got through her concentration and grabbed her attention. She turned up the volume.

"...the bodies found in the old Salt Works well in Gallatin County. As reported previously, police were alerted Saturday around 10:00 a.m. by two people researching the site who were visiting that morning. Neighbors, Louis and Mildred Vincent, had noticed the absence of normal activity or lights in the Duncan home the evening before. An untended gate again drew their attention close to midnight Friday night. The official cause of death has been designated as drowning. The couple appeared to have been battered before being restrained and placed in the well.

The sister of the deceased woman lives in Harrisburg and was notified by law enforcement officers Saturday afternoon. She states that she has no additional information which might indicate a motive and there are no suspects at present in the double murder." The blond anchorwoman paused, then continued, "In local quarter-mile racing news, the season's last race at the Harrisburg…"

Perri switched off the television. She knew she needed to get to bed, but her thoughts raced as she made plans to research the house and family. She knew what she wanted most, though, was to get a look at the house, preferably the inside as well as the outside.

Chapter 9

May 29, 1819, 2:07 p.m.

Francis McCade led his bay horse off the ferry on the Illinois side. He ran his palm gently over her muzzle and spoke quietly to keep her calm while walking her down the rickety ramp to the sloping, rocky shore. She balked a little when the chains of the ramp jangled as she stepped to the packed dirt of the road. "Come on, Fiona, you did fine. All over now." The sienna-colored bay shook her head back and forth, her black mane tossing, not yet willing to be placated after the river crossing. Francis reached in his coat pocket and pulled out one of the dried apple treats he had made over the winter. Fiona loved them and it went a long way to soothing her affronted attitude.

Francis retightened the cinches, having loosened them during the ferry ride to give Fiona a breather. After making sure everything was secure, he took the reins and walked in front of her, "Let's go girl, I'll walk with you for a while until you calm down." The horse nodded her head up and down, but stayed put. Francis reached back into his pocket for another treat. "Last one for now." She snuffled as she accepted the peace offering, then placed one hoof forward as if to say, 'Ok, I'm ready to go.' Francis ran his hand down her withers and walked ahead, leading her gently. Fiona followed but retained an air of injured reserve. One big, round, brown eye fixed on Francis and conveyed, 'I'm doing you a favor.'

Francis laughed out loud as he turned a full circle while walking to get a last expansive view of the Ohio River. Once more facing ahead, he walked for a quarter of a mile before climbing into the saddle and riding north on Ford's Ferry Road.

After two or three miles, he became aware of the sound of hooves clopping up the road behind him. He turned in the saddle and saw several men steadily gaining upon him. He felt a twinge of fear and reached inside his coat to be sure his knife was within reach. He continued to watch them as one man broke away from the group, holding up one hand, and called, "Hello, friend. We don't mean to alarm you, but are traveling the same road. Shall we ride together?"

Francis eyed the man suspiciously, who again spoke before he could respond, "There is far greater safety in numbers." He tipped his head toward the others, six men besides himself. "We are all fellow travelers sticking together for our time on the road." He now pulled level with Francis.

Tipping his hat, the man said, "I'm Alexander Samuelson."

"Francis McCade, sir."

"A pleasure to meet you, Mr. McCade. May I ask where you're headed?"

Francis glanced again at the other men, who remained several yards behind. "I'm headed for Shawneetown."

"Oh! Shawneetown. Well, now, you must be a businessman."

"I am hoping to be, yes." Francis drew himself up a bit in his saddle. "Shawneetown has a chartered bank, the first in Illinois, and I'd like to take a position there if I can."

"You a banker?" Alexander asked earnestly.

The saddle creaked a little as Francis adjusted his posture, "I have a little background with bookkeeping and hope to be a success in the new territories. I'm from Kentucky, but I want the chance to make my own way. Shawneetown is up and coming, now is the time to get in on the development. I've heard there is a chance to become a wealthy man if one is wise with one's decisions."

Alexander glanced back over his shoulder and nodded for the others to join them. As they approached he gave a discreet negative shake of his head to Joshua, then said to Francis, "We are presently all heading in the same general direction. There is an Inn ahead, only about four or five miles, where we plan to put up for the night. There is nothing beyond that until you come to Shawneetown, so you might consider lodging there and continuing in the morning."

"You appear familiar with the area. Are you also going to Shawneetown?" Francis asked.

"No sir, my party is bound for St. Louis but we plan to overnight at Pott's Inn and start fresh in the morning. While it isn't exactly late in the day, night will be here before too many more hours. There is a lot of land between here and where we are going with few inns, and we need to be alert for our journey. It would be the wisest choice to stay in a safe and comfortable place, with good food, when we can, isn't that right?" The other men murmured their agreement.

Joshua Rutledge understood Alexander's signal. They were to allow Francis to advance to the Inn, essentially to delay a decision regarding robbing him until more information could be gathered. Ford's Ferry Road was already known for thieves. With the recent pressure from settlers for enforced protection for travelers, Alexander didn't want to risk drawing undue attention to their activities by attacking indiscriminately on the open road or too often. The best marks were those who were not only alone, but who possessed something to make the robbery worth the risk and who didn't have people waiting to hear from them at their journey's end. The stretch of road from the ferry landing to the Inn provided the perfect set-up for assessing the potential of travelers.

Amiable chatter made the miles pass quickly. Alexander pointed to a gently sloping hill they were just beginning to ascend. "That's Pott's Inn ahead. Almost there." He flashed a comfortable smile toward Francis.

Francis ran an appraising eye over the Inn which was set back from the road at the top of the hill on their left. It was a two-story clapboard building with a porch running along the front of both levels. The two porches were supported by whitewashed wooden posts, the ground floor porch was open to the lawn in front of it with the second floor being enclosed by a railing. Caned rockers sat on both levels. Smoke curled from a chimney at the back of the inn scenting the air with a combination of wood smoke and cooking fat.

Francis hadn't planned on stopping at an inn for the night, but the prospect of a meal and an evening in good company sounded mighty good to him right then, not to mention a chance for Fiona to rest. She'd been agitated since the ferry ride, the rolling of the ferry in the waves of the Ohio River had unsettled her.

After seeing his horse installed in a lean-to style stable behind the Inn, with food, water, and her own blanket over her back, Francis had obtained a room on the second floor. It was small but serviceable with a narrow iron bedstead, one chair, a somewhat rickety washstand, and a pitcher, basin, and towel. He had splashed the road dust from his face, brushed his coat and trousers with a bristle brush he kept in his pack, and gone down to the dining room located at the front of the building.

Francis was seated at a table next to one of the front windows. He requested ale from a man who briefly emerged from the kitchen. There was no one else in the dining room. The view was pleasant and calming. The flowering dogwoods and red buds had shed their spent blossoms and, along with the plentiful maples and oaks and hickories, were starting to fill in their skeletal winter frames with soft green leaves. The fields extending from the base of the hill across the flat bottom of the valley were plowed and may have been already planted, Francis couldn't tell.

A middle-aged woman who introduced herself as Mrs. Potts served Francis a supper of meat stew with chunks of squash and potatoes, a loaf of dark, coarse bread with butter in an earthen pot, and a second tankard of beer. When she took his bowl away, Mrs. Potts brought Francis a fluted glass containing a rich syllabub made with cider. The fluid in the bottom of the glass sparkled amber in the firelight, the curds frothy on top. As the sun lowered behind the hill and the tentative daytime spring warmth gave way to the still receding cold of winter, Mr. Potts lit the fire in the cavernous field stone fireplace at the end of the room.

The warmth and sound of crackling flames were winning Francis over to the side of sleep. He wasn't ready to retire just yet. To combat the drowsiness, he removed a small leather-bound notebook and pencil from the pocket inside his coat. He turned to the first blank page and entered the date, May 29, 1819, and followed with a brief accounting of his day, including his shared travel with Alexander Samuelson and ending with what he had for supper at Pott's Inn. He swigged down the last of the beer and looked to the window again. The scene outside had disappeared into the opaque blackness of night in the mostly unsettled land where no other cabins or signs of civilization were visible. He could see only his reflection in the slightly wavy panes of glass.

Francis returned the notebook and pencil to the depths of his coat and was about to rise when Alexander and another man entered the room.

They stepped between the empty tables by different routes to make their way over to where Francis was still seated. Alexander spoke, "Mind if we join you for a bit of a talk?"

Francis was a little disappointed: his belly was satisfied, the beer had relaxed him, and the fire warmed him. He was ready for bed. Despite that, he stood and said, "Certainly, have a seat, gentlemen." He sat back down once the other two men were seated. "Is there anything in particular you would like to discuss?"

"Business. Francis, this is Abrahm Stegall...Abrahm, Francis McCade."

Francis and Abrahm shook hands. "What type of business do you want to discuss, Mr. Samuelson?"

"Call me Alexander, please. May I call you Francis?"

"Yes, of course." Francis leaned back in his chair and waited.

Alexander began, "I passed on to Abrahm your hopes for success in business in Shawneetown — he wasn't able to hear all of our conversation on the road. We thought we'd talk to you about possibly doing business together."

"I'm flattered, Alexander, but I have yet to make a start and have no idea what business we could conduct at this point."

"That's why I wanted to talk to you. We're just getting started too, that's why we are headed to St. Louis. Abrahm and I are the investors and the others are going to work for us. We all have to start somewhere, don't we?" Alexander flashed a brilliant smile, marred only by one lower tooth which didn't quite line up with the others, but projected forward a bit. "Now, I understand that Shawneetown is on its way to becoming a bustling river city, which St. Louis already has become. Since I still have family in these parts, I tend to travel back and forth. It would be mutually beneficial to have contacts in other thriving centers of business, especially ones located on navigable rivers."

"I can't disagree with that." Francis looked from Alexander to Abrahm and back again. "What are you suggesting?"

Alexander surreptitiously glanced around the otherwise empty dining room, more for effect than need. He smiled, scooted his chair further up to the table, and leaning toward Francis, said, "My true name is Alexander Mason." Francis's eyes grew wide. "Here's what I propose."

Against his better judgement, Francis leaned in to listen.

## Chapter 10

October 11, 2016

"Mr. Tollander. Mr. Tollander! Please, wait, stop." Perri dodged the patient's flailing arms to avoid contamination or being clocked in the head by an elbow. She hoped he wouldn't also contaminate the sterile field she had just set up around his leg wound, but it wasn't looking good as the chux pad under his lower right leg creased and moved around on the sofa.

The old man's voice rose shrilly, "You're a'killin' me. You hafta stop." He slapped at Perri's arms with both hands.

Perri drew back from the line of fire, held both sterile gloved hands up between waist and shoulder level to keep them sterile, and waited while her patient wound down. His drama continued for another fifteen seconds or so before he noticed she was standing three feet away from him. "You're supposed to be taking care of my leg and there you stand, just doin' nothin'. I'm going to tell…"

"You're going to tell who? And what are you going to tell them?" Perri tilted her head and grinned just a little bit. "Are you going to report me for trying to redress your leg wound, which is why I'm here?" She stepped back to the patient's side. "What exactly are you going on about? How am I killing you?"

He glared at Perri and clucked like a ruffled hen.

"Mr. Tollander, I am not a new nurse. I've seen plenty of hissy fits in the last eleven years and not once has it helped anybody feel better or heal faster."

The elderly man dropped his skinny arms, his hands plopped into his lap. He frowned, his assault thwarted and obviously trying to decide what to complain about next. It didn't take him long to zero in on something. He pointed at Perri, "It's that Pearl Gentry, she turned you against me afore you ever got over here, I just know it." His dentures clacked as he snapped out the words. "Did Pearl say something about me? What'd she say?"

Perri decided on the quietly sympathetic but firmly authoritative approach. "I can't comment on anyone else. I can't even say if I know them or not. Privacy laws, you know? Now, let's get this dressing changed, my arms are getting tired holding them up." She grinned and reached for the bottle of irrigation saline. "Why don't you tell me something about yourself, Mr. Tollander?"

He turned his diluted blue eyes to Perri in surprise. The lower lid of his left eye turned outward, an exotropia. It revealed a road map of vessels in the conjunctival tissue. His expression softened. "Did you hear about Pearl's sister and her husband getting killed?"

Careful to keep her responses neutral, Perri said, "I heard about the deaths of a couple from Old Shawneetown on the news last night, is that who you mean?" Holding a towel beneath the patient's leg, Perri moistened the dry, soiled gauze covering the ulcer with saline solution and carefully unwound the dressing."

"That was Pearl's little sister, Ruby, and her husband, George. Good people. Somebody killed 'em and turned their house upside down. It's disgusting, tying 'em up like Christmas turkeys and tossin' 'em in the salt well out in the woods. I wish I knew who was responsible." He fumed, making and releasing a fist.

"That's horrible. Do they know why yet? Or who?"

"I ain't heard nothin' new today." Mr. Tollander winced as the last of the gauze came away and Perri peeled the 4 x 4s from the wound. "I used to date Pearl, way back before she married Charlie. Yeah, I used to drive over there to Old Town and pick her up at that big estate on the hill. Her and her sister Ruby were something else, both of 'em pretty as could be. I can't believe Ruby's gone, murdered!"

"It's awful. I hope they catch who did it." Hoping to probe into any suspicions her patient might have, Perri prompted, "I wonder if they have any suspects yet."

Mr. Tollander shook his head. "You said you used to date Pearl, Mr. Tollander. Why did you stop dating, if I can ask?" Perri asked.

"Call me Stanley. Mr. Tollander was my dad." He shifted slightly on the couch as Perri applied fresh gauze pads. "Pearl's daddy didn't want her datin' a miner. No, they were better than that, I guess."

"Did the family have money?" Perri asked as she realized Mr. Tollander might also be a source of contemporary information about the McCade house decades ago.

"They did, at least at one time. They must have. Had that big old house that's been there forever. Everybody always made over it being a grand place. Supposed to still be full of antiques and treasures and money."

"Really? Full of treasure?" Perri kept working on the dressing, filling the debrided wound with fresh sterile gauze sponges moistened with solution. She glanced at Stanley.

"Well, that's what the stories said. Supposed to be stuff in the family, been passed down for generations, worth all kinds of money. And it would be if it'd been in the house since it was built and I don't think they ever got rid of anything. Everyone said Old Man McCade, not Pearl's daddy, but his daddy, Pearl's grandpappy, buried a bunch of stuff on the grounds somewhere."

Perri stopped and looked at Stanley. "Do you think people ever really buried valuables? It seems like there are so many stories, but I'm not sure many people actually did it. Look at all the tales about Cave-in-Rock. I know people sometimes buried mason jars with money in them, but large amounts of money or valuables... I don't know. You don't often hear of someone finding those kinds of stashes. It seems there are far more theories than actual finds." She went back to wrapping pristine white gauze around Stanley's leg.

With a smirk, he replied, "Well, I think they might've over there at McCade Manor."

"McCade Manor? Was the house called that?" Perri asked.

"I don't know if the McCades called it that, but most everybody else did. There's gotta be some reason so many people asked Ruby and George if they could metal detect on their property."

"Metal detecting? Really...has anything been found?"

"They never have let anyone do it, but where there's smoke, there's fire."

"Well, it's an interesting idea though, isn't it?" Wanting to find out as much detail as possible, Perri asked, "What do *you* think they might have buried on their property?" Perri pulled off her gloves, one inside the other, flipped the wadded gloves inside out and tossed them in the red biohazard bag along with the old dressing.

Stanley pressed his lips together then opened them with a smacking noise. "Well, that's a question been going around for donkey's years. I remember stories when I was a kid that the family's been there so long they have chests of gold coins buried in different spots around the grounds."

"Hmm. I can see how that would draw a lot of interest. Chests of gold seems a little unlikely, don't you think?"

"Yeah, maybe it's just a little gold. Or maybe it's just coins. But they never said, and now it might be too late to find out unless Pearl knows about it."

Perri excused herself to wash her hands in the aqua-tiled bathroom. The sink and toilet matched the tile and ceramic mermaids hung on the walls, probably having been in place since the 1950s. When she returned to the living room, she didn't repeat aloud her worry that the possibility of Pearl knowing, or someone *thinking* that Pearl knew about family treasure, could be a problem for her safety. She packed her supplies back in her bag. "You said you were a coal miner back then?"

"Oh yeah, yeah, but that was the strip mining they did in the 60's. I didn't have to go underground like my dad, back before the mines all flooded in '37. We used giant shovels above ground. That thing was huge. We had one of the biggest ones in the world at Sahara Coal. Thing was eight stories tall." He was staring out the window, a vague wisp of a smile on his lips, his thoughts very far away.

"I'd like to hear more about it, Stanley, maybe on my next visit?"

The old man smiled and nodded as close to enthusiastically as he probably ever did. "I'd like that young lady, what'd you say your name was?"

"Perri Seamore."

"Seamore. Hmm, mighta known your grandpa." He squinted at Perri while he searched his memory. "Bill....William?"

"Yes, that's him. You knew him?"

"Somewhat. He worked at Sahara for a while. I might forget a lot of things, but I don't forget a name."

"I'd love it if you could tell me anything you remember about him. I am always working on my family tree and writing down stories. I'll look forward to that!" Perri picked up her bag and moved toward the front door. "Take care, Mr. Tollander."

"Stanley!"

"Ok, Stanley."

"You be careful, now." He held one hand up in the air, not waving, just a gesture.

Perri left feeling pleased that, at least for now, she wouldn't have to dread visits with this patient. Instead, maybe a little selfishly, she hoped she could hear some stories from a person who knew her grandfather long before she had, back when he was a young man. She had long felt that family history was more than simply charting names and dates or racking up numbers of names in a tree. Stories about family members from people who knew them were gold and Perri documented any stories she collected.

The rest of Tuesday went by uneventfully. It already was beginning to feel routine as she grew more comfortable in her new role.

After her last case, she threw dietary caution to the wind and picked up supper from a drive-through burger joint. The day had been warm and she drove back to the apartment with the windows down. The char-grilled aroma had reached in, grabbed her by the nose, and forcibly dragged her to the drive-up window. 'I'm my own worst enemy,' she thought to herself as she shifted into drive and left the pick-up window, the bag on the passenger seat.

Once back in her apartment, she put the food into the toaster oven to keep warm while she showered, which she always did after a shift no matter where it was. After a steamy shower and a handful of cocoa butter lotion, she climbed into a corner of the couch, tucking her robe under her feet. She used a pillow to prop herself up with her back against the arm, her food in her lap on a plate, and a glass of unsweetened iced tea on the coffee table. Unsweet tea was her one concession to moderation. She dragged her laptop over and entered her daily timecard, charting, and notes.

Finished with the wonderfully smoky blue cheese burger and onion rings, as well as her job-related online paperwork, Perri decided to see what she could dig up on Pearl's family. Pearl had told her the family name was McCade. Stanley's tales about buried valuables and the house had piqued her curiosity. She couldn't help but wonder if the deaths of Ruby and George Duncan were connected to the rumors of valuables on the property. But if they were, why take them to the salt well. She had very few puzzle pieces, but that piece didn't fit anywhere, not yet.

Perri opened her browser and clicked on the Genealogy file in her bookmarks. Knowing she would likely find the most useful information on the McCade property and family history in the genealogy society's library, she planned to form a basic outline of the family to work from, and take note of anything interesting that might show up from sources online.

She went to Genweb first. She could look up the family on Ancestry, but wanted to check the Gallatin County content first. Ancestry would certainly have some of the more commonly available online information, but by checking a smaller local database first, she figured she might be able to narrow her search for the McCade family given names before using the larger database on Ancestry and having to wade through possibly thousands of results. At any rate, since Francis McCade went back to the very early 1800s, it was less likely she'd easily find the types of records she could expect for the latter half of the century, birth or death certificates or detailed census records. There may be tax records or land patents though. Being in the area where Francis and his family lived, she hoped she'd be able to find more personal information, like church directories or local newspaper articles.

The USGenWeb Project was created to provide information for genealogists with every county in each state being represented by their own web pages. Each county site was maintained by a volunteer, so the content could vary significantly. Perri had found some very valuable information on the site while researching her own family. Often, unexpected records not otherwise available online could be found there, like scanned images of family Bibles, letters, diaries, clipped newspaper articles, personal family photographs, items that had been kept for generations by families and were submitted to the site by individuals.

Some of the county pages had evolved into what amounted to community projects. As more people learned about the site, more documents were shared. She'd found a treasure trove of information on the Clinton County page, including the exact location of an ancestor's burial and directions on how to get there. Without that information, she would never have known where to look for her x4 grandfather's burial location, especially since he died in the Civil War and the bodies of many soldiers never made it home.

The Gallatin County page looked very promising with links to records for local deaths, marriages, land records, old church documents, maps, military service, and cemeteries. Perri clicked on *Deaths* first. It wasn't a searchable database, but the names were listed in alphabetical order.

The data was listed in columns for name, sex/race, age, death certificate number, death date, county, city, and the date the death was filed. There were two listed.

McCade, Thomas R., M/W, UNK, 31026, July 20, 1921, Gallatin, Shawneetown, --

McCade, Morgan E., M/W, Y-64, 31569, December 14, 1952, Gallatin, Shawneetown, 52-12-17

Perri jotted down the information, noting that Morgan McCade was a candidate for Pearl's 'grandpappy,' as Stanley called him. Based on his age at death, he would have been born in 1888. He would have been 58 when Pearl was born in 1946. She would have been six years old when her grandfather died and may or may not remember him, but she probably would know his name to verify the information.

Thomas R. McCade was a likely father to Morgan, but Perri would need to confirm it with documentation. Even though Morgan would only have been around two years old in 1890, Perri couldn't expect to find Morgan and Thomas listed together until the 1900 census. Except for a few remnants, the 1890 census had been destroyed. It largely escaped the fire in the Commerce Building where it was stored, but it was heavily damaged by the water used to put it out. Still, a large portion of the census could have been salvaged, but it would have taken time and money, so as is typical with bureaucracies, it was allowed to sit and rot until it was in deplorable condition. Someone made the decision to destroy the entire collection only weeks before an effort to save them was scheduled to start. Now only a few fragments remained, a handful of counties from an even smaller handful of states. It made Perri angry all over again every time she thought about it.

Since Morgan would only have been twelve years old in 1900, he probably would be listed in his father's household, but Perri liked having as many opportunities as possible to find someone on a census, and the loss of 1890 reduced the chances by half. By 1920, Morgan may have married and/or moved away from home, and while he was most likely on the census, the certainty of finding him listed in Thomas's household as his son would be lost. She'd have to be happy with 1900.

After working her way through various spellings of McCade on Ancestry, Perri had come up with a record for a Thomas McQaid living in Shawnee Township, 47 years old, born in August of 1853 in Illinois. The information given indicated his father was also born in Illinois and his mother in Pennsylvania. Thomas was listed as a merchant. His wife was named Hattie, possibly a nickname for Harriet, born March of 1852 in Illinois, with both her parents being born in New York.

There were two children in the McCade household. The eldest was Margaret, born in June of 1886, the second child was Morgan, born in July of 1888. The census information for this township had been gathered on June 1, so unless Margaret was born before June 1, neither she nor Morgan had celebrated a birthday yet in 1900. Margaret was listed as 13 and Morgan as 11. Given the age of the Morgan in the death record listing as being 64 at his death in 1952, this matched up with the Morgan on the census. Perri was very pleased to find Morgan and Thomas in one household. She sent the page to her printer.

Checking the time, she decided on one more site before bed. The Illinois Newspaper Project was hosted by the University of Illinois at Urbana-Champaign. Its searchable database provided information about each newspaper, such as the year published and where, as well as the range of dates the paper was active. Locations were given where the newspapers could be viewed, either in original format or as microfilm. Perri noted that several of the papers were available in both the Shawneetown and Harrisburg libraries. One of the papers had been published as early as 1819. "I definitely need to see that one." She printed the page of newspaper titles, placing it in her satchel with the census record.

It was getting late and she had an early start the next morning. Perri tossed her trash in the wastebasket and washed the few dirty dishes that had accumulated. After falling into bed, she was asleep in only a couple of minutes. She didn't wake up repeatedly through the night like she had the two previous nights, but slept like the dead.

## Chapter 11

October 12, 2016

Wednesday morning broke clear but windy. Sudden gusts scuttled leaves across the apartment parking spaces like a leaf blower. A discarded potato chip bag pirouetted in a spiral dance as the air eddied between the building and the brick wall around the trash disposal area.

After Perri's normal morning chore of trying to get her ultra-straight hair to do something other than hang in her eyes, the wind maliciously whipped it straight up, forward, and back again while she piled her bag and purse in the back seat. 'So much for that,' Perri thought to herself and climbed into the Cooper, slamming the door shut to block out the rush of air. She leaned over and looked at her bedraggled image in the rear-view mirror. "Yep. Hair all over the place. Oh, well." She blew upward to get the strands out of her eyes.

She turned left out of the apartment driveway and headed south. The patient list was similar to Monday morning with Pearl scheduled first, but Perri's afternoon was free. It was a nice break in the week and she planned to take advantage of it by visiting the genealogical society.

The field along the southeastern edge of highway 45 was covered in standing water from the rain a few nights ago. The wind buffeted the surface giving the impression of a lake rather than cropland that, two weeks ago, had been full of corn and pumpkins waiting to be harvested. Fields on the opposite side of the highway were dotted with honey-colored straw, chopped up by the harvester and strewn about the furrows, not yet disked under for the winter.

Geese stood in groups looking around continuously as though they'd lost something and crows picked through the rows looking for remnants of corn. A short distance ahead, Perri could see a few crows doggedly chasing a Cooper's Hawk which had brazenly entered their territory. The hawk turned and dived then rose again, changing directions, screaming out its distinctive call. But the crows followed relentlessly until the hawk decided it wasn't worth its time and flew away to the east.

When Perri knocked on Pearl's door, she was greeted with the door being swung partially open by a woman who looked to be in her 50's. She was thin, wearing the kind of jeans that Perri associated with the 1970s, the kind with rhinestones edging the pockets, and a flannel shirt tied in a knot at her waist. With one hand propping the door open, she drew heavily on a cigarette and let the smoke curl out, one eye closed against the sting. "Yeah?"

"Hello. I'm Perri, the home health nurse." Perri waited. The woman kept staring at her, frowning. "I'm here to see Pearl?"

The woman looked past Perri, to where her car was parked in front of the house, then said, "Alright." As Perri climbed the remaining steps, the woman walked away from the door, letting it slam shut behind her.

The door quivered on its hinges. Perri drew in a quiet breath and opened it, following the woman into the main house. Her nondescript hair could have been brown, dark blond, or gray, or a mixture of all three. It was pulled very tightly back in a thin ponytail that was just long enough for the tip to hang inside the worn collar of her shirt. Once she reached the center of the living room, the woman turned to face Perri, standing squarely with one arm folded across her abdomen and the other elbow propped on her forearm. Perri's expectant look was met with a blank stare. Finally, the woman took another deep tug on her cigarette and said, begrudgingly, "I'm Stella Paulson, Pearl's daughter. You here to check her sugar?" A puff of smoke burst forth from her thin, dry lips with every word. A whiff of lingering alcohol accompanied the exhaled smoke.

Perri resisted the urge to wave her hand in front of her nose. "Yes, and to check her medicine supply, do a quick assessment." Perri didn't see Pearl and didn't hear anyone in the back part of the house. She gave the room a pointed look around and with growing impatience asked, "Is Pearl awake?" She'd never been good at concealing how she felt, either her face or her voice betrayed her and she could hear it in her tone now.

The house was an older floorplan where each room opened into another with no hallway. Perri could see into the dining room, then the kitchen. By the configuration of the exterior, the bedroom would be accessed from the dining room. The bathroom most likely had been added somewhere after the house was built.

"Hang on." Stella ran her tongue over her lips and walked over to the coffee table, brutally crushing her cigarette on a dirty plate left to harden. Despite the force she used, it didn't quite go out and an acrid smell emitted from the smoldering butt. She left the plate on the table. "MA!" She shouted in a craggy voice as she walked through the doorway into the next room. Perri saw her turn right as she called again, "Ma! Wake up. Nurse's here."

Perri felt uneasy. She shifted her weight from one foot to the other, walked forward a couple of steps and listened, then called, "Hello? Stella?" Quiet. "Is Pearl ok?" Perri's uneasiness worsened and her palms started to sweat.

"Come on back," came Stella's lazy drawl.

Perri quickly rounded the corner of the dining room and entered the darkened bedroom. Pearl was in bed, but was stirring, which Perri was relieved to see. "Good morning, Pearl, it's Perri. How are you doing?"

"Oh, yes, it is, I'm sure. Why do you ask?" Pearl looked up sharply at Perri in the dim light.

Perri sat her bag on the blanket chest at the foot of the bed and cast an assessing eye over Pearl. "Well, because I'm here to check your blood sugar and see how you are doing."

"I just don't understand that at all. Why are you causing all this trouble?" Pearl's voice became angry and she nervously moved her hands over the quilt.

Stella picked at her teeth with a jagged pinky fingernail without expression or reaction. Perri glanced questioningly at Stella, who insolently shrugged and left the room.

"Pearl, do you mind if I raise the blind? It's a little dark in here." The old-fashioned roller blind didn't respond at first, then finally twirled up to the top of the window, the end slapping around against the frame several times before coming to rest.

"I will not tolerate any more of this monkey business. Take your friend and get out of here, right this minute! I've told you I made up my mind and I mean it. I mean it, I'm telling you!"

Perri quickly put a hand on Pearl's cheek, then her forehead. Her skin was cold and clammy. Pearl swatted at Perri's hand on her cheek. Perri snatched her bag up onto the bedside.

Pearl was in a near-seated position in bed, propped up against the headboard by several cushions and pillows. "I gave you my answer! Leave me alone, I'm tired of your pestering!" Her head then wilted back on the pillow and she gazed blankly forward.

Knowing Pearl's blood sugar was likely very low, maybe dangerously so, Perri rapidly unzipped her supply bag and pulled out gloves and the portable glucometer, hastily turning it on to start the self-check routine while she swabbed Pearl's middle finger with an alcohol wipe then tugged on a pair of gloves. Grasping Pearl's finger firmly, she struggled to keep hold of it while Pearl tried to pull her hand away. She lanced it and gathered the sample on the strip, a little sloppily because of the motion, then inserted the strip in the meter and set it on the bedside table. Again, Pearl relaxed against the pillows. Perri applied the blood pressure cuff and took Pearl's blood pressure. She didn't resist this time. Her BP was a little low. Her pulse was elevated.

By the time she had the BP, the glucose test was finished. 42. "Crap." Perri opened the glucose gel and applied a blob to a tongue depressor and pressed on Pearl's jaw to open her mouth. She needed to get the gel inside Pearl's mouth without getting bitten. She slid the depressor out against the tongue to deposit as much of the gel as possible. Pearl was moving her tongue in and out of her mouth and was swallowing without difficulty. Perri readied another test strip and set the meter back on the table, ready to recheck.

"Stella! Can you hear me?" Perri shouted.

"Yeah?" Came the disinterested response.

"Do you have some sugared soft drink, not diet? Or orange juice? Also, some peanut butter or cheese crackers if you have them, for after her sugar comes up enough for her to eat something. Perri heard an impatient sigh, but got no answer. Pearl's languid expression slowly shifted to slightly more focused but still bemused. Perri took her BP again, 100/70, normalizing.

The recheck showed Pearl's blood sugar was up to 88. Perri relaxed a little. Stella walked in with a mason jar drinking glass half full of orange juice and a couple of crackers with peanut butter on them sitting on a paper towel.

"Thank you." Perri set the crackers on the table. She tapped Pearl's shoulder and asked, "Pearl? Pearl, do you know who I am?" Pearl looked at Perri. She didn't answer verbally, but she nodded yes. "Can you take a sip of juice for me?" Pearl reached out for the glass, but Perri held it to her lips for her as she took a couple of swallows, then laid her head back against the pillow. Perri looked around, Stella had left the room.

Twenty minutes later, Pearl's blood sugar was in the upper normal range and her blood pressure was stabilized. She had finished the juice and eaten the crackers. Stella peeked in the bedroom, so Perri quickly asked, "Can you come in for a moment, Stella?"

Stella stepped into the bedroom and crossed her arms without saying anything.

"Can you tell me what Pearl had to eat this morning for breakfast?"

"Far as I know, nothing." Perri waited for further explanation. "Said she didn't want anything."

"Being diabetic, she has to have something to eat at each meal."

"She said she didn't want anything. I can't force her." Stella rolled her shoulders and turned her palms outward as if to say, 'What do you expect me to do?'

Perri breathed in and out a couple of times. "Do you live here with your mother?" Perri asked.

"No. I came in … early. I guess. Middle of the night. Sometimes I stay here if I don't want to drive all the way home. I live in Equality."

Perri understood that it probably meant she couldn't drive home without the fear of getting breathalyzed. Stella added, "I work over here sometimes, at the raceway, in the concession stand. Gets late, ya know?"

"I see. Where are your mother's supplies? I need to see that she has enough to follow up on her glucose herself." Not trusting Stella's vigilance or will to help her mother, Perri asked, "And, can you show me what she has to eat for lunch, if you know?"

Stella didn't sigh this time, likely sensing it would be over quicker if she didn't resist. Instead, with a barely-there eyeroll, she waved Perri into the kitchen and pointed to the refrigerator, saying, "There it is, help yourself."

After making sure there were adequate amounts of food, Perri collected the dirty dishes from the living room, plucking them from around Stella's booted feet on the coffee table. She put them to soak in hot soapy water in the kitchen sink then went back to the bedroom to find Pearl putting on her robe. "Are you feeling better?"

"Yes, honey, I'm so sorry. I usually can tell when those spells are coming on, but this one just crept up on me. Where's Stella?"

"In the living room." Perri could hear audience applause from one of the morning shows.

Pearl smiled at Perri and gestured toward the living room. As they walked, Perri asked, "How are you doing today otherwise? I mean, after the news on Monday."

"Well, I'm getting by." Pearl sat in her chair and propped her feet up on the hassock. "I can't say I understand it any better than I did Monday. They still don't know who did it."

Stella pointedly made a not so subtle reduction in volume of the television.

Perri asked Pearl, "Do you and Stella have other family around the area?"

Stella answered for her, "No, it's just us." Her eyes moved only enough to glance at Perri, then shifted her attention back to the talk show melodrama.

Keeping one observant eye on Stella, Perri said, "I'm sure it's a difficult time for both of you." She was rewarded with a smirk from Pearl's daughter. Perri continued, "Pearl, you said you would tell me more about your family home. I'm very interested in hearing about it."

Pearl's visage brightened at the thought of talking about the past. "Did I tell you that our house was a very special house?"

"You did say that it was one of the first brick houses in Shawneetown. What makes it special, other than that it was built so long ago?"

Pearl settled in to tell her story. "That house has been there since the early 1830s, not sure exactly what year. They weren't building too many houses in brick yet. I have heard it was the first one, but I don't know about that. It might have just been my granddad telling a story. He liked telling stories. The McCade who built it, Francis, was the first one to live in Shawneetown. Somebody told me once that it was quite the showplace in its day. It's a little run down and needing some work now, but it's got good bones."

"Do you remember your grandfather's name?" Perri asked.

"Oh yes, I do. I have a family Bible that my grandmother gave me and it has a lot of names in it."

"That's great, Pearl. I'd love to see it."

Stella interrupted brutally, "Why are you asking her these questions? What business is it of yours anyway?"

"Stella!" Pearl gasped.

"It's ok, Pearl." Perri turned to Stella. "I'm very interested in genealogy. It sounds like the McCade family has lived here for a very long time, and in a very special house, so it would be interesting to see how far back through the family tree the Bible goes." Stella didn't respond, just scowled.

Pearl continued. "I'll be glad to show it to you. Stella..."

"I'm not getting it out to show Nosy Nancy Nurse! Let her get it if you want her to know all about our family."

Perri's sense of knowing when to leave was overwhelmed by her curiosity. She would also have to admit to a strong desire to thwart Stella's attempts to discourage her too. Ultimately, it mattered what Pearl wanted. "If you want to show it to me, I can get it for you if you tell me where it is."

Perri located the bible in the blanket chest at the foot of Pearl's bed, tucked away in one corner beneath two hand-stitched quilts in classic honeycomb and log cabin patterns. The black leather-bound bible was dry and crumbly around the edges, the layers of paper inside the leather binding separating and flaking away. She gingerly handed the decaying book to Pearl.

Pearl settled the book on her lap. "Now, let me see."

Perri quickly got her notebook out of her satchel and pulled a pen from her scrubs pocket. "Do you mind if I make notes? I would love to help you find out more about your family and the house." She cleared her throat a little then said, "I wanted to ask you about writing an article about your family's home for a genealogy magazine too."

"An article? What the hell are you taking about now?" Stella dragged her attention away from the histrionic talk show and dropped both booted feet down to the floor. She sat bolt upright, frowning.

"I'm supposed to write an article for an online genealogy magazine. The McCade family and their home in Old Shawneetown sounds like a great subject for the article."

"Well, I don't know about that. Maybe we don't want our business put out there for everyone."

"I wouldn't write anything personal, at least nothing that the family didn't want, but telling the story of the old house would be..."

Stella stood and glowered down at Pearl. "No. I say no. Mom? You don't want her yammerin' on about our personal family stuff in some online rag, do you?"

"Well, I think it'd be nice. And she just *said* she wouldn't put anything private that we didn't want in there." Pearl's voice gained some assertiveness. "I have pride in the family and I'd like to find out what we can about the house. I don't know how to do that, and you sure as heck won't do it, so yes, I do want Perri to write about it, Stella."

Stella stood, jangling her keys without saying anything.

"Isn't it about time for that no-account boyfriend of yours to show up? Why don't you just go on?" Pearl and Stella glared at each other for a few moments.

Stella tossed the remote on the coffee table. It bounced and slid across the top, fell to the floor and scooted under the couch. "Sounds like a good idea to me. I don't like snoops poking around in everybody's business." Stella threw a dagger look at Perri and jerked her thumb, and her head, at her. "You'd better watch out Ma, this one is after something." She stomped out, slamming the screen door, leaving it rattling in its hinges.

Perri was torn between sadness for Pearl, surprise at Stella's outburst, worry that she might get in trouble with the agency, and excitement that Pearl was willing to tell her about the house. "I am so sorry! I had no idea ..."

Pearl appeared wholly unconcerned about the altercation. "You just forget her. She's got a bad attitude about everything anymore and that house is at the top of her list. And since she's been running around with that hoodlum — he's too old to be a hoodlum I guess — she's been worse than ever."

"Oh?"

"My sister left the house to me. I grew up there just like she did. But Stella had some wild idea that she'd get the house or at least part of it. Thinks I'm too old to inherit something, that it might as well go on to her. She and her husband are getting a divorce, bless his heart. He's living in their house in Equality. I think he finally threw her butt out. That's why Stella stays here sometimes. I have no idea where she stays the rest of the time. Don't want to know. But probably with that greasy-haired bum she's taken up with. She even showed up at Ruby's house the very day they found her. Can you believe that?"

"Why did she go there?"

"She wanted in. Said it was going to be hers and she wanted to make sure she knew what all was in it, as though the police were going to steal stuff from the house." Pearl fluttered her hand to dismiss the incident. "Ok, where was I? I'll start with me and go back as far as I can. My maiden name was Pearl Edwina McCade and I was born in 1946 right there in Shawneetown, the old one. My sister's name was Ruby Allison McCade, she was born in 1950, so I was four years older than she was." A little shadow flitted across Pearl's face, but she continued. "Ruby was my little sister. Dad named us both after jewels. Ruby and Pearl. Know why?"

Perri looked up from her notebook and shook her head.

"Well, his first name was Abner, but his middle name was Jewel. Abner Jewel McCade. He thought it was a great idea to have his little girls named after jewels since we weren't boys and he couldn't name one of us Abner, Jr." She laughed quietly to herself. "Now, Jewel's not as strange a name for a man as you might think. Oh, it is by today's standards, but not so much then. There was a man daddy knew that used to work at the salt works who was called Emerald."

"My dad was born in 1916, there in that very house too. Our mother was Dorothy. She died in 1968, after I got married and before Ruby did. I married Charlie in 1965 when I was nineteen years old. Stella is the only child we had. Charlie died a few years ago from a stroke. When we got married, Charlie and I got our own house here in Harrisburg. When Ruby married George, momma was already gone from cancer, so Ruby and George lived in the house with daddy. He didn't do too well after momma was gone."

"I'm sorry to hear that, Pearl."

"Long time ago now." Pearl waved her hand as if to shoo the bad memories away before they made her cry. "My granddad died when I was still pretty young. I had started school then, but only just, because I remember momma coming to get me from school that day. His name was Morgan McCade. Oh, he was a character, everybody always said. What I remember was that he knew everybody. There wasn't a person he could pass on the street that he didn't know and say hello to or have a chin wag with. He used to walk me down to the little neighborhood market and buy me a piece of candy, and I remember it always took forever to get there because we stopped so many times."

"That's a great memory, Pearl, do you mind if I mention that in the article?" Perri asked.

"I don't mind at all. I think he'd be pleased to know people remembered him that way. Like I said, he was a character, so there are a lot of stories about him, I'm afraid." Pearl considered for a moment. "You know, the things that might be scandalous at the time end up being thought of as funny or quaint, don't they? And people like remembering them."

Perri took a surreptitious peek at her watch and realized she should have left twenty minutes ago. She didn't want to stop Pearl but wanted to get as much information as she could. She encouraged Pearl to tell her more about Morgan. "Other stories?"

"Oh yes. He had his finger in a lot of pies in the 1920s and 1930s. And my grandmother too!"

"What was your grandmother's name?"

"Lucinda. They called her Lucy. She was a force to be reckoned with, as they say. She was one of the few women in Gallatin County who dared march with the Suffragettes. And from what I've heard, she spoke out a lot. Got arrested a couple of times not too long after my dad was born. Caused a big scandal and raised seven kinds of hell with Grandpa's business, but I think they did alright in spite of it."

Perri automatically looked at her watch again. She couldn't delay any longer. Pearl noticed and said, "Perri, you should run along. I'm sure you're running behind schedule now."

She wasn't wrong, Perri was already late for the next patient. She had gained quite a bit of information by staying, so it was worth it since she'd be hard at the research books that afternoon and this gave her a head start.

Perri sprang up from her perch on the ottoman, "I've so much enjoyed talking to you. You have some colorful stories and I'd love to hear more sometime."

"I'd like that too. Um, I don't want to be forward. I know this is your job, but if you want to, come by when you aren't working some evening, we'll talk some more. Then you won't have to worry so much about the time."

"Are you sure you wouldn't mind?"

"I think it would be the best thing in the world for me right now. They still don't know any more about what happened with Ruby and George and it upsets me, and scares me too. And I don't even want to start thinking about what I'm going to do with that house!"

Remembering something Pearl said while her glucose was low, Perri asked, "Had you thought about selling it, or has anyone suggested that to you?"

Pearl's face clouded over. "There's always been someone wanting to buy the old place. Ruby and George had troubles with some man a few years ago who kept after them to sell. They didn't want to sell and he tried to set fire to their barn. George caught it before it got very far and the police caught the man before he got very far too!"

It was an answer and yet not an answer. Not completely convinced that it hadn't started up again, Perri said goodbye and let herself out, closing the porch door carefully so it didn't slam shut.

Pearl watched Perri walk to her car. She had thoroughly enjoyed chatting about the old house and her family, more than she would have expected. It made her feel somehow less alone, less sad, to relive the good memories. She found herself yearning to talk more about the McCades and their house. The idea of an article being written about it gave her something to look forward to, as well as helped take her mind off all the things that would have to be sorted out over the next few weeks. She watched the red Cooper pull away from the curb and disappear down the narrow street leaving a roiling wake of red and gold leaves.

## Chapter 12

May 7, 1825

Repercussions from the twenty-four-gun salute bounced back and forth across the expanse of the Ohio as the steamboat approached the landing. A receiving line formed on each side of the walkway, a layer of calico fabric covered the path from the dock to the hotel a couple hundred feet from the banks. Local Shawneetown officials and socialites, as well as out-of-town luminaries were eagerly awaiting the arrival of Gilbert du Motier, Marquis de Lafayette.

The door of the Rawlings Hotel stood open, festooned with sprays of May flowers gathered by a group of ladies from the local Presbyterian church. Clustered about the entryway was a collection of those ladies tittering with excitement and whispering to each other behind their hands. The satins and silks of their expensive party gowns rustled so constantly in their nervous agitation that it sounded like the wind through a wheat field.

Nearly fifty years after General Lafayette had fought with the Patriots in the American War for Independence, reverence and admiration for the great man had not dimmed, but rather prospered, being instilled even in the descendants of those who had lived through the war. The Marquis, now sixty-eight, was in the midst of a visit to the United States in which he planned to visit each of the twenty-four states in the Union. Tonight, he was visiting Shawneetown and a lavish reception had been planned for what the town knew was most likely a lifetime opportunity.

A concerted, and quite furiously enacted, refurbishment of the hotel had been completed by the new owners with help from the populace. Fresh paint in all the rooms, repairs and finishing to the plank flooring, and bolstering of the supply of fine linens, glassware, and tableware turned into a community project in anticipation of such a venerable guest. The second brick building in the town, it had quickly fallen in stature at the neglect of the previous owner who preferred drinking at all hours of the day or night as opposed to hotel-keeping. His wife and three daughters had done their best to keep up the hotel by cooking, cleaning, and catering to guests, but the proprietor and his son-in-law proved too much even for their valiant efforts.

The General had been greeted by Mayor William Docker upon disembarking from the steamer, the Natchez, and now walked slowly through the greeting line, nodding, shaking hands, and speaking briefly with the town's governors and top businessmen. Francis McCade gave a courteous bow and flushed with pride as he shook the General's hand.

Once Lafayette had progressed down the line far enough for Francis to be out of his notice, he gazed past the General to covertly seek out Arminda Grey in the clump of ladies eagerly awaiting the honored guest's arrival at the doorway. She was standing close to the hanging bower of daffodils. Francis thought she looked radiant in her brilliant blue dress, a delicate cream-colored shawl draped around her shoulders. Francis wondered if Arminda had noticed him and his brief exchange with the Marquis in the receiving line.

Once Lafayette reached the portico, he bowed to the ladies, who bobbed and curtsied like mad. They accepted his gracious complements with blushing cheeks and shy giggles. He then turned to face the crowd as Judge Hall gave the welcome speech, after which General Lafayette thanked the people of Shawneetown and entered the hotel.

Several hours were spent partaking of the light meal, champagne, and wine. Many tales of wartime glory were recounted for the appreciative crowd. After an enjoyable evening, the distinguished elderly Frenchman returned to his steamer and continued his journey down the Ohio River, his departure accompanied by another twenty-four-gun salute. The guests watched the boat, through the drifting haze of gunfire smoke, until it blended into the dark expanse and the sound of the paddle thrashing the water had finally faded away.

Francis McCade returned to his room in the Rawlings Hotel. He'd been living there since his arrival in 1819, taking a room in the then-ramshackle inn because it was the cheapest accommodation he could find within the limits of the town itself. The circumstances of the hotel had now greatly improved and he wondered if his board would see a corresponding increase. He wasn't quite ready to purchase property. Francis wanted to owe no man and was determined to wait until he had the cash in hand.

After riding into town on the back of Fiona, Francis had taken the first job he could find, loading presses in the printing office of the Illinois Emigrant newspaper, which ceased printing due to lack of funds shortly after he started work. He was fortunate to be picked up by the Illinois Gazette within the month. Eventually, through introductions made via contacts with the newspaper, he interviewed and was hired at the Bank of Illinois. It was the first chartered bank in Illinois Territory, having been established in 1816.

Francis had saved every penny he could from his salary over the last six years while continuing to develop other sources of income during his evening time. He figured the more streams of money he could establish, the more he was protecting his future. And Francis had big plans for his future: buy land near the river, marry, build a fabulous house, and have a family. His daydreams were often of himself as a Lord of the Manor and, after a stellar business career, enjoying a genteel retirement with grace and easy wealth.

Not included in his plans was the bank suspending operations the year before, in 1824. Plans to extend the charter and rename the institution to the State Bank of Illinois were in process, but the wheels moved too slowly for him to wait without taking another position. Francis increased his involvement in his side partnerships and, after a few months of financial planning and discussions, had become an investor, and one of the lessees, of the United States Saline salt works.

The salt works had been operating since 1803 when the Shawnee Indians ceded the Great Salt Springs to the still-young Union. It was currently leased from the government by the group of investors who agreed to produce a minimum amount of salt each month or pay a penalty.

Obtaining the salt was an impressive production. Water from the salt wells was heated in large kettles over trenches dug in the ground and filled with timber from the surrounding forest. The fires burned day and night. A lot of labor was needed to fell trees and transport them to the site, to keep the fires stoked, finish the processing, and packing the salt in barrels. Illinois was a free state, but it's first constitution, written in 1818, still allowed the use of slaves for the salt works.

Francis was not involved, thankfully, but he was concerned over the pending outcome of the recent arrest of three men, one of them from Shawneetown, accused of kidnapping for the purposes of supplying slaves to the salt works. The case was in court presently, the outcome not yet known.

The salt wells, both the natural well and the drilled wells, were located in the dense forest along the banks of the Saline River, a good ten-mile ride from Shawneetown, but Francis didn't need to be on site often, only to attend the meetings and participate in the company business. And, of course, to collect his salary, which was turning out to be much more rewarding than the one he had from the bank. He also operated one of his additional businesses from Cave-in-Rock. A long day's ride for him but he needn't go there often. His business partners were more than adequate at managing the operation and he preferred keeping his business transactions separate from his family life. He and Alexander had an agreement that business was not to impinge upon or interfere in any way with family members of either partner and this principle had been strictly maintained for the years they had collaborated.

Thinking of his salary, Francis took his account book and a diary from the writing table drawer. He added the amount of his monetary contribution to the night's extravaganza in the debit column and brought down the balance. He was doing very well, but he had spent more in the last two weeks than he had in the previous two months, having acquired a new suit and shoes for the gala. But, he knew it was well worth the money to have his name included in the list of donors that would appear in the newspaper. Arminda Grey's father was an avid reader of the Gazette. If Francis held any hope of courting his youngest daughter, he would need to impress the influential businessman.

After recording his account of Lafayette's visit in the diary, he returned both books to the drawer with a satisfied smile. Someday, he would write his memoirs and include this piece of history. Francis devotedly kept a daily record of his experiences, business, and any other noteworthy news. But, the time for a memoir was for the future, at the dusk of long life. Now he needed to go to bed.

He would have an early day tomorrow setting out for Pott's Inn. He had requested the stable have Fiona saddled and ready to depart thirty minutes after daybreak. The trip would be at least fifteen miles, considering he would have to ride two miles further west than he needed to in order to cross the Saline, then travel southeast to get to the Inn. His satchel was already packed since he planned to stay the night. At least once a month, Francis met Alexander Mason at the Inn. Their business partnership had continued unabated since their first meeting six years ago. Alexander lived with his family in Elizabethtown. Potts' Inn was roughly midway and served as their meeting place. Francis was looking forward to it, he always did. With the possibility of trouble with the Salt Works, while remote, he wanted to bolster the business with Alexander Mason.

He carefully hung his new suit in the small wardrobe, smoothing the wool so it wouldn't crumple against the other clothing, then climbed into the narrow bed. He pulled the linen sheet up and over the top of the coarse wool blanket to keep it from scratching against his skin. Francis McCade fell asleep to his mind's eye image of Arminda Grey in her blue gown, her auburn hair shining in the firelight.

\*\*\*

Their meal finished, Francis and Alexander sat back in their chairs in familiar, companionable silence while Mrs. Potts cleared their table in the corner of the Inn's dining room. The two men faced the room and the burgeoning fields visible through the line of windows that stretched across the front of the building. The May evenings were still turning cool and the Inn's owner, Hiram Potts, was stoking up the fire. When the flames rose to his satisfaction, Hiram nodded at the two men and left the dining room to them, quietly closing the paneled door that led to the kitchen behind him.

"Now then, Alexander, it's been a long winter. Has your business improved with the break in the weather?" Alexander nodded affirmatively.

Francis leant both forearms on the table in anticipation. "What have you for me?"

Alexander reached to the floor next to his chair then dropped a well-worn leather bag onto the table with a brilliant smile. "Let's see."

## Chapter 13

October 12, 2016

    The Saline County Genealogical Society resided in the basement of the city building on Locust, just down the street from the courthouse. Perri turned the Cooper onto Locust Street, and searched out a parking space between the courthouse and the Society library. Perri had never seen the original courthouse, a post-Victorian brick behemoth with a clock tower built in 1905. It was long gone, having been replaced in 1967 with a smaller brick and concrete building on the same site.

    After parallel parking, Perri hopped out, hoisting her purse and satchel with her camera, laptop, and notebook on her shoulder. The blip of the lock sounded behind her as she headed down the sidewalk toward the city building. The entrance was through a door in the alley, just around the corner from the main building entrance.

    A tarnished bell attached to the top of the door jangled as she stepped through. A man's head appeared over a filing cabinet between a potted spider plant and a row of bulging magazine storage boxes. Perri stepped down the two stairs into the office. The man had been seated at a giant old desk covered with dozens of books, piles of papers, envelopes, notebooks, and folders. He looked up and smiled. "Hello there. Can I help you?" The voice belonged to a man probably in his 70s who angled his head downward a little and looked at her over the tops of his plastic gray-rimmed reading glasses.

    The corners of Perri's mouth turned up just a bit. She thought it wouldn't be hard to convince herself she had just stepped into a shop in Diagon Alley. The sight of the racks of books gave her that rub-your-hands-together anticipation of searching through some unique records.

"Hi. I'm Perri Seamore. I'm a member of the Society. I'd like to have a look at some of your records. I know it is in Gallatin County, but I'm hoping you have some references that would include any information or history of original houses remaining in the Old Shawneetown vicinity. Do I need to show you my membership card?" She tugged at the zippered pocket on her purse with one hand.

"No, no, that's fine. I'm Martin Sloat, by the way." He took note of her scrubs and asked, "You live around these parts, do you?" He rounded the desk.

"I'm Perri Seamore, and no, I live over in Vailsburg, Indiana, but I had family who did live here, well, mostly in Eldorado. I'm here working a temporary job."

Martin nodded, "I've heard the name Seamore, but I don't know anyone by that name now." With his chin in his hand, he tapped the side of his cheek with his forefinger, thinking. The light shining through the office from the high windows filtered through Martin's fringe of longish gray hair that seemed to defy gravity to a certain degree and some strands floated horizontally next to his head. He asked her, "There were some Seamores here in Harrisburg too, weren't there?"

"Yes, that would have been my grandfather's or my great uncle's family."

"I thought I knew the name." Martin side-stepped around the desk, avoiding a few piled cardboard storage boxes precariously leaning into the aisle. "Excuse me." He edged between Perri and another filing cabinet and padded down the center aisle of the stacks. He was wearing a pair of well-worn leather suede house slippers that had formed to the same shape as his feet. The nap of the chocolate brown suede had worn over his little toes and were now shiny tan spots. "I think we have some materials that might have what you want right over here. Most of our comprehensive volumes include more than just Saline County, so you may find what you're looking for."

Martin ran his eyes over the rows of books, plucking one from the top shelf, another from a lower section, then moved on to another row.

Perri talked as she followed along behind him. Martin handed her each book as he selected it, freeing it from its place on the shelf. "I'm so glad I'll be able to come here often. I've been once before, but I didn't get to stay long."

"I'll be happy to help you out however I can." Martin turned and handed Perri three more books of various sizes. "These might have the information you are looking for. They've been popular lately." He pointed at the teetering stack of books in Perri's arms. "What you have there: an illustrated History of Old Shawneetown; Portrait and Biographical Record of Gallatin County; History of Gallatin, Saline, Hamilton, Franklin and Williamson Counties; a plat map; and some other general histories about the area and its industries. Not sure if that'll help, but you never know."

"Oh, I nearly forgot, do you have a book of censuses that would include Gallatin County, starting with 1820?"

"Sure do. Right over here." Martin went straight to the census collections, ran his finger down the row, pulled out one large cloth-bound volume and a thinner book covered with marbled paper. "One is 1800s, the other is 1900s up to 1940." He balanced the two books on top of the heap Perri was already carrying. "Did you know there's been talk about doing up the old bank building?"

"I hadn't heard that, but I hope so. It would be a huge shame to let it just fall into total ruin." Perri shifted the stack of books. "This is great, thank you."

Martin pointed past Perri, back toward the front, of the room to indicate a table against the far wall. "You can have a seat at the table. I'll be right over there at my desk if you need something. I'm getting the monthly newsletter ready to mail out."

Perri pulled out the folding metal chair. She set out her notebook, pen, camera, phone and laptop, which she switched on. She located an outlet on the wall to her right and plugged in the cord. She often used her phone to take photos of information if it was easy to read and only a page or two long, but for this Perri wanted to use her camera. The high resolution would be important for enlarging sections of print.

She started with the large tome that included history on Gallatin County along with four other Illinois counties. Gallatin County was formed in 1812, so before the McCade house was built. The aging leaves of paper were the mellow color of perfectly done toast. The language of the prose was both very formal and yet, at the same time, somehow managed a casual flavor to the treatment of the subject matter. Reports of legislation and land grants were very structured and methodical then were immediately followed by a report of a murder with a hint of Victorian gossip column fodder.

The plethora of unusual stories was distracting. One that highjacked Perri's attention was an account of how a woman's husband killed a man with an axe after discovering his wife had been "criminally intimate" with him. The locals figured the man had left the area, but a couple of weeks later, *'his body was found under the smokehouse, some say by means of an old lady's dream.'* Neighbors deduced that the man had been murdered by the owner of the smokehouse. The guilty party, seeing the tide turning against him, fled. Following a pursuit on foot and horseback during which the scoundrel ran through woods, leaped over a creek, surprisingly clearing it, running into a herd of cattle and hiding behind a steer, he was eventually cornered and carried to justice via the hangman's noose. The book continued with records of early settlers, one of whom, Solomon Hayes, attempted to achieve perpetual motion but decided friction had got the best of him. And John C. Reeves, a cashier at the bank, who used to sleep on top of the barrels of silver to prevent theft. "That's dedication. If it's true," Perri murmured.

"Come again?" Martin asked, turned half way around and peering over his glasses.

"Just me babbling. These stories could distract me all day." Martin grinned and nodded knowingly, then went back to his work and Perri guided her attention back to her intended task.

She paged through the thick book, glancing at subtitles and headings until she came upon a section about early settlers to the area and the first citizens of Old Shawneetown. She was amazed to find a few paragraphs about the early homes of note and their owners. According to this account, Francis McCade didn't have the first brick house in the area. That honor belonged to John Marshall in 1822. There were two subsequent houses mentioned, the second and third brick homes were built by Moses Rawlings, also in 1822, and Robert Peeples in 1823, although from time to time there was speculation Mr. Peeples could have built his house by 1819, but this had never been substantiated.

Perri had heard of the Rawlings Hotel and the John Marshall home. The Rawlings Hotel had managed to survive on the bank of the Ohio River until fire took it down on June 23, 1904 and the Marshall home had been demolished at some point, but she couldn't remember why or when.

Turning to her laptop, her fingers tapped in the key words for a quick search on the Peeples home. An application for it to be added to the National Register of Historic Places had been filed in 1983. The house was gone now, as well as the 1846 house built adjacent to it by Robert's son, John. Perri would check on it later to find out what had happened to the buildings, but whether or not they had been added to the Register, they appeared to have been allowed to decay and eventually fall down or be knocked down.

While searching the database of historic places, she came across another application, this one for the McCade home. It had been submitted in 1984, the year after the application for the Peeples house. The application had been approved the following year and the house was now Listed as a National Historic Place.

Perri sat back in her chair, a bit confused by that, since Pearl hadn't mentioned it. It didn't seem likely that she was aware of it since she was worried about how she was going to manage the house, saying it needed a lot of work. If the house was Listed, she should be able to get funding assistance for preservation. She poked around on the government websites and found a preservation directory that listed various funding sources, grants and programs, a list of State Historic Preservation Offices, complete with all contact information, and even a source of information about historic preservation easements that could possibly help Pearl with the property taxes and ensure the home was looked after in the future, no matter who owned it.

Perri bookmarked the page, determined to go over it with Pearl when she could visit her one evening. Maybe it would ease her mind a bit about inheriting the house and all the responsibility that went along with it. Perri felt it was vitally important since the McCade house appeared to be the only survivor of the early 19th century brick homes in Old Shawneetown.

Many other homes were described in the pages of the book: family homes, mansions, Victorian wonders...all gone. Lost either to the ravages of time, flooding, or neglect. There wasn't much left of the original Shawneetown. The Shawneetown Bank, built in 1840, was one of the last vestiges of the once-prosperous city. Perri recalled seeing the impressive Greek Revival building several times during childhood and into adulthood. It always seems a little creepy to her, so tall and lonesome, looking out over the river. She knew that, at least for now, it still sat on the corner, nearly alone, with only one other building standing on its block of Main Street. She hoped fervently that it could be restored and not disappear the way most of the rest of the town had done.

After scanning the remainder of the book, Perri turned to the land purchases and ran her finger down the list of names and plot descriptions. She found two entries for Francis W. McCade from 1829. He had purchased both the southeast and southwest corners of the southeast quarter of Section 45. She pulled the book of plat maps over and thumbed through it to Section 45. Yep, that was it, two parcels together, the southeastern edge running along the Ohio River.

The camera shutter seemed loud in the now quiet room as Perri snapped a photo of both pages. But before she had completely closed the plat book, something else on the page caught her eye. A couple of parcels to the west was a quarter marked, not with an owner's name as the others were, but 'Gold Hill Cemetery.' Its proximity to the McCade property encouraged Perri to hope for the possibility of finding some family burials there. With Pearl's permission, adding photos of family stones, along with photos of the house, if she could get them, would lend more interest and authenticity to her article about the McCade house. She made a note on her To Do List to check out the cemetery.

Featuring no roads or other landmarks recognizable to her other than the river itself, the plat map was not so useful for finding the cemetery's current location, so Perri clicked the icon to open Google Earth. She framed the general area on her screen and slowly zoomed in while comparing the location of the river on one side of the McCade property and a stream on the other, both of which were represented on the plat map, with the cemetery situated just beyond the stream. As street names appeared on her screen, the obvious moniker of Gold Hill Road made the old burial ground easy to locate. 'I'm sure I can find that fairly easily.' Saving a screen shot of the area, she moved on to the next book in the stack.

The Portrait and Biographical volume, compiled in 1840, not only had a biography of Francis McCade, but a fabulously rendered woodcut portrait. How closely it resembled Francis was anyone's guess since many times these likenesses were created from a verbal description, often written by the person themselves or a family member and mailed to the artist. While the arrangement of features may have been guesswork, probably some characteristics were true to the details given. He appeared to have light hair, maybe sandy brown or dark blond, although it could also have been of a reddish hue. The length was just to the top of his collar and was depicted with errant curls framing his face. The irises were only lightly shaded, so possibly blue, gray, or even light green eyes. Even though the woodcut artist probably never met Francis, he gave him a slightly mischievous, barely-there smile. "I bet you were considered quite the catch, Mr. McCade," Perri said to the illustration.

Francis's biography was written in the grandiose verbiage typical of late 19$^{th}$ century volumes. The summaries flattered the subject to the point where, if it was taken at face value, every man was a saint who was generous, benevolent, kind, wise, and smart in business, having built his own livelihood with his bare hands and bleeding knuckles from nothing more than dirt and sheer will power. Perri read it anyway, hoping to pick the actual kernels of truth out of the saccharine narrative.

Something else the bios were good for was that many times the flamboyant summaries would include a fair amount of information about a man's wife and at least some of his children. Sometimes it was even accurate. The information would need to be verified, but at least it gave a researcher some names to start with, something to look for.

In the social paragraph of the article about Francis, it was revealed that Mr. McCade had been betrothed to the delicately beautiful, and much sought-after, Arminda Grey in the summer of 1830. Arminda was the youngest daughter of the esteemed Bank Manager of the Shawneetown Bank, Mr. Hubert Grey. The lovely couple had built a magnificent home on a hilltop overlooking the river and raised four well-mannered, talented, and extremely well-behaved children: Martha, Hugo, and Jane and Jubal, who were twins. The author was quite certain each of the them would become pillars of the community in business and polite society.

There was also a short family history, including a couple of reproduced newspaper items about Francis and his father. 'That's what I need.' Perri kept reading. The earliest was a short notice that had been published in the Illinois Emigrant, dated May 31, 1819: *The Emigrant would like to welcome Mr. Francis W. McCade to our printing staff. Mr. McCade joins us from his former home in Muhlenberg County, Kentucky. We expect him to be a valuable addition to our town.* According to the archive listing, the Emigrant began publishing in June of 1818 but ceased in 1819, so when this item was published, the paper had seven months or less to go before it closed.

The next quoted item was from the Illinois Gazette which began publishing in 1819, perhaps starting up from the remains of the Emigrant, or at least taking over the circulation. This item was announcing the appointment of Francis McCade to a junior management position with the Bank of Illinois in February of 1822. He had started as a teller, although it didn't say when, and through his exemplary work and attention to detail was being promoted to Junior Assistant.

There was one item about Morgan's father, Thomas McCade, who began a newspaper himself, The Gallatin Reporter, in 1875. Per the list, the Reporter published until 1920, so it had a forty-five-year run. Thomas died in 1921. Perri wondered if the paper folded for some reason or was shut down due to his ill health. She also wondered if his decline had something to do with the newspaper closing.

After documenting the information and also photographing the portrait, Perri moved on to the census books. She located Francis on the 1820 census as a tenant in a boarding house operated by Mr. and Mrs. Kinsall. In 1830, Francis was living in the Rawlings Hotel. Per the census records, Francis was in Shawneetown but still unmarried on August 7, 1820, as well as on June 1, 1830, the official enumeration dates.

In 1840, Francis McCade was listed in his own dwelling. His was the only name given for the household. Family members would not be named until the 1850 census. He was married by this time, and with children. Following his name spelled out in a decorative cursive hand, the remainder of his family was represented only by numbers in the columns pertaining to their age at the time of the census. Perri jotted down the information, writing in parentheses the name of the person who most closely corresponded to that age. One male under 5 (Jubal); one male between 5 and 10 (Hugo); one male between 40 and 50 (Francis); one female under 5 (Jane); one female between 5 and 10 (Martha); and one female between 30 and 40 (Arminda). This totaled six people in the household, Francis and his wife and four children.

On the 1850 census, which was done in September, all family members were listed. With the exception of one, the names and ages here matched the ranges of people on the previous census, so Perri could be fairly confident of the names of those in the family in 1840. Francis was noted as 54 years old and his occupation was given as Merchant. Something interesting was that his wife was noted as Nancy J and her age as 33 years old. Unless Arminda was also called Nancy J, which didn't seem too likely, and her age was off by quite a bit in one census or another, Arminda must have died and Francis remarried a younger woman sometime between 1840 and 1850.

The children in the household were Hugo at 17, Jane and Jubal at 14, and Lavinia at 5 years of age. There was no way to know, at least not yet, if Lavinia was a child of Arminda or Nancy. If Arminda was her mother, she could have died when Lavinia was born, which wasn't uncommon. Absent from the household was Martha who had most likely married and gone. A marriage record would help; without one she'd be more difficult to trace, since her surname would have changed and there was a surfeit of women named Martha in the census.

Perri looked at her watch. Nearly three hours had passed while she read about the McCades and the town as it existed nearly two hundred years ago. She felt she had accomplished quite a bit having successfully found some information about the man responsible for building Pearl's house, as well as his family. She couldn't wait to tell Pearl on Monday. She wanted to print out the sketched portrait of Francis, even if it might only be a whimsical representation of him.

"Mr. Sloat?"

"Call me Martin, please." Martin slipped a folded newsletter into a brown half-sheet-sized envelope as he turned in his chair.

"Ok, Martin. I'm done with these books."

"Were they helpful to you?" he asked.

"They were very helpful, yes. I'm wondering if you happen to have any books that might have marriage records for Gallatin County?"

"I think we might. Most of our books here come from donations, and sometimes when we get donations, they aren't necessarily books about Saline County. Some counties don't have a physical repository, and in that case, or if the other Society has duplicates, we keep them." As he got up from his chair, Martin licked and closed the gummed flap of the envelope then pounded his fist along the back to make sure it sealed.

While he was running his hand down a row of books, Perri calculated how much more time she could spend here before she'd need to take off. She figured on at least a couple of hours, plenty of time to look through the marriage records and maybe even stop in at the library to look for those newspaper articles.

Martin had just placed a book bound in a coarse-woven, navy blue fabric on the table when her phone vibrated on the surface of the desk. It was Nick. "Speak of the devil." She picked it up and silenced it as she stood and indicated to Martin that she was going to step outside to make a call.

Martin said, "You don't have to go outside to use your phone, unless you just want the privacy."

"Oh." She looked at Martin uncertainly. She swiped her phone and quickly said, "Hold on a sec," then covered the phone while she spoke to Martin. "I feel like I'm in a library here and shouldn't use the phone inside."

"There's no one here but you and me anyway, darlin'." Martin stood up. "Besides, I need to go to the back room to run postage on these envelopes, so feel free. You can holler at me if someone else comes in because I don't always hear the bell over that infernal postage machine. It sounds like a wood chipper running." He hefted a wire basket full of newsletters and disappeared through a doorway behind his desk.

"I'm here, hello!"

Nick's voice came through the phone, "Hey! Are you busy? Are you still at work?"

"No, I'm in the research library."

"Oh, sorry, didn't realize."

"No problem. What's up?"

"Just calling to let you know my time off was ok'd. I plan on leaving here Friday morning."

"Awesome! So glad you got the time off." Perri tried to keep her voice down regardless of what Martin had said.

"Me too. I won't keep you, I'll talk to you tonight."

Perri ended the call and set her phone back on the tabletop. She riffled through the pages of the record book to 1830 and began looking for marriages after June, at which time she knew Francis was not yet married. A few pages later, midway down the page was a marriage between Francis Washington McCade and Arminda Eloise Grey on September 3, 1830 in the Presbyterian Church in Shawneetown, Rev. B.F. Spilman officiating.

Perri decided to pack it in here for the day and move on to the city library to check for newspaper items about the McCades. She gathered her belongings and walked up to the desk. "Mr. Sloat?" Perri called. "Martin?" There was no answer, but Perri could hear the rhythmic clunking sound of the postage machine. She walked around the desk and stuck her head through the open door. She called loudly, "Martin?"

Martin looked back over his shoulder and shouted, "Hang on" over the mechanical clattering.

Perri hollered back, "I'm going to head out for now. I've left the book on the table. I'll probably be back next week, if not sooner." Martin had turned the machine off, and the sound wound down slowly.

"Sorry about that. Blasted thing needs replacing."

"I'll be back, probably next week."

"That sounds fine. Look forward to seeing you then." Martin turned back to the stack of envelopes and hollered, "Bye for now."

Perri fast-walked back to her parked car, mentally arranging a list of what to look for at the library. She sighed with exasperation as she tossed her bag in the backseat. The luxury car in front of her had parked over the line of its parking space so that even her Mini Cooper was hemmed in between the fancy-mobile and a van behind her. She finally got the Cooper out of the spot after inching back and forth about twenty times. Free of the parking space, she gunned the engine and whipped around the corner without stopping at the stop sign. She nervously glanced into the side and rear-view mirrors a couple of times. "Well that was dumb. Run a stop sign right in front of the court house."

While she was busy scanning for lurking police cruisers in the rearview mirror, another stop sign loomed ahead which she only saw at the last minute. A car in the crossing street had already entered the intersection and Perri had to stomp on the brake quickly. The red Cooper skidded just a little bit on the rocks in the street where they had migrated from the gravel parking lot of an electrical supply store on the corner. The driver of the other car stopped directly in front of her, eyes and mouth open wide. Perri waved an embarrassed apology and the driver cleared the intersection, glaring at her the entire time.

Perri continued down the road, shaking her head, both mad at herself and wondering why people stopped directly in the path of an oncoming car rather than kept going. Smoky barbeque aromas wafted from a bar and grill as she passed and she pondered stopping for something to eat. But, in considering that she wanted to continue to fit into her new jeans, she settled for a suspicious energy bar she had made that was still drifting around in a baggie in the bottom of her purse. She tried to remember when she had made this batch, but wasn't sure, so she ate it anyway.

The library was only a few blocks away and soon she had requested the microfilm she needed at the reference desk. She took the three spools to a viewer and settled in. After a couple tries, she got the first one loaded and advancing properly.

The first spool contained issues of the News-Gleaner, which had been published from 1905 through 1923, and contained papers from August 1921 through July of 1922. She needed February 17 of 1922 and fast-forwarded until she was close, then scanned to the front page for Friday the seventeenth. Each issue was only four pages long so it didn't take long to find the article which was above the fold. *Local Man Arrested for Bootlegging.* "Bingo."

The article read: *A local man was arrested at his home last night. Morgan McCade, 34, was apprehended by local policemen after being observed loading and driving a truckload of bootlegged liquor from his home on Ridge Hill to a restaurant he owns in the Whiskey Chute section of Harrisburg. McCade has owned the restaurant for three years and previously operated it as the Shot Glass saloon. The saloon was transformed to a restaurant in 1920 with the advent of Prohibition. Acting on information from a caller, authorities were affronted to discover the cellar of the establishment being used as a speakeasy where both liquor and gambling were taking place. It is yet to be determined if the alcohol was distilled on Mr. McCade's own property, or brought in from somewhere else. There was question as to whether other illegal activities were occurring but this will not be commented upon by this reporter until more information is available. Mr. McCade is expected to be released by this afternoon and will be assigned a date to appear before a Judge in Saline County regarding this blatant violation of the law.*

Perri grinned just a little at this. It was against the law at the time, but she couldn't help but see Morgan McCade as a bit of a character, knowing that her own great-grandfather had dabbled in cooking up a bit of homemade hooch in their cellar too in order to provide a bit of extra family income when it was needed. She wondered what other 'illegal activities' the police might have suspected. She ran her finger down her notes. Morgan bought the Shot Glass in 1920, which was the same year The Gallatin Reporter had stopped printing. She wondered if Thomas had indeed been ailing and shut down the paper, maybe selling off the equipment, so Morgan could buy his own business.

She enlarged and printed the article before moving to the next one. Almost two weeks later, on March 2, Morgan had appeared in Saline County court and was fined $175 and released. This wasn't the most interesting part of the article though. Much more compelling was the mention of Morgan's wife: *Mrs. McCade, nee Lucinda Corcoran, known to her friends as Lucy, was present for the hearing and accompanied Mr. McCade's lawyer, Wyatt Pumphrey of Harrisburg, into the courtroom, taking a seat just behind Mr. Pumphrey. She was seen brazenly leaning forward at various times to speak quietly with the attorney. The* *public will recall that Mrs. McCade is no stranger to the courtroom herself, having become familiar with them, as well as the police facilities in Gallatin County, where the McCades reside, following two separate arrests three years ago, prior to the passage of the right to vote for women. She was first seized and jailed for distributing suffragette pamphlets to businesses in downtown Shawneetown after being asked to stop. The second incidence was a mere week later when she organized and executed a plan to block the steps of the Bank of Illinois, along with seven other women, carrying signs and shouting. All the women were taken into custody. Mrs. McCade has continued to present her outspoken opinions regarding numerous controversial issues. Mr. McCade was assigned a fine of $175 by Judge Sparks and released. This reporter is of the feeling that perhaps Judge Sparks gave Mr. McCade a light punishment out of sympathy for his predicament.*

'Boy, I would love to have met her.' Perri thought to herself as she printed this article as well. She hoped that this would lighten Pearl's spirits just a little, to read these details about what a strong and courageous woman her grandmother had been. She made a note to try to find articles about Lucy's arrest when she had time, but it wouldn't be today since she still had a couple of other things to look up.

The next reel contained articles from other newspapers about Morgan being arrested again in 1926 for being involved with Charlie Birger and his gang of bootleggers. 'You'd think he'd learn.' Perri printed the article too, but wasn't sure if she'd give it to Pearl. Perri recalled seeing a copy of an article featuring a smiling Charlie on the gallows about to be hanged, as he was on April 19, 1928. The rope that was used had eventually surfaced in a museum in the St. Louis area when she was young. Morgan McCade appeared to have retired from the bootlegging life just in time to keep his own neck out of the noose.

She rewound the last spool of microfilm, replaced each in its small carton, and put them all in the returns box. In light of the adventurous life led by many of the McCades, Perri wondered if there wasn't something in the rumors of money or valuables being stashed away somewhere. If someone was convinced of it, the hope of finding the valuables might have precipitated the murders of Ruby and George Duncan.

Walking back through the parking lot, Perri couldn't get her mind off Gold Hill Cemetery. She didn't have anything she had to do tonight and it was still relatively early. It wasn't dark yet, it was only 5:28 p.m., she had another hour or so of daylight. If she hopped onto highway 13, it was just a hair over twenty miles to Old Shawneetown. The drive would do her good after sitting inside hunched over books and microfilm all afternoon. She wouldn't try to get out and search for headstones tonight of course, but she could locate the cemetery and get a feel for the area. That was completely reasonable.

She snapped her seat belt closed and rolled the window down just a little. As she nosed out onto West Logan and turned right, she mused about maybe just driving past the Duncan house. Rationally, it made sense. She's be *right* there. It would practically be on her way home. Logistically, she would already be headed in that direction, heck, she probably would have to go past it anyway to get back to highway 13 because turning around on a country road at a curve wasn't the safest idea. She wouldn't stop or try to peek in any windows. She wouldn't even have to stop the car. She'd be perfectly safe inside driving past the house, she'd even lock the doors. Why not?

Once through a couple of stoplights, the Mini revved up and swept through the open farmland, passing fields and retention ponds and little else. Moments later she crossed the low and slow Middle Fork of the Saline River and had the straightaway to herself.

## Chapter 14

July 21, 1831

"I just can't wait, Lissy, I really can't." Arminda bubbled excitedly to her friend as she watched the last of her packed trunks being carried out of the bedroom.

"I can't wait to see it all finished, but I know it will be a delight." Malissa Beauchamp bubbled with enthusiasm at her friend's good fortune to be moving into a newly built, two-story house. She had only seen it from the outside as it was being put up, but it seemed like a mansion to her.

Arminda sat and settled her new, expensive cotton dress and many layers of petticoats around her on the window seat next to Lissy. She crossed her legs at the ankles and sat admiring her new kid leather slippers which were dyed green to match her dress. The vivid green was the current rage in London. Not only had Francis obtained the dress and shoes for her for their first anniversary, but he had perfectly timed the move-in for their new home to be on the very day. The room was barren of furniture, having already been loaded on carts and transported to the new address. She sighed a little dramatically, "I have good memories of Francis's and my first year of married life in this house, but I just know that everything will be so much more agreeable in the new one.

Arminda Grey had married Francis McCade exactly one year ago. Her family was well off already and her parents had been very satisfied in her match with Francis, a notable businessman and upstanding society figure in Old Shawneetown. Her father had strongly approved of Francis's decision to defer marriage until he had established himself in business and was financially secure. His new son-in-law's professional success, coupled with his primary role in bringing new banking business to Shawneetown via the salt works, had brought about a meteoric rise in esteem for Francis from the communities of southern Illinois. His actions had also assisted some funding for the upkeep and periodic patrol of the road from the south. While some bandit activity was still a risk, and the main gang of bandits were still eluding capture, incidents were less frequent. The possibility of being caught by enforcers afforded a somewhat higher level of security for travelers using the road that lead north from Ford's Ferry in Cave-in-Rock, at least it was perceived that way. Commerce on the Ohio River and the states which bordered it had been increasing steadily over the last few decades. Even though Shawneetown was located on the Ohio, it was upriver of the crossing from Kentucky, so a safe and reliable road through Illinois was vital.

Mr. Grey felt that Francis, as a mature man of thirty-five, was at the optimum age to begin and provide for a family. At twenty-two, Arminda had been the last of the available Grey daughters. Becoming Mrs. Arminda McCade had erased the vestiges of her father's anxieties about matching his daughters to respectable men. Life was now settled, upright, and satisfactory, as it should be.

Work had recently been completed on the expensive brick house Francis had built for Arminda, a progressive design in the area for 1831. The bricks had been ordered from the east coast and were shipped down the Ohio River along with an experienced mason to direct the local men in the technique required for the patterned areas of the exterior.

The home had been constructed on top of a picturesque rise in their property where it would be clearly visible from downtown as well as the surrounding rural area. It faced the river and was surrounded by plenty of their own land. Francis had set aside a tract of land behind their house to be planted as a decorative garden. There were no worries about someone else building a house too close to theirs.

"I'm certain it will be Minda. I can't help but wish that Theodore will be able, someday, to build a house like it for us."

Malissa Beauchamp said wistfully, unfolding and refolding a lace-edged handkerchief in her lap.

"Your house is a perfectly good one, Lissy." Arminda smiled contentedly. "But, I do understand." She smoothed her skirts and said, "Francis is so thoughtful. There is a grand room for a nursery, just next to our bedroom. He ordered a connecting doorway be built from our room into the nursery."

Malissa took Arminda's hand and held it in hers. "He's so considerate. I'm glad that we both have found such doting husbands. You said that Francis had some of your furniture made for you. Has it all arrived?"

Arminda's eyes lit up, "Oh yes, you must see it. There are some beautiful pieces, including a crib for the nursery. He also purchased silk dressings for the crib. He's such a marvel to me, because he has ordered new silver cutlery and trappings for the horses. There will be a barn for the horses too. Francis has had the portrait framers busy with our wall hangings, including all of my favorites which are to be hung in the dining and drawing rooms. I'm sure the cook will enjoy using the new cookware shipped directly from London. I was able to order new curtains, tablecloths for the dining table, fine cotton clothes for the baby that should be here any day."

The two friends sat and chattered away about the new house until footsteps were heard in the hallway and Francis put his head through the doorway. "Ready ladies? It's time to leave. We'll be turning this house over to the new owners momentarily. Shall we go?"

They both quickly retied the ribbons of their bonnets. Arminda gingerly lowered herself from the window seat, with her friend's arm for support, and glided across the floor to her husband's waiting arm. Malissa followed, admiring the handsome figure of her friend's husband. From the gossamer sheen of his silk hat, the deep cuffs of his fine shirt, to the expensive cut of his frock coat and trousers, he was every bit the successful gentleman. Francis McCade assisted his wife and Mrs. Beauchamp into the waiting carriage then climbed into the compartment and closed the door. He reached one arm through the window and tapped the roof of the carriage, signaling to the driver they were ready to depart.

## Chapter 15

October 12, 2016, 5:20 p.m.

On the eastern outskirts of Shawneetown was a right hand turn off for Gold Hill Road. Perri squinted at her phone clamped into its bracket and suction-cupped to the windshield. Judging by the map, she'd have an S-curve, then the cemetery entrance would be on the right side of another curve, just before Gold Hill Road tee'd into Ringgold Road.

There was not going to be a sign for the graveyard at the roadside, not that she could discern from Google Earth, so she slowed the Mini and scoured the grassy verge for an opening. The light was rapidly fading on the western side of Gold Hill, making it difficult to see detail in the shadow of the hill after driving in the bright sunshine. Finally, a hundred feet or so from the upcoming intersection, Perri could see a break in the vegetation lining the road. A mown area left the road and turned sharply right, following the contour of the hill where it disappeared into the cover of trees. Checking her rearview mirror for other cars on the road and seeing no one behind her, she came to a complete halt in front of the grass covered, once-gravel lane.

Gazing up the hill into the dim interior of this narrow, protruding finger of the Shawnee National Forest made Perri's 'hackles' stand up at the nape of her neck, but she persisted in her effort to get a gander at the old burial ground tonight. She cautiously pulled into the gap, halfway expecting the front end of the car to drop into an unseen culvert camouflaged by weeds, but it was solid ground. She angled around the immediate right turn and warily climbed the hill.

Edging the Cooper along a few feet at a time, Perri crept forward the short distance until she reached the edge of the trees. The lane disappeared into the gloomy interior where the wooded area reached out and enveloped the road on both sides and from above, shielding the old resting place from the prying eyes of passersby or satellites. The car idled quietly while she sat peering through the windshield. The lane twisted to the left inside the trees. She couldn't see any stones or portion of the cemetery from where she sat.

Perri checked her watch, 5:57 p.m., and made a sudden decision that the sensible part of her brain knew full well she shouldn't. However, the curious part of her brain was much more assertive and pushed the sensible part away. She told herself she only wanted to see the layout of the cemetery and would only take a few minutes, if even that. Obviously, it would soon be too dark to be stumbling around over uneven ground trying to read stones that were most likely difficult to make out at the best of times. Perri scrounged in the glove compartment for her Maglite and stuffed her purse under the passenger seat. She left the car just outside the tree line and locked it, tucking the keys in a pocket of her Galaxy Blue scrubs.

Within a few steps, the fading light was further dimmed by the thick canopy of leaves and the temperature was noticeably cooler. She pushed the button on the end of the flashlight and followed the road under the outstretched arms of huge oak, maple, hickory, gum, and sycamore trees. Despite the grass growing directly in the lane having been mown, the ground beneath it was lumpy and hard from a couple centuries' worth of foot traffic, horses, carriages, wagons, and cars. The ground was dry in most places, but soft and damp spots lurked in low areas in the perpetual shade.

Perri instantly located one of these spots. As soon as she put her weight on her forward left foot, it sank several inches. Not wanting to bury the other foot in mud, she stood awkwardly, leaning her weight back on her right leg while attempting to extricate her foot, preferably with her shoe still on it. She could feel the cold mud close over the top of her foot and tried not to think about her $120 nursing shoes.

She couldn't even budge her foot if she kept it flexed, so she risked her shoe coming off by extending her toe and pulling. The mud, largely comprised of dense river clay, made a sucking noise. She felt it give and pulled harder, then landed on her butt with a sudden thump and pain shot through her hip. Shifting to one side, she swept a couple of hard, spiky gum balls, courtesy of the nearby sweet gum tree, from beneath her rear. She shone the light on her foot. No shoe. Just a bright white sock circled by a ring of grayish-brown.

"Uhhhh." She groaned. "Well, crap!" Perri took a few deep breaths staring at her muddied sock, acknowledged that the shoe wasn't going to crawl out by itself, then knelt close enough to reach the slowly closing gap in the mud. She pushed the long sleeve of the jersey shirt under her scrub top above her elbow and reached into the chilly ooze to retrieve her shoe. After pulling the no-longer-new shoe from the sludge, she plopped it down and tried to scrape as much mud onto the grass as she could. Her hand was now covered too but a thick patch of kudzu provided enough leaves to bundle together and wipe most of it off. The leaves were large, so she hoped it was kudzu and not exceptionally healthy poison ivy. "Guess I'll find out."

She looked at the mud-covered shoe. Not wanting to walk around the graves with only one shoe, she reluctantly shoved her foot in without untying it, hoping not too much mud had glopped inside as she pulled it from the mudhole.

The lane tee'd ten feet away from the first appearance of stones. A footpath led to either side. Perri followed the path to the left aisle where it then turned again toward the rear of Gold Hill Cemetery. The remaining daylight, while subdued, was still golden where it shone through an occasional opening in the high branches, but was misty everywhere else, giving the appearance of smoke wafting through the cemetery.

All was quiet save for a few half-hearted cricket chirps, a leafy/branchy shuffling sound, and fluttering of birds, disturbed while settling into their roosts for the night. Blurs of motion passed in front of Perri just above the illumination from her Maglite, which was noticeably weaker than it should be. Evidently, she hadn't changed the batteries in longer than she thought. A few more blurs passed directly over her head, probably bats. Hopefully, nothing more sinister than bats. She remembered the tales the kids in her neighborhood had told each other when they were playing outside after dark in the summer. Tales about bats flying down and getting tangled in your hair and not being able to get loose. There was always one kid who knew someone it had happened to. Perri knew that wasn't true about bats, but she still remembered it and it was a bit more difficult to shrug off standing here, alone, in the dark, in a cemetery, with a not-great flashlight, and things flying over her head.

Shaking off her fairly successful attempts to spook herself, she was distracted from her discomfort by nearly tripping over a grave marker closest to the path. It was only about a foot high, appearing to have mostly subsided into the earth, leaving only the top portion visible. Perri crouched down to see if she could read it. Most of the inscription looked to be below ground level and the face of the stone was overgrown with vines clinging to the surface by hundreds of tiny determined tentacles burrowing into every available crevice. Only a few scattered letters were visible, not enough to read a name or epitaph, although she could make out '_83_' on the far right edge. She hoped this was a 19th century date and an indication the cemetery was old enough to be the final resting place of a McCade family member or two even back from Francis's time, so it was encouraging.

Her plan wasn't to locate specific graves that evening, but since she was here anyway, Perri was curious to see if she could recognize any names. Maybe she could get a return on the time she would surely spend cleaning her left shoe later tonight. She slowly walked down the left aisle, playing the light across the stones. Her teeth suddenly jarred together catching the tip of her tongue as she stepped into an unexpected dip, probably an old wheel rut. At least it was dry.

The surviving stones were scattered around like a handful of marbles rolled across the grass and abandoned, setting down roots where they came to rest. The visible markers were in barely discernable rows. Many were completely unreadable, the soft sandstone wearing and eroding to smooth, sparkly lumps of white and gray, the only identifiable part often being a carved willow tree centered at the top, usually for an adult. It signified deep loss and mourning.

The earth undulated beneath her feet from time-worn graves that sank further as the years passed. She ambled from one stone to the next. Several of the markers in what would be the south half of the graveyard were from the mid-20th century. Many of the older ones, on the north half, were still readable, even with only the flashlight to illuminate them, but Perri didn't recognize any names. A Civil War marker, a white marble slab, curved at the top, with a recessed shield that should bear the person's name, although it was nearly smooth now, was set immediately next to a faded stone that had broken off a couple of inches above ground level and was now lying flat behind the remnant. The harsh glare of the Maglite, held at an angle, was sometimes an aid to reading worn lettering, but between it being rather dark in the cemetery and the flashlight battery getting low, it did little to help read the closely-lettered, worn italic script. Better to check the broken slab in the daytime and use a sheet of foil to see if the name on the government memorial was readable by that method.

Walking further toward the back, Perri stood still and held the Maglite above her head, trying to illuminate as much of the grounds as possible. Her hope sank along with her resolve when she saw the grass and other vegetation, mowed down in the portion nearest the road, had not been touched for ages in the remainder of the lot. She murmured, "Maybe this is the extent of the burials," trying to resurrect some hope, but without confidence as she swept the light side to side, trying to locate the cemetery boundary.

Her optimism was further dampened as the beam reflected off the face of stones peeping through the brush and vines, struggling for space beneath bushes and saplings across the entire width of the cemetery going back as far as she could see in the darkness. Better to know ahead of time, she reasoned. When she and Nick came back on the weekend, they'd be armed with gloves and pruning shears to cut back the growth around the stones.

A little disheartened, knowing that the stones she was searching for usually ended up being in the most difficult to read or least-tended portion of a cemetery, and in this case, it was more than a little bit of a jungle, she stepped as close as she could get to the nearest stone. She couldn't begin to read it, but did see that it was topped with a reclining lamb. This figure was usually reserved for children, and their graves were often located in a section for babies and children only. It could be that the rear portion of the cemetery was such a section.

Telling herself she probably wouldn't have to search the overgrown area, Perri turned back toward the entrance. A wave of goosebumps sprouted along both arms, the hair prickled again on the back of her neck, and a frosty finger of apprehension flickered its way up her spine. She was uncomfortably aware that it was no longer gray dusk or twilight. It was now truly dark and she couldn't make out the opening in the trees through which she had entered the graveyard. She'd stayed longer than she intended to and the night had swallowed the graveyard.

Suddenly feeling exposed, the malevolent blackness became smothering, like a wet wool blanket. Perri had a moment of panic and had to fight down the urge to run screeching toward the car, or where she thought the car was. She hadn't intended on walking back this far tonight. Behind her, she imagined the untouched foliage creeping forward, reclaiming the cemetery and her, sending curling tendrils along the rough ground toward her ankles. She shuddered once from her waist up through her neck and head, like a wave rolling upward.

"Get a grip! There's nothing here that wasn't here when you arrived," she told herself, "you just can't see it right now." Perri took a few slow, measured breaths. The anemic flashlight beam was going to make it harder to see how to get out. Again, she had to battle her flight reflex and take several more breaths. She focused on planning her exit to minimize the chance of tripping over a stone and breaking her neck. Her thrumming pulse slowed acceptably close to its normal rate. She intended to walk along the row she was in, such as it was, to the path along the north edge of the cemetery, since it was closest. Then make a right turn onto the path and walk to the front, thereby avoiding most of the stones. She picked her way cautiously forward, fighting the urge to run since her only source of light was beginning to dim suddenly, then brighten, and dim again, signaling impending battery death.

Completing the first leg of the trip uneventfully, no hands reaching from the ground to grasp her ankle, or arms embracing her from behind, she felt more courageous. She turned a sharp right toward where the entrance and her car should be. Satisfied she was on the clear side aisle next to the burial plots, Perri picked up her pace and cast the rapidly fading beam slightly to her right, searching for the opening in the trees as she went.

She had no recollection of the abrupt trip from upright to prone. Some things, like car accidents, can seem to occur in slow motion. This wasn't like that. Perri had spotted the lane and was heading toward it and then she was no longer standing for the second time that night.

She was lying on the ground, her arms crumpled beneath her. She pushed herself up a little and realized she couldn't see her hand in front of her because she either didn't have the flashlight anymore or she'd finally killed it. She lay perfectly still for a few seconds. Nothing. There was another moment of panic when she thought her ankles had been tied because she couldn't move them and they felt restrained. She heard a yipping noise that sounded very much like her great-grandmother's elderly Chihuahua but realized the squeaks were coming from her own throat as she struggled.

Her already high level of anxiety turned to horror when she reached forward, expecting the stubbly grass or stones, but her hand contacted the side edge of a hole. The hole she was in. "No, no, no!" Perri writhed onto her back and saw stars in the sky through the branches. Simply having something to focus on, something in the blankness other than solid, impenetrable darkness, helped. Then she realized what she thought was a newly dug grave, wasn't. It wasn't very deep and it certainly wasn't the length of a grave. She puffed out several lungsful of air.

The hole was about two and a half feet deep at the end where her head was located. The opposite end was much more shallow. Her legs stretched over the edge of the hole from the knees down. She pulled herself upright in one of the best unassisted sit-ups she'd ever done. Her hands scrabbled around her ankles. They weren't tied, they were just tangled up in whatever had tripped her. She could see the feeble glow of her Maglite from the opposite side of a hairy, rangy, out-of-control yucca planted a couple or three decades ago next to a gravestone. Probably meant as a nice clump of white flowers in the summer and some greenery throughout the winter. Right now, it looked more like a haggard sentinel in the eerie light.

Perri reached down to extricate her feet from the jumble of metal. "What is this, an animal trap?" Part of her left scrub pant leg was firmly snagged on something sharp on her right side, keeping her ankles bunched together. She ended up just tearing it to get loose. This was going to be an expensive trip for a simple glance around. Scrambling over to the flashlight, she whirled back around to inspect the area, sure she felt eyes on her back.

The 'trap' she had stumbled into turned out to be two spades, one flat shovel, a weeding claw, and a 3-inch paint brush jumbled together in a pile. The weeding claw was now sporting a swatch of Galaxy Blue fabric. "What on earth is someone doing digging..." Perri's head snapped up as the hot fear returned again. She might not be alone. Maybe those really *weren't* birds shuffling around in the yew trees and bushes when she first arrived.

She came as close to sprinting as she dared, up on her tip toes and panting like she'd already run a 5k. As she neared the opening in the trees, Perri had a bad moment fearing her keys may have dropped out of her pocket while she was wallowing around in the hole, or worse, even further back in the cemetery, but they were still there. She nearly sobbed as she fished them out and unlocked the car. Launching herself into the driver's seat, she hit the lock button three times, the sound of it a concrete assurance that she was safe. She jabbed the button to turn on the dome light and spun around to check the back seat, flinging the now dead flashlight onto the floorboard of the passenger side. No one there. She was safe. She flipped it off just as quickly, not wanting to be in a spotlight.

Fear seeped away, giving in to chagrin, both at having been scared witless of a pile of tools someone left behind and for having gone there at all too close to sunset. Eyes closed, she tipped her head back and exhaled in exasperation. She half-opened her eyes, looking through the sunroof at the stars, just in time to see the gleam of a flashlight flicker jaggedly across the huge lobed leaves of a gigantic oak overhanging her car.

"Damn it!" Perri jammed the key at the ignition, taking a couple of stabbing tries before she managed to fit the key into the slot. She started the car, which revved loudly since her foot was already close to flooring the gas in fright. "Nope. Not being silly. There *was* someone there. Gotta go, go now!"

She talked to herself in a faltering voice at least two registers higher than normal as she began the backwards descent, one hand on the wheel, the other arm gripping the edge of the passenger seat as she twisted around to see where she was going.

"Stupid, stupid, stupid. Why did I do this? Why did I park so I'd have to back out? What the hell was I thinking?"

It wasn't terribly steep, but it was pitch black. The taillights weren't enough, but her brake lights provided at least a few feet of visibility, so she had to keep them on while she let the car roll gently backward down the hill in what felt like painfully slow progress. Perri kept glancing back toward the cemetery to see if someone was approaching her. Her imagination thoughtfully created a deadly horror movie-like creature, lumbering slowly out of the darkness, carrying another wicked garden implement, toward her car which would get stuck in a ditch if this really were the movies. In reality, she saw nothing else.

She gratefully spotted the access to the road on her right as she reversed slightly past it. Throwing the car in drive, Perri spun her wheels on the rock-strewn weeds as she zoomed out onto Gold Hill Road once more. There was a shorter, straight road leading back to highway 13 only about a half mile away, but it was gravel and she didn't want anything smaller or more forlorn than the road she was already on. She zipped around the set of s-curves without slowing her speed at all and skidded to a halt at the stop sign at highway 13.

She had never been so glad to see the lights of a tavern as she was at that moment. Even though she wasn't going to stop and go in, she certainly didn't want to get back out of the car, there were people there. People who weren't skulking around in graveyards with flashlights and shovels in the dark. Ok, so she had been skulking around in a graveyard in the dark with a flashlight, but she wasn't digging the place up. Someone was though.

No way she was going to drive past the Duncan house, not tonight, and not alone. Once her hands were no longer twitching like they carried an electrical current and her breathing wasn't coming in ragged gasps, she looked back and forth several times for cross traffic and pulled onto the highway. She'd follow 13 to Highway 142, just past Equality, which would take her straight into Eldorado less than a mile from her apartment.

Back on the familiar road, Perri gave some thought to what she'd seen in Gold Hill Cemetery. It would be easy to dismiss the digging tools as being there for normal cemetery work, but it didn't look like any gardening work fine enough to require a weeding claw was being done, and why a paint brush? Also, the hole hadn't been dug in the burial area, where a grave might have been. She'd tripped over it because it was in the aisle. Had she entered that way, she would have seen it and probably left right then. Well maybe not. While the collection of tools did seem odd, there really hadn't been anything material to scare her other than her own imagination…at least not until she saw the flash from someone else's flashlight. There was that to consider. Everything else could be explained away except that.

It sent shivers crawling up the flesh of her back all over again thinking about someone hanging around the cemetery, regardless of the fact that she had been hanging around the cemetery. She would have spoken to someone had there been another person enter the grounds while she was there. Were they coming after her as she left, or was that just a coincidence? Maybe they had taken a break from whatever it was they were doing. Maybe they didn't even realize she had been there.

Maybe it was a park ranger wondering who was poking around the cemetery in the dark. Of course, that was it! The cemetery *was* located in an outlying part of the Shawnee National Forest. It was right at the edge of it, but still within the boundaries of the forest. That made sense to her. Perri realized there was no way she could tell Nick about it or she'd never hear the end of it.

Perri abruptly felt extremely weary, her eyelids drooped as though weights hung from her lashes. After the adrenaline had receded, the safety of the car and warmth from the heater were lulling her to sleep. She turned off the heater and flipped on the CD player, turned the music loud to keep herself awake, and decided no more thinking about the cemetery that night.

## Chapter 16

August 16, 1831

Francis stood in the open doorway, staring out into the darkness, watching for any movement to signal the arrival of the doctor. He had hung a lantern on the peg outside the door to light the approach for Peggy Logsdon. Her house was not far from the McCade home, both located in the Sandy Ridge area south of Shawneetown. The ground still radiated heat from the August day's sunshine. Arminda's friend, Malissa, was with her upstairs in the bedroom adjacent to their own which was set aside for her confinement and the nursery. They'd been in the house now for a few weeks and, fortunately, had time to furnish the nursery and make sure all was in readiness.

Arminda's health was good and there had been no problems, there still weren't, so Francis was perplexed why he should feel so flustered and anxious in the face of a happy occasion. His life was orderly and planned, and he generally knew what to expect. He had not expected this. But everything would be fine once Peggy arrived. She had served as physician and midwife to residents on both sides of the Ohio for many years. There was no one more experienced than her anywhere near Shawneetown and she was afforded the admiration and respect of the male physicians in the entire region. Francis knew Arminda was in the best hands available.

He could hear the clopping of the horse's hooves before he saw any indication of movement in the pitch of the night. His forceful exhalation broke the silence; he'd been breathing shallowly and the relief at hearing Peggy's horse flooded Francis's limbs with warmth and a bit of weakness. She rode right up to the door and dismounted, slinging her bag off the roan's pack and handing the reins to Francis with the flash of a smile as she deftly stepped around him and through the doorway.

Peggy pivoted on her boot heel in the wide foyer and asked, "Which room, Mr. McCade?"

"Up the stairway, turn left, it's the next to last room on the right." Francis watched her take the stairs two at a time. Before she disappeared beyond the open railing in the corridor above, she leaned over the painted, scrolled bannister and, smiling, said, "Why don't you find someone to visit you while you wait? Or have a nice brandy. With that pallor, I'm going to need to attend to you too if you don't relax a bit."

Francis looked at the reins in his hand as though he'd no idea they were there until that moment. Even the horse eyed him with what he imagined to be reproof. He lifted the lantern from the peg and guided the horse to the stable behind the house where it could shelter with Fiona and the two other horses for the time being.

After several hours of fidgeting, sipping a finger or two of whisky to calm his nerves, checking and rechecking his accounts, Malissa Beauchamp descended the stairs looking haggard and rumpled. Stray strands of hair were plastered to her forehead and her dress showed patches of sweat beneath her arms, across her chest, and down the center of her back. She merely waved her departure to Francis as she crossed the foyer and left the house. Dr. Logsdon called down from the top of the stairs, "Mr. McCade, would you like to come meet your daughter?"

Francis jumped out of the comfortable wing chair and bounded up the stairs. It was stifling in the room, but they didn't dare open the windows for fear of the baby or Arminda catching a cold. The pink little thing in the blanket wiggled and squirmed, making faces, but not too much noise. Francis was grateful for that. Arminda was tired but smiling. Running her finger very softly over the baby's brow, she whispered, "Do you like the blanket your Uncle Alexander and Aunt Celie sent you?"

Dawn was starting to creep in around the drapes. Dr. Logsdon had finished packing her bag and now faced the couple and their new baby. "I'll be going. Minda, you send someone for me if you have any problems at all. I'll be back in the early evening to check on you both." Noting Francis's look of panic, she added, "Malissa will be back in a few hours to help out. She needs some sleep first, as do the rest of you. I'll let myself out."

Francis sat on the side of the bed and touched the baby girl's fine, wheat-colored hair. "What are we going to call her?"

Arminda answered, "I thought we could call her Martha, like we talked about, after my mother?"

Francis nodded, "Martha it is. A middle name?"

"Well, your mother's name was Rose, how about Martha Rose McCade?"

He smiled. "She'd like that. How about you, Martha Rose?"

## Chapter 17

October 13, 2016

"Thanks for having me, Pearl. I've been looking forward to this all day." Perri settled on the large, high sofa with her laptop and notebook. There was a silver tray on the mid-century coffee table with what surely had to be an antique tea set. Pearl's house was a hodgepodge of styles, some most likely family heirlooms and some probably purchased when Pearl and her husband first bought the house. There were not many truly modern items in the house, other than the stainless washer and dryer which dominated one corner of the kitchen.

Pearl pointed to the tray with the bone china teapot painted with cabbage roses and its matching cups and saucers. She shyly said, "I made tea. I haven't made tea for company in so long. I hope it's alright."

"That's so thoughtful of you, Pearl!" Perri's voice conveyed true appreciation. "Thank you!"

"And I have to confess, all the talk about the old days made me think of this tea set and I wanted to use it again. It was stored in a box in my closet, but I got it out and washed it."

"It's beautiful."

"This set was my Mama's. I'll pour." Pearl bent over the dovetailed, surfboard style coffee table and poured tea into each thin, delicate cup. "I'm sorry I don't have sugar in the house. But I found this honey in the cabinet if you can use that."

"That would be perfect." Perri squeezed honey into her cup and, as she stirred, watched it swirl in the bottom until it dissolved. She took a sip of the strong black tea and closed her eyes, savoring it before swallowing. "I needed that." Setting her teacup back into its finely painted saucer, Perri said, "I absolutely want to find out more from you about your ancestral home, but first, I have a few things I found about the McCades to show you."

"Really? You found information about my family? Where? How?" Pearl settled back into her armchair with the clawed arm rests and legs, holding her saucer and cup on her knees.

Perri explained about the Society research library. "I can't believe I didn't even know about that place." Pearl said in astonishment. "Right here in town, not but a couple of minutes' drive from here."

"Well, if you hadn't done any genealogy or checked into your family history yet, it would be easy to not realize it was there. The important thing is that it is there and I found some information for you." Perri gathered the copies of the information she had found, including the woodcut of Frances, which she would save for last. "There could still be more information to find. This is what I got from the books I looked at yesterday."

Pearl set her tea on a small occasional table to her left, jammed firmly between the chair and the sofa. Perri scooted to the end of the sofa closest to Pearl and shared what she had found about the McCade house and Francis McCade. She read through the biography and showed Pearl the family tree she had put together.

"I just can't get over this," Pearl exclaimed. "I'm so amazed to find out this much information about Francis, and, um, Arminda, is that right? What a lovely name."

They moved on to the newspaper clippings about Pearl's illustrious grandfather Morgan, and her grandmother Lucy, the Suffragette. Pearl had a wry smile on her face as she shook her head slowly in endearing dismay at her grandparents' escapades. "I knew they were a mess, but my grandmother was a pistol, wasn't she?"

Perri nodded and smiled warmly at Pearl's response. Her face was alight. She looked happier and younger when she smiled than Perri could have expected. She was obviously delighted with the family history Perri had uncovered. "And I saved the best for last. Well, I think so anyway."

Pearl leaned forward in anticipation. Perri handed her the printed copy of the woodcut. "This is Francis McCade, your great-great-great grandfather, the man who built your family home. At least, it's an artist rendering of him as he was described at the time."

Pearl took the sheet of paper as gingerly as though it was an original drawing. "Oh my." She brought the paper close to her face and lost herself in it. "He's real. He was real. This makes it seem real now, I mean."

"Oh, he was real, alright." Perri smiled. "I still have some work to do if I want to find out more about his businesses, but I do know he owned part of the old ..." Perri hesitated, realizing the Salt Works were not the best topic to bring up right now. "Rather, I'm just not sure yet which businesses he owned or at least in which he was part-owner. But we do know that at one time he worked in the Shawneetown Bank building that is still there. That was right after he came to Shawneetown from Kentucky."

"Oh, yes." She ran her hand over the face looking back at her. "I didn't know our family ever lived in Kentucky, but I guess it shouldn't be a surprise. They had to come from somewhere before Shawneetown was there."

"Exactly. And somewhere before Kentucky, too, if you keep going back through your family line." Perri paused to change the subject a little. She continued. "I haven't seen your family house yet," she paused a moment, "but I do hope to drive by and see what I can before I write the article about it. The more I know the better, and actually seeing it, maybe even getting a few photos would be best. Inside and out?"

Perri waited tensely. Pearl looked up, distance still reflected in her eyes, then they cleared and she said, "Oh! Well, you should see the house, of course. I mean, it's mine now so you can see it whenever you want. Well, whenever the police say it is ok to go back into it. They've called me a couple of times asking lots of the same questions. I don't know more now than I did. They seem to think someone was after some priceless old thing George dug up at an estate sale or something. They want to know who he did business with, but I don't know that stuff. When I was with Ruby, or we talked on the phone, we didn't discuss George's haggling partners.

The oddest thing too, they wanted to know if George had brought anything to my house to store recently, like they thought he was hiding something."

"But he hadn't?" Perri asked.

"No. I do have some things from home but they're ones I brought with me when Charlie and I moved here when we got married. I brought some dishes that were to be mine anyway, a few pieces of jewelry, those two framed embroidery samplers hanging in the dining room that mama said were done by one of the early ladies in the family, and a dresser and chest of drawers. That's what I remember anyway.

Anyway, I think they may be finished with the house soon. I'll have to ask." Her gaze was drawn back to Francis McCade. "You know, I can't help but see my sister in him. Ruby had that same unruly, curly hair. Same nose. Oh, I know it's a long time but family traits are passed down. I think I looked more like Momma. But Ruby, she looked like Daddy. Isn't it funny how some traits continue down the line for so long?"

While it was possible, Perri knew that the curly hair could have come from any number of relatives in the family tree over two hundred years, and she wasn't about to dispel Pearl's pleasure in it. "Yes, isn't that amazing?"

Then, as gently as she could, Perri tried to steer the conversation to more recent information. "Pearl, can you tell me about Ruby? What was she like?"

Pearl sighed a heavy sigh and held out the print to Perri, who put both hands up, "Oh no, Pearl, you keep that. I took a photo of the print from the book and can print as many as you would like. And the other information too. All of this is for you to keep."

"Thank you, this is just such a comfort right now. Let's see, what can I tell you about Ruby? She was a quieter girl than I was. Not that I was loud and rude of course, but Ruby was just more…genteel, you know? I guess she was the lady and I was the tomboy. She liked helping Mama in the kitchen and I like climbing the trees in the orchard. The orchard's mostly gone now."

She paused sadly for a moment. "Nothing much riled Ruby up. She and George were a good match. George was level-headed and mostly laid back, as they say now, but that man did have a stubborn streak. And I hesitate to say it, but he was a little frugal. Oh heck, no, he was tight as the skin on a drum." Pearl chuckled. "You couldn't have pried an extra penny out of his hands with a crowbar."

"What was George's occupation?" Perri asked.

"He worked at several jobs. When he was younger, most of them involved loading cargo onto barges down at the river front. Grain, coal, whatever needed shipping. Living right on the river made it handy too. He also did some farm labor."

"Did they do any farming of their own? There are a lot of farms in the area."

"No, they didn't farm themselves. The family land used to extend farther from the river, but in the late 1940s, not long after I was born, but before Ruby, Daddy sold the back half of the property. They needed the money, I think. Not long after that, another house was built on that land. That's where the Vincent's live now. They bought the house when it was new and are still there. Most of their kids have moved all over the country it seems, but they still have a son and grandkids in the area."

Perri nodded. "That explains the map. I could see on the old plat map that the property consisted of two lots. At that time, the boundary of the McCade property was closer to Gold Hill Cemetery, wasn't it?"

"It probably was. I don't remember exactly where our property ended before it was sold, I was too young. Even so, it wasn't all that close to the old cemetery, you still had to follow the track that ran by the stream and then out to the lane to get to it."

"Do you know if any of your family is buried there?"

Pearl considered the question before answering. "Mama and Daddy are, yes. Other than them, well, I'm not for sure, but I would imagine there must be, wouldn't there? I've never really thought about where those people further back were buried, but they had to be buried somewhere. That would be as good a place as any being as close as it is."

"I would like to go there, probably this weekend, and look. My boyfriend will be here and we are going to visit a few sites around the area. If it's alright with you, would it be ok to publish a photograph of a McCade memorial if I find one? With the article, I mean."

"Sure, honey. Wouldn't that be just wonderful? I would love to see the graves if you find them. Maybe you could show me sometime?"

"I'd be more than happy to do that!" Turning back to the subject of Ruby, "Did Ruby have an occupation outside the home?"

"No, Ruby didn't work outside other than at home, and of course we all know that's more than a full-time job in itself, isn't it? But...I don't know if this counts, but she and George did do a lot of that...oh, what do they call it? It's on TV all the time." Pearl pressed her fingers to her lips in thought. "Those guys who drive all over the place and poke through people's barns and buy their stuff so they can resell it."

"Pickers?"

"That's it, pickers. That's what they did. Ruby helped with that a lot."

"Did they travel mainly around southern Illinois or did they branch out to other areas too?"

"Mostly it was around the area: Shawneetown, Cave-in-Rock, Elizabethtown, Rosiclare, and I think once or twice they went as far as Golconda. Most of the places were right on the river, they didn't wander inland too much."

"Did they sell online, from their home, or...?"

"Mostly through auctions or summer flea markets. George had an old van and they'd load it up and travel to weekend fairs or the auction barn in Equality, places like that, to sell what they'd found. I guess they did alright at it because they kept doing it, and George wouldn't have done it if it wasn't making him a dime. Oh, that van will be in the barn at the house. Anyway, they didn't do any business on the internet, I don't think. I mean, I could be wrong, but I don't remember Ruby saying anything about that. I don't think they would have wanted to fool with packing and mailing things."

"I've watched some of those shows about pickers and the things they find. I can see why it would be fun to do if they had the time. Did George and Ruby specialize in any certain type of finds, or did they go for anything they could sell?"

"Hmmm. George liked to find old ship parts, you know, stuff like old helm wheels, anchors, capstans. Whatever he could find. He liked anything to do with boats and ships, the older and the stranger the better." Pearl smiled sadly. "He would be so excited with a new discovery. He was always walking around on the river bank too, looking for stuff that might wash up."

"Did he find many artifacts washed up on shore?" Perri asked.

Pearl chuckled. "He found lots of junk, I tell you. But he did come up with some bits of old anchor chain, pulleys, or pieces of crockery that sometimes had the name of a ship on them. Most times it was broken or at least chipped."

Perri didn't want to be blunt, but wanted to know, so she asked, "Collectors can sometimes be eccentric and intense. Do you think there's anything to the idea that George found something unusually valuable that could have been the reason for someone searching the house and that might have resulted in his and Ruby's death?"

"Well, I can't say it didn't happen. We talked at least once a week, but not every day. Ruby didn't mention anything like that, but she might not have unless they'd already sold it. George liked to keep his good finds quiet until they came up for auction. He thought he got the best take that way, surprise everyone with it and they'd be eager to get it, not have time to wheedle."

"Does your family still have many of the things Francis McCade might have furnished the house with when it was new?"

Pearl replied, "Yes, yes, there are some things. I'm sure there's some I don't recall right off the top of my head. We do still have an old cradle, probably a lot of glassware and silverware, and a couple of small samplers, you know the needlework young girls used to do to show off their sewing?" Perri nodded. "There's a lot of stuff in the cellar and the attic too, but I can't remember what's up there. For all I know, they sold off what was worth selling."

"I hope not all of it, for your sake." Perri continued, "The last thing I wanted to talk to you about is the house itself. I know you expressed some concern over inheriting the house and what you would do with it."

"Yes, that's a big weight on my mind right now. I find myself with a family home that means the world to me but that I never dreamed I'd have to take care of myself. I always figured George and Ruby would live in it, take care of it, and pass it on to someone when they died, and then I thought it would be after I was gone."

"They had no children to leave the house to?"

Pearl made a soft, throaty noise, then said, "They had a son, Chris, but he passed away in a car accident when he was only twenty-six." She blew out a long, slow breath, calculating. "That would have been in 1995."

"I'm so sorry to hear that."

"Well, I say car accident, and I guess technically it was." Perri didn't say anything, just waited for Pearl to continue, and she did. "He'd crossed the Ohio into Kentucky on the ferry at Cave-in-Rock early in the day and was on his way back in the evening. He'd been waiting in line to get on the ferry. His was the only car waiting. Just as he was driving on deck, a truck came up behind and couldn't stop. It hit Chris's car and pushed it right off the end of the ferry, into the river. The truck stopped just short of going over, it got hung up on something on deck."

"That's horrible! Did they...couldn't they..."

"No, it was winter and the water was so cold, and it was dark. He never made it out of the car. They did recover it the next day. Even then it had drifted down river a ways."

"I'm so sorry. That's tragic."

"Yes, it was tough on George and Ruby. But...long time ago now."

"That's why the house came to you."

Pearl nodded. "About the house, I hope you don't mind me having checked on this for you. The house is nearly two hundred years old, and as we now know, it's also the only remaining original brick house built in the Shawneetown of the early 1800s. According to the information I read about it in the research library, the brickwork was unique to the area as well. Since those things qualify it for consideration on the National Register of Historic Places, I looked up the process of application. When I did, I found that one had already been completed for it in 1984 and it was approved in 1985. I checked the online database and your house is listed. It's already on the list."

Pearl was listening, but her face registered no comprehension.

Perri explained. "What I'm saying is that since your house is already approved, there may be assistance resources for you to apply for in restoring the house and helping you with the taxes so it can be preserved. At the very least, you would have access to expert advice."

Pearl was just staring at Perri. "I'm saying that your house is a real treasure and it may be historically very important. I will help you however I can to check into those resources. Also, I didn't think of this at first, but writing about the house in the genealogy magazine may be a good way to get its story out there, too. You never know where help may come from."

Tears welled up in Pearl's eyes and she gripped Perri's hand, squeezing it tightly. "I would never have imagined there would be something like that. But I would love to try. I don't want the house to fall apart. I've been so afraid it would be bulldozed like all the other old houses. I know a lot of them had to go because they were so flood damaged, but our house has always been up high enough that it managed to avoid the worst of that."

"I tell you what. I'll check with the Illinois State Historic Preservation Office and find out what to do next."

"That would be just great. It would take a load off my mind. As it is, I've been afraid I'd have to let the house sit there, or worse, sell it to one of those vultures who keep circling around. And I worry about vandals and robbers too, especially since someone already broke in there and killed my sister in the process."

"Vultures?" Perri asked. Are people pestering you to sell the house already?"

"Yes, well just once since Ruby died. But in the past, it seems like there was always someone leaving cards taped to Ruby and George's door, knocking and asking to talk about selling. Ruby said those people didn't want to take no for an answer sometimes. Once, she even had to threaten to call the police if they didn't leave them alone about it. Another time, she got a little scared because one guy was showing up while George wasn't around and got awful mad that she wouldn't change her mind and talk George into selling. She said he wanted it really cheap and kept telling her it was turning into a dump and was going to go to ruin if they didn't sell it to him."

"Was the man someone she knew?"

"She didn't say she did. I think she would have told me his name if she knew him."

"Unless she was afraid of him. But she didn't call the police? He left her alone after that?"

"As far as I know." Pearl replied.

"How long ago was that?"

Pearl though about it. "Gosh, it was probably the first part of the summer. It had to be before it got too hot outside because Ruby said she had all the windows open and only the screen door to the kitchen, which wasn't latched. I mean, in broad daylight, we never had to worry about latching doors. Anyway, the man startled her by opening the screen and calling in to see if anyone was home, then stepped right into her kitchen."

"That was bold, to just walk into someone's house. I wouldn't like that at all either."

"Ruby had a knife in her hand so she shooed his hind end right out of the house and told him she'd call the police. He left." Pearl set her empty tea cup back on the silver tray. "So…you think that I might get a little help with the house?"

"I hope so. I'll certainly try to find out." Replacing her own cup and saucer on the tray, Perri stood and said, "Pearl, I really enjoyed talking with you tonight and I appreciate you letting me come by." She picked up her satchel.

"It was just what I needed and I'm so glad you came. I guess I'll see you in the morning for my glucose check, right?"

"Yep. You're first on my list. I'll let you know what I find out about your house, but I might need a few days."

"You take the time you need. I'll find out when you'll be able to go inside the house to have a look too."

"That sounds great. Thanks, again, and I'll see you tomorrow."

Perri had a lot to think about after her conversation with Pearl. She was especially interested in getting to see the inside of the McCade house and trying to find out if George had sold any high dollar items. She could check with Wanda about that. If he'd sold them privately or at a flea market, she had no idea how to find out.

For now, she could look forward to Nick arriving tomorrow and going out together Saturday for a bit of exploration. She also might want to check out whatever information she could dig up on

Chris Duncan's fatal accident on the ferry, just in case it seemed a bit off.

## Chapter 18

October 14, 2016

    Perri had finished seeing her morning patients and was just about done with the sloppy pulled pork sandwich she was having for lunch at the Vine Street Cafe. She had fully intended to go back to her apartment and eat the spinach and arugula salad with tomato and cucumber that she had put together the night before. But, here she was, ensconced in a green leather booth, listening to old country & western, not having that salad. She also was not regretting it one bit. A frosty cold beer would have been great to go with it, but, still having two patients to go, it would have to wait until tonight when she and Nick would most likely be eating out again. So much for the diet. Maybe they'd get a lot of hiking mileage in the next day and this would all be a wash.

    Her phone, still on vibrate, buzzed in her scrub top pocket. Perri ripped open the little packet containing the moist towelette to get the barbecue sauce off her fingers then grabbed the phone and answered it. "Hello?"

    Nick's voice answered her, "I'm on the way. I left about thirty minutes ago, just hit I-69 north."

    "Yay!" Drawing attention from the tables nearest her, Perri toned down her voice. "Well, I just yee-hawed to the entire restaurant. Anyway, can't wait for you to get here. Where are you crossing the river?"

    "I'll cut through to the river at Morganfield and cross at Old Shawneetown. I'll be taking some back roads, but it's a beautiful day."

    "Sounds good. I'll finish up my schedule in the next hour and head back to the apartment."

    "I can't wait to get there, I've been looking forward to this all week." Nick replied.

"Me too." Perri was getting antsy now that she was talking to Nick and he was on his way.

"Well, I'd better get off the phone. I'm doing ninety-five and..."

"You are not!"

"Why not? I want to get there."

"Don't, Nick."

"But I want to get there quickly."

"And what, spend your time in the hospital?" Perri could hear him laughing. "I know you're just saying that. You aren't driving ninety-five." She paused and waited, nothing. "You aren't, are you?"

"No! Of course not."

"Why do you say stuff like that then?"

"Because you take me seriously every single time." Nick laughed.

"No, I don't."

"You do. Every. Single. Time."

"Alright, yes I do, because you might actually mean it. How would I feel if something happened and I thought you...?"

"Ok, ok, I get it. I'll stop doing it."

"No, you won't."

"You're right. Sorry."

"No, you aren't."

"Right again. You're on a roll today."

Perri intentionally sighed dramatically. "Why do I want to put myself through more of this?"

"Because you love it, and you know it." Nick laughed again.

"I'll concede. Hey, I've found some interesting information on the house I was telling you about." Perri waited but only heard silence. "Come on, I told you I wanted to write about it."

"And?" Nick asked warily.

"I want to go by and see it."

"I knew it. Do not go without me, ok? I'm on the way, so just wait."

"I don't mean today. I'm thinking, you know, tomorrow."

"Alright, we'll *drive past* it tomorrow, but promise me you won't go alone."

"Promise. Besides, I am going get to see the inside at some point soon anyway."

"Really? Why?"

"Um, I'll have to tell you after you get here. We'll talk about it. Don't drive too fast!"

"Yes ma'am. Hanging up now to focus on safe driving with my hands at ten and two o'clock." Nick's voiced softened. "I'll see you in a couple of hours."

"Be safe. See you soon."

\*\*\*

Perri had just walked into the living room from the bathroom when she heard tires crunching across the gravel lot. She jogged up to the window and looked out in time to see the rear end of Nick's black Jeep pull around the corner of the building to the parking area. She'd taken a shower, dried her straight hair, and fooled around with it for several minutes before putting on an outfit she bought before she left Vailsburg but hadn't worn yet. This was probably the fifth time Perri had checked the mirror.

She brushed imaginary lint off the new dark jeans and straightened the purple and black sweater. She hadn't seen Nick for a couple of months and had the fluttery feeling in her midsection again like she did each time she saw him.

She decided not to wait for him to come up the stairs, but to meet him at the entry door to the building. She bounded down the first set of steps and collided with Reuben Webb, who was coming up the stairs, as she rounded the turn. The group of magazines he was carrying fell to the stairs, some sliding down several steps.

Perri gasped. "Oh! I'm sorry, I wasn't paying attention."

He laughed, "That's ok." He stepped back down a couple stairs and bent forward to retrieve his magazines.

"No, good grief, let me get those. I'm sorry." Perri zipped past Reuben to retrieve the magazines.

Reuben chuckled good-naturedly, "You seem to be in a hurry, I can do that."

"No, I just…my boyfriend is just getting here from Kentucky for a visit, I was going to meet him outside…here he is." Perri smiled broadly and hopped down the remaining few steps. She gave Nick a kiss, a little self-consciously, then turned back to Reuben. "Nick, this is Reuben Webb. He lives in the apartment across the hall upstairs, and I just mowed him down as he was coming up. Reuben, this is Nick Silver."

Nick slung his duffle over his shoulder and set down a gym bag next to him. The two men shook hands and exchanged pleasantries. Reuben said, "Nice to meet you, Nick. Enjoy your Friday night." He nodded and climbed the stairs.

"Do you have anything else to carry up?" Perri asked Nick.

"No," he laughed, "I pack lightly. I don't have encyclopedic collections of research materials to..."

Perri playfully slapped him on the arm. "Come on up."

\*\*\*

Two hours later, Perri and Nick were settled in a booth at a pizza place in Eldorado. They ordered a large pizza and worked on their first beer while waiting. Perri said, "This is a fairly new place, I believe. It's supposed to be pretty good. I'm glad they have local beers, too. Perri poured her Saluki Dunkeldog into a frosted pint glass and Nick sampled his Big Muddy Monster straight from the bottle."

"The food sure smells good." Nick took two more gulps of his beer then let out a long sigh of relief and slid down in the booth, crossing his long legs next to Perri's. "It's fan-tas-tic to be off work for a while and be here with you."

Perri raised her glass and said, "I'll toast to that."

Nick tapped her pint glass with his beer bottle.

Perri set the glass back down after a drink of the draft. "How's Lesley? Everything ok in Cambridge?" Nick's sister lived in Massachusetts.

"Oh yeah, she's fine. Doing well. She started her own business, some sort of ... shop, I don't know."

Perri shook her head at him. "Some sort of shop. That's informative."

"Cut me some slack. You know she'll tell me more about it later. Over the holidays, I'll hear enough about it to feel like I work there."

Once he'd updated Perri on his sister, Lesley the Shop Owner, and her husband, Doug the Accountant, she told Nick about her week and what she knew of the double murder of the couple in Old Shawneetown. She had to choose her words carefully so she didn't reveal that the sister of the woman killed was one of her patients, at least until she could get permission from Pearl. Since she'd gone to her house, off duty, and done some research for her, it would be hard to avoid mentioning it.

"Oh man, that's horrible." Nick's face was a mixture of shock and concern. "Do they have any idea who did it?"

"I don't know anything else about it. When I was there...in my car I mean, when I was listening to it on the radio, and on TV, they said they didn't have any suspects yet, nor any motives."

The pizza was brought to their table. Conversation stopped while the waitress set the still-bubbling pizza on a metal tripod in the center of the table, giving them room for their plates which they loaded up with pizza, sprinkling Parmesan and red pepper flakes over it.

After a few bites, Nick said, "This *is* good. I like the sauce. Tastes homemade."

"Mm, hmm." Perri agreed as she savored the spicy pizza and crisp crust. "It kind of reminds me of pizza from that place back home. I don't know how they make their sauce here, but the one at home puts a touch of honey in theirs."

Nick finished his first piece and took another drink of his beer. "Hey, whatcha thinkin'?"

His face came into focus and Perri realized he had asked her a question and was waiting for an answer. "I'm sorry, what?"

Nick squinted at her. "You've got that...you know, Nancy Drew-ish look in your eyes. You aren't planning on trying to figure something out about this murder on your own, are you?"

"Why would you say something like that?" Perri busied herself shaking Parmesan all over her next slice.

Nick watched her for a few moments. "You gonna cover that completely?" He nodded at her plate. "I said it because I think you've caught a little of the investigation bug after the couple of escapades you've been involved in over the last year or so."

"I'm just...I just want to help figure it out. It must be awful for the family to have no idea who or why."

Nick leaned forward, around the pizza and said, "That's what the police are for. We don't have to solve this." He stared at her, waiting, then said, "You know what they say about curiosity."

"Yep, but I also know that cats have nine lives, so I'm good."

"In case you haven't noticed, you aren't a cat. And you didn't know these people, they didn't live in this town, and not even in the ones you are working in. They could have been involved in anything. They could have been drug dealers or involved in some other kind of stuff. You never know anymore."

"I don't think so, Nick. They were in their late 60s and had lived on that property their entire married life. The woman, Ruby Duncan, had never lived anywhere else, it was her family home."

He studied Perri's face. "How do you know all that?" Realization creeped into Nick's expression. "You *do* know something else about this! You have an inside source, Nancy?"

Perri sat with her mouth slightly open, unsure what to say. Then finally, "I can't tell you."

"You can't tell me."

"No."

"Why not?"

"Because."

"Because why?"

"I can't say."

"You can't tell me why you can't tell me?"

"Correct." She nodded and took a big enough bite of pizza to occupy her mouth for long enough to think of something else to talk about. A blob of hot pizza sauce squeezed out of the corner of her mouth. She quickly grabbed a napkin to wipe it away.

Nick continued to watch her, which made Perri squirm. "Ok. I think I get it. You can't tell me why because some, I don't know, rule or regulation somewhere about something, says you can't. And you can't even tell me if I'm right. I get it."

Perri stared back at Nick, eyes a little wide. He said, "You haven't told me anything. I know if you can, you will. Let's talk about where we're going tomorrow."

"That's a good idea." Over Nick's shoulder, Perri saw Reuben Webb and a dark-haired woman come through the door. "Hey, there's Reuben again."

Nick looked over his shoulder and turned back to ask, "Do you want to ask them to join us?"

"Sure, but I don't want you to think I'm not enjoying your company and having you all to myself," Perri replied. "We haven't seen each other for a while."

"I don't think that, and I'm here for a week. It might seem a little unfriendly not to ask. They may not want to join someone else, but we can make the gesture anyway."

"I agree."

Nick turned around again and waved to get their attention as they stood, waiting to be seated. Nick mouthed, "Want to join us?"

Reuben turned to the woman and spoke. She nodded and the two slalomed through the tables to get to the booth where Perri and Nick were seated. "We don't want to intrude." Reuben said.

"No intrusion. Have a seat." Nick moved to sit next to Perri, freeing the other side of the booth. He and Perri moved their plates and pizza stand as far down as they could to make room.

Reuben introduced the woman, "This is Carmen Blubaugh. Carmen, this is Perri Seamore and Nick...sorry, I forgot your last name."

"Silver." Nick and Perri both shook hands with Carmen, then she and Reuben slid across the red vinyl upholstery of the booth, Carmen scooting to the wall, seated directly across from Perri.

Reuben said, "Carmen is a, well, not an *old* friend, I guess," he laughed, "but rather a friend of some years."

"Reuben and I met at Purdue, on highway 231 just outside of Lafayette, to be precise." Carmen chuckled. "He was working there for a semester to fill in for a professor on sabbatical and I was still in the throes of my doctorate research project."

"In what field is your PhD?" Perri asked.

"Entomology. I was driving my old, beat-up car out to the research site where I knew I had at least four undergrad students waiting for me when the radiator blew. Steam was belching out from under the hood, just about obliterated the car in a cloud of steam. I was standing there on the side of the highway staring at it and grumbling when Reuben pulled over to see if he could help."

"I couldn't believe she was trying to drive that car. Only the proverbial rust was holding it together." Reuben tilted his head toward Carmen. "Definitely a risk-taker, this one."

"So, Reuben gave me a lift out to the site. We've been friends ever since."

"What happened to the car?" Perri asked.

"Towed to its final resting place. The cost of fixing everything that was wrong with it was more than getting another used car, provided I didn't expect something snazzy."

The waitress came to take their order.

Reuben nodded to the menus tucked into the ring clasp of the condiment tray and said to Carmen, "I've been here before and know what I want."

"Ok, Mr. Adventurous." Carmen grabbed one of the menus and hastily opened it while Reuben ordered. "I'll have the spicy stromboli with a side of pepperoncini and a glass of iced tea."

"Do you want the full or the half strom?" The waitress asked, pen poised.

"The full strom." Reuben replied.

Carmen was tapping her forefinger on her chin, trying to decide. She looked up to see the waitress waiting, and said, "Um, I think I'll have the baked ziti, an order of onion rings, and a Ski."

The waitress jotted down the orders. She removed the empty plates and pizza pan with its stand, then said to Carmen and Reuben, "Be back with your food shortly."

Wiping his mouth and scrunching his napkin into a little ball, Nick asked, "Do you live in the area, Carmen?"

"No, I'm on a working visit to Southern Illinois University, over in Carbondale. Their environmental sciences department is doing a project on the role of insects in prairieland and ecosystem management. They're using ground beetles in one of their test fields. I did my doctoral thesis on the ground beetle, so I was asked if I'd take part in getting it set up. And here I am. It isn't too far away, so I drove over to have supper with Reuben. I didn't want to leave the area without having a better get-together than the one we had Saturday."

Reuben added, "Carmen lives on the west coast and I live in Michigan now, so this was a good chance to meet and gossip about all the people we used to work with."

"I went to Purdue also, Nursing." Perri said to Carmen.

Carmen smiled and, in unison, Carmen and Perri said, "Boiler Up!"

"That's great, it's a small world, isn't it?"

"That it is." Perri couldn't contain her curiosity any longer. Her elbows on the table, she asked with anticipation, "So...if it bothers you to talk about it, I totally understand, but I heard you were unlucky enough to find those bodies in the salt well."

Carmen looked over at Reuben then shook her head as she replied, "That was one of the most ghastly mornings I've ever had. I'm thankful the weather hadn't been ninety-eight degrees in the shade, because it was terrible enough as it was. Although, had we noticed a smell, we may have had a suspicion there was something dead in there, but I still wouldn't have expected to find two human bodies bobbing up like corks once we moved that big limb.

Nick joined the discussion. "Perri told me about it when I arrived this afternoon. She said the bodies were tied together?"

Carmen answered, "Yes, back to back. They were tied with rope, looked like polypropylene rope, or at least that's what I think it was." Perri and Nick both looked at Carmen with inquiring expressions, and she explained, "I recognized the type because I used it a lot to mark off test plots. It's fairly common. Why I took the time to notice that, I don't know, but I was fixating on the rope instead of looking at the woman's face."

"After that, we hightailed it back to the car and Reuben called the police. We had to stay for a while, long enough for them to talk to each of us, separately. Not a place I ever want to visit again, which is too bad because its history is fascinating. On the bright side, when Reuben told me he was researching land titles, the history of the area, and disappearing towns, I pictured ghost towns, abandoned houses with doors hanging on their hinges, and the wind whistling through jagged glass in broken windows. I didn't realize he meant villages that literally disappeared from the landscape entirely. I've seen some of the photos he's taken and I think they will make a compelling collection once he's finished. The black and white ones are the most haunting, I think."

Reuben replied, "Thanks, Carmen. I appreciate it." He looked at Perri and Nick. "She's right, I'm here to tramp around through trees and weeds, search for remnants, and photograph them. Several small communities left when the salt works petered out after the Kanawha production started up in West Virginia."

"Why did the local salt works close completely, was it because of the one in West Virginia?" Perri asked.

Reuben nodded. "Kanawha was able to produce huge volumes of salt much quicker. Saline just couldn't keep up with them."

Perri commented, "I'd like to compare notes on Old Shawneetown with you sometime, Reuben, if you wouldn't mind. I'm doing some research on the only remaining brick house in town."

Nick interjected in a wry tone, "She's activated her snooping mode." Perri gently elbowed him in the ribs. "The house she's talking about is where the murdered couple lived. She's bound and determined to find out all about that house, and is hoping, just by accident, she'll figure out who might have done it." Perri turned sideways to look at Nick full on. He quickly added, "To be fair, the house *is* supposed to be one of the first brick houses in the area and she's supposed to write an article for a genealogy e-zine." He shrugged apologetically to Perri. With a bare whisper of a smile, she turned back to Carmen and Reuben.

The waitress arrived and set Reuben and Carmen's food and drinks on the table. "Anything else for you guys?"

"I'll have a cup of coffee, please." Perri replied. Nick shook his head that he didn't want anything else. The waitress headed for the drinks station.

"Nick and I are going to do some hiking and exploring around the area south of here this weekend. We were going tomorrow, but something else has come up for part of the day, so we'll probably hike on Sunday, or maybe a short one Saturday afternoon. I'm looking forward to getting out in the fresh Fall air."

Reuben asked, "Where do you plan to go?"

Nick answered, with arched eyebrows. "Initially, we were going to the Shawnee forest area, including checking out the salt well, but those plans have changed."

"Good idea. Did you see on the news about the vandalism at Cave-in-Rock?" Reuben asked as he unwrapped the foil enclosing the stromboli. Steam issued forth and he yanked his hand back.

The waitress deposited a cup of coffee and a saucer with several creamer cups arranged on it. Perri shook her head, "No, I didn't. What happened?"

Pulling his scalded knuckle out of his mouth, Reuben said, "Fortunately, nothing that permanently damaged it, but someone dug multiples holes, some pretty deep, in the soil-covered floor of the cave." He commented just before he bit into the still-steaming sandwich. His eyes opened wider and he took a quick sip of the tea.

Carmen laughed and said, "You just burned your hand on it, then you stick it in your mouth without letting it cool?"

Nick responded to Reuben's statement. "Holes in the floor of a cave? Why would anyone do that?"

"Holes, like big holes or little holes? You mean like they were digging, looking for something?" Perri asked Reuben, thinking about the tools left in Gold Hill Cemetery.

"Yeah, like that. Who's to say if they found what they were looking for or not. You stop looking when you find it, but there's no way to tell if they stopped because they found something or they ran out of time."

Nick looked puzzled. "What could they hope to find in a cave?"

Perri explained. "The cave isn't underground. It's basically a channel worn into the limestone just above ground level. The mouth looks out over the Ohio River. It doesn't go very deep or have multiple chambers. I've been there lots of times. It was one of my favorite Saturday trips back in the day. It isn't remote or secluded, people are in and out of there all the time."

"I still don't get it. Why would someone dig up the floor?"

"That's a long story, but in a nutshell, the cave has been a lot of different things through history. In the distant past, it was sometimes home or a temple-like place for Native Americans. Over the past, oh…two hundred plus years, it has served as a hideout for criminals, a base for ambushing travelers, a work site for counterfeiters, and even an actual Inn at one point. That's hard to imagine when you see it now."

"She's right," Reuben said, "there have been so many rumors about what might be buried in that cave, and every now and then interest in it flares up again and people go treasure hunting."

Nick listened attentively as Reuben continued, "Every decade or so, someone emerges who gets it into their head that there is gold or bags of money buried in the cave." Reuben snorted a laugh. "Like after two hundred years, they'll be the one to dig a few shallow holes and find the treasure when no one else has. I'm glad they didn't destroy any of it. I don't understand the mentality of people who do things like that."

Carmen finished off her last onion ring and piped up, "Ooh, buried money. *Has* anyone ever found any?"

Perri added, "Not the kind of money these people expect. Two hundred years ago, travelers did often shallowly bury their valuables overnight while they camped, but unless they were killed or got scared away and couldn't go back, they would have dug it back up the next day and taken it with them. Not that no one got killed in or around the cave, that definitely did happen, but they were generally killed for their belongings and the bandits responsible would have been watching them. Any valuables would have been dug up and taken. Over the years, there have been odds and ends found, like an old pistol or tool, but adherents to the theory believe there are vast amounts of buried treasure in the cave, hidden there by river bandits. Kind of the inland version of buried pirate treasure on islands along the Atlantic Coast. I just can't see that being the case, at least not after all this time."

"It doesn't seem likely," replied Nick. He turned to Perri, "I'd like to see this place. How about we go there this weekend instead?"

Perri's eyebrows lifted at the thought. Thinking her job of convincing Nick to go through Old Shawneetown on the way just got easier, she answered, "Sure, sounds good to me. I'd love to see it again." Turning to Reuben, she asked him, "Is it open? Do you know, or is it closed because of the vandalism?"

"I think they said it was supposed to be open again by the weekend. Not much to put right, they were just going to fill the holes back up and make sure there was no danger to anyone."

"Alright then, that's settled, we'll go there." Nick smiled.

Perri changed the subject, saying as matter-of-factly as she could, "You know, Old Shawneetown has a thick history of underhanded deeds, rumors, and intrigue too. Reuben probably knows all of this, but most of the buildings from before 1937 are gone. There was a lot of water damage, some houses just swept away, and people didn't want to bother, or couldn't afford, to fix them. So yeah, it is interesting that the McCade house is one of the only remaining ones."

"McCade house?" Reuben asked.

"The original owner, the man who built it, was named Francis McCade. The Duncans, the murdered couple, lived in it. Ruby Duncan was a descendent of Francis McCade."

"You've done more than just a little research on it. I did hear that the house is very near the river. Do you know if the McCade house was ever flooded?"

"I haven't found any evidence that it was. It supposedly sits up on a hill, so it may have escaped the flood waters, even in 1937. The house itself has some rumors of its own, though."

"What kind of rumors?" Nick asked.

"Oh, a lot of the usual: that it was a brothel at one time, that one of the owners ran a moonshine business out of the cellar during Prohibition, which I think is probably likely, or that this or that famous gangster stayed the night there. There was even a time when it was thought to have been a stop on the Underground Railroad. But, that happens a lot with old houses placed near river ways, doesn't it?"

"You're right, it does." Reuben drained the last of his tea. "If every house said to be part of the network truly was a part of it, every other house along the major rivers of the Mason-Dixon line would have been involved and the banks would be riddled with tunnels. Would've been hard to keep a secret then, wouldn't it?"

Perri asked Reuben, "You've been doing some research of your own, do you think there may be some truth to any of those rumors about the town's criminal activity?"

"I don't know which stories are true, but my guess would be that if any are true, it would be the ones about Prohibition, some prostitution, and maybe a gangster or two." Reuben winked. "But who knows, they could all be true. This part of the country had a lot going on during the early 19th century, and before. As far as rumors about the house you're referring to, I don't know anything specific about it."

"It would be interesting to find out." Perri lifted her cup for a sip, but it was empty so she set it down again. Placing a hand on Nick's knee, she said, "Well, time for us to go and let you two have that time to catch up." Perri and Nick slid out of the booth. "It was great to meet you, Carmen. I hope we meet again sometime."

"Good to meet both of you, too." Carmen responded.

Reuben wiped the corners of his mouth and laid his napkin in the red plastic basket his sandwich had been in. He stood and brushed the crumbs from his jeans and flannel shirt. "We may as well get going too. I'm looking forward to a cup of tea. How about you?" he asked Carmen.

"Sounds great."

Nick suggested he and Perri have supper with Reuben again before Nick left town and Reuben replied, "I'd like that. You know where to find me. Well, I hope you have a pleasant outing tomorrow, wherever you end up going."

Nick tossed several bills on the table. When Reuben opened his wallet to do the same, he said, "I've got it," and added a few more.

"Thanks." Reuben replied.

"After you." Nick and Perri got in line behind Reuben and Carmen at the register. Reuben paid the bill at the counter and left, waving as he held the door for Carmen.

Nick and Perri followed suit. A gust of wind fought its way in as Nick opened the door for Perri, bringing a few leaves with it. She commented, "Feels like it's getting frosty out here."

As Nick pulled out of the parking lot, Perri said, "Thanks for agreeing to go to Cave-in-Rock."

Nick smiled the just slightly crooked smile that Perri loved and said, "That's no hardship on my part, I want to see it too, and I don't feel comfortable about blundering around in the woods near the salt well right now." Nick reached over and squeezed Perri's knee then left it resting on her thigh. It felt warm and comfortable in the chill air of the car. She put her hand over his and smiled.

## Chapter 19

February 28, 1836

Francis had closed his eyes, willing himself to remain calm, to not sound irritable. "Arminda, it was at your bidding that I amended my practice of traveling to my places of business that are more than five miles away whenever I am able to do so."

"I know that, Francis, but I'm curious about who all these men are who keep coming to the house. Some of them look…unsavory, and I'm worried about the children."

He was losing the battle with restraint. "Shall I instruct everyone who comes to our house for business purposes on their manner of dress and personal care? They will think me a lady!" Francis's face began to darken. "What would you have me do, pray tell? I must conduct business but if you don't want me to venture far from home, or overnight, I must do so here and I cannot require that every business contact be attired for a fancy-dress party."

Arminda's face flushed. Francis added, "I've already restricted all business to the carriage house, shall we meet in the orchard in the snow?" Francis paced back and forth in front of the sitting room fireplace. The toe of one highly polished shoe connected with a painted wooden block which flew across the room and cracked one of the glass panes of a leadlight cabinet. The colorful design of the toy had blended almost seamlessly with the expensive carpet on the floor, rendering it invisible. Francis strode quickly to the bottom of the staircase and shouted "Hugo! Hugo, come here this instant."

Francis returned to the sitting room and faced Arminda. She set aside her embroidery and picked up one-month-old Jane who fidgeted restlessly in her arms. Jubal was sleeping through the commotion in his cradle near the fire. "He is old enough to put his toys away. Why don't you make sure that he does?"

Arminda calmly stroked Jane's fine, downy coating of golden hair and replied, "He's four years old, Francis. He's been told. He'll learn but he's going to forget at times. Let's not be too harsh on him."

Hugo could be heard clomping down the stairs, his small boots striking each step with force. Francis said in a lower tone, "That pane of glass must be replaced and I'll have to remove the contents of the case and take the door off for now, before the rest of the pane falls out and seriously injures someone." As Hugo entered the room, he hissed "*Talk* to him."

Francis began removing books and other items from the case. Arminda decided it was probably better that Francis wasn't the one to talk to the child right now. As the pile of books on the carpet grew with each thud, she explained to Hugo the problem his carelessness had caused. Hugo's lower lip stuck out further as his mother talked and his nose began turning red as the tears pooled in his eyes and squeezed through his thick black lashes.

"Now don't cry, Hugo dear. It will be alright, just be more careful next time, won't you?"

His fleshy lips scrunched together, the tow-headed child nodded. Arminda leant forward and whispered into his ear, "Go tell your father you're sorry and everything will be fine."

Hugo swallowed, but bravely crossed the room to where Francis was kneeling. Each hand clutching a fistful of trouser leg, he stopped just behind his father's feet and said, "I'm sorry I left one of my blocks on the floor, Papa. I didn't mean to break the furniture."

Francis sighed deeply, then stood and turned to Hugo with a deep frown. Hugo's eyes widened. Francis smiled and picked the child up. "You know better, right? You won't do it again?" Hugo shook his head energetically back and forth, obvious relief on his round face. "Ok. Your mother and I are about to leave for dinner at your grandparents' house. Will you be a good boy for Annie while we are gone? You'll go to bed when she tells you to go?"

"Yes, Papa, I will."

Francis set the boy back down on the carpet and mussed his hair. "Go on, then, back to your room."

Once Hugo had returned upstairs, Francis asked, "Are you ready to go?"

"Yes. Let's have a pleasant evening, Francis. I don't like to bicker. I'm sorry, I know you are trying to please me and I'll try to be less concerned. I know you wouldn't risk our safety by exposing us to miscreants."

"Absolutely not." Francis walked to the front door and, taking a long, black velvet cloak from the settee, held it out for Arminda. She gathered the skirts of her bright green dress, her favored color and one that was costly, therefore making a statement about the McCades' wealth. She turned, allowing Francis to drape the cloak over her shoulders. She clasped the carved pewter closure at her throat, reached through the front openings and placed both hands into a fur muff. After donning his heavy woolen coat, Francis opened the door and stepped onto the cobbled portico to assist his wife to the carriage. The wind whipped and blew spits of snow in their faces. The driver was hunkered down in the seat, eager to get started, the sooner they started, the sooner it would be over. Two black horses snorted their warm breath which turned to icy mist.

The carriage creaked as it traveled over the frozen, rutted street. The carriage was fitted with the newest suspension system, but the cold made it less flexible and the ride bumpy. Arminda was glad it wasn't far to the Grey home, just on the other side of Shawneetown. They were soon bustling through the wrought iron gate and into the house while the carriage was taken around back for the horses and driver to be sheltered in the stable until it was time to make the return trip.

The Greys were meticulous about creating an elegant home in Shawneetown, at times spending staggering amounts of money on landscaping and furnishings, many of which were imported. The roaring fire warmed the sitting room and lent a cheery atmosphere.

After exchanging news about the children and Arminda's sisters, dinner was served in the formal dining room. The teardrop chandelier sparkled in the candlelight, the white table linens dazzled, and the burnished silverware gleamed.

The consommé had been finished and cleared away. Roast venison with steamed potatoes was served on fine English china, rich red wine glowed in Italian crystal goblets. Martha Grey cleared her throat and asked, "Francis, did you know that Hubert was robbed yesterday on his way back into town?"

Arminda gasped and Francis asked with great concern, "What? Yesterday? Where did this happen?"

Mr. Grey threw a slightly annoyed glance at Mrs. Grey for bringing it up. "I had been to Red Banks for a week and was traveling back along the ferry road, probably less than an hour after I came off the ferry on the Illinois side."

Francis's scowl deepened. "What did the robbers take from you? I hope you didn't have many valuables with you."

"Just my wallet and my pocket knife. I had a pocket watch, but they didn't take it. Maybe because it was engraved with my name. Harder to sell? Definitely a recommendation for engraving, I would think." Hubert resumed cutting his potatoes, "The money is not of as much concern as the knife." Hubert Grey cut a piece of venison, sopped it in the gravy, and said, "I liked that knife."

Francis clutched his silver utensils tightly. "How many were there? How many men, I mean?"

"Oh, heavens, at least three I would imagine, a couple on horseback, one came walking from the underbrush. I can't say as I took time to count them precisely. Just wanted to get away with my hide." Hubert laughed good-naturedly.

Arminda shot a look of concern at her husband who was still gripping his silverware and glaring at his plate as though it had offended him. Sensing her eyes on him, he returned her gaze and gave a faint shake of his head, but appeared to make an attempt to relax.

The rest of the meal was spent discussing more mundane matters and enjoying an after-dinner glass of sherry. Arminda and her mother repaired to the parlour to talk while Francis and Hubert Grey puffed on pipes and discussed business ventures in the sitting room.

## Chapter 20

October 15, 2016

There was no rain Saturday morning, only crisp and clear. Perri and Nick spent a leisurely half hour drinking coffee, talking, and listening to the leaves rustle in the field behind the apartment through the open bedroom window. The morning chill gave a bite to the air in the room which made snuggling beneath the flannel sheets feel luxurious.

Finally breaking away from the comfort of being huddled under the covers, Perri said, "I'd better get a move on. Why don't we stop by the grocery on our way out of town and pick up something to drink and maybe some snacks for later?"

Nick stretched, dangled one lanky leg over the edge of the bed and said. "Yep, we should definitely get a move on." He threw back the covers and grabbed his clothes and a towel from the linen closet just inside the bathroom.

An hour later, Nick swung the Jeep into the grocery parking lot at State and 45. The Big John store had been there since Perri could remember and it had been there long before her memory, although she didn't recall the gas station/convenience store now sitting directly in front of it on the corner. Still standing firmly in position next to the entrance, the giant statue of Big John holding four bags of groceries in his burly arms had mesmerized her as a child. It looked like it was kept in good repair; the red and blue of his shirt and pants looked relatively fresh, as well as the bright colors of the groceries in the bags. Perri gaped up at it as they drove beneath it to the parking area.

"Hard to miss this store, isn't it? Good idea." Nick exclaimed, slowing down and craning his neck out the window. "Wish we had one of those, it's kinda cool." He flashed a big, toothy grin.

Having wandered up and down the aisles, the decision-making process finally complete, Perri and Nick lined up at the checkout with bottled iced tea, spicy peanuts for Nick, and wasabi peas for Perri. The store was busy, so four of the five lanes were open and had customers waiting.

Perri and Nick perused the covers of self-improvement and celebrity magazines, recipe booklets printed by brand name companies, and then, reluctantly, the bizarrely outrageous tabloids. Perri squinched her nose, elbowed Nick, and pointed at the headlines on a couple of them. She wondered how anyone could believe the claims made, whether about celebrity brawls, the 'last days' of an actor, or strange mutant humanoids found living in Cleveland right under everyone's noses. She ran her eyes over the incidental items sold in grocery lanes: lighters, chapstick, gift cards, and batteries.

Finally exhausting the entertainment value of the items on display, Perri eyed the customer with the spiky blond hair standing in front of her. She had one of the small carts, as they did, with a gallon of orange juice, a mondo-sized can of coffee, a jar of mixed nuts, and several containers of bakery cookies. Perri leaned around the woman's left side and asked, "Beth?"

The woman turned around, stood motionless for a moment, then recognition dawned. "Oh, hi! Perri, isn't it?"

"Yes, I thought I recognized you." Perri pointed at her cart, "Looks like you have a party to go to today too."

"I do, well, not a party but an open house."

Perri made introductions, then explained, "Beth is from the rental agency that manages the apartment building I'm in."

Nick reached across their shopping cart to shake Beth's hand. "Nice to meet you, Beth."

Beth's flushed. "It's nice to meet you too."

Perri asked Beth, "You had mentioned you were also into selling real estate. You have a listing to show today?"

"Yes," Beth gestured to her cart, "that's what all this is for. I like to have some refreshments at the showings. Makes it a bit more homey and keeps people happy."

Not wanting to be overly nosy, Perri offered their plans, "We're heading out to do a little hiking, a little exploring."

"Great day for it, where're you going?"

"Probably down to Cave-in-Rock, maybe drive through Old Shawneetown. I want to show Nick the old bank building there." Perri side-eyed Nick who was giving her a first-I've-heard-of-it look.

"Oh, yeah. I wish they'd be able to fix it up. Hell, I wish I could buy it, but that's not gonna happen anytime soon."

Nick asked, "Were you thinking of buying it sometime?"

Beth fluttered her hand around her face, and replied, "I'd love to, believe you me. I'm ok with the property management and regular real estate sales, but I want to get into buying and refurbishing older properties."

"You mean restoring them, or updating to a more contemporary design?" Perri asked.

"I mean more like restoring them. When you first came to get the key, you mentioned that you were interested in the older buildings being restored too. That's why I wanted to get in on buying that old building downtown, the one that burned. The bank in Old Town is irreplaceable."

"I read up a little on the history of the town. I'm interested in seeing the Duncan house while we're there. It's a survivor in a town where there aren't many."

"I'd love to get my hands on that house too." Beth sucked in a breath, "Sorry, I didn't mean that the way it sounded. I guess I'm just worried about what might happen to it now that the Duncans are, well, gone. You know how these things go, people put a stigma on a house where someone was murdered and then no one wants it or they just let it go to ruin."

"I hope that doesn't happen. The Duncans did have family, right? I mean, someone is inheriting it?" Perri quickly added, "I thought I heard that on the news."

"Yes, the murdered woman's sister."

"Since the house is going to family, maybe it'll be taken care of. It sounds like there are a lot of rumors around the property too, about valuables being stashed away, stuff like that."

The conveyor belt had been inching forward and was now clear. The customer in front of Beth was loading her last bag in the cart. Beth shifted her items onto the belt. "I've been hearing that since I was born. No one's ever found anything."

"Has anyone actually looked? I mean done a planned search with metal detecting and such?"

"Not that I know of." Beth pushed her now-empty cart to the end of the counter. "I know the Duncans were asked lots of times, but they never allowed anyone to do it. Good grief, there's so much junk in that barn and storage shed that it would take an army to go through it. Mr. Duncan was an avid flea market consumer. There's no telling what's in there."

"What kinds of things did Mr. Duncan buy?"

Beth sighed, "Ohhh, I don't know for sure. You could ask Tim or Wanda though, they might know."

"Tim and Wanda? You mean from your office?"

"Yeah. Tim's brand spankin' new in the real estate business and isn't listing houses yet. He lives over in Equality, so he still works part-time out at the auction barn there. This is a hard business to get established in, especially in a small town or rural area. It takes a while, and there's very little money in it if you aren't selling houses yet. Wanda's father owns the auction business. She works in the office on Saturdays to help out because her mom's got rheumatoid arthritis and can't do it full time anymore. George Duncan used to sell stuff through there a lot, most weekends come to think of it." Beth flashed her phone under the scanner to pay for her order. "If you're headed to Old town, stop in and ask for one of them, it's on the way."

"Good idea. I'd love to look around. Do they have an auction every weekend?"

"Most weekends, but they have a consignment section too, so there's always plenty of stuff to look at." Beth took her receipt. "Have a great day you two."

"You too, and good luck with your open house."

"Nice to meet you, Beth." Nick said.

"Same here." Beth lifted her two bags, pushed the cart back to the entry area, and clicked across the tiled floor and out through the automatic doors.

\*\*\*

Nick loaded the grocery sack in the floorboard behind his seat and hopped into the Jeep. Starting the engine, he asked, "Where to now?" Before Perri could reply, he added, "I figured I'd better ask since plans may have changed or been added that I don't know about yet." He raised his eyebrows and widened his mocha-colored eyes.

"Ha. Ha." Perri pointed to the side exit on to State Street. "Turn left there and go straight. This road leads directly into Equality."

Nick accelerated traveling southeast down route 142. "I was just nudging you, you know that right?" Perri acknowledged with a nod. He added, "I don't mind going through Old Shawneetown. I want to see this place."

"Ok." Perri gazed out the side window, watching the farmland flicker past. "I forgot to mention it, I guess. I wanted to go and had thought about it so much that I didn't remember I hadn't yet said something to you."

Nick reached over and squeezed her arm. "Not a problem. You want to stop at the auction place first?"

"Let's do. I can't help but wonder if George Duncan may have stumbled upon a cache of something valuable on his property and was auctioning it off bit by bit and alerted someone to the fact. Maybe that's why he would never let anyone else metal detect on their property, he knew they might find something. Maybe someone decided they wanted it and they wanted it all at once. Maybe it was something George was trying to sell and George wouldn't sell at the price they were willing to pay for it."

"Could be. Sounds like those are all plausible theories. You think someone went to their house about it and argued with him, then ended up killing him and his wife in the process?"

"It's possible. I don't know. The police aren't saying anything about motive. The report last night said they had been beaten but the cause of death was drowning, lungs filled with brine, so someone hauled them all the way out there. I still don't get that. There had to be some reason not to kill them at home and leave them there." Perri was thinking about the digging she saw in the cemetery, the vandalism at Cave-in-Rock, and wondered if there had been any digging at the Salt Well site. It hadn't been mentioned, either on the news or by Pearl.

"Did you hear me?" Nick asked.

Perri turned to see an expectant look on Nick's face. "Sorry, no, I was thinking."

"What about?"

"Wondering how Beth knows how much stuff is in the barn and storage shed at the Duncan's house. How does she know that?"

Nick's brows knitted together. "I didn't think about that when she said it, but that's true."

"Hm, well, I'll keep it in mind. What were you saying to me before?"

"I said it seems strange that if the killer had his or her heart set on drowning them, why not do it in the river. Would have been a lot quicker and easier, I would think, if the river runs right past their house."

"It does, all that's between the house and the river is the road and embankment. And the embankment is steep, easy to roll someone off. But...you'd have to worry about them getting hung up on the way down and having to pick your way down the side to finish the job."

"Maybe that's why they were taken to the well. It might have been too easy to get caught trying to cross the road with two people."

"I wouldn't think it would be easy to take two people ten or fifteen miles in a car then herd them into the woods either, not without motivation. Maybe the killer had a gun and the Duncan's thought if they did what he wanted, they'd get away. People always think that, or hope that, don't they? And it almost never works out that way."

"True. The road by their house isn't a busy area, but it isn't completely abandoned either. Maybe too much chance of someone coming along and seeing them."

Nick looked sidelong at Perri and risked saying, "I knew you wanted to poke around in this." Before she could protest, he lifted one hand and said, "I know, I just mean let's try to be low key, under the radar if we can. I don't want to become a suspect or get arrested for interfering. Or worse, have us become the third and fourth body in the well." Seeing Perri's furrowed brow, he continued, "I'd like to try to piece together what might have happened, as long as we don't get in anyone's way."

Perri turned to face Nick, held up two fingers in the traditional scout salute, and said, "Scout's honor!" She smiled and sat back in her seat as she slipped a printed map from her purse. "I know where the bank building is, but let's see where the house is."

She scrutinized the map and, without looking up, said, "Stop shaking your head, I can see it out of the corner of my eye. It's not like I'm going to get out and run up to the door and ask to look around."

"You might, I wouldn't put it past you. Just in case, let's remember that you just said that under oath." Nick chuckled and nodded at the paper Perri was peering at. "I see you were assured of convincing me, since you already have the map to the house printed out."

"I'd never go up to the door…only if I thought they'd let me, which I know they won't. Not yet anyway."

"What do you mean not y—"

Perri quickly continued. "Also, one of the Scouts' fundamental principles is to 'Be Prepared' so of course I have a map."

"Mm hmm."

Perri laughed and said, "Once a Scout, always a Scout, buddy." She pointed straight ahead and said, "Cross highway 13 for now and keep going straight until you get to a left-hand curve onto old highway 13."

Nick nodded and asked, "Is there a New and an Old for everything here?"

"Not everything." Perri leaned forward, peering out the windshield. "Right up there, there's a big white and red sign, see it?"

"Got it." Nick turned into the chat-covered parking lot and pulled into a spot facing the pole barn. Its corrugated metal siding was fading to a chalky blue from many summers of heat and sun.

Nick pushed open one of the double doors and held it for Perri. The mixed aroma of leather, engine oil, the fustiness of old furniture, and popcorn rushed to greet them. There were several people milling around through long tables arranged in rows and covered with small items. Larger items were displayed on metal shelving units behind the tables. The auction podium was bare, a lectern sat at the back of it, too early for any auction that might be scheduled for today. There were no windows, at least none that were visible. Lighting was provided by rows of rectangular fluorescent fixtures suspended from the high ceiling.

Through a window in a small office enclosure built a few yards inside the main doors, Perri saw the woman she had seen in Fuller's Rental Agency crouched over a stack papers on the desk, a pencil clamped between her teeth while she operated an adding machine from which a long scroll of paper curled. Her glasses were perched down near the tip of her nose. Perri tapped lightly on the door frame. "Excuse me."

The woman looked up and blinked. Perri said, "Are you Wanda? Beth Trammel told me about the auction barn and said I could ask for you here." The woman continued to study Perri, trying to decide from where she knew her. "I'm Perri Seamore, I'm renting an apartment through the agency. We haven't officially met, you were on the phone the last time I was in the office, when I came in to get my mailbox key, and —"

"Oh yeah, yeah, I remember now. Lordy, I knew you were familiar but couldn't place you." Wanda pushed back her well-worn rolling office chair and stood up, reaching toward Perri for a handshake. "I'm Wanda Harrison." Rather than the mint green pantsuit and blouse she had been wearing in the office, today the short, roundish Wanda sported stretchy knit pants with a long-sleeved tunic and a brightly colored scarf around her neck.

Perri shook Wanda's warm hand. "This is Nick Silver."

Nick also shook Wanda's hand, nodded and said, "Glad to meet you."

"What can I do for you? You looking for something in particular? Goodness knows we probably have it here somewhere." Wanda chuckled and shook her head. "Tim would be the one to find what you need, but girl, I can barely find a clean pad of paper in here. Look at this clutter." Wands swung her hand around in exasperation at the office full of filing cabinets, mismatched dining chairs from numerous decades, and piles of paper covered with an impressive layer of dust.

"Your parents have owned this business for a long time, I take it?" Nick asked.

"Mm hmm. Since I was a little girl. My brother and I used to play in here. Heaven only knows how we didn't get tetanus and die from playing with all the junk that came through. Oh, there's some good stuff, don't get me wrong, but there's a lot of junk too.

But you know, some people collect things others wouldn't think twice about keeping."

"That's what makes it fun, poking around through stuff though, doesn't it?" Perri said.

"You aren't wrong. Half the fun is in the looking, that's for sure."

Wanda indicated a couple of chairs and motioned for Perri and Nick to have a seat. She settled into her chair and reared back in it, putting her feet up on the CPU tower sitting on the yellowing linoleum floor that curled up at the walls, no baseboards to help hold it in place.

Getting to the point of her visit, Perri took a seat and asked Wanda, "Do you happen to remember anything about George Duncan or the types of items he used to sell through your auction or consignment business? Beth said he was a frequent seller here."

"Oh, George Duncan. God rest that man's soul, and his wife too. Poor Ruby."

"Did you know Ruby Duncan too?"

"I did, but not near as well as George, of course. He was here every weekend, and sometimes during the week. He'd bring Ruby with him occasionally, but that was ordinarily when they had jewelry to sell. I think Ruby took charge of it, that and other things like sewing machines or craft supplies. George always had something to sell. Weekends aren't gonna be right without him here."

"Did he tend to sell things that were mostly junk or did he have some items of real value? Do you remember?"

Wanda regarded Perri while she thought about the question. "Well now and then, he did have some very nice items. George was one of those people who had a special knack for pickin', you know what I mean?"

Nick asked, "You mean he had a good eye for valuable items that someone else might overlook?"

"Yes, that too, but I mean he just always seemed to know where to go to look. Anybody who looks often and long enough will eventually stumble onto a few sought-after items stashed away in someone's unused barn, but George was consistent in coming up with stuff that people clamored after. Things that would go for top dollar. Always finding a honey pot somewhere, seems like."

Perri tossed a meaningful glance at Nick.

Wanda shifted in her rolling chair. "But you wanted to know what kinds of things George sold, is that right?"

"Yes."

"Well now, let's see." Wanda pressed her lips together and stared past Perri, thinking. "Nautical stuff. Old river boat parts and pieces, like he had an anchor one time. Rusty and dirty, but he acted like he'd found a real prize, and somebody paid good money for it so maybe I'm the one who doesn't know what I'm talking about. He'd have old tools and machinery and I didn't know what half of the stuff was for, but he did, and people seemed to want it." Wanda pointed to the ceiling and nodded, "Now, sometimes he would have jewelry, old jewelry, you know? Like cameos, hairpins and combs that were decorated, pocket watches, even some lace hankies or fans like the ladies used to carry a long time ago."

"It does sound like he knew where to find things. Did he ever have any old coins or gemstones, anything like that?"

"Hmm." Wanda considered. "I don't recall anything like that coming through here." She pulled the pencil from behind her ear and tapped the eraser end on the canary yellow legal pad on the desk. "The thing is, if people have old coins or gems, stuff like that, they tend to take it to a coin dealer or a jeweler, not an auction, not of this size anyway. Now, if it's known someone is looking for that type of thing, they might offer it to a private collector."

Wanda laughed. "Sounds fancy, doesn't it? It all depends on what it is. We do have people who collect very specific items and we keep a list of names and what they collect. If one of the things on the list shows up, we call the collector to see if they're interested, provided the person who brought it to us agrees."

"Do many people opt to go to a collector?" Nick asked.

"Some people want as much money as they can get for an item with minimal fuss and that's that, but there are those who enjoy the bidding process and don't want to go for a single buyer, unless it was something really valuable that they probably couldn't get top dollar for on the block. Most of the goods we see that get sold privately are from estate sales, things like antique furniture or dishes, silverware, paintings, unique books, old military medals or things like that."

"You have a complicated business to run here, don't you? How do you have time for this and your job at the rental company?" Perri asked Wanda.

"I don't come here much during the week, just on a Wednesday evening maybe, to keep things from getting too far behind."

Footsteps could be heard approaching the office across the gritty floor. A head popped in around the door jamb, "Hey, Wanda, where do you want that...I'm sorry, I didn't realize you had someone in here."

Perri smiled and said, "Hi, Tim, right? We met at Fuller's on Monday."

"Yes, I remember. Are you coming to the auction this afternoon?"

"No, we — uh, this is Nick — we're not staying long, but we might have a look around."

Wanda spoke up, "Tim, since you're here, you might be able to help."

Tim stepped into the office, wiping rusty iron residue from his hands with a shop rag then stuffing it into his back pocket. The knees of his Levi's were white with dust. A wad of lint coated with sawdust clung to the hair above his ear. "Sure, what can I help with?"

We were talking about what kind of items George Duncan used to bring in to sell here and I told her what I could remember." Wanda ran through the list of things she had listed, then asked Tim, "You remember anything different?"

Tim breathed deeply and thought about it a moment. "Well...there was the time he brought in that half-dollar die plate. Said he got them from someone down around Cave-in-Rock who dug it out of the ground on the shore near the ferry dock. It went to old man Carrier up in Junction."

"That's right, I forgot about that."

"A counterfeiter's plate? Like from the early 1800s when there were counterfeiters around the cave?"

"Yeah, exactly, late 1790s-early 1800s." Tim nodded eagerly in agreement.

"Wasn't there a coiner named Duff who was supposed to have lived in or around the cave in the 1790s? I read about him, and some other counterfeiters too, but he was supposedly killed and buried somewhere near the salt spring, wasn't he?"

"There was a Duff, yes. They think he could have been the John Duff who helped direct George Rogers Clark back in, oh gosh it was earlier, like in 1777-1778 or so, from Fort Massac to Kaskaskia, but no one really knows if it was the same guy. And no one's sure exactly where he's buried. There are all kinds of stories. Some have him being buried in a river cavern downstream from Cave-in-Rock or in somebody's yard next to their flower garden."

"Yeah, I remember reading that too. I wonder if the plate was truly that old."

"George thought it was. Apparently, Mr. Carrier thought so too, because he bought it for a pretty penny before it could go to auction."

"I see." Perri thought a moment. "Did George belong to the group of people who thought maybe there was buried treasure in the cave too?"

Tim looked surprised and then laughed. "Probably. He never said but I can see him at least wanting to find out for sure. He would have been disappointed if it wasn't true."

Nick asked, "Was George into all the legends and tales about the cave?"

"Definitely."

"Do you have anything left for sale that George brought in?"

Tim looked at Wanda and contemplated the question. "I think everything sold except for a pair of scissors."

"A pair of scissors?" Perri asked, uncertain if Tim meant just a plain pair of scissors or something more specialized.

"Yeah, the little kind, for sewing." He held his fingers apart by about four inches. "Only about this big."

"Oh, ok. I wouldn't mind seeing those if you know where they are."

"I think I do. I can get them if you want to hang on a minute." Tim turned and left the office.

Perri said to Wanda, "We've taken up enough of your time, Wanda, we should let you get back to work. But I really appreciate you taking the time to talk to us and answer our questions."

"No problem, honey, not at all." Wanda used her hands on her knees to push herself out of her chair. "You didn't say why you were asking."

"I'm sorry. I'm writing an article about the Duncan house and the family who built it. I want to include some of their more recent history for an online genealogy magazine. I knew that George Duncan had been an avid picker and sold antiques, so I wanted to get a little first-hand information. I'll certainly credit you as a source, if that's ok with you."

"Suuure, it is." Wanda drawled. "You need anything else you just come on back and ask me."

"That would be great, thanks! We'll leave you be and I'll go have a look at these scissors. Might be something I'm interested in having. I'd kind of like to buy something George brought in and I knit when I have time so I can use a small pair of scissors."

"Alright then, hope you like them." Wanda sat back down and rolled up to the paper-strewn desk. As they walked back into the main area, the clattering resumed on the adding machine.

Perri and Nick were waiting near the tables when Tim emerged from between two rows of heavily laden shelves. "Here they are. Come over here to the table, you can look at them under the lamp."

Tim placed the scissors on the table and pulled the chain to turn on the lamp. There was an arm with a magnifier attached to the column. The scissors were indeed about four inches long. Most likely silver, they were uniformly tarnished, giving them a matte gray color. Perri swiveled the magnifier over and peered through it. She wasn't an expert but could see there was a design around the surfaces and the edges of the oval finger loops. After adjusting the magnifier, she could see the loops were decorated with flowers and tiny bumblebees, very finely wrought.

Perri commented, "The engraving detail has been rubbed a little smooth at the contact points from a lot of use, but otherwise they appeared in good shape. The hinge is a bit loose but could be tightened. The points are still sharp. Someone must have taken care of these." She looked up at Tim, who had watched her study the scissors. "What do you want for them? Or, are they scheduled to be auctioned?"

"Nah. They've been here for a month. We put them on the shelves to see if they'd sell. Twenty bucks."

Perri looked over the scissors again. Nick remained silent, not wanting to interfere. If the scissors were 19th century, which they appeared to be, although she couldn't narrow it down more than that herself, and they had been brought in by George Duncan, she wanted to have them. "Done." She stood up and handed the scissors to Tim. "I'll take them."

"Good! Alright then, I'll ring you up over at that register," Tim pointed to the other side of the auction stage. They crossed the room together, Tim pulling ahead of them as they neared the check out.

Nick gently nudged Perri's arm. "You didn't try to get a lower price?"

"You know I'm not a haggler. I hate doing that. If I'm not willing to pay it I usually just don't get it. But I do want these. They're worth it to me, and I'll use them."

"Ok, I'm not trying to tell you that you're wrong." Nick grinned mischievously. "But I would have offered $15, just to see."

"I know. And you probably would have gotten them for that price, too! Oh well."

"Well...you could have maybe winked at him and gotten them for $18."

"Seriously? My wink is only worth two bucks?" She needled back at him.

"Kidding, remember? I'd sorta rather you didn't wink at other men."

"That's good to know. Glad you shared that with me." Perri set her purse on the counter and pulled out her bulging billfold. It was so full of items other than money that the snap had strained against the leather and a small hole was forming. Without turning to look at Nick, she said, "Don't say it. Don't even go there."

She paid for the scissors and Tim said, "I'll wrap these for you so you don't stab yourself, or...someone else, with them."

Nick laughed, "Hey, he's got the same kind of sense of humor I do."

"Oh goody. Two of you."

Tim asked, "Did you know George or are you family?"

"No, I didn't know him."

"Oh. I thought maybe you were related."

"You left the office to get the scissors when I explained to Wanda." Perri related her story, and added, "I hope I get to see the inside of the house when the police release it to the family. I think it'll make an interesting story, what with all the history around it and the town itself."

Tim nodded and said, "There's certainly enough material to write about, that's for sure." He slipped the paper-wrapped scissors into a second-hand hardware store plastic bag and handed it to Perri. "Enjoy them. I'm glad someone is going to get some use out of them rather than sitting around on the shelf here until they get broken or lost."

"Me too. Thanks, Tim."

Tim waved and strode off across the pole barn. Perri and Nick waved at Wanda as they passed the office window. Perri held up the bag and Wanda smiled and gave her a thumbs-up.

Back in the Jeep, Perri tucked the sack into the glove compartment, Nick backed out of the space and turned onto old highway 13. The north fork of the Saline River was to the right and the road no longer crossed the water, it just petered out from pavement of the old highway, to the narrower and cracked surface of a previous farm road, to gravel, and finally into grass. "Where to now?"

***

Almost as soon as they left Equality they passed a turnoff for Junction. Nick jerked his head toward the sign and asked, "Isn't that where Tim said the guy lives who bought the money plate?"

"That's it. I wonder if this Mr. Carrier's interest is mainly in relics of the thieves and gangs that used to frequent the cave. It sounds like he wanted the plate badly enough to purchase it outright."

Within five more minutes they had passed the newer city of Shawneetown and arrived in Old Shawneetown. "Turn left here." Perri pointed. "You have to turn here or you'll be on the bridge into Kentucky.

"Wow, the town really is nearly gone, isn't it?" Nick's head swiveled back and forth, looking out each side of the Jeep. "I knew most people moved out, but ... the big open spaces between the remaining buildings emphasizes how much is missing now."

As they approached Main Street, the last street running parallel with the river, the three-story Greek style bank building soared upward on their left, its regal bearing enhanced by the absence of a single neighboring building.

Nick turned onto Main Street. He parked the Jeep and he and Perri walked up to a decorative iron fence that now surrounded the building. "This wasn't here the last time I was. If it helps protect the building even a little bit, it's worth it." Perri squinted at the front of the building. "If you look...just...there, on that column, that's a high-water mark from the flood."

After several minutes of walking around the building and studying it from every angle, Nick said, "I can see why you feel the way you do about saving it. It's a fantastic building."

They walked down Main Street, nearly to the other end, where the only other surviving building on the block stood. The two stories were narrow, but deep. It retained its decorative architecture and appeared to be in use. The wide sidewalk continued to the end of the block and turned, becoming more of a standard width and proceeding along the side street, completely devoid of buildings, no houses or businesses. Back in the Jeep, they circled the block. Perri pointed at a large, rectangular area of concrete, now exposed to the sunlight, grass growing in the cracks. "I could be wrong, but I think that's where there used to be a grocery store."

They followed Market Street and stopped before driving beneath the now-elevated highway 13 as it approached the bridge. Perri pointed toward the river. "Over there, somewhere along the bank, is a concrete marker for the Riverside Hotel that used to be here. It was huge, a grand place. She pulled her map out of the cubby on the door and directed Nick, "Ok, go straight and then take the curve to the left."

The Jeep followed the narrow but paved country road. After looping around several grain silos, the road twisted toward the river, climbed gently to a ridge, and ran very near the edge overlooking the Ohio as it traveled between Kentucky and Illinois. Nick commented, "I can see how this area could have avoided the

1937 flood. It's elevated significantly more than the main part of the town."

"You're right, it could be that the McCade house never was flooded. Probably why it's still there and most everything else has vanished." Perri slid forward in the seat as the road leveled out. Pointing, she said, "Up there. See that rooftop over the trees? I think that's the house! I can't wait to see it."

As they drew past a hedge that was turning from dark summer green to its autumn cloak of fiery red, the house came into view. "It's beautiful!" Perri exclaimed. "Oh, my gosh, I love it! Look at that brickwork." Perri put her hand on Nick's arm, "Slow down. I want to look at it." There was a blue pick-up truck in the driveway, parked behind an older model Buick in the carport.

Nick slowed to a crawl, but Perri said, "Stop. I want to take some pictures." She fished her camera from under her seat. Unzipping it and fumbling to get the camera out in her haste, she said, "I would so love to go through that house."

The brickwork was stylized, bordered sections formed a herringbone pattern around the windows. The design was so perfectly done that the windows didn't need shutters, which would have detracted from the appeal. The front door was sheltered in a portico supported by two ionic columns painted bright white. The steeply pitched roof was obviously new but in keeping with the original style of the house. "Stop, please."

"Perri, I don't want to block the road."

Perri grinned and looked at Nick. "Block it from what? Traffic? There's no one else here. If someone comes, we'll move on. I just want to look at the house, I mean, it's like one hundred eighty-five years old almost. There aren't many houses that old in this area."

"Ok, if you say so." Nick stopped directly in front of the house. "But there's someone here." He nodded at the truck. "Or did that belong to the Duncans too?"

Perri didn't know and she didn't answer because she was busy rolling down her window. She got up on her knees in the seat and leaned on the open frame to gawk at the house. She chattered away about different aspects of its architecture, snapping photos, while Nick kept one eye on the rearview mirror.

When the front door partially opened, Nick nudged Perri, "Hey, maybe we should get going."

A man stepped out onto the porch. His shoulder-length dark hair fell in greasy strands framing an unpleasant expression only partially masked by an untrimmed beard and mustache. He shoved his hands in his pockets and glared daggers at the Jeep's occupants.

The man appeared in Perri's view through her camera. She reflexively snapped a photo then immediately lowered it and replied, "Oh. Yeah, maybe so." She smiled winningly and did her best princess wave as Nick shifted into drive and continued down the road. Perri laughed.

Nick looked incredulously at Perri. "Why did you do that?"

"Didn't know what else to do. He'd seen us. It isn't like I drew his attention, he was looking straight at us."

"Yeah. I don't know who he was, but with my luck, he'll call the police and say we were snooping around and maybe we're the murderers. I'm sure he got my license plate number. And I'm from out of state, which probably makes me more of a target."

Perri was quickly reviewing the photos she'd taken. "I don't know who that was at the Duncan house, but the photo turned out clear." She pointed the camera screen toward Nick, who couldn't see the photo in the glare and while driving.

"You took his picture?" Nick asked.

"Yup."

After rounding another curve, the road turned them away from the river. Nick commented, "You are enjoying this a little too much."

Perri turned the camera off and laughed. She lightly thumped him on the leg, "You are such a fuddy-duddy today! Usually, it's the other way around. We haven't done anything, what are you worried about?" She looked back out the window. But, she whispered, "Just don't drive over the speed limit. We can take my car next time."

"Next time?" Nick's eyebrows arched upward, forming lines across his forehead.

"I mean, if we ever come back by here. You never know."

Nick knew to pick his battles, so he simply nodded and said, "Ok, Navigator, which way do we go now?"

"Turn right at that T-intersection."

"Where are we going?"
"Go slow, we need to turn onto this gravel pull-in. See it?"
"Yeah, but where does this go?"
"This is Gold Hill Cemetery."

Chapter 21

October 15, 2016, Early afternoon

Perri didn't feel quite as eager to revisit Gold Hill as she had been to see the McCade house. Even with Nick beside her, the fear she had felt Wednesday night in the old burial ground hadn't completely faded away and it put a damper on the prospect of exploring it.

After Nick had parked the Jeep at the edge of the cemetery, they climbed out into the brisk shade of the old trees leaning protectively over the graves. Armed with her camera around her neck, a notebook, and pen, Perri told Nick she was looking for any stone with the name McCade. "If you can't read it, or it even looks like it could be McCade, let me know and I'll bring the foil and brush over and we'll see if we can read it."

She glanced over the stones and said, "Normally, I'd say let's each walk every other row, but the stones aren't exactly in orderly rows anymore. Let's divide it in half from here," she walked to a gap between two front stones, "back to that cluster of honeysuckle by the tree line. That ok?"

Nick agreed. "Let's get started."

Nick, now on Perri's right, turned to the right to start on that side, but Perri quickly trotted past him and said, "I'll take this side." Seeing Nick's quizzical look, she answered, "I already saw a couple of these stones when I walked up, so I'll just go ahead and do these." Nick didn't look completely convinced, but turned and started on the opposite side.

Perri knelt in front of the first stone and pulled back the periwinkle vine growing over the corner. She hazarded a glance at Nick to make sure he wasn't going to ask her about it again, but he was kneeling down and was busy pulling long grass away from a stone on the opposite side. She didn't want to draw his attention by immediately darting back to the spot where she'd fallen in the hole, but tried to get a glimpse of it from where she was. She couldn't tell if the hole was still there, but the tools were obviously gone.

Perri was wrapping foil around an unreadable stone when a ballpoint pen suddenly floated into her vision and hovered in front of her eyes. As she finished securing the foil behind the stone, she didn't look up but asked, "What's that for?"

Nick replied, "Found it."

"You found a pen? Ok." She smoothed the foil over the front of the stone with one hand.

"Yeah, it was on the ground right over there." Nick pointed to an area midway down the first row, an area with no grass and where now-dry mud was churned up in one spot. "Funny."

"It's funny?"

The pen rotated in front of her eyes until the printed insignia of the nurse staffing agency Perri worked for was visible. She sighed a hopefully inaudible sigh and sat back on her heels, reaching up with one hand to snatch the pen away from Nick, but he pulled it away too quickly and said, "Uh uh."

Perri said, "Ok, great, you found it."

"I did. Thing is, you weren't over there to have dropped it today…"

"It could have rolled, or bounced."

"…and this pen has dried mud on it, which makes sense I suppose since it was in an area that looks like it was muddy after the rain, but isn't muddy now." Nick looked over his shoulder. "It's dry now." He looked back and squatted down very close to her. "Like the mud on this pen." He rolled the pen around and smiled.

"Yeah, that would make sense." Perri kept her eyes averted by digging through her duffle bag for the brush she used to coax the foil into the crevices of unreadable stones.

"The mud looks churned up a little bit, almost like, I don't know, someone stepped in the mud. Maybe they fell, dropped their pen."

Perri flopped her hands into her lap. "Ok! Alright, alright. I lost it there Wednesday."

"Wednesday." A statement, meant to encourage the continued flow of information about Perri's previous visit.

"I was coming right by here anyway on my way home."

"On your way home from where?"

"From work."

"I guess it was getting late. Was it dark?"

"No!"

Nick narrowed his eyes and pursed his lips.

"It wasn't dark...when I got here." Nick held his concerned gaze. "Ok, I'll tell you. Now, remember, ok, that I never promised I wouldn't come *here*. I said I wouldn't go to the Duncan house, and I absolutely did not, didn't even drive by it. And I said I wouldn't go to the woods."

Nick pivoted on the balls of his feet and briefly surveyed the area, held one hand up indicating the thick areas of surrounding trees. "This counts as woods."

"But it isn't the woods you meant, you said the woods where the salt well is located. And I didn't go anywhere near there."

Nick plopped down and sat cross-legged in the scrubby grass while Perri told him about her previous visit. His initial concern faded at first but was restoked when she told him about falling in the hole and the light she had seen as she left.

"Someone was here, digging in a cemetery, and they came back before you left? Or worse, they were here the whole time, watching you."

"I doubt they were here when I was. Probably they just came back as I was leaving. But I never saw anyone and they probably didn't see me either. They didn't come out of the woods, I just saw a flashlight beam as I was backing down the lane."

"I'm not going to argue with you about it, you already know I worry. But if you think someone didn't see your headlights as you backed out of here, you're being overly optimistic. Let's have a look at the hole, see if it's still there, how big it got."

Perri jumped up and took off, eager to check it out. "It was right about here. Yes, here, see?" Clods of dirt and sod were dumped back in the hole upside down. No real attempt had been made to hide the fact that digging had been done.

"It's off to the side of where the graves are, in the path." An enormous sassafras tree grew right up into the edge of the path and leaned over it toward the graves, the lobed leaves dangling like dozens of oven mitts reaching for them. Nick hopped over the loose dirt of the hole to view it from the other side. "There's no way you could have avoided falling into this. There's a gravestone on one side and the tree on the other. Why here, where it was taking up the entire path?"

Perri replied, "I have no idea. I don't know if it's good or not that they didn't seem to be digging up an actual grave."

Nick turned toward the burial plots. "Let's finish checking the stones and keep an eye out for any other areas like this."

They spent nearly two hours in the cemetery. Many of the stones had degraded so completely they were unreadable. A number of them took time to check by methods other than simply reading the inscriptions. They quickly burned through one roll of foil and started on another. Besides using foil or a flashlight to highlight difficult to read lettering, Perri found that sometimes viewing the stone through her camera or taking a photo with adjusted lighting could bring out an inscription. There were some stones she couldn't read until she'd been able to load the photo to her computer and use a photo manipulation program to enhance it.

The readability of gravestones depended on the predominate material used in the area and the weather. Sandstone markers could serve as a long-lasting memorial, unless moisture got between the layers of the stone. It would freeze in the winter, thaw in spring, then refreeze and thaw every year. The stone would eventually delaminate over time; the outer layer would expand, crack, and flake off, taking the inscription, and any hope of identifying the grave, with it.

Gold Hill Cemetery was probably initially on a sunny hilltop, either naturally or by purposeful clearing, but over the decades, trees grew and encroached on the plots, eventually becoming a forest surrounding the cemetery. The canopy shrouded the graves completely, allowing the rain, dew, and humidity to permeate the stones. Indirect light promoted the growth of lichen, moss, and clinging vines which assisted in the destruction.

They didn't venture too far into the rear of the cemetery. After cutting back clumps of kudzu and honeysuckle and pruning away saplings pushing against the fragile stones, the stones in the rear section were exclusively infants and children, as Perri had suspected. They were often the smallest stones and at least for now they were the ones first being overtaken by the forest.

When they were finished viewing every stone they could, their efforts had paid off. The gravestones of Arminda McCade, as well as Francis and his second wife Nancy, were found. The McCade family stones had probably been quite expensive at the time, and it was their saving grace. While they were among the oldest in the cemetery, the letters of the inscriptions had been deeply carved in granite and had survived the elements in much better condition than the later sandstone markers.

Perri had photographed every stone and marked its location on a piece of graph paper. Those that were readable were labeled with the name for reference to the photo. Those that were unreadable were marked as such. Most rural cemeteries that began almost two hundred years ago were on private land and were for family or the immediate community. More than likely, as she researched the McCade family, unfamiliar names on some of these stones would come up as neighbors or relatives. No matter how sure she was she remembered precisely where a stone was, it could still be hard to find if she went to back for another look without a map. They found no other holes dug in the area like the one Perri had fallen into.

Sitting in the grass outside the path of the cemetery, Perri read from her notes. "Here's what we've got. Francis McCade shares a stone with his second wife, five rows from the front. According to the dates on the stone, Francis was born in June of 1796 and died in October of 1868, which puts him at seventy-two years old. He lived a long life for a man of that time. Nancy Jane was born in November of 1818 and died in January of 1879. She was twenty-two years younger than Francis and she was only sixty when she died."

Arminda's stone is in the first row. It has a little more detail than the others, except no months are given. She was born Arminda Eloise Grey in 1808 in Philadelphia and she died here in Shawneetown in 1843."

Nick said, "She would only have been 34-35 years old. I wonder what happened."

"I don't know, but maybe I can find some information about her, but that's a huge maybe. When Arminda died, the reporting of births and deaths was voluntary. Doctors were required to report births and deaths that they witnessed which was relatively few at the time. The public could report events themselves with a witness, but they weren't required to, so there are almost no records to be found."

Nick asked, "Isn't there some other kind of register where you can find when or how people died?"

Perri shook her head, "Seems incredible to us now, doesn't it? Rarely, you get lucky and find a death recorded on a Mortality Schedule, but the earliest one was taken was in 1850 and it only includes deaths for the previous twelve months. Arminda died seven years too soon for that possibility."

"That won't help then. It does seem hard to imagine things like that going unrecorded. Times have changed. Think how much time people spend now documenting things: birth, death, first word, first food, school photos, the dates we worked every job in our life, taxes..." He let the list trail off. "...but something as important as a family member's birth or death went unrecorded not so long ago."

"True. A lot of people couldn't read or write, and that has a great deal to do with it. Also, the working class didn't have loads of extra time on their hands. Many of the personal records that were made come from wealthy, educated families. It's more likely to find tax records from 1810 or 1820 than a birth record. Money's always important. A lot of people didn't even know their exact birthdate, especially if one or both parents died before the children grew up. People back then didn't necessarily celebrate birthdays the way we do now." She laughed, "Can you imagine having eight, or ten, or sixteen children like some families did, and having a celebration for each one? People didn't have the time or the money."

"I guess still being alive was celebration enough."

Folding the graph paper map, Perri said, "Other than these three, we also found the other generations of McCades: Hugo and his wife Arminda, born 1832 and 1834, respectively. The name Arminda was popular at the time or this Arminda was the daughter of family friends and they named her after Arminda McCade. And it makes sense since there weren't that many families in the area to choose a bride from, at least not that would have had a similar social status as the McCades."

"Then there's Thomas and his wife Harriet, Morgan and Lucinda, and Abner and Dorothy. There were at least seven children's stones with the name McCade but we may not be able to connect them to their parents if they weren't living when a census was taken in 1850 or after."

I have clear photos of each of the McCade stones, so we're good on that. The military stone turned out to be a Matthew Grey, most likely related to Arminda's family. Perri stood up, "You ready to move on?"

Nick joined her and they headed back to the Jeep. As they neared it, Perri heard her phone ringing from her purse in the floorboard. Nick unlocked the car but the caller hung up before Perri could dig her phone out of her purse. She didn't recognize the number, but after climbing in her seat and snapping the seat belt, she said, "Let's see who this is," and tapped redial.

"Hello?"

"Hi. I just received a call from your number on my phone, but didn't get to it in time to answer."

"Perri? Is that you?"

"Yes?"

"It's Pearl. I hope I'm not bothering you. You gave me your number so I could call you if the police released the house and they have. They called me yesterday evening. I didn't want to call you then since I knew your beau was coming in town."

"Oh, that's great. I'm glad to hear it. Nick and I are in Old Town at Gold Hill and we drove past the house on our way here. I saw someone come out of the house so thought maybe they'd turned it over to you."

There was a pause, long enough that Perri asked, "Are you still there?"

"I'm here. I suppose it might have been a policeman, locking up or something."

Perri hedged at first, but, decided Pearl should know if someone was in the house, finally said, "He didn't look like a policeman."

"I can't imagine who it would be then."

"He looked middle-aged, hard to tell from the distance. Black hair, kind of stringy, beard and mustache, there was a blue pick-up in the driveway."

Perri heard an intake of breath. "Well, I never!"

"Is something wrong?"

"I don't know what's going on here but that sounds like the no-good boyfriend my daughter has been running around with. The one I told you about. Was he there by himself? I can't imagine how he got in there!"

"I didn't see anyone else, but that doesn't mean he was alone. He stepped outside as we were driving by. Someone else could have been inside."

"I'm gonna talk to her and find out what they were doing there. They have no business prowling around without telling me. They didn't waste time, did they? I wish I could get in there, but I don't drive anymore."

"Well," Perri looked at Nick and raised her eyebrows in question, "I'm sure we could bring you to the house one day if you wanted to see it." Nick didn't know who Perri was talking to but nodded nonetheless.

"I don't want to impose on you two, I couldn't do that."

"Pearl, honestly, it would be a pleasure. I've wanted to see the house, you want to see the house, why not see it together? A guided tour from someone who lived there would be a plus."

"If you're sure about that, I'd love to."

"Alright then, would you want to go tomorrow, or is that too soon?" Perri bit her knuckle in anticipation, hoping she didn't sound over-eager.

"That sounds fine. Would you be able to come by here around 10 o'clock?"

"We'll be there! I'm looking forward to it. See you then. Oh, wait! Pearl? I need for you to give me permission to talk about…it would be hard for me to avoid…with Nick, I mean."

Pearl caught on to Perri's meaning. "Oh sure. That's just fine, you can tell him how you know me. It would be tough to talk around that, wouldn't it? Heck, I'll tell myself tomorrow. Don't you worry about that."

"Thanks. See you tomorrow."

"Bye-bye."

Perri put her phone back in the pocket inside her purse and said, "Well, we've got a ticket into the McCade house tomorrow, courtesy of Pearl McCade Gentry."

"Is Pearl the person you have been extracting all your insider information from that you couldn't tell me about?"

"That would be her. I'm not great at secrets, am I?"

"This is a special circumstance. But, truthfully, you're right. You suck at secret-keeping. You manage to out yourself somehow just about every time." He grinned and fired up the engine, then held up the mud-slathered pen. "Don't forget this."

Perri snatched the pen, smiling, and tossed it into her cemetery kit bag.

Nick began backing down the lane. "Why don't we have our drinks and snacks, my stomach is rumbling."

Perri's phone rang again. As she answered, she said to Nick, "Keep on this road until you get to Route 1, then turn left. Hey, Nina. What's up?" A pause, then "Right. Nick is here and we're on our way to Cave-in-Rock. Going to do a little more poking around." She listened for a while, smirked, listened some more, then replied, "Yeah, I know, I saw it. She's just trying to stir the pot. If she was as happy with him as she says she is, she wouldn't need to be on social media talking about me." Perri puffed out her cheeks, "Pfft. Who's she to talk? Really. I guess if she's monitoring my page, what little of it there is, just so she can make snide comments, she must be desperate. Who am I to deprive her of a little drama?"

Nick could hear the rise and fall of Nina's voice as she recounted some obviously juicy story to Perri, but he couldn't make out the words. "Tell Nina hello from me," he said.

"Hey, Nick says hello." She paused, then, "Nina says, 'Hello handsome.'"

Nina changed the subject. "As you know, I intended to come over there a couple of weekends from now."

"Problem?" Perri asked.

"Oh hell, yeah, there's a problem, and I'm Eventually Mad."

"You're 'Eventually Mad'?"

"Sure am."

"Ok...what does it mean?"

"You know, when you say to your husband, 'Honey, I'm going to visit my best friend on such and such date.' And he says, 'Ok, that's fine.' But then later, he suddenly spits out, 'Oh, I forgot to tell you. My Mom's coming to visit for a couple of weeks and she'll be arriving that day and I sorta need you to pick her up at the airport.' Then you say, 'You forgot to tell me?' And I got really mad and all."

"Yes, I can understand that." Nick looked over questioningly. Perri just shook her head and shrugged.

"Exactly, right? So then after I expressed my displeasure at Tom not telling me about this sooner, he says, 'Why are you so mad?' Then I said, 'You know how when someone does something that ticks you off and you ask them to stop, they say they will but just keep doing it over and over?' He said, 'Yeah.' And I said, 'Wouldn't you be angry about it?'

Perri began nodding, seeing where it was going. Nina said, "So Tom answers, 'Well, yeah, *eventually*.' Then I said, "Well, I'm *Eventually Mad!*' The long and short of it is that I can't come over there when we planned."

Nina waited, then asked, "Are you laughing?"

"Oh, my gosh, of course I'm laughing. Sorry, I know it's irritating, but that's hilarious. Look, we'll make it another time. I'll still be here for a while after that. But I get it, you thought you had it planned out and now it all has to change."

"You got it, sister. Oh well, things'll cool off by then. I gotta run, I haven't seen Aaron for at least five minutes and heaven knows he's probably behind the dryer crawling out through the vent or dismantling the plumbing. Have a good weekend, you two!"

Ok, thanks, we will, you too. Bye." Perri dropped the phone back into her purse.

Nick alternately looked at Perri and back to the road. Finally, he asked, "Well? What's going on?"

Perri told Nick about Nina's surprise in-law visit. Nick said, "Well, before that. There was something else before that."

Perri sighed. "Oh, nothing that matters."

"Someone bothering you online?"

Perri hesitated, then said, "Yes. It's my ex's new girlfriend. Her name's Sondra Lamey." She chuckled, "That's appropriate, huh? But yeah, she made a remark about me on a mutual friend's page a couple of weeks ago, which I just ignored. Obviously, that isn't what Her Hatefulness wanted so she's been stepping it up over the last few days. I started commenting back at her. I have no idea what she's got stuck in her giant craw, but she can't seem to unstick it. I don't even know her."

"What does she say?"

"She took a few jabs at a couple of vacation photos I had posted months ago, but mostly name calling and heart-rending, sob-worthy declarations of how terrible I treated Alan while we were married. She brays like a donkey, but she leaves out the parts about all his extramarital girlfriends, if she even knows about it yet. Then, after she feels enough people have seen it, or I finally make a comment that embarrasses her, she deletes it and pretends to be all innocent. She's one of those pot-stirrers who purposely posts stuff she knows will just get people into an argument, gets her friends involved in the attack, and then acts all offended that someone 'took it wrong.' She's a typical Harpy."

"Doesn't Alan ask her to stop harassing you?"

Perri looked at Nick over the top of her sunglasses. "Are you kidding me? He's probably enjoying it. He'll milk it for all the attention he can get." She pushed the sunglasses back up her nose. "Who knows, maybe if the offending object stays stuck in her craw long enough she'll form a giant pearl. Alan would love that, something he could make money from. He'd make her sign a contract though. 'X' amount of pearls per quarter, with his cut being fifty percent or more."

"He sounds like a gem. Pun intended. Has the mutual friend said anything about the comments?"

"Nope, she coolly stayed silent."

"Oh. This mutual friend just lets the other person sling mud at you?"

"Yep."

"Not much of a friend. I'd clear that one off my list."

"I probably will. I got busy with this trip and figured it would stop, but she seems to be self-agitating, like a washing machine that just works up more and more lather."

"Well, it's easier said than done, but try not to let losers like that bother you. If they had a happy, meaningful life, they wouldn't be trying to cause trouble with everyone else. I think there's something wrong with a person who gets fun out of setting other people at odds. Sounds like those two have some emotional issues of their own."

Perri agreed and the conversation turned back to their next stop.

In another twenty-five minutes, homes, churches, and small businesses began to dot the roadside as they entered the small town of Cave-in-Rock. Many of the cottage-style houses were decorated for Halloween with pumpkins and cornstalks adorning porches and displays in front yards. As they entered the town proper, the road dipped down, ending in a line of cars waiting to board the ferry, which was about two-thirds of the way across the Ohio coming from the Kentucky bank.

"Hey, we should cross over to Kentucky on the ferry one day, if we have time." Perri said hopefully.

"Sounds good." Nick turned left onto Water Street and followed it as it curved back north to intersect with Main Street.

They drove to a lot where they could park and walk down to the cave. After getting out her camera and locking her purse in the footlocker in the trunk, Perri and Nick headed down a gravel path which led to a steep flight of steps with segments of metal railing. At the bottom, the walk led through two stone columns onto a sandy path which curved around a sheer limestone bluff to the rocky beach in front of the mouth of the cave. The remains of wakes from passing barges licked at the stones. The muddy water had patches of foam on the surface in places and there was a distinct whiff of fish now and then.

Perri looked west down the river and saw a barge heavily laden with coal slowly chugging along. The ferry had reached the Illinois shore. A handful of cars and trucks were exiting down the ramp and driving up Canal Street.

She turned back and jogged around to the cave mouth. "Here it is!" She was more excited about seeing the cave again than she'd expected. "I know, it isn't huge, but I always loved coming here. I think it makes such an impression when you first see it. It's kind of cool to come back to a place and find it looks exactly like it did when I was eight years old. I still have a photo of me standing right…there."

Nick grinned broadly and walked through the narrow keyhole opening between two giant slabs of limestone. He craned his neck and looked up to the ceiling and around the walls. Perri darted past him, "Come on, let's get up on the ledges."

Nick followed her toward the back of the cave where the ground rose enough to step up onto the flat layers of stone. They walked back to the opening and sat on outcroppings of rock, surveying the expanse of Ohio River stretching away into the distance. Cave-in-Rock island sat almost directly across from them. To the east, the river bent and traveled north, and to the west, the tip of Hurricane Island was visible, its remaining fringe of trees turned to gold.

"I can see why you loved coming here as a kid. I would have too." Nick said.

After a solid five minutes of enjoying the scenery in contented silence, they explored the back of the cave. Scuffing the loose dirt with the toe of his boot, Nick commented, "I can see where they filled in the holes the vandals dug." He looked up through the opening in the cave roof. In the interior dimness, the pattern of the metal screen covering the opening formed a black grid against an oval of startlingly blue sky.

"I love being able to visit sites like this, but those few people who have no respect for monuments, historical places, or natural formations almost make me wish they were off limits to everyone, just to preserve them," Perri said as she peeked into the cubby-hole in the east wall of the cave then pointed them out to Nick. "When I was little, I was convinced something would be hiding in there and jump out at us."

Nick studied the filled holes again, "What do *you* think they were looking for?"

Perri was arched back, looking up through the opening. "Who knows, the rumored 'buried treasure' again, I suppose."

"I can't imagine anything important being left here after a couple centuries though, can you?" Nick asked.

"No." Letting her eyes adjust back to the dimness inside, she scuffed the toe of her boot along the broken soil just as Nick had done.

The beam of overhead light flickered momentarily throwing a shadow over the chamber. Perri and Nick both looked up but caught only a glimpse of movement. "Just someone looking down through the opening. I used to be afraid I'd fall through if I leaned over too far." Perri stated matter-of-factly. "But no, I can't imagine there being anything left either. I know they were still digging things up or finding them lying around in the late 18th and early 19th century, but not lately."

"Tim said someone recently found a counterfeiter's mold over by the ferry ramp, is that the kind of stuff they found inside the cave?"

"That and Native American tools and broken pottery, tools left behind by settlers, some animal bones. If I remember right, a farmer near here found a small Native American statue in his field, just sitting there, probably turned up by the plow. It was unbroken, but I can't imagine how."

They walked back out into the sunshine. Nick said, "Mileage-wise, I don't live that far away from here, but I didn't realize there was so much history behind this cave. The criminal element part sounds a lot like the history of Russellville, minus the river and the cave of course."

Perri looped her arm through Nick's as they headed back up the stairs to the parking area. "Its past is long and extremely checkered and some of the people notorious in those stories, both from Russellville and here, are the same people."

"Yeah?"

"The Harp brothers, the Masons, they were back and forth all over this area for years."

Back in the Jeep, Nick pulled over in the paved area near the dock. They watched the cars loading on the ferry.

Perri tipped her head toward the ferry, "Can you see a vehicle being pushed off the edge of a ferry by accident because someone loading behind them couldn't stop? I realize the accident I told you about happened a long time ago and this is bound to be a different ferry, but, what do you think?"

Nick studied the vessel for a few moments. "Well, if the vehicle that couldn't stop was heavy enough and had enough speed on it, I think it could push a car through that barrier, yes. It isn't a fixed barrier at either end. They have to be raised and lowered, so they're hinged. Yeah, I can see that happening. Why?"

I was wondering about the death of Pearl's nephew. I'm probably reading things into it. It happened decades ago most likely it was exactly what they said, an accident."

"It *was* over forty years ago. If you are trying to tie it in with his parents' murders, it would need to be a vendetta on the scale of the Hatfields and McCoys, and either carried out by a younger family member or a very spry elderly person."

Perri laughed and shook her head. "True. I just feel like there's something going on with these murders that I can't grasp and I'm grabbing at anything out of the ordinary that comes along. I don't have enough information to make the pieces click."

"Like what?"

"I don't know exactly. These may be unrelated instances, but somebody digging in both the cave and the cemetery, the house being ransacked, the Duncans killed, people keep trying to buy the house, even in the week after the Duncan's were murdered. It's a lot of focus on that house, or maybe on that family. There's an underlying theme but I'm not catching on to it yet."

Nick kept silent, thinking. He watched a tug push another string of coal barges down the Ohio. "They call them tug boats, but they don't tug, do they? They push."

"I know. It's contradictory." Perri answered. "So much for hiking today, huh? Maybe tomorrow when we go through the house we can find out more from Pearl."

Nick agreed. "We'll give it a shot." He put the Jeep in gear and turned to Perri, "You ready to head back? I'm starving. We've only had snacks since breakfast and I'm ready for a cold beer and some of the BBQ you told me about."

The last car had been loaded on the ferry and it was repeating its cross-river trip to the Kentucky side. "Me too. Let's go."

Nick pulled the Jeep back onto highway 1 and started the trip back to Eldorado.

## Chapter 22

October 16, 2016, 10:00 a.m.

"I'm glad we got our outdoor wandering done yesterday. It looks like it's going to start raining any moment. I brought an umbrella." Perri scanned the sky. A churning wall of dark clouds was building, marching across the otherwise gray cloud cover and she could just hear the far-away rumble of thunder. "Once that lets loose, we'll need it just to get from the Jeep to the house and back."

Nick parked the Jeep in front of Pearl's house, lining up the passenger side door with the walk. As they approached her door, Nick said, "I'll help her get in if it's a little high for her. Your car is low and mine's high, so I hope this was the better choice."

"I think so. It might be a little cramped in the Mini."

Pearl appeared at the porch door before they reached the stairs. She pushed the door open wide and immediately turned, bustling back through the living room. "Step inside, I'm all ready to go, I just need to get my raincoat on." She laughed, obviously tickled to be going to see her old family home. Perri and Nick stood just inside the front door while Pearl went to get her coat.

Nick looked around the room. He was making comments about something, but Perri didn't hear what he was saying. Her eye was caught by a business card lying on a tea table placed in front of the window that looked out onto the porch. The card was turned away from her, but she could read the writing upside down. *Bethany Trammel, Real Estate Agent, CRS, ABR.* Perri was frowning over the card when Pearl re-entered the room, fastening a large buckle on the belt of a tan raincoat with voluminous pockets and wide lapels.

"Ok, I'm ready. I can't wait to see the house," Pearl chattered. "I barely slept last night. I didn't realize I'd be so excited, but I guess it's been a few years since I was there. Time sure does get away from me."

"I didn't know you hadn't visited at the house for so long. Did you ever have holidays or family gatherings here?" Perri asked.

Pearl held on to Nick's arm as she descended the seven stairs to the walk. "Sometimes, but mostly we met somewhere for dinner. You know, that way nobody has to do all the work of having company for dinner and then cleaning up. Once you get as old as we are, all that fuss just isn't very appealing."

Perri opened the door of the Jeep for Nick who helped Pearl scoot into the seat and get her feet inside just as fat raindrops began plopping on the sidewalk and windshield. "Here it comes."

Nick hopped into the driver's seat and Perri climbed into the back behind Nick where she could see Pearl while talking to her. As they made their way through Harrisburg, Perri asked her, "Everything been going ok? Has anyone been asking you about the house?"

"Oh, you know, the usual. Nothing much. The obituaries were in the paper, so a realtor came by asking if I was wanting to sell but I said I absolutely did not at this point. I may not need two houses but I'm not going to rush into anything. I haven't even looked the house over yet. And since you found out it's on that Register thing, I want to try that route first." Deftly stepping around further discussion of the realtor, Pearl pointed at a restaurant and made a comment about it.

She gave Pearl a gentle reminder. "I'm glad no one's bothering you. If anyone does, speak up, ok? You shouldn't have to go through that."

"Don't you worry, I will, honey. I'm old but I can be a brassy old broad when those varmints come around."

Perri caught Nick's eye in the rearview mirror and narrowed her eyes. She didn't believe for a moment that it wasn't a problem.

The rest of the trip was taken up with chit chat. As the Jeep neared the old house on the hill, Perri could see Pearl tense and her expression tighten. "You ok?" Perri asked her.

"I'm ok. I've been so excited about seeing the house again that I forgot that Ruby wouldn't be here. I didn't forget she was gone, I don't mean that, I mean I just hadn't let myself dwell on it."

Nick pulled into the driveway and stopped, turning to Pearl. "Do you want me to pull into the carport so you can get out where it's dry?"

Pearl's face showed confusion. She didn't answer.

Nick and Perri exchanged glances. Always cautious about diabetics who began responding unusually, Perri leaned forward to get a better view, looking for signs that Pearl's blood sugar might be dropping again.

Pearl saw her look of concern and waved her hand to dismiss Perri's worry. "I expected the car to be here. It's gone." She turned in the seat and looked over her shoulder at Perri. "Ruby and George's car is gone. The police said it was in the carport."

Thinking back to the day before, Perri responded, "You're right, it was in the driveway. Remember, I said Nick and I drove past here yesterday and it was there then." Nick was nodding in agreement.

"And is that when you saw that good-for-nothing scum boyfriend of Stella's coming out of the house?"

"Yesterday late morning, yes," Nick answered.

Pearl smacked her hand on her purse. "That no-good…you can be sure Stella's going to hear about this. They've stolen that car. It wasn't a sports car or anything valuable, but they can't just come in here and take things like that!"

Perri blinked a few times, then asked, "Do you want to call the police?"

Pearl sighed. "Let me talk to her first. That girl." She shook her head. Nick looked at her uncertainly, the engine idling. "Sorry, yes go on and pull into the car port. *Now that it's empty* we may as well make use of it."

Nick pulled the car under the shelter and turned off the ignition. "Hang on, I'll help you get out, it can be a big step down and the runner will be slippery from the rain."

Perri exited as Nick jogged around to the passenger side and helped Pearl out. She had a set of keys in her hand. There was no entry door to the house on the driveway side. When the house was built, there were no cars and visitors entered from the front door whether they arrived on foot, horse, or in a carriage. Horses and carriages were taken to the rear after the passengers entered the house. The back entrance was most likely reserved for servants and service deliveries, or family if they wanted to use it. The carriage house no longer stood, but the old horse barn was being used for equipment and storage.

"Nick, lock the Jeep if you will." She gave him a knowing look. "Good idea." Nick blipped the key fob, locking the doors. Perri opened her umbrella and held it over herself and Pearl as they sloshed through the puddles to the front door.

Pearl unlocked and pushed the door open. They stepped into a foyer-like area and stopped to wipe their dripping shoes on the mat. Perri turned to close the door on the slanting rain but paused to take in the view of the river from the hilltop where the house perched. Dark, steely gray against a heavy sky, it looked like an iron serpent winding its way through the fields lined by trees. The wind was strong enough to dot the water with white frothy waves. She shut the door on the wet and dreary day, thunder rattling the old windows.

A few feet into the foyer, on the left, was a wide entrance to a front room, probably called the parlour or sitting room when the house was built. Along the right wall of the entryway rose a staircase. The finish on the decoratively carved bannister a bit dull, but all the balusters were still intact. A carpet runner was tacked on the stairs but, having been done with very little skill, it looked like it might provide an easy way to plunge to one's demise.

Next to the stairway, a chandelier hung from the second-floor ceiling. Not the showy piece with cascades of crystals that is often seen, this one looked like it might be an original candle type that was converted to electricity. There were now ten electric candles in the corona. The chandelier was understated, the candles being seated in cast leaves and the modest amount of gilt was still relatively unblemished. Perri was already thinking it wasn't any wonder people were itching to get hold of this house and/or it's furnishings. She didn't know what the asking price for a vintage chandelier like this would be, but it might be enough to serve as a motive for murder if someone did realize the value of even this one piece with an eye to more goodies being in the house.

Perri wondered what other original features the house still possessed. She found Pearl slowly navigating around the living room, studying the furniture, the trinkets on the fireplace mantle, the paintings on the walls, and the books in the old cabinet as though she'd never seen them before.

Giving the appearance of French doors, two very tall windows, nearly floor to ceiling, provided the occupants a sweeping view of the river. The fireplace was opposite the windows. Perri had seen a double chimney in the center of the roof when they drove by on Saturday. No doubt there were other fireplaces upstairs and in the kitchen area. Many older houses had their nonworking fireplaces covered during remodels. She wondered many were still visible.

Perri walked behind one of the wing chairs positioned on the area rug in front of the fireplace. "This is an amazing bookshelf." Hinged glass-paneled doors protected the books from dust. "It's beautiful."

Pearl replied, a little absently. "I'm glad it's still here."

"Were you expecting it to be gone?"

"I think I did expect that. I know that George had sold a couple of things. Ruby mentioned it to me a couple years ago. He sold one of the old bedsteads and a dressing table that had been my grandmother's. I don't know if they needed the money that badly or he just got greedy."

It was the first time Perri had heard Pearl talk about George in a negative light. "Was that…a problem, do you think?"

"I don't know how much of a problem, but I think it was a problem. Ruby didn't like to talk about George that way, of course, but she did let slip once or twice about George selling things she wanted to keep or hated to see go."

"That's why you're studying everything so closely, you're looking for things that were here before but are now gone?"

"Mm-hmm. I won't know for sure until I've seen the rest of the house because stuff may have been moved around, but I don't see our mother's sewing box in here. She always had it next to her chair right there," Pearl pointed to the chair opposite the one in front of the bookcase, "and it isn't there now."

"Would that be something George would want to sell?"

"It had been my mother's grandmother's. It wasn't just a box, it was on legs and was hand-painted. It wasn't just old, it was one-of-a-kind. George wanted to sell anything the market would churn out money for. The older he got, the worse about it he got, like he was addicted to selling things." Pearl brooded for a few moments and added, "More like addicted to the money he got from it, even if it wasn't that much. Maybe that's the same kind of thrill a gambler feels. It isn't the amount of money won, but playing and then winning."

Perri suddenly recalled the scissors she bought at the auction barn. She felt a sense of dread that the sewing box had, indeed, been sold, probably with all the contents being sold separately. She suspected one of them was in her purse right now. "Um, Pearl, will you take a look at something for me?"

"Ok."

Perri pawed through her purse until she found the paper-wrapped scissors. "I bought these yesterday. I haven't even taken them out of the paper yet. Your talk about George selling things, and then saying the sewing kit is missing makes me wonder if you'll recognize these."

Pearl watched with apprehension as Perri unwrapped the scissors.

"These came from the auction barn in Equality." Perri slid the scissors out of the paper and handed them to Pearl. "I was told they were probably the last item they had from George."

She watched Pearl's face, seeing recognition there, quickly followed by anger. "I don't believe it!" Pearl turned a hard gaze on Perri.

Perri saw the flicker of rage in Pearl's eyes and quickly said, "I knew George was a picker, getting stuff from all over southern Illinois, but I certainly didn't know…"

"No, no, I'm not mad at you. How could you possibly know? I'm mad at him. I'm sorry he's dead, and he was a good man to my sister, but he just got too dadblamed greedy as he got older."

Pearl held the scissors out to Perri. Perri very gently pushed her hand away, "You keep those. I bought them because they were so unique and beautifully done, but if they were your mother's, you should have them. I don't want to keep them."

"I'll pay you what you bought them for, more if you want." Pearl offered.

Perri felt terrible for Pearl. "I'd rather give them to you. I'm just glad they're back where they belong. I wish they'd still had the sewing box, but I don't think they do."

Pearl nodded. "I thank you. She tucked the scissors into her short-handled, navy blue handbag, her eyes a little bright with moisture.

Nick quickly suggested, "Let's have a look around the rest of the house.

The upstairs showed more obvious signs of the search than the living room. Drawers were partially open with socks and underwear draped over the edges. Closet doors hung open with discarded clothing and shoeboxes lying in the floor. The only room on the second floor that wasn't totally disheveled was the bathroom, with only a few drawers and no closet, there weren't many storage or hiding places.

Pearl told Nick and Perri that Ruby and George had used the smaller bedroom adjoining the master for their son, Chris, when he was a baby. Once he was older, they'd moved him to the bedroom at the end of the hall and Ruby then used the connecting room as her craft room. "Ruby loved to sew and do all kinds of needlework. Momma taught us both to crochet and knit, and I still do that, but Ruby liked everything. She did embroidery, made quilts, and that other kind of needlework, uses floss…what is it? It was popular in the 70s, everybody had landscape scenes over their couch."

Perri suggested, "Crewel?"

"That's it. There's a framed panel Ruby made in the dining room. I'll show you when we get back downstairs."

"Did Ruby make the quilts you have at your house, the ones in your blanket chest?"

"Yes, she did. She was very good at it. She won ribbons at the State Fair a couple of times, but that was a long time ago. Her eyesight had dimmed and she had trouble with the tiny, little stitches. She'd use a good bright light to help her see the stitches on the fabric but she said it just made the glare worse. She was thinking about having cataract surgery soon, but …"

Nick pointed to a narrow door at the end of the hallway. "Is that a closet?"

"That's the door to the attic."

He opened the door then looked back at Pearl. "Would you like to go up there and look around?"

Perri truly hoped she would want to, but instead, she hesitated, a little dispirited by the state of the house. "You know, I think I'll maybe wait until another day for both the attic and the cellar. Maybe you and Perri could come back with me another time and we'll look, but today I think it might be too much."

"No problem, you just say the word." Nick closed the door. "Are you ready to go back downstairs? I guess we have the kitchen and dining room still to see."

The three of them descended the stairs and turned right, passing the living room, walking beneath the old chandelier and through a doorway into another, smaller, foyer area. Perri could see the kitchen straight ahead. Pearl turned right again through a door under the stairway that led into a dining room. It was a large room, and, like the living room, it had tall windows on the front wall, although three rather than two. There were an additional four windows along the side wall that would have faced the approach to the house. Built-in cabinetry along the back of the room was painted white, but had a layer of dust over it making it appear dingy. A fireplace was centered in the wall in the middle of the house, exhausting through one of the multiple chimneys.

The long table seating eight was covered with embroidered dimity. "One of Rubies creations?" Perri asked lifting the corner of the linen edged with delicate picots of crochet.

Pearl nodded yes.

Gazing through the leaded glass doors of the cabinets, Perri asked, "Does it look to you like all the plate and crystal is here?"

Pearl opened each door, one by one, looking over the contents. "As far as I can tell, it does. That's a relief. I was afraid of what I'd find in here."

Nick said, "Doesn't it seem odd that the house was apparently gone through but these things," he waved a hand at the cabinets and the silver, crystal, and pewter items sitting neatly in place on the shelves, "are still here?" He peeked in at the dust on the shelves and reached in to lift one thick goblet, noting a clean circle underneath. "They don't even look like they've been moved around."

Pearl asked Nick, "What do you mean?"

"Well, it seems to me whoever did this was looking for something specific, not just something of value to steal. If they were," he nodded again towards the cabinets, "a lot of this would be gone. Those candlesticks on the dining table look like silver too. They would bring a good price if someone wanted to hock whatever they could find and they're easy to carry off."

"I didn't really think about that. I guess you're right though. Let's have a look at the kitchen."

The kitchen stretched the width of the house across the back with a smaller dining table occupying one end, probably the one used by the family except on occasions. There was a bookcase of a more utilitarian design against the outer wall, near the corner. Pearl pointed to the empty wall next to it and said, "There's a hutch missing from there. It was a Hoosier cabinet and sat right there." She pivoted around, surveying the rest of the room. "Now it's gone!"

"Surely, whoever…was here last week didn't take a cabinet that large." Perri said.

"No, but I have to wonder if it didn't go the same way as the car. I remember George talking about it a few Christmas's ago, saying the right kind could bring three-thousand dollars or more. Stella was there, of course, and it interested her very much. She asked some questions about it then." Pearl's face flushed with anger. "I told George that Christmas that I didn't like the idea of him selling that hutch, and Ruby agreed with me. She didn't do it often, but she put her foot down on that one, so I don't think I can blame George for it being gone. I guess after Ruby was gone, Stella couldn't wait to get in here and start picking off the prize items. Well, I guess it turned out to be *the right kind of cabinet*, wasn't it?"

Nick asked, "You don't think George just went ahead and sold it anyway?"

"I thought George abided by what Ruby said on that. I could be wrong of course but I think she would have raised a stink about it if he sold it. But I do think him selling things could be one reason he started wanting to have holidays somewhere besides the house! Didn't want me to see what he was doing. But I still don't think he sold the cabinet. I think it was the other stuff he didn't want me to notice. Silly thing, I guess he didn't think Ruby would tell me."

Nick asked, "You think Stella and her boyfriend, what is his name anyway, took both the cabinet and the car?" Perri grimaced at Nick from behind Pearl.

Pearl pressed her lips together so firmly, new wrinkles formed all the way around her lips. "That I will be taking up with my daughter. Stella has problems, but I think that boyfriend of hers, and the little greaseball's name's Eric, puts her up to some of the things she does. She's always had a rotten attitude, I can't put that on him, but I'm bettin' you he's behind taking the car. The cabinet was probably Stella and she got him to help her." She turned to Perri. "That's what they were doing here when you saw them yesterday. Came in the house and got the keys to the car, and you said they were in a pick-up truck, right?" Perri nodded yes. "They used that to haul away the cabinet."

"Maybe they still have it. Unless they already had a buyer for it, maybe it isn't lost yet."

Pearl's eyes lit with a little hope. "Maybe. Eric works for that hauling off company too, the one Stella works for, and they usually take their stuff to Equality."

Nick suggested, "We could notify the auction house to let you know if they turn up with it."

"Let's do. I don't want to get my hopes up, but I sure would like to get that back." Pearl fidgeted with the clasp on her purse.

"How did they get in? Did Stella have a set of keys to the house?"

"Not that I know of. They must have broken in, unless someone left a door or window unlocked. There have been police in and out of here, so it could happen."

During this exchange, Nick crossed the kitchen to the back door. "No, whoever came in forced the back door. Look." He was holding the back door open, splintered wood surrounded the striker plate. Pearl just shook her head. Nick stopped short of saying the murderer could have been the one to break in before Stella and Eric got there, giving them easy access.

Dispelling that theory to an extent, Pearl added morosely, "The police didn't say anything about the door being busted before they turned it over to me."

Trying to lift the dark cloud, Perri commented as lightly as she could, "It looks like Ruby liked to cook. She's got a huge collection of cookbooks." She was crouched down reading the titles in the bookcase next to the empty spot where the antique cabinet had been. "Wow, there are some great old books here, very nice collection."

"She liked cooking too. Ruby was happy as a big sunflower being home, cooking, doing her sewing. She wasn't one for going places all the time."

"Is it ok if I look at a few of these?" Perri asked.

"Sure, go ahead. You can have some of them too because heaven knows I'm not going to use them. I don't cook a whole lot anymore anyway, but with my diabetes, half the fun of cooking has gone out of it. I always like to bake, and I can't have the things I used to have."

"That makes it tough." Perri turned her attention back to the bookcase.

To continue to distract Pearl from her disappointment and anger, Nick asked, "Was this the stove that was here when you grew up?" The huge cast iron stove had been fitted into what was the original kitchen open fireplace, the vent pipe running up a chimney at the back of the house.

"It was. That thing made the kitchen so warm and cozy in the winter when it was all fired up. I didn't like cleaning it though, and I always had to help do that. Our dad brought in the wood every day, all chopped up to small pieces so they fit in the opening. There's plenty of room in that to cook a holiday meal, bake your bread, and keep water hot. Our mama could time everything to turn out at the same time."

"Hey Pearl, what's this?" Perri rose from her kneeling position with a small black leather-bound book in her hand. "It isn't a cookbook. I thought at first it might be a personal recipe book, but I don't think so. It's pretty old and fragile" She carefully handed it to Pearl. "I didn't open it, it might be private."

Pearl opened it and slowly turned the first few pages. Finally, shaking her head, she said, "It looks like a diary, or something like one. The writing is hard to read, I can't tell what some of these words are. Where was it?"

Perri pointed to a small empty spot on the bottom shelf. "Right there, between Julia Child's *The Way to Cook* and James Beard's *Beard on Bread*."

Pearl handed it back. "I'm not sure. Maybe you can read it better than I can. My eyes aren't so great anymore either."

Perri took the book to the kitchen table and settled into a seat with the book in front of her Nick and Pearl followed suit. The small volume was about four inches wide by six inches tall, bound in black leather. The front cover extended into a flap closure that wrapped over the edges of the pages and around to the back.

Attached to the front cover flap, through a tooled loop in the leather, was a badly frayed remnant of what appeared to be a silk ribbon meant to secure the book closed. Perri carefully opened the cover, a few motes of dry leather floated onto the table top and she made a pained expression in response. Inside the cover, where the flap folded, a tapered pocket was fashioned in the same leather to accommodate a small writing implement that would fit snugly when the journal was closed, but it was empty. Tucked behind the leather cover and what would be the paste down end paper was a pocket, lined with marbled paper, for storage of small items, maybe receipts or calling cards.

The first few pages were thick stock in a creamy color that had darkened around the edges. The writing may originally have been black but now was a rusty brown. Overall, it appeared fragile, like it would crack and flake off if the page was bent too much. The penmanship was ornate, at least on this page. The capital letters were large and embellished with flourishes.

Getting impatient, Nick asked, "Well? Can you make out any of the writing?"

"It looked like a bunch of swirly lines to me." Pearl said quietly, shaking her head slightly.

"It's definitely fanciful script, but I think it may be confined to the opening pages. Hopefully, the main text will be written in more simplified cursive." Perri felt the urge to shout, just a little bit, but kept it under wraps.

Nick prodded her, "You waitin' for a drum roll?"

"Maybe. Ok, ok. The first line of the inscription on this page says: *Journal of F.W. McCade* and on the next line *For June 1836-March 1837*. The ink of the second line is slightly different than the first line because he added it after the book was full."

Pearl gasped, her hand to her throat. "Really? Does it really say that, or are you just messin' with me?"

"I wouldn't do that! It really says that. Unbelievable that it was pushed between two cookbooks," Perri glanced back over to the bookcase containing cook books and recipe card files, "just sitting there." She ran her gaze quickly over the rest of that shelf and the others to see if she spotted any more like it.

Pearl offered, "It's my guess Ruby did that to keep it safe."

"To keep it safe? Between two cookbooks probably isn't the best place, too easy to rough it up or crush it."

"I guess what I meant is she wanted to hide it from George. Maybe she thought he'd try to auction it off." They were back to that. Pearl's dander was rising up again.

Nick replied in a calming tone, "Hmm, that's a thought. If it was written in the 1830s, it's considered a historical document, and being written by a contemporary living in the Shawneetown of that time period would make it pretty sought after, I would think. But it's still here, so she kept it safe, if that's why she kept it here."

"You're absolutely right." Perri answered. "Judging by the information I found so far on Francis McCade, he settled in Shawneetown in 1819, so this journal was started sixteen years after he'd settled here." She looked around the kitchen.

Pearl asked, "What are you looking for?"

"I want to use something to slip between the pages to turn them, not use my fingers. I'm afraid I'll crumple them. I probably shouldn't even try to…"

"Oh no, I want to know. Please, let's look at it. What kind of thing do you need? I'll see if I can find something."

"Something flat and thin maybe."

Pearl foraged through a couple of kitchen drawers. She turned, holding a long metal letter opener, and asked, "Will this do?"

"That should work. I just don't want to get the oil from my hands on the pages or crinkle the edges trying to get hold of them." Perri took the letter opener from Pearl. "Let's see what else it says." Perri very carefully slipped the slender piece of metal beneath the next page and, supporting it along the length of the letter opener, gently lifted and turned the page.

"This says, *'Orchard Parke'* then on a second line, *'Sandy Ridge, Shawneetown, Illinois.'*"

"Where is Sandy Ridge?" Nick asked.

Perri looked up, her gaze unfocused while trying to place it. "I don't know the exact boundaries, well, I don't know loosely either, only that it was an area just south of Shawneetown. There was a second house, in addition to the Crenshaw House near Junction, where slaves were imprisoned, usually for labor in the salt works. It was known to have been in Sandy Ridge."

"You aren't saying our house was used for…"

Perri assured her, "No, not this house. That house no longer exists. But I think your house may be in the area that was considered Sandy Ridge at that time."

"Oh, ok. What else?" Pearl scooted her chair further up to the table in anticipation, the shadow of her black mood disappearing just as swiftly as it had returned.

"Next page. This page starts the journal entries with June 14, 1836. It says, *'Back from meeting with AM. Very successful. Next meeting two weeks. Pleasant day, river crossing easy today. Home a little later than expected.'*"

"Meeting *with AM* or *in the a.m.*?" Nick asked.

"*With AM*, as in someone's initials."

"Another McCade, do you think?" Nick paused, then said, "His wife's initials were AM, weren't they?"

"Yeah, but why would he have to go somewhere else to meet with his wife? It sounds to me like the meeting was some distance from home, and he says across the river. Then he returned home afterward."

"You think he crossed the Ohio River to meet someone? Where would he cross? There's nothing directly across the Ohio but farmland, not even now, and the bridge wasn't there then." Pearl asked.

"Unless he went down to Cave-in-Rock, there was a ferry there at that time and the road was dangerous on both sides." Perri considered a moment, then said, "He could have been referring to the Saline River, which seems more likely. Maybe there'll be more information further in the journal to clear that up."

Perri turned the book over and opened it from the back. "Hmm, the back section is a ledger."

"A ledger?" Nick came around the table, behind Perri, and leaned over her shoulder. "Yeah, it has columns for Particulars, Payables, and Receipts."

"This is the 1836 equivalent of our checkbook registers. Francis kept his accounts in this and it looks like he was very meticulous about it."

Pearl smiled and asked Perri, "Will you take it with you and read it? There's no way I could read that but I am so curious about what it says. This is my something-something great grandfather. Isn't that just amazing?"

"He's your great grandfather times three. I made a family tree for you in my genealogy program. It was easier to keep track of the people that way. Heaven knows I've been over it enough times. I have trouble remembering my own people, much less others. But to answer your question, you have no idea how pleased I'd be to read this.

Perri closed the book and asked Pearl what she wanted to do next, but her mind was occupied by the tantalizing prospect of where other journals might be located. What were the chances this was the only one?

"Well, I think I've seen most of the house now. At least I have a better idea of what I'm dealing with."

"This back door needs to be fixed, Pearl. It looks closed and locked but, as you can see," Nick lightly tugged on the door handle using only two fingers and the door swung open, "it isn't. I can repair this and replace the broken lock for you if you like."

"Would you? That would be a weight off my mind if you could, but I hate to put you out."

Nick generously responded with, "I'll be glad to contribute something. Otherwise, I'm just here for my charm and good looks."

Perri expressively rolled her eyes. "You fill that role perfectly fine, too."

Pearl stood and slid her chair back under the table. "I've really wanted to see my family's graves at Gold Hill. Do you think we could do that too?

"Sure, we can, if you don't mind slogging through some possibly mucky ground?" Pearl nodded enthusiastically. Perri carefully picked up the journal. "Ok, are you ready to go now?"

As Pearl nodded that she was ready, Nick added. "I'm glad it's still early because that door needs to be dealt with in some way today. I wouldn't feel comfortable leaving it like this overnight, especially since someone knows that it's open and they may come back."

"You're right. I didn't think of that." Perri hesitated, not sure whether to go to the cemetery or take care of the ruined door first.

Nick continued, "Tell you what, let's drive over to new Shawneetown and make a stop at the hardware store so I can get what I need to fix this. We can pick up some drive-through food and come back here to eat. I'll do what I can with the door, although it might be temporary, and we'll go by the cemetery afterward. There should still be plenty of time and, that way, the house isn't sitting open for any longer than necessary. Maybe you and Perri can go through more of the journal while I'm working on the door."

"That sounds perfect."

"It's settled then, let's get going." Perri said. "I'm still taking this with me," Perri indicated the journal in her hand, "because I don't want to risk losing it if someone shows up in the meantime."

Pearl's brow furrowed. "Do you think someone might come back that soon?" She was starting to look worried, and a little scared, her eyes darted to the windows and back.

Nick looked around the kitchen thoughtfully. "It wouldn't stop them from getting in if they were determined, but if we drag something over in front of the door, they'll know someone is aware of the break-in and it may scare them off, not being sure how soon we'll come back."

"I wonder if the person, or persons, who broke in here are the same ones who were digging in the cemetery."

Pearl pivoted back and forth between Nick and Perri with an even more alarm. "What? Digging? In the cemetery?"

"Not in the grave area, Pearl, there was a hole dug in the side path."

"What for?"

"We don't know. We figured it was probably just someone acting on the rumors about buried treasure, especially since the digging at Cave-in-Rock has been on the news lately. With a name like Gold Hill, it's inevitable that someone takes it literally, right? Then again, it could all be the work of the same person." Perri mused.

"I guess so." Pearl hesitantly agreed.

Perri didn't want to say she was wondering if Pearl's daughter, Stella, and her boyfriend were involved, but it seemed like a real possibility. They'd been in the area and were undeniably up to no good. In her opinion, they were good for the break-in at the house, since she and Nick had seen them coming out of it just yesterday and today the Duncan's car was gone.

Nick, still contemplating the door, said, "We can use the bookcase to block the door, but all the books would have to come out before we could move it." He felt around the end of the bookcase and pulled gently while trying to peek behind it, then removed a handful of books from the top shelf to get a view of the back of bookcase. "That's what I thought. It's bolted to the wall to keep it from falling over. I don't think it's worth the time investment to move the bookcase. We could use the table with a couple chairs on top. It's the startle factor we're going for anyway."

Perri and Nick pulled the chairs away from the table and scooted it against the door. They stacked two of the chairs atop the table, tipped up on their rear legs with only the tops of the chairbacks touching. They'd easily slip and make a racket if someone moved the door even a little. "That'll do until we get back."

"Let's get going. The sooner we go, the sooner we'll get it done." Perri said.

## Chapter 23

October 16, 2016, 12:30 p.m.

Perri and Pearl waited in the car in the parking lot while Nick was in the hardware store getting supplies. Nick wouldn't let Pearl pay him and she'd been concerned he was going to spend too much money on tools in addition to the supplies, but Nick always kept a full toolbox in the footlocker in the back of his Jeep.

"Tools are not a problem, believe me." Perri tried to reassure her. "He's in his element, good grief, let him enjoy it. He's probably relieved to have something to do. I'm surprised he doesn't want to replace the whole door, and that is a distinct possibility since he called this a temporary fix."

Pearl was a little flustered, no longer used to having a family member around to help out or do odd jobs that came up. "Well, if you say so." But she continued to look worried.

Nick came out of the hardware store carrying a sack and grinning. Perri was still amazed that a man of his height, over six feet, could have such a buoyant step. She murmured softly, "I wonder if he can dance."

Pearl turned around in her seat, smiling a little impishly. "I think you should find out. Wouldn't that be fun? Put that man in a suit and go out for a nice dance."

Their shared laughter was still lingering when Nick climbed back in the driver's seat. He looked at them both and said, "What?"

"Nothing. Just girl talkin' in here. Let's go get some grub, I'm starving."

Nick nodded toward a chicken joint with a drive-up across the street from the strip mall where they were parked. "That place ok?"

With everyone in agreement, he crossed the street and joined the line of cars waiting to order. Each of them straining to see the posted menu, they mulled over the choices while creeping forward in the line. There would be plates and silverware available at the house, so they decided on a bucket of chicken with sides rather than individual meals. Pearl insisted, "It won't take but a couple of minutes to clean up and it'll be much nicer than eating out of Styrofoam. I can't stand that squeaky noise it makes. I always end up sticking my fork through it and making a hole."

There were two cars left in front of them, including the one at the window, and a few cars now behind them. Suddenly, Pearl sat up very straight in her seat, her face turned toward her window, intently watching something.

"What do you see?" Perri asked.

Pearl tapped her finger against the window and whirled around in her seat. "That's them! There's my sister's car. I'll be damned. It *is* Stella and that rotten boyfriend."

Nick said, exasperated, "There's a concrete barrier along the side of the drive-up or I'd pull out and follow them for you. He reached in his jacket pocket and pulled out his phone. "Do you want to call the police and report it?"

The car drove out of site. Pearl turned back around. "No. I want to, but I'd better talk to Stella first." She shifted uneasily. "Oh, I know you probably think I'm being silly since I was so mad about them taking it."

"We don't think you're silly. You don't want to turn your daughter in to the police, at least not without talking to her. I get that." Nick looked at Perri in the rearview mirror. Perri continued, "So…this boyfriend. You said he's no good. Do you know much about him? What's his name again?"

Pearl drew herself up and huffed out a sigh of disgust. "His name is Eric Massey. He's been in trouble since he was seven years old, I think."

"This is someone you have known for a long time?" Nick asked.

"Oh yes. That little twerp lived on the same street as us, just down a couple more blocks. Always in trouble in school, he was. He stole Stella's lunch money one time and he borrowed her bike another time and wrecked it before giving it back to her. I guess I should be surprised he gave it back at all. Charlie had to replace the front wheel." She pointed back over her shoulder, the way the car had gone. "And that isn't the first car he's made off with. He spent a little time in the government system for auto theft. Here he is, doing it again. Always was too dumb to learn anything. Stella must be losing her marbles to be hanging around with him."

Perri was leaning between the seats. "You said Stella was in the midst of a divorce, right?"

"Yes, she..."

Conversation halted while Nick paid for the food and handed the bags back to Perri. The smell of hot, spicy fried chicken filled the interior. She set the sacks on the seat beside her and covered them with a blanket from the back to keep it warm then leant forward again so she could see Pearl's face clearly. "Go on."

"Stella and Scott have been married about, oh, eight years or so." She could see Perri's look and explained. "Scott was married once before. I don't know the details of that breakup."

Perri nodded, but didn't say anything, wanting Pearl to continue.

"And...well, he and Stella met at the racetrack where she works part of the year and started going out. She works in the grill and Scott was there a lot of nights so they got to talking. Scott's not a bad man, just a little aimless sometimes. She's messed it all up now though and he's done."

"Where does Stella work the rest of the year, when the track closes for the winter?"

"She works some nights at the Mini-Mart in Harrisburg. Most of the time, though, she works for The Cleaning Crew." Pearl didn't explain and her expression made it clear she figured Perri knew what that was.

"Is The Cleaning Crew a type of ... maid service or cleaning company? Sorry, I don't know."

"Oh, I guess I thought you would know. It's a company that goes into houses that are going to be sold or rented out, usually when the previous tenant left without taking all their stuff or left it damaged or dirty. They haul away whatever's left and then clean the place. If repairs have to be done, another group does that stuff, painting and the like. It's the place Eric works for."

"I see. Do that many people leave stuff behind when they move that a whole company exists to deal with it?"

"I wouldn't have thought so, but evidently they do. Sometimes it's just trash they didn't want to clean up themselves. That's usually what gets left in apartments and rental houses. But they do a lot of work for realty companies too."

Perri could feel Nick's eyes on her as he glanced over, then back at the road. They were nearing the turnoff for the house.

"The real estate companies?"

"Yeah. Stella said a lot of times people have to move several states away or something, like for a job, and they can't or don't want to take all their stuff. Sometimes it's a house full when someone dies and there's either no family or the family doesn't want the stuff, so after they've picked through and taken what they do want, they hire the Cleaning Crew to come in and sell what can be sold, then haul away the rest."

"What do they do with it? Where do they haul it?"

"I expect some goes to the dump and some gets donated. I suspect they're probably careful about what they get rid of. The better stuff goes to auction or at least to flea markets. The owner gets the bigger part of the money but the company gets a percentage of the sales."

"It's in their best interest to sell as much of it as they can at the highest price they can get."

"Right. And I'm sure that not all of the stuff that gets sold is known by the company. I can't think of any other reason Eric would stay at it this long. He's quit every other job after a month or so."

They arrived back at the house. Nick pulled the Jeep into the carport. The rain had stopped and the sun was out, washing all the autumn colors clean and leaving them vibrant and bright. The sunlight glared off the surface of the Ohio in a shimmering blanket of flashes.

"Do you think Stella was coming by the house again today? They were headed in this direction."

Nick said, "We might be about to find out." Perri took the sacks of food and she and Pearl followed Nick to the door. They waited while he unlocked the front door and headed straight for the kitchen. The chairs were no longer in their original position. One was on the floor, the other lying on its back on the table. Seeing Pearl's face darken, Nick quickly said, "This doesn't mean for sure they tried to get in. We had them balanced so they would fall easily, and they may have fallen on their own. The table doesn't look to be moved much from where it was, although, maybe a bit. At any rate, they didn't get in. Even if they did, they just left again because it hasn't been long."

"Oh, don't try to keep from upsetting me. I'm sure they were probably coming back to haul off anything else they could. Ha, I'm just glad they didn't get to! Bet they weren't expecting that." She plonked her purse down on the counter. "Now, let's get some plates and forks and eat this food before it gets cold and we have to heat it up." Plates and utensils were soon clattering on the countertop while Nick and Perri put the table back where it belonged.

"You mind if I stick the mashed potatoes and gravy in the microwave?" Perri asked Pearl. "They've cooled off quite a bit."

"Go right ahead." Pearl's spirits lifted as she bustled around, wiping the table off and setting it for three.

Nick retrieved the tools he'd need for the door from his Jeep and was busy organizing the supplies so he could get started as soon as he ate. "You know you probably should have this door replaced?"

Tossing the dishtowel over one shoulder, Pearl laid out the utensils. "Perri said you'd say that."

Nick, on one knee on the floor threw Perri a look under his arm and winked at her. "She was right."

After eating, Nick started on the door, serenading the others with the shrill whir of a drill, the hammering punctuated with a couple bouts of expletives when the striker plate wouldn't line up with the latch because of the splintered wood.

Perri and Pearl sat at the kitchen table and scanned through portions of Francis's journal. Pearl was eager to know what story the diary entries had to tell, but seemed to enjoy looking at the account entries most, since they were neatly printed and easier for her to read for herself. She was delighted to see the prices Francis had paid for pairs of boots, new breeches, saddle repair, or one of the best entries, payment to a woman doctor for delivery of the McCade twins.

Perri was astonished. "Wow, that's a really great discovery!" She peered closely at the entry. "It doesn't say midwife, it actually says physician. I wasn't aware there was a female physician living and working in this area so far back."

"Isn't that something?" Pearl seemed both amazed and somehow proud. Maybe it was pride that her ancestor had not harbored ill feelings toward a woman who wanted to work, to provide a service to her community, to use her intelligence to better the lives of those around her no matter the adversity and to do so in a historically male-dominated profession. Peggy Logsdon probably had to face adversity to do so.

There was a reprieve from repair work tension when the hardware finally matched up enough that Nick could repair the damage with wood fill. "This needs to cure for twenty-four hours, so let's hope no one screws around with the door again in the meantime. It really needs to have this section of the wood jamb replaced, or a new frame, because it'll never be right otherwise and always a hazard for easy break-ins. You could keep the original door if we fix the frame."

"Hey, maybe we can find a frame at that Auction Barn place." Perri suggested.

At first Nick opened his mouth to say something about Perri just wanting to go there to ask questions, but instead said, "That's not a bad idea. They did have a lot of old doors and wood stacked up along the side. These older houses, especially one this old, don't use a standard size…anything. I'll take the measurements and we'll see if we can find anything that will fit."

Nick measured the frame then put all his tools back in his toolbox, washed his hands, and said, "All ready to go to the cemetery? It's only a little after two o'clock so we've got plenty of time."

"I'm ready." Pearl scrambled out of her chair as quickly as she was able, obviously eager to go.

"Let's go, then." Perri gathered up her purse and the journal. "Are you leaving your tools here, Nick?"

"No. I like to have them with me in case I need them. As soon as I leave them behind, I'll need something." He hefted the long, black toolbox with one hand and pulled his keys out of his pocket with the other. He turned to look out the door at the backyard. "Sun's out now." He turned back. "I'm ready."

The sun reflected on the puddles in the road in momentarily blinding flashes. The smell of earth and water mixed with pavement and sunshine filled the air. The drive to the cemetery was over in a matter of minutes. Nick parked the Jeep at the edge of the grassy area, near the first row of stones. He nonchalantly glanced over his shoulder then said to Perri, "We might want to steer clear of some of the low areas at the front, they might be muddy after the rain." He smiled endearingly. "Don't want anyone to fall."

"Thanks." Perri answered dryly.

Perri walked next to Pearl as they strolled along the first broken row of stones. She had brought the cemetery map to make it easier to identify the family stones without having to try to read each of them again. Perri stopped and laid her hand on a stone and said to Pearl, "Right here, in the front row, is your great-great-great grandmother's grave. I think she was likely one of the first people buried here. The date is certainly early enough and the burials progressed backward."

Pearl bent forward, Perri held on to her arm to steady her. "Arminda Elouise Grey McCade." She read the remainder of the inscription and stood, just looking at the stone for a while. "She had such a lovely name. I wonder what she looked like." Pearl turned to Perri. "That book didn't have a drawing of Arminda in it, did it?"

"No, it didn't. Occasionally, they do include a woodcut of a wife, but I don't think Arminda lived long enough for that. By the time Francis passed, he would have been married to Nancy longer than he was to Arminda, and Nancy outlived Francis by eleven years."

"How do you know that?" Pearl asked.

Nick answered as he walked through the broken rows. "Because Francis's stone is here. Nancy is buried next to him. Francis died in 1868 and Nancy in 1879."

Pearl seemed disappointed by this, so Perri went on. "It wasn't uncommon at the time. Since Arminda died in 1843, the twins would have only been around seven years old. Men and women both tended to remarry quickly after the death of a spouse. Long courtships just weren't practical, especially not for a single parent with four children."

"I wonder what happened to Arminda. She was only, what, around thirty-four or so?"

"Yes. That wasn't uncommon either. People died from things we don't worry much about. Simple colds could turn to pneumonia. There were no vaccines or antibiotics and many times doctors contributed to a patient's death. Not purposely, but through ignorance of basic things like hand-washing. Aseptic technique would have saved countless women and babies, as well as injured soldiers."

Nick agreed, "I've read about Civil War casualties and how many soldiers died from wound infection rather than directly from the injury itself."

After looking over Francis and Nancy's stone, Pearl pointed to a stone behind it and a few plots down. "What does that stone say? It looks like another 'A' name."

Perri moved through the leaning stones to crouch down next to the stone. The first letter was fairly clear because it was larger and deeper than the other letters, but the rest of the inscription was badly worn. "This is one that we foiled to be able to read. We got the name and dates, but this inscription down here," Perri pointed to at least four lines of italic script, "was unreadable except for a few characters. I can try to enhance it on my computer and I'll check the archive of the most popular epitaphs for the time period to see if we can figure out what this said. Most of these poetic inscriptions were stock phrases, poems, or Bible verses that the family chose from when ordering the stone."

Perri shifted on the wet grass and consulted her map, running her finger along the rows until she found the location of this stone. "The name is, oh, I remember this now. This top part, up here under the vine hanging down, says, *'Wife of H.B. McCade.'* Going by the family tree and another stone in the cemetery, this would have been Hugo Bernard, eldest son of Francis. His wife's name was also Arminda McCade."

"Really? Another Arminda McCade?"

"Yes. This Arminda was born in 1834, no month given, and died in 1892. I haven't had time yet to discover her maiden name. There's a good chance their marriage will be listed in the Illinois

Statewide Marriage Index, depending on where they were married. I can check tonight. If it is listed, her maiden name will be there."

Pearl nodded and said, "Ok. So...wouldn't Hugo be my great-great grandfather then?"

"Yes, he would. You had two grandmothers in succession named Arminda. Hugo's son was Thomas, the one we talked about a little the other day, then on to Morgan who you knew and remember."

"When you put it that way, it doesn't seem like it should be so long ago that Francis lived here, but it was. Of course, I'm constantly made aware that I'm older than I think at times. Lots of daily reminders," she said wistfully. She moved on to the next stone. "Now who is this, do we know?"

Referring back to her map, Perri answered, "This is a Nathaniel Mason and his wife Jane. Going by the birth year for Jane, 1836, I'm wondering if this might be one of Francis's twins, Jane and Jubal. The birth year is right, remember the journal mentions the twins too. Jane is a common name, so it may not be, but it's likely."

Pearl looked thoughtful. "Is the other twin, Jubal, in here somewhere too?"

Nick replied, "If he is buried in this section, which is the adult area, the stone was either unreadable, even with foil, or it's missing. It's also possible he could have died young and is buried in the children's section," Nick pointed to the overgrown area of the cemetery, "back there. There's no telling how many burials are back there and we don't have the time to tackle that jungle."

Perri explained, "A lot of children's stones were quite a bit smaller than those for an adult, and you can see how far down some of these large stones have sunk. I would imagine a lot of the children's stones are completely underground now."

As they finished their walk-through of the cemetery, Nick cautioned Pearl about the loosely refilled hole in the path. She spent some time at her parents' and grandparents' graves. Once on the opposite side of the graveyard, they began working their way back to the front. Pearl stopped and turned to look at one last stone, right on the aisle near the path where Perri had fallen in the open hole.

Perri and Nick stood behind Pearl. *Christian Lee Duncan, b. Feb 13, 1969, d. Jan 08, 1995.*

"Chris's grave must be one of the last, or even the last, in the cemetery. We didn't find any later than 1995," Perri said.

Pearl nodded sadly. "Ruby and George are buried at Elmwood up at Equality. I know Ruby wanted to be here, but..."

"Cemeteries eventually go inactive." She glanced at Nick, then said, "Would you like us to take you by Elmwood to see the grave on the way home?"

"No." Pearl's answer came quickly and sharply. "I thank you, but I just saw it fresh and I don't need to see it again for a while."

"I understand. If you want to go there while I'm still in town, just let me know."

"I appreciate that. I'm sorry, but I think I'm a bit tired."

"We should go." Nick gently took Pearl's arm and supported her back toward the Jeep.

"An old woman needs an escort, doesn't she?" Pearl laughed.

"It has nothing to do with age. Perri took a tumble in here twice in one day. Maybe I should be holding on to her." Nick grinned and Perri smirked playfully in return.

## Chapter 24

October 16, 2016, Afternoon

As Nick was reversing out of the cemetery lane, Pearl started a couple of times to say something, but was hesitating. Stopping at the roadside, Nick asked. "What is it, Pearl?"

"I'm just being fussy. I'm worried about the house. I know it sounds...oh, I don't know. I'm not someone who worries a whole lot about material things except that they're my family heirlooms. I could lose just about everything and I'd make it, but the thought of someone carrying off the things that have been in that house for decades, or a hundred and more years, makes me mad, and sick. It's bad enough that someone would do that just for money, but to think my own daughter might be involved in selling off the family things upsets me. What if she gets arrested? I mean, she'd deserve it, but she's the only family I have left. I keep hoping things will get better someday."

Nick responded. "You're afraid someone will get back in, aren't you?" Pearl nodded. "To be honest, you have a real concern there, because if it is your daughter and her boyfriend who broke in, they know no one is staying there. If they want in, even a new door wouldn't stop them."

"I guess you're right. I just have to … hope they don't go back."

Perri listened with sympathy and not a small amount of anger at the daughter who was willing to plunder the family treasures, most likely because of her boyfriend's influence. "Um, look." Nick looked back over his shoulder. Perri decided to be somewhat opportunistic and take the chance. "Pearl, I don't know, this is just a suggestion, but would you be more at ease if Nick and I stayed at the house for you tonight?" Nick raised his eyebrows in question.

Pearl struggled a bit with her seat belt to turn and be able to see Perri. In an apologetic tone, she said, "I couldn't ask you to do that! I really appreciate it, though, but that's just too much to ask." But her hopeful and somewhat pleading expression was at odds with her words. Perri looked to Nick, who made a face indicating he wasn't against it.

"I don't think it would be too much to ask. After we take you home, we can stop by the apartment and get what we need for the night. I do work tomorrow, but I have a patient in Equality in the morning and it isn't very much further from here as it would be from Eldorado. It isn't like the house has been abandoned for years. It has everything we need. The water and electricity are still on."

Pearl's lips parted into a silent 'oh' as she looked from Nick to Perri. She asked Nick, "Would you be alright with that? I don't want to put you out."

"I'm living out of my suitcase already. I'd be fine with staying at the house. While Perri is at work tomorrow, I'll replace the jamb. There is probably some wood out in the barn, I would imagine, and if not I'll go get some. I can just remove and replace the damaged section rather than look for a frame to fit. I doubt we'd find one and a new frame would have to be custom made anyway."

"Well, I just don't know what to say. I'm all teary-eyed. But, if you really want to do that, there's that guest room at the end of the hall upstairs. It's always made up so it should be fine. But check it and if it needs cleans sheets, the linen closet is in the joining room next to the main bedroom. There'll be some sheet sets in there."

Nick took this as an indication the matter was decided, and turned out on to the road toward Harrisburg.

Cozying up to the idea, Pearl added, "And if you get cold, the thermostat is in that hallway right next to the dining room door. I can't tell you if it needs a pilot light lit or not," she looked at Nick, "but I'm sure you can manage that if you need it and it didn't seem cold in there today. You might want to pick up a little food, or take something with you from your place so you can have coffee and breakfast in the morning before you go to work."

"Alright, then, we'll do it. It sounds fun to me. Can I ask if you would mind if we had a look around, say in the attic or cellar? It would be a great chance to get to know the house more closely, and who knows, maybe I'll find some more of those journals." Perri waited and hoped Pearl would say it was ok.

"I don't know why not as long as you promise to be careful. I don't know what's in the attic or the cellar and I don't want either of you to get hurt."

"We'll be careful."

"If you are wanting to do some of your work, I know you do a lot online, there's probably still the internet in there."

"Ruby and George used the internet?"

"Yes. George didn't sell online but Ruby had told me how he was always talking to people on there and checking on the value of things he found, or trying to find out what ship something might have belonged to."

"That would be great. Thanks for telling us." Perri turned that information over quickly, wondering if the computer was still at the house or had been taken by the police.

After seeing Pearl inside and settled, Perri and Nick headed for Eldorado to pick up what they would need for an overnight stay.

"I can't believe we get to stay in Orchard Parke," Perri said happily. "I wonder how long it's been since that name was used for it."

Nick was grinning and slowly shaking his head. "I don't know how you do it, but you somehow managed to finagle a way, not only into the house, but to spend the night. You'll be up all night."

"It'll be worth it if I am. Think about it though, a two-hundred-year-old house and we get to poke around in the attic! Imagine what could be up there."

"You say that with the same glee many people would use to say they get to go on a weekend trip."

"This is just as good, or better. You know I want to look for the rest of the journals."

"The rest of them?" Nick asked. "I meant to ask you about that when you said it to Pearl."

"There have to be more somewhere. Anyone who writes down a summary of each day and keeps meticulous records of purchases and expenditures didn't do it for only one year. And Francis McCade had been in Shawneetown for seventeen years when he wrote the journal we have."

"That's true, I wouldn't think he'd pick it up and just as suddenly drop it."

"And the journal we have isn't just for 1836, it covers some of 1837 too. Journaling surely was a habit of his." Perri bit her lower lip, then said, "The next thing I have to wonder about is, why did Ruby put just that journal in her cookbook case? Pearl said she figured Ruby was trying to keep George from getting hold of it and selling it, but if that was the case, she'd have to hide all of them."

Nick replied, "Unless she didn't have the others, didn't know where they were? Maybe that one was stored separately. Or George had already sold them and she managed to hang on to one."

"Well, I hope that's not it." Perri nodded slowly, contemplating. "It's a little awkward to aggressively snoop when the owner is there with you, especially after a tragedy like that. I can't help but think we might be able to understand the murders better if we can get an idea what the murderer was looking for, and I just have the gut feeling they didn't find it."

"If he, and let's say 'he' for convenience, was looking for the journals, what are the chances he didn't find them but we will? And if he did find what he was looking for, why take the Duncans all the way to the Salt Well and kill them there?"

"I don't know, unless they came home and caught him, or he had worn a disguise but they recognized him. No one seems to be connecting those particular dots, or any of the dots really. If the police have, I haven't heard of any arrests or any more news about it. Always the same, 'ongoing investigation.' Pearl hasn't mentioned anything about them contacting her to ask more questions or show any progress."

"Sounds like they are just as baffled. Did they search the house?"

"Yes, but according to Pearl, they weren't looking for anything specific, just clues of any sort. Guess nothing seemed to jump out at them. One thing I do wonder about is George's computer. Pearl said George used the internet to chat with people and research his items. I wonder if he told the wrong person about something he had?"

"That's very possible. Lots of scammers and weirdos on the internet." Nick agreed.

"I would think the police took George's computer to check it out and they may still have it. If we see a computer there, I'm going to have a look at it."

It took less than ten minutes to get together the supplies they'd need and load them in the Jeep. Since Perri would need her car in the morning for work, they drove separately back to Old Shawneetown.

Evening had arrived when they arrived back at the house. It was getting dark and, in the dusk, the house with an unsecured door didn't seem quite as inviting to Perri as it had in the daytime. They carried in their bags and a couple small sacks of groceries from the apartment. Perri was turning lights on in the living room when Nick came back from the kitchen. "Door's intact. If anyone comes back tonight, the lights should put them off. I say we leave a few lights on. I'd prefer not to have to fend off an attacker."

"Agreed. I'm going upstairs to get the bedroom ready."

Nick was holding his phone and studying it. "I'll go with you. There's wi-fi here because my phone detects a connection. We'll need to find the password to use it though. If we need to plug into the router, I have an extra ethernet cable in the Jeep."

"A well-prepared man is so sexy!"

"Thank you! Good to know. I'll be even more attentive to that in the future."

Nick took Perri's hand and drew her back toward him as she headed for the stairway. "Let me go first. I want to make sure there are no surprises." He led the way up the stairs, Perri close behind him, both listening as they went.

They had checked each room on the second floor and were satisfied no one else was in the house, at least not on the main or second floor. Perri stripped the sheets off the bed in the guestroom, put them in the washer in the laundry room off the kitchen. The bed didn't appear to have been slept in anytime recently, but while the room was made up and ready for guests, it hadn't been aired or cleaned in quite a while. There was an impressive layer of dust on the furniture and probably the bed also. "No need to use another set. I'll just put these back on the bed. I'll wash them again tomorrow if we only stay tonight."

"If we only stay tonight?" Nick asked as they climbed the stairs back to the second floor.

"I'm just trying to look ahead, you know, in case you can't get the door frame fixed tomorrow or something else comes up. Repair jobs always, always take longer than expected."

"Uh huh." Nick changed the subject. "While you were fixing up the bed, I looked through all the books in the kitchen bookcase to make sure there wasn't another journal there. I didn't see one. I also didn't find a computer in any of the downstairs rooms."

"Ok. Let's look around the bedrooms for one."

A search of each bedroom and the bathroom failed to turn up a computer. Perri declared the search futile. "I don't think it would be hidden if it were here. The police surely would have found it and taken it. If they'd returned it, it would be in an obvious spot, not buried under clothes in a drawer,"

Their footsteps down the length of the upper floor hallway were barely muted by the threadbare carpet runner. Nick placed his hand on the battered knob of the attic door and turned to Perri. "You ready?"

"Are you kidding me?" Perri lightly elbowed Nick in the ribs and darted past him and up the stairs. Each step was tall and shallow because of the steep angle. There were footprints in the dust and dirt on the stairs, but there were many sets that all looked recent, so probably they belonged to the police. Any footmarks left by the murderer would have been photographed and studied, but they were long since muddled by law enforcement traffic.

Perri and Nick stepped a few paces into the attic and looked around. Nick spoke first. "Where do you think we should start?"

Hands on hips, Perri ruminated over the most likely place for journals. "Well...I'm going to say we should start with the small humpback chest and that steamer trunk.

"Which would you prefer to look through?" Nick asked.

"I think I'd like to look at the steamer. It might have some clothing in it and I'd be interested in seeing that too, as long as nothing is making a home in it."

Nick sat down on the floor, his long torso hunched forward, his head bent over the open chest.

Perri knelt in front of the heavy steamer trunk. It was framed with hardwood and reinforced with metal corner caps. Leather bands stretched across the top and sides, now parched and cracking. The domed top and front featured panels of hammered metal with a leaf design. The square metal closure was engraved with an elaborate scrollwork 'M' just below the clasp.

Perri pulled open the now rough and pitted clasp and carefully lifted the lid to its fully open position. The fabric lid restraints on each side had long rotted away, leaving only frayed remnants. Pulling her hands away slowly, the lid remained in place. The stale air of the trunk was sucked out into the room with the motion. She leaned forward and took a long, slow breath. The mixture of paper, cloth, wood, leather, and a lingering powdery echo of perfume drifted up her nostrils.

On the top of the contents was a shirt of loosely woven cotton and decorated with embroidery around the neckline. It was a neatly folded man's shirt in a style popular in the 70s for both men and women. Perri thought perhaps this had belonged to Christopher Duncan and was kept by his grieving parents. She blew away the greater part of the dust on the floor then lifted it out and gently set it down next to her.

Next was a scrapbook that looked like it hailed from the 60s. Held together by slender braided cords with frazzling tassels at the ends, its green and brown cover was unblemished. She opened it just enough to see Christopher's name written in a boyish hand and his birthdate printed beneath it. It had probably been a birthday present. Keeping in mind that her foremost purpose was to find the journals, Perri made herself set it aside, making a mental note to go through it later. Below the scrapbook were two pairs of baby shoes that had been bronzed and mounted to a wooden plaque. The obviously well-worn shoes had belonged to Ruby and Pearl. Worn laces and creases in the leather were preserved for all time in their sheath of metal.

Two cigar boxes were next. The outside was mainly yellow with a red and blue border. Around the border and prominently in the middle was the logo and wording 'King Edward the Seventh, Mild Tobaccos.' They both contained odds and ends: old dog tags, a small magnet, a tin of pencil leads, an old-fashioned lighter, several odd keys, a plastic Ford logo keychain, and several of the largest, most wicked looking safety pins Perri had ever seen.

The second cigar box held, in addition to the detritus of daily living, two pairs of handknit baby stockings. They were in the style of the late 1910s or early 1920s, the main color was black, one pair with pink heels and toes, and the other with red. Either moths or time had gotten to them, they both had a few small holes. The stockings weren't sized large enough for the intended child to have worn them out by walking. They were too early for Pearl or Ruby but they were the right time for their father, Abner, born in 1916. That long ago, pink was not reserved solely for little girls, so it was likely these belonged to him.

"Hey, Perri." Nick's voice broke through the fog of Perri's wonder at the items in the boxes.

"Yeah? Find something?"

With a pleased expression, Nick answered, "Only a bunch of black books like the one you found downstairs."

Perri closed the cigar boxes and set them next to the scrapbook. She crawled across the dust-layered floor and settled next to Nick, peering into the chest. "Isn't that the most beautiful sight?"

Nick looked at Perri, her chestnut brown hair falling forward as she leaned over the chest. She wasn't putting on, she was truly entranced, and so was he, just not for the same reason. He smiled. Perri's delight in discovery was one of the things he loved about her. She wasn't concerned with the material trappings so many women he had dated found of the utmost importance. Besides being an RN and working in the high-tech medical field, Perri was involved in history, family stories, artifacts and she spent time tromping around old cemeteries battling bugs and brambles just to get photographs and information.

He realized Perri was looking back at him with a perplexed look. She asked, "You feeling ok?"

"Yes, just thinking." Nick leaned back toward the contents of the chest. "Are these the other journals?"

"Looks like it. I peeked in a few of them and they're in the same handwriting and are dated. Let's take them downstairs to the dining room table. I want to put them in date order. I wish it wasn't Sunday so I didn't have to work tomorrow. I just want to read through all of these."

"When is your last patient?"

"Three o'clock, and it shouldn't take too long. I have a ninety-minute break between the morning and afternoon, so I could come back here for that too."

"If you think you can do it without cutting it too close, but you wouldn't really have much time to read with the driving time back and forth. They'll be here when you get finished, you know?"

"I know. Well, I can at least get some done tonight." Perri leaned back on her heels while Nick gathered up the small chest, ready to go downstairs.

"As we go, we should make a list of the journals and the dates they cover." She looked at the steamer trunk. "First, I need to put this stuff back in the trunk." While hurriedly replacing the contents, she turned to Nick and said, "You know what, though? Finding all these up here makes it less likely Ruby was trying to hide that other journal from George by putting it with her cook books." She gestured toward the chest full of diaries. "If they were valuable to anyone else, these would have been easily found, either by George or by the person who searched the house, but they're still here. Look how quickly we found them."

"That's true. Maybe she was working her way through reading them and that's the one she was on at the time."

"Could be." Perri closed the trunk lid and latched the rusty clasp. "We may never know that."

Nick carried the small chest down the steeply pitched attic stairs. Behind him, Perri pressed the round doorbell-like button to turn off the attic lights and shut the door.

Once in the dining room, they arranged the leather covered books in a double row along the table. Nick commented, "That is a lot of reading. I don't think it matters that you have to work tomorrow, it's going to take a while to get through all that."

Perri nodded in agreement. "They may have been stored in chronological order. You can tell which are probably the oldest by looking at the covers. Those at that end are more worn. The black leather looks almost brown, lots of wear, maybe from the newer books being stored on top of them. Let's start there."

They each pulled a chair up to the head of the table. Perri selected one of the volumes that had been on the bottom of the chest. "I need to get that letter opener that Pearl had." She shifted forward in her chair to scoot back but Nick got up first.

"I'll go get it." Nick offered. "You go ahead and get started."

"Ok, she put it back in the small drawer at the end of the counter."

Nick returned in a few seconds and handed the letter opener to Perri. "This kind of makes me nervous all over again. This one may be sixteen or seventeen years older than the one we've already looked at. I don't want to damage them. If these earliest volumes look too fragile to read I'll have to talk to Pearl about taking them to a conservationist, or at least someone qualified to handle them. I'm hoping it's just the cover that's in this shape and not the inside."

She slipped the thin blade under the cover and lifted.

## Chapter 25

October 17, 2016, 4:00 p.m.

Perri sped down the highway toward Old Shawneetown. The work day couldn't go fast enough for her. She was glad it was finally done. She had seen Pearl in the morning and told her about the other journals. Pearl was eager to find out what they said and Perri had explained to her that it might take some time to do that. She promised to make notes as she went along so she could give Pearl a summary of the story as it unfolded. Then she could fill in with more detail about the parts Pearl wanted to hear.

Nick had called and left a message around noon. When Perri called him back, he described his morning removing the damaged door jamb. His next step was to collect the materials he would need to replace it, but he'd found a lot of rot behind it where water had seeped in over the years and deteriorated the framework around the door. He said there was nothing substantial enough to serve as an anchor for the new wood. He wanted to know if Pearl wanted him to do that or contact someone certified to work on historic homes. Pearl had said to go ahead and Nick decided he'd temporarily remove the jamb on the undamaged side and do his best to mirror it. Provided it wasn't also water damaged, it shouldn't be too difficult a job. Famous last words, Perri thought. That was like saying, 'It'll only take ten minutes' or uttering the forbidden words, 'Sure is quiet on the Unit tonight' in a hospital.

She felt a twinge of guilt that she was just a little thrilled that she and Nick got to stay in the house another night. She wouldn't have been as happy there by herself, murderer aside. The aged house creaked, popped, snapped, and groaned throughout the night as the temperature changed. The roof timbers had the ability to sound exactly like someone landing on the roof after jumping out of a tree. The odd noises had kept her awake for a while, but she'd eventually fallen asleep, snuggled next to Nick who appeared to have zero difficulty, falling asleep in about thirty seconds.

She pulled the Mini behind Nick's Jeep. The day had been chilly and damp and was getting colder. She was met with a rush of warmth as she stepped through the front door, closing it quickly behind her, suddenly getting a shiver. "My gosh, it feels good in here."

She heard Nick's steps coming toward the living room. "Hey there! How'd your day go?"

"Uhh, good, but I'm chilled." Nick wrapped his warm arms around her and gave her a hug. "That feels a lot better. I could just stay right here...but I need to get these scrubs off and get a shower. I always feel like I'm dragging home a thousand organisms, which I am."

Nick backed away. "Enough said. I picked up something for supper when I went to get the wood for the frame. Why don't you go get your shower? I'll put on some coffee and get the food in the oven?"

"I could get really used to this."

"All I need now is an apron." Nick headed back to the kitchen, calling over his shoulder, "Get me the ruffly kind. I like those."

Wrapped in her warm robe, her feet ensconced in thick socks, Perri settled at the kitchen table opposite Nick. As they ate their hot and spicy stir fry and rice, they went over what they'd read in the journals the night before.

Nick started. "We know that Francis McCade came to Illinois from Kentucky, because he described crossing the Ohio on the ferry."

"Right. It would have been Ford's Ferry at that time. He talked about meeting several other men on the road, which we also know would have been a dangerous place, especially that one. Ford's Ferry Road was infamous for bandits. I'm stoked that he mentioned Potts' Inn. There are lots of stories about that place. Local stories claim the owners of the Inn would kill guests so they could take their money and valuables."

"Travel back then was a gamble, including staying at an Inn apparently."

Perri reached for her notebook, still on the table, and flipped it open. "So far, in May of 1819, we have Francis arriving in Illinois and spending the first night at Potts' Inn, but leaving unaccosted the next morning, unlike many travelers who had the misfortune to stay there and never leave."

"A nineteenth century Hotel California." Nick quipped.

Perri smiled in agreement, "Sort of, yes, just minus the pink champagne." She took another bite of her food and chewed. Eager to talk about it and comfortable enough with Nick not to adhere to strict dining etiquette of swallowing all her food before talking, she said, "He mentions having a conversation with AM and AS that night in the Inn and doing some type of business with them, although he doesn't describe it in any detail. What he does say is that he had to unpack his bag and rearrange it before he could fit in the packet of papers. Hopefully, the other journals will help us determine who AM and AS are. He doesn't say it outright, but he doesn't appear to have known them beforehand. It sounds like they may have been part of the group he met on the road, since they were all staying in the same Inn."

"Either Francis didn't have anything worth taking or there was another reason for letting him go"

"Based on 'AM' showing up regularly in other entries, I'd say after they met on the road they worked out some sort of arrangement because Francis mentions meetings with AM fairly regularly. Their meetings continued through the years, sometimes with longer stretches in between, but so far they always resume."

"It never says exactly what they talked about or did though. You think it was something under the table and Francis didn't want to commit it to writing or he just didn't think it important enough to write down?"

Perri swallowed her bite of food and took a sip of water. "My gut tells me it was under the table. He obviously held other jobs that were respectable and above-board. He worked for a couple of newspapers, then a bank. I already knew that from the archived newspaper articles I found and in old bios at the research library. Francis had been doing rather well for himself. I do have to wonder if some of the income is coming from a source other than his day job. And too, he isn't one to skimp on words when it's something he wants to describe."

Nick agreed, "That's true, he gave a vivid account with a lot of historical information when he described General Lafayette's visit to Shawneetown. Pearl will be pleased with that."

"I think she will too, especially because Francis met him and shook his hand. And it's a bit romantic that Francis mentions Arminda in 1825 because they didn't marry until 1830. We'll see if he mentions any other ladies, but he seems to have homed in on Arminda early on."

Nick asked, "What date are we up to?"

"We're scanning through quickly. I intend to take the time to read them word-for-word, but since we're looking for anything that'll help us understand what might have led to the Duncan's deaths, and not just having an enjoyable read, it would take too long. I think Pearl will give me the chance to study them longer." Wiping her mouth with her napkin and taking her plate to the sink, Perri sat back down and reviewed her notes so far. "We've gotten through five journals, ending in September of 1830. Arminda and Francis were just married in July of 1830, they were newlyweds at the time, and are living in a house somewhere in Shawneetown. He doesn't give an address in the front of this one, maybe he will in another, but I doubt it. The article I read about the house said it was built in 1830-1831, so they probably lived in this first house a short time, maybe only while they were building Orchard Parke."

Referring to her abbreviated notations, she continued, "Francis was obviously distressed that his job in the bank was put on hold when it temporarily ceased operations. He was doing well for himself and this was a big stumbling block in his plan for success. He doesn't mind prattling on about *that* in his diary. That's when he bought a share in the salt works. Coincidentally, his meetings with AM picked up the frequency around then."

"Right," Nick mulled over the limited information they had on AM. "I'm wondering. This AM doesn't appear to live in Shawneetown or Francis wouldn't have to go to Potts' Inn to meet him. The salt works were northwest of Potts' Inn, but still the meeting frequency increased. I would say AM lived somewhere west of Francis, and when Francis became involved in the salt works they were able to meet more often."

"That makes sense, I agree. Around this time, the two seem to have had a couple instances of arguing, not agreeing on something, whatever, because he writes a little ambiguously about continuing their business relationship. But I have to wonder if they were also friends, because Francis seems to be musing over it more than someone would an arrangement that was strictly business. It sounds more like a personal squabble is the cause of the discord. Without coming out and saying it, they had a falling out for a while and it bothered Francis. He mentions a man in his employ accompanying him on his trips to meet with AM."

Giving Nick the date, he found the appropriate journal entry and read it aloud, "*Meeting today tense. WR accompanied me. AS with AM. Not pleased with need to involve others in meetings. Settled amiably enough today, but AM must come to realization we had an agreement and it stands. No need for continued controversy.*"

"Sounds like he was worried about something, whether it was having a witness or just someone else physically present. For whatever reason, he thought it best to have company even though he didn't want to."

"It appears AM felt the same way, since he's bringing along AS again. At any rate, it didn't stop them from meeting and they must have cleared the air because they resumed meeting alone in the future. Whatever they were doing was profitable enough to get past a disagreement or two."

"Which is weird, because Francis seems to have been held in such high esteem by ... well everyone, as far as we can tell from all the sources you've found."

"That doesn't mean he wasn't doing something illegal or unsavory."

"True."

Perri stood and took their plates and utensils. "I'll wash up. Why don't you get the next journal and start reading it aloud? It won't take me long here. We can get our coffee and I'll take it from wherever you leave off."

Nick left the room to retrieve the next unread journal from where they still lay in chronological order on the dining room table. Perri stood at the sink which was situated in front of a window overlooking the back yard and field between the Duncan and Vincent houses. It was pitch black outside and all she could see was a rectangle of light from the Vincent's kitchen window across the backyards and shared field, and her own reflection. She tried to imagine looking out of this window over the orchard, garden, and horse stable as it might have looked in 1831. The water turned hot, she pushed down the drain stopper, added dish soap, and swished her hand around to make more bubbles. As she was scrubbing the first plate, she looked back up to the window just in time to see a face quickly vanish from within a couple feet of the glass.

Nick was walking out of the dining room when Perri's startled scream pierced the otherwise quiet calm in the house and brought Nick racing back.

He skidded to a stop directly behind her. "What? What happened?" Perri didn't answer right away, just stood still, hands covered with suds and dripping. "Did you cut yourself, or…?"

"No. Someone was just outside. Someone was looking in the window. I was…" Before she finished, Nick was dashing through the doorway. He was back in a few seconds. "Damn! I need a flashlight. It's like being underground out there tonight."

"There's one under here." Perri bent and opened the cabinet beneath the sink, her hands dripping spots of soapy water over the floor. "I saw it when I got out the dish detergent. Here."

Nick snatched it out of her hands and ran back out the door. Perri wiped her hands on the flour sacking dishtowel. A little worried that someone might try to come back through the less than stable door while Nick was outside, she pulled a carving knife out of the wide utensil drawer and stood with her back to the corner of the cabinets.

She could hear Nick shouting. "Oh, good grief, what now?" She hesitantly put the huge knife on the counter and ran on tip toes through the short hallway. She didn't want to be a typical horror movie cliché, but she also didn't want to trip and stab herself. She passed the stairs and into the living room and peeked out through the tall windows. The front porch light was on, so a portion of the front yard was visible. She couldn't see Nick, but she could see the flashlight he carried bobbing up and down as he ran along the road away from the house. She chewed on her thumbnail, hoping he wasn't going far and wondering if she should go back and get the knife she'd left on the counter. What if the man returned and came in the rear door then picked up the handy knife she'd kindly left lying out for him. If it was the same person who killed the Duncans, it could turn out badly.

She didn't have to fret for too long. Before she turned to hightail it back to the kitchen, she could see the wobbling round glow of the flashlight returning to the house. She opened the front door for Nick as he got nearer. "What happened? Who were you yelling at?"

Nick was slightly out of breath, not so much from running but from the adrenalin glut. "Damn it! I wish I could have caught that slimeball. You saw him, right?"

"Only briefly. I mean, like a split second. It was enough to see it was a male, dark hair, but that's it. Even then, his face was a moving blur."

"I don't think there's too much of a mystery about who it was. He ran out to that same silver Buick Century. He wasn't alone and I'm sure his companion is someone you would know. The car started moving before he got the passenger door all the way open, so he had to jog with the door open for several feet. When the dome light came on, I could see a woman with her hair in a ponytail behind the wheel and the guy with the black stringy hair jumped in beside her. They took off. I was trying to get a license plate number but the lights around the plate are so dim I couldn't see it."

Perri's jaw was set in resolve. "Let's call it in. The police could easily find out the plate number. We know the car belonged to the Duncans so it'll be in the BMV records. Call it in for skulking around the house and peeping in and for stealing the car! Pearl said they had to have broken in to get the keys, so maybe they can be charged with breaking and entering too."

Nick looked at Perri for a moment. "Do you think we should call Pearl first? Remember, she didn't want to report it until she talked to her daughter."

"Yeah, I'm startin' to not care too much about giving the daughter a chance to explain herself. She's a loser. Sorry, but she is." Perri frowned, her brows drawing together. "And this is getting tiresome."

Nick raised his eyebrows in an expression of uncertainty. "Why don't you ask Pearl tomorrow and if she agrees, we can call then? It won't change anything tonight, and those two aren't going anywhere. They probably came back here to get in and take things, or whatever they plan on doing, but when they saw the cars and lights they knew they couldn't. Apparently, curiosity got the better of the guy…what's his name…why can't I remember it?"

"Eric. Because Eric is just a loser and completely forgettable, that's why." Perri answered indignantly.

"He couldn't resist having a peep in and got caught. Kind of funny, really. I don't think they're coming back tonight." Nick tried to lighten the situation.

Still sober, Perri asked, "Nick, do you think they may have killed the Duncans? I know they were Stella's aunt and uncle, but judging by the way she treats her mother, she doesn't seem like someone who cherishes familial relationships. And they keep turning up at this house like turkey vultures circling roadkill. They can't wait to get in here and haul things off. So far, they've at least taken a car and the Hoosier cabinet that Pearl said was missing. And by the way, I wonder if the truck they used was from that hauling business Stella works for sometimes to move the Hoosier cabinet. Those things aren't small and they seem to be driving the car all the time."

"If he's the car thief Pearl paints him as, maybe he stole the truck to do the hauling."

Perri huffed in exasperation. "No telling what else they've made off with that hasn't been noticed yet. And Pearl did say that Stella thought the house should have been left to her. I guess she feels she is entitled to sell off what she wants."

Nick thought about it, then replied, "As far as the Duncans go, they can't be ruled out, but they aren't exactly professionals, are they? I mean, they've been driving around for days in a stolen Buick Century that's a decade or more old. If they have a truck, why drive the stolen vehicle?" Nick chuckled a little. "I'm sorry, but what are the chances those two clownhorns pulled off and would get away with a double murder without leaving enough clues to get them caught?"

Perri relaxed a tiny bit. "True. For Pearl's sake, I won't call tonight, but I'll nail that Stella character to a wall the first chance I get."

Nick grinned but declined comment. Perri added, "And her greasy boyfriend too."

"Come on, let's read some more diary entries."

\*\*\*

Two hours later, Perri was yawning and struggling to keep her eyes focused on the spidery handwriting.

"Why don't we stop for the night?" Nick stood up and stretched his six-foot-two frame and rolled his head from shoulder to shoulder. "I'm about done for and I still need to secure that back door for the night."

Perri screwed her face up in concern. "Oh yeah. What are you going to do since there's nothing to secure it to?"

"I'll have to put a piece of plywood over it, or at least a couple two-by-fours across so the door can't open. I don't like blocking an exit, but I can't leave it unlatched and open all night."

"No, don't do that."

"I'll leave the tools on the table so I could easily get the boards off in an emergency."

Perri sighed and stretched her arms over her head. "Alright, I'm going to turn in while you do that. I have a shorter day tomorrow, thank goodness. Before I come back here, I'm going to stop by the library in Harrisburg and look for any newspaper reports of this incident we read about tonight, the one where Francis organized a search party for the guys that robbed his father-in-law. Wouldn't you think that would be big enough news to make the newspaper, especially in 1836?"

"I would think so. It's worth checking out. Having newspaper documentation to back up the journals will be helpful. It gives credence to the other things Francis talks about. We know the story about Lafayette visiting the town was true because that's been documented. So far, he seems accurate."

"What I'm wondering is why the meeting between Francis and AM stopped suddenly. Does it have anything to do with the 1836 incident? Because there are no more meetings after that and he hasn't mentioned AM again."

"True. Maybe it will answer your question about what Francis was up to, or it may create more questions. I hope you find something."

"Me too." Perri gave a protracted yawn, pushed her chair under the table and gave Nick a kiss. She headed for the stairs. "Good night."

"I'll be up shortly."

## Chapter 26

October 18, 2016

Eager to find something reported in the old papers, Perri loaded the reel of microfilm at the same viewing station she'd occupied the last time. It wasn't a very big reel of film. The Illinois Advertiser newspaper had only been published from 1836-1837. Another newspaper, the Western Voice, had begun publishing in 1836.

The incident had occurred in late February. It didn't take long to find what she was looking for. This event had probably been the highlight of the season and the headline screamed from the page in bold letters. As she read, she could feel her heart rate revving up. After printing the article and confirming it was clear and complete, she quickly scanned the remaining days on the film. The entire volume of the Advertiser was not present, most copies probably having been lost. Mainly, the articles were about the bank resuming its business, agriculture reports, and saccharine accounts of social life in Shawneetown. However, toward the end, there was a concise paragraph stating that Francis McCade had been found completely blameless in the death that resulted during the arrest of the bandits and was honored by society as a hero for the town.

After printing the last article, Perri placed the film in the returns box and was just about to leave when she had an idea. Stepping into the restroom so she wouldn't bother the other patrons, she called Nick.

It rang several times before a slightly breathless Nick answered, "Yeah? Hello?" This was followed by a loud clunk and a curse.

"You ok? Sorry, did I call at a bad time?"

"No, yes, no, just hopping over tools to get to the phone. What's up?"

"I'm at the library but, before I leave, I thought I'd check for something else if you can do me a favor."

"Sure, what do you need?"

"I think I left in a daze this morning and didn't bring all my notes with me. Will you look at my map of Gold Hill Cemetery and tell me exactly what year Arminda McCade died, the one married to Francis? I know it was after 1840 but can't remember if it was 1842 or 1843 and I don't want to spend time scrolling through the wrong roll of film. My bag is still in the dining room."

"Ok, hang on." Perri heard tools being moved around, footsteps, then rustling. "Here it is." Nick flipped through the notebook to find the map. "Ok…Arminda McCade, front row and center. She died in 1843. Doesn't give a month."

"That's good enough. I'm going to check for a paper from that time, see if they have the microfilm and try to locate an obituary. Maybe we can find out what happened to her. Something that I did find is an article about Hubert Gray's attack, Arminda's father."

"Great! What did it say?"

"It's an interesting story with Francis McCade right in the middle of it. I have a copy of it to show you when I get home. It'll have more impact if you read it rather than me tell it."

"Ok, I'll get back to work. See you soon."

Seated at one of the computer stations, Perri searched the Illinois Newspaper Project for papers published in Shawneetown in 1843. The Illinois Republican and Western Voice were most likely published then, and the Illinois State Gazette certainly was, but the Harrisburg library didn't have those issues on microfilm. Per the information about the extant copies, she'd have to either go to the Abraham Lincoln Presidential Library in Springfield, IL or she could order an interlibrary loan for the microfilm. The latter was clearly the best option, so she filled out the request form and turned it in at the desk.

Since they didn't have the wi-fi password at Orchard Parke, she did a rapid check of the Illinois Statewide Marriage Index on the Illinois Secretary of State's website. No entries for Hugo McCade or Arminda Mason came up in Gallatin County, or any other county in Illinois. Groaning inwardly, she figured they either married somewhere else, maybe in Kentucky, or the record was lost or overlooked when the database was input. Or, one or both names were misspelled, which meant a lot of trial and error to make the same mistake the transcriber had made. She had also found records where the given name and surname were reversed, such as a James Allen might be entered as Allen James. It didn't seem likely in this case, but she tried it anyway before she left. No cigar.

On a whim, rather than go directly back to the house, Perri drove to Eldorado first. She stopped in at the apartment and checked her mailbox, which was empty, of course. She picked up another pair of scrubs, in case they got to stay another night. She hoped they did. It was probably imposing to stay. Even with the unwanted visitations from Stella and Eric, she was thoroughly enjoying the old house and reading the journals in the very rooms where Francis may have written most of them.

As she sat in the left turn lane at the stoplight at the intersection of highways 142 and 45, she was dumbfounded to watch the silver Buick Century pass through the intersection right in front of her, headed toward downtown Eldorado. Stella Paulson sat in the drivers' seat with the confidence possessed only by those unfettered by sympathy or conscience. She breezed through the intersection completely unperturbed to be driving a murdered couple's stolen vehicle. Perri had broached the subject with Pearl when she saw her to check her blood sugar, but Pearl still didn't want to call the police, not until she talked to Stella, but she hadn't been able to reach her and she certainly hoped nothing was wrong. Perri grumbled to herself that the only thing wrong was she didn't want to be arrested. Stella obviously didn't want to be contacted. Perri had resisted an impatient sigh and what would have been a thoroughly satisfying eyeroll.

She watched the car as far as she could. Then, looking over her right shoulder and seeing no approaching traffic, Perri cranked the wheel hard and scooted over from the turn lane, squeaking just behind a car in the forward lane, making it into the right turn lane just as the light turned green. She drove slowly up State Street, looking left and right at the intersections. When she reached Locust, she turned right, since this was the main access to the downtown area. If she didn't find Stella here, she could drive a little further down State Street, but it seemed most likely she'd be going downtown.

She drove past Watson Funeral Home, where she'd come for the funeral of several family members over the years. No sign of the Buick yet. She paused briefly at the stop sign where five streets intersected. From her vantage point at the stop sign, Perri could see the Buick parked smack dab in front of Fuller Properties on the street just ahead.

"Uh huh! I knew something was fishy." Perri exclaimed aloud to herself. She passed the car and parked in the next available spot, five spaces down. "I knew there was something going on. Realtors don't leave their card with someone for nothing." She sat in her car, eyeing the second story windows, not sure what she wanted to do next. "Come on, think. What excuse can I use to go inside?" She tapped the fingers of both hands on the steering wheel to the beat of the Green Day song playing on the radio.

Deciding on a ruse, Perri jumped out of the car and bounded up the stairs, eager to find out what Stella was doing there. She swung the door open, almost with the expectation of revealing a clandestine meeting between people who should not be meeting, to find Wanda at her desk, on the phone as usual. She looked up and waved at Perri, giving her a wide, bright smile. Timothy, or what was probably Timothy, visible only as a khaki-covered rear end sticking out beyond the edge of a desk as he struggled with the contents of a bottom drawer in a filing cabinet. No one else was in the room, so Stella must be back in Bethany's office. 'Mm hmm,' Perri thought to herself.

Hearing the door whoosh shut, Timothy stood up, his face reddened from the exertion of bending forward, his glasses rested near the end of his nose. He pushed them back up and greeted Perri. "Hi." He dragged his hands through his sandy brown hair to smooth it. "What can I help you with?"

"Hi Tim, how are you today?"

"Oh, I'm good. Thanks. You?"

"Doing great, thanks."

Timothy stared at Perri, obviously a little perplexed, and waited.

"The reason I came by is just to ask a quick question. I was on my way home from work so I figured now's as good a time as any."

"Yeah, sure. I've just been, oh, well, no, it's fine. What is it you wanted to ask?"

"It's nothing urgent, really. My washing machine, in the apartment I mean, just shut off while I was doing a load of laundry the other day. I've done a couple loads since then, and it was fine, but I'm wondering, if it happens again, does Beth have any specific repair shop she prefers that I call, or should I just call here?" Perri kept an eye and ear on the hallway leading to Beth's office. She could just hear the murmur of voices, but couldn't make out what was being said.

"Let me see if I can get you a phone number. We have a book of vendors that we use for repairs and cleaning, things like that. Hang on, I'll look."

"Ok, thanks."

Perri meandered toward Beth's office, as casually as possible, while Timothy unearthed a large 3-ring binder from beneath his desk. She walked over to a potted rubber plant situated at the entrance to the hallway where it struggled toward the light of the windows. She toyed with the leaves for a moment, listening, but still couldn't discern anything being said. She heard a chair scrape across the floor and the door flung open unexpectedly.

With no time to scuttle back to Timothy's desk, within a couple of seconds, Perri was face-to-face with a very flustered-appearing Stella who stormed out of Beth's office. Stella stopped dead in her tracks and glared at Perri. She snorted and took off again. Perri feigned total surprise, although she was a little startled at being caught out so close to the office door.

Beth appeared in the doorway behind Stella. She stopped short when she saw Perri. Just as Beth opened her mouth to say something, Timothy said, "Here it is, Perri."

Perri dodged any questions from Beth by darting back over to the desk. Timothy was scribbling the name of an appliance repair shop on a piece of paper, along with the number. Stella's footsteps were pounding down the stairway. Perri hastily took the paper from Timothy and thanked him as she backed toward the door. "Thank you so much! I appreciate it, I'm sure it may have just been a fluke and won't happen again, but I'm glad to have this. Thanks." She shut the office door behind her and ran down the steps after Stella. If she lost sight of her, she could always follow the malodorous trail of stale smoke.

Perri reached the outside door just as it slammed shut. It pushed her back a step. She regained her balance and flung it open again, lurching out onto the pavement. She was looking up the street, toward the parked cars, trying to spot Stella, when her head was snapped back by someone grabbing a handful of her hair and yanking it. The paper Timothy had given her floated out of her hand, remaining poised in the same airspace it had previously occupied as her hand disappeared, jerked along with the rest of her. Her purse dropped from her shoulder to her forearm and slid down. She caught it in her fist and swung it around. The gratification of the solid thump the contact made with her attacker renewed her resolve to keep a purse containing something for every situation.

"You nosy bitch! I knew you were trouble the first time I saw you. Why are you following me?"

"Hey! Let … go … of my hair." Perri swung around and was winding up to hit Stella with her purse again. The fist tightened in her hair and yanked her head up. Obviously, this was not Stella's first rodeo as far as catfighting went. "Shit." Perri's eyes watered.

"I asked you why you're following me?" Stella wrenched twice, hard, on Perri's hair. "I didn't hear an answer," came her taunting voice, accompanied by breath tinged with Eau de Cheap Wine and something fried and greasy.

"Ok, you asked for it." Perri had twisted to face Stella and, even though her head was up and back, nearly immobile with Stella holding two fists full of her hair, Perri had full use of her own hands. She had a clear view of Stella's bony chest where the stretched-out neck of her t-shirt hung low, worn under a conveniently unzipped jacket.

Stella yanked upward again. "Yeah? Come on, I'm waiting, Nosy Nurse." Her laugh was more of a dry rattle.

At that moment, the door flung open behind them and Timothy and Wanda squeezed through the door together, popping out onto the sidewalk in unison.

"Ok, then." Perri brought up her fist with two knuckles raised and dug them into Stella's superior mediastinum. "There you go! Sternal rub for Stella!" Stella immediately let go of Perri's hair. Perri's face was flushed and tears brimmed in her eyes. She shouted back, "Hey Stella, that worked for me! That work for you?"

"What's going on?" Timothy asked.

Perri glared at Stella, who threw her a scathing look in return. "You alright?" Wanda asked, walking to Perri and put a hand on her arm.

"Yes, I'm fine." Perri tried to smooth her hair down. "Thanks, Wanda."

Beth stepped through the door and joined the others. "What's happening here?"

Timothy asked again, "What's this about?" and eyed Stella warily.

The way Stella puckered her lips together, Perri thoroughly expected her to spit on the sidewalk. Instead, she said, "None of your business."

"We were ironing out a previous disagreement, getting some things off our chest, so to speak. That's all." Perri rubbed her scalp on the crown of her head while squinting at Stella through narrowed eyes.

Stella poked a finger close to Perri's face and said, "This nosy-ass bitch has been poking around my family's house and asking my mother all kinds of questions."

Three pairs of eyes turned on Perri, awaiting a response. "I have not been poking around uninvited, Stella!" Perri turned to Beth, Timothy, and Wanda. "I'm getting information to write an article about Stella's mother's house…"

"Oh, shut your pie hole! I'm sick of hearing that. You just want to get inside and stick your nose in everything. What are you going to do? You stealing from my mom?"

Amazed that Stella went there, Perri retorted, "Not at all, but let's talk about stealing, shall we, Stella?" She turned and pointed toward the Buick. "Let's talk about that car you drove up in."

Stella shook her head side to side, smirking, but didn't say anything.

"Look, this is silly. Let's just stop it. Your mother wants to talk to me about the house and her family history. She enjoys it and so do I. You certainly won't have anything to do with it unless there's something in it for you. She invited me to do the research and she's the one who gets to make that decision. So just cut the crap."

"What research is her mother having you do?" Beth asked, ignoring Stella.

"Some family research, her genealogy, historical information about the family home in Old Shawneetown."

Beth nodded, "I see. You said you're writing an article about it? For a magazine or …?"

"For an online genealogical magazine, yes. A friend of mine co-owns the website and asked me to write something. Anyway, the house now belongs to Pearl Gentry, Stella's mother, and she has authorized me to…"

"Blah, blah, blah. You're a nosy pig."

"That's not really called for here, Stella. This isn't a dive bar at last call." Timothy said sternly. Perri swiveled her head around in surprise. Then to Perri, he asked, "You're gathering information about the house for the article? And Mrs. Gentry wants you to do this?"

"Yes, that's right."

Tim nodded thoughtfully. Beth asked, "What kind of things are you looking for in the house?"

Perri tried not to betray that she knew Beth had been talking to Pearl about the house, but she carefully watched Beth's face as she answered. "The house's general history, special architecture, information about the family and their history in the area, any remaining artifacts from the early days of the house. They were an interesting bunch, especially the man who built the house, Pearl's ancestor. He was apparently quite a character."

Timothy remarked, "That would have been quite a long time ago, are you able to find out much about it?"

"Surprisingly, yes, considering limited sources." Perri didn't want to mention the journals.

"It sounds like a good idea, Stella. Why are you opposed to it?" Beth remarked.

Stella looked from each person to the next. Abruptly, she brazenly shoved her way between Beth and Wanda, causing Beth to take several quick steps backwards, then marched off toward the car. "Just piss off, all of you. You're all alike. Bunch of meddling morons."

In the wake of Stella's abrupt departure, as the stunned knot of people watched her come as close to squealing out of the parking space as the Buick was able, Wanda softly asked Perri, "What did you mean about the car? 'Cause I recognize that, it was George Duncan's car. He drove the van if he was bringing stuff to be sold, but he drove that car the other times."

Beth and Timothy both turned to Perri in anticipation as Stella roared off down the north end of Locust Street at 30 mph, blue smoke chugging out of the exhaust pipe.

"So, the car?" Beth prompted.

"According to Stella's mother, the car was taken from the Duncan's house without her knowledge or permission."

"Have the police been called?" Timothy asked, concerned.

Perri shook her head. "Her mother doesn't want it reported, not yet anyway."

"Have they stolen anything else?"

"They?" Wanda asked Beth.

Beth replied, "Oh, come on, everybody knows Stella hangs around with that Massey dude. He's bad stock. And I can't see Stella stealing a car on her own. Right?" She gestured the direction Stella had gone. "She had trouble getting it out of the parking spot."

Perri said nothing but nodded affirmatively. Wanda murmured, "Sober drivin's probably new to her."

"That's not right!" Timothy looked genuinely shocked and offended. "Have they stolen anything else?"

"As a matter of fact, they have. They took an antique cabinet from the kitchen. And they broke in the back door to do it. Nick and I are staying there, at Pearl's request," she added quickly, bending it just a little, "until it's fixed. The entire frame has to be replaced because the jamb just splintered to pieces."

"You're staying in the McCade house, the Duncan house rather?" Beth asked.

"Yes, Pearl was worried about it sitting unsupervised with the back door accessible. I think she was afraid to ask us, so we offered and she took us up on it. Oh, and the original official name of the house, at least during the mid-1800s, was Orchard Parke."

"It's nice of you to do that. I'm sure Pearl appreciates it. How do you know what the house was called?" Beth asked.

"It was written in … um, an original ledger that was left in the house."

"Oh." Beth replied, thoughtfully. "That's great, to find something contemporary to the house."

"I agree with Tim, honey," Wanda said to Perri. "The police need to be called. Maybe you can convince Mrs. Gentry to do that before those two rob her blind." She patted Perri's arm again and sighed. Reluctantly, she said to the others, "We'd better get our pitooties back up to the office."

The trio lingered a moment, then made for the door, hesitant to return to work. Perri said, "Sorry for the dustup. I had no idea she was going to waylay me."

"Girl, don't you worry about it, it was the highlight of our day. Least I think so." Wanda snorted a laugh and the others chuckled along. "Why don't you and that man of yours come by the barn again some evening? Give me an excuse to take a break."

"Will do." Wanda released the door behind her, but before it closed, Perri reached for it and called out to her, "Hang on, Wanda, that reminds me." Wanda turned and stopped the door from closing, poking her head back out. "We intended to call you about it. The Hoosier cabinet that was stolen from the house…if anyone shows up with it wanting to sell it, could you go ahead and accept it but call either me or Pearl Gentry? That's a cherished heirloom and she would really like to get it back if she can."

"I sure will, you can count on it. And I gotta tell ya, if they do, I'm tempted to call the police and report someone bringing in stolen property, but I'll hold off on that and call one of you first," Wanda agreed as she waved and started the climb up the stairs, using the worn railing to pull herself along.

Perri retrieved the dropped paper with the appliance store information on it from a grate in the sidewalk. She ducked into the Mini, suddenly self-conscious and wondering how many people had watched the brawl from store and office windows. She rested her forehead on the steering wheel. "Oh, good lord. Just don't let it get all over town." Realizing it was doubtlessly already all over town, she started the car and aimed for Orchard Parke. As she drove, she ran through the encounter and conversation, trying to glean any information from the responses.

Back at the house, Perri chucked her work bag into the corner of the foyer, kicked off her shoes, and headed toward the sound of an electric drill. Nick was finishing up the new fortified door frame. He turned toward her when she entered the kitchen, a light coating of wood dust on his hair and face. "Just have to rehang the door now that the new hardware is installed." He brushed his hands off on his jeans and gave her a kiss. "How did your day go?"

"Oh, it was ok." Perri didn't look him in the eye. Instead she took a glass from the cabinet and filled it with tap water, taking a long drink.

"Uh huh. That was noncommittal. Anything interesting happen?"

"No." Unpleasantly aware that she wasn't going to be able to avoid telling him about the fracas with Stella, she sighed and said, "Not unless you call getting into a knock-down-drag-out on Locust street interesting."

"You? You got into a skirmish?" He was obviously trying not to laugh. "With who?"

"Stella! She ambushed me as I came out of the door from the rental agency."

"Ambushed you?" Nick thought a second. "What were you doing at the rental agency?"

"Alright, I was following Stella, but she didn't know that."

"It sounds like she did."

"Hey, I had developed a very plausible reason for being there."

Nick pulled a chair out from the table for Perri and said, "Let's hear it," then deposited himself in another.

Perri flopped down in the chair, and crossed her arms and ankles. "I said the washing machine shuddered to a stop the other day and I wondered if the agency had a preferred repair shop in case I needed to call one." Nick didn't say anything, just stared at her, smiling. Perri dug the paper out of her scrubs pocket. "See! Here's the place they recommend."

"Ok, alright. How did you come to be following her?"

Perri described seeing Stella swan through the intersection, plain as day. "Now, why do you think Stella was there talking to Beth? Do you think Beth might be trying to get Stella to put some pressure on Pearl to sell the house? She's obviously been there to talk to her since she left her business card on the table. And they didn't seem buddy-buddy with each other. They certainly weren't making plans for a cozy lunch together."

"Could be the other way around, too." Nick brushed the dust from his hair and leaned forward, elbows on his knees. "Stella could be going to Beth to enlist her help in convincing Pearl she needs to sell the house in Shawneetown. Who better than a realtor to conjure up dismal images of old houses needing lots of repairs being hard to sell, and getting harder to sell as time goes on if expensive repairs aren't made.

"True."

"And if it were me trying to convince her, I'd also talk about the comparative isolation of that house as opposed to where she is now."

"There's the Vincent house right behind it though. It's not like there's no one anywhere close."

"Right, one house, with two backyards, two gates, and a field between them. It didn't stop two people being murdered in the house."

Perri nodded. Beth did tell us she was trying to get into buying and refurbishing old houses and buildings. I wonder if she's the one who wants to buy the house."

"Could very well be."

"Pearl told me there had been people who pestered Ruby and George about selling. She said once, a man just walked right through this back door and into the kitchen while Ruby was here alone. He got very aggressive about buying the house and got angry when Ruby insisted they didn't want to sell."

"That would mean Beth either has someone doing the intimidation work for her or it was an entirely different situation. No description on the man?"

"No, Pearl said Ruby just told her it happened, but didn't say she knew him or not and didn't describe him." Perri sighed. "And I can't see Beth killing the Duncans, even if she wanted to. Had they been shot, maybe, but not physically herding them around. She's shorter than me and probably weighs...a few pounds less."

Nick wondered, "Unless she had a gun and the Duncans complied with what she asked them to do thinking they'd be let go eventually."

"Maybe. I don't know. Could she have managed to keep a gun trained on two people, George being a tall burly guy, albeit older, and tying them up at the same time? I'd think she'd have to have help with that. The most obvious choice would be Stella and/or her boyfriend, that Eric guy. He's a seedy looking individual and he's got a record to go along with his bad reputation. It wouldn't surprise me if he was involved."

"Me either. It would be easier to manage with more than one person, of course. But, just like we said last night, what are the chances Stella and Eric could pull off anything without screwing it up somehow?"

"True. It would also be more difficult to hide, to leave no evidence. You get two or three people together, especially when a couple of them are almost comically inept thieves, and there's bound to be some evidence singling someone out, but so far, it's all been inconclusive."

"Yeah, I saw on the news that the fingerprints they identified all belonged to people who had a valid reason for being in the house at some point." Nick asked.

"Even Stella and her boyfriend could make a case for being there, since Ruby and George were Stella's aunt and uncle."

"And...it can't be checked out to make sure it's a legitimate story since they are both gone."

"Right. I asked Pearl if Stella was in the habit of visiting Ruby and she said sometimes she does, but she thought it had been a while. It doesn't mean that Ruby informed her of every single visit from Stella, so nothing there."

"Were there prints from anyone they can't identify?"

"I suppose they would have come up with some, they haven't said. If they have anyone in mind, they can fingerprint them and see if they get a match, but they haven't publicly named any suspects." Perri ran through the possibilities in her mind. "I suppose it could be possible that someone George communicated with online killed them. It would be hard to know who to even fingerprint if that's the case. Although, they do still have his computer, and everyone can be traced, eventually. There are some psycho people on the internet."

Nick nodded. "If that's the case, the police may discover something but we don't have the resources to find out that sort of information."

"What if George had a potential buyer come to the house to take a look at an item he was trying to sell? They could have decided to kill both of them and take whatever they could find that was valuable, and easy enough to steal." Perri stopped and shook her head slightly. "No, that doesn't make sense either because the house was so thoroughly searched but so many valuable items that were easily portable were left behind. It always goes back to a person looking for something specific and not finding it, getting angry, angry enough to kill over it."

"Right. But searching the house for something specific also makes the theory of wanting to convince the owner or owners to sell the house less plausible. Would someone want to buy a house just to be able to look for something?"

"I guess it depends on what it is. Or not, who knows, some people's actions don't make sense."

"And...the cause of death was drowning, so they were still alive when they left, or were taken from, the house. Which raises the question of why drive them ten miles away. Maybe they went willingly."

Perri simply nodded, focused on her thoughts.

Nick shook his head. "I got nothin' else. I don't know."

"So...could there be a clue in the journals?"

Nick said, "They were written an awfully long time ago. What type of clue are you thinking about?"

Perri sat upright. "Oh, I got so caught up in the incident with Stella that I haven't shown you the article."

"The one you found at the library this afternoon?"

"Yeah. Hang on, I'll get it." Perri went back to the foyer where she'd dropped her work bag, pulled out the two sheets of paper, then returned to the kitchen.

"The article I found describes how Francis's father-in-law was robbed but didn't tell anyone at first. It goes along with what Francis said in his journal, that he found out about it when he and Arminda were at the Grey's for dinner. His personal account lacks the most interesting details, though." She handed Nick the article and said, "I'm going upstairs to get out of these scrubs and cleaned up. I'll be back down in a jiff."

"Ok." Nick started reading.

Across the top of the sheet, Perri had written 'Western Voice, March 4, 1836.' The clock spun backwards as he read the article, written in the more flamboyant/embellished style of days gone by.

### Vile Bandits Meet Their End.

*A gang of bandits who have terrorized the ferry road from Cave-in-Rock for the last couple of decades finally met their match this week. For years, travelers who crossed into our state from Kentucky were besieged by thieves who robbed them, and in a few cases of inhuman lawlessness, injured or killed their innocent victims. Many lawmen have tracked and pursued these vagabonds, but none were able to apprehend them until a posse of men from Shawneetown gathered together on Monday and routed the scoundrels from their lair.*

Nick smiled and shook his head slightly, "Wow, this reads like an old-time western." He continued reading.

*A great man of our community, Mr. Hubert Grey, was accosted and relieved of his valuables on his way home from Paducah, Kentucky while traversing the ferry road just over a fortnight ago. Being a private man and knowing the long, futile history of catching the bandits, Mr. Grey did not burden anyone with the knowledge of his losses, other than necessarily telling his wife. Fortunately for all of us, hearing of this atrocious act over Sunday dinner at the Grey's home, his son-in-law, Francis McCade, worked tirelessly to discover information about the brigands. Through Mr. McCade's extensive business connections and wily investigation, he cleverly discerned where to unearth the thieves. He then supplied this valuable information to our Sheriff.*

*A group of able-bodied men, including generous participation from Mr. McCade, gathered and swiftly rode to the home of the head of the gang, Alexander Mason, taking him completely unaware as he slept.*

*Alexander Mason has long been known to be the son of the famous brigand, Samuel Mason, who terrorized the banks on both sides of the Ohio before and after the turn of the century. Samuel Mason was put to death by hanging in 1803, ridding the area of this noxious person and his deeds. Sadly, this son of his followed in his footsteps and was as terrible a scourge as his father. Alexander will not be jailed and tried, as many people have inquired, since he was killed as a result of a well-placed gunshot by Francis McCade in the skirmish at his house in Elizabethtown. Mr. Mason's wife and children remain to fend for themselves now that his life of crime has ended. Mrs. Mason, nee Celie Ann Hartsaw, intends to continue to live on the property with their son and daughter, Nathaniel and Arminda, ages five and three, respectively.*

Nick pondered the information, dark stubble rasped against the palm of his hand as he rubbed it over his chin.

A few minutes later, Perri returned to the kitchen in jeans and a sweater. She sat at the table. Seeing Nick's expression, she said, "After reading that, I wondered about the nature of Francis's business connections that he was so quickly able to find out what no one had been able to discover for decades. It's highly suspicious and I figure he already knew."

"That was my thought too. It's starting to make some sense now. Disturbing sense."

"Right. Alexander Mason has to be AM from the journals, don't you think? It explains why the meetings stopped when they did. AM was dead."

Nick nodded. "Mmm hmm." He gave a lopsided grin and said, "Wow, a Mason. That's amazing. Oh, I know, he was a criminal, but you know how kids are, they like stories about Jesse James and Billy the Kid. I used to read stories about the Samuel Mason gang. I didn't know about Alexander though. He must have been the youngest, too young to be part of his Dad's gang, because his elder brothers were part of it. Didn't help him much. The books I read left off soon after the execution of Samuel Mason. Most of Alexander's brothers ended up dead or in jail, except one who turned out alright and lived with his mother in Mississippi. I believe his name was either Magnus or Samuel, Jr. Alexander doesn't seem to have ended up any better than the others."

"I want to go back through the journal that covers this time period. We can look at it with different eyes now and see if there's anything we missed or didn't understand the first time through. Francis McCade was instrumental in not only ending the reign of that particular group of thieves, but personally killed Alexander Mason, someone he had done business with for years, regardless of how nefarious it was. That's quite a betrayal. Why kill him? Provided Alexander Mason *was* the AM from the diaries, they knew each other very well for many years. Why not just talk to him?"

Perri considered while she located the journal covering 1836-1837, then said, "Firstly, is it significant that this is the same volume Ruby Duncan had secreted away with her cookbooks?"

"I hadn't thought of that, but you're right. She held this one out for some reason."

"Secondly, doesn't Francis's reaction seem melodramatic, even rash? All accounts of him describe him as level-headed and in possession of himself. I mean, even for the slanted writing of the time, if Francis had been a man who was easily agitated or lost his cool, I think it would have been mentioned in some way, but he's always portrayed as calm and a competent leader."

Nick considered. "It does seem like an overreaction. Maybe Francis was the excitable type but didn't want bad press about having a quick temper or bad disposition and had enough influence in town to discourage it. He owned a lot of land and businesses that employed people in a time when there weren't a whole lot of places to work."

Perri thought about that, then said, "Yes, it seems unlikely though. Even if it were true, that might only last up until the time of his death. Posterity sometimes has a way of sharing a few secrets. He can't have outlived *all* his contemporaries."

"He certainly didn't seem to want Mr. Mason to be taken alive. If he was the A.M. in the journals that Francis met with so often, it's pretty cold and calculating to kill the guy after their long history."

"It is. There had to be something Francis didn't want known. When Mason's bunch robbed Francis's father-in-law, it tipped the scales and Francis ratted on him. Maybe that's all it was. I mean, why reveal who Mason was and where he could be found if Francis wanted to keep it secret?" They contemplated in silence for a few moments, then Perri said, "Unless…unless when Hubert Grey told about being robbed at dinner, Francis got so angry that the gang had robbed one of his own family, he lost his head and in eagerness for revenge, he said things he would rather not have said before he regained control of himself."

Nick nodded. "That could be. How long was it between Francis finding out at that dinner and the night he shot Alexander?" Before Perri could respond, he asked, "I can't see what bearing that would have on the present, though, do you?"

"No, not yet. But right now, it's the only thing I have to go on." Perri opened the journal to February 1836. I'll read it out loud. It's harder to go too fast and miss things if one reads and the other listens. Perri started with the first February entry.

The first three weeks of the month were routine, with nothing outstanding. Mostly information about making trips to the salt works to pay the workers and check on the processing and inventory. Francis and Arminda held a dinner party at Orchard Parke on the twentieth, a Saturday. Attending were Theodore and Malissa Beauchamp, William and Phoebe Tuttle, and Zilpha and John Groves. It was described as an enjoyable evening with lively discussion. Zilpha played the piano for the party after dinner.

Nick took a turn at the beginning of the new week. February 28 had been the Sunday dinner at the Grey's home. He read: *'Very cold, blowing snow. Too cold to snow much. Tense day. Shouted at Hugo over mishap. Need to go to Potts' this week for old business matters with AM that should have been settled long ago. Dinner at Hubert's tonight. Excellent as always but ended badly. Shock. Will rectify.'*

"Discovering his father-in-law had been robbed, and by his shady business partner's men to boot, ruined the evening for him." Perri remarked. "Maybe he was simply afraid someone would solve the robbery and in the process Alexander would let the cat out of the bag that Francis was involved in an illegal business. Maybe it became a battle of who points the finger first."

"But what illegal business? Let's go through the next week." Nick read a few more innocuous entries. "Here, I can see why we didn't get its meaning the first time through, before you found the article. It's March 3. All it says is this, *'AM Meeting failed. Cannot continue.'* After that AM is not mentioned again."

"Francis didn't let any moss grow on him, did he? He met with Alexander on March 3, maybe confronted him about Mr. Grey. Whatever happened, he decided their issue couldn't be worked out and set out for Elizabethtown the very next day with a group of men. I wonder why he didn't write about that?"

"Maybe he didn't want to allude to any knowledge beforehand and felt it would be easier to just not talk about it at all. It probably wouldn't have set too well if it got out that he had been partners with the guy."

"No." Perri checked the time. "Time to pack it in for the evening. Tomorrow I'll see what else I can dig up on that relationship. Now that we know who is on both sides of the partnership they seem to have had, we know what connections to look for. After I read the article, I checked with the Hardin County Clerk's office about how far back their records go. Elizabethtown is in Hardin County. I thought maybe I could find something about Alexander there. The original court house burned in 1884 and again in 1921, so lots of information has been lost. The earliest marriage, death, and probate records are from 1884, so no way there's anything about him there."

"Their land records start in 1814, but I don't think that would help us much right now. We already know he had a house and land there, but his widow and kids did continue to live on the property, at least for a while. There might be a chance of getting some information about Alexander's family because the birth records start in 1844. We know from the article that he had two children when he died, Nathaniel and Arminda. If we can find a birth record for a Mason, we likely can find out who Nathaniel married, if they stayed in the area. Arminda would be more difficult since her surname would have changed and we don't know what to look for. It's a starting point."

"You're wanting to go over there? When?" Nick asked.

"I've emailed them, and I can call if I need to. I'm going to try to at least find out if there is a record before making the trip. It isn't like it's a long trip, but it isn't super close either and I'd rather not chase my tail. Hopefully, I'll hear from them tomorrow."

## Chapter 27

October 19, 2016, Morning

Wednesday was Perri's shortest work day, her last patient was scheduled at 11:30 a.m. She and Nick would be moving back to the apartment this afternoon; the new door was installed, and had been tested and passed muster. Nick had included a dead bolt along with the new locking knob to make it less likely someone would kick in the door. Pearl gave the thumbs up for taking the diaries with her so she'd have time to get through them all.

Before leaving for work, Perri had tossed the sheets and dish cloths and towels in the washer. Nick had already packed away his tools and cleaned up the mess. He'd promised to get the linens out of the washer, put them in to dry, then put them away and head back to the apartment as soon as he was finished.

That morning's visit with Pearl had been a trifle tense. Impatience was overtaking Perri. Impatience with trying to puzzle out the murder, with writing an article she hadn't even started, Pearl's continued complacence regarding Stella and Eric's obvious thefts, and with an irrational feeling that work was always in her way when she wanted to be doing something else.

To attempt a calming exercise she'd watched online after a particularly heinous week at the hospital, she raggedly drew in a breath and was steadily exhaling to the count of four when her ring tone interrupted. Her nerves jangling, she blew out the breath in frustration and answered the call in a waspish tone she hadn't intended. The caller hesitated before saying, "Hello? I'm calling from the Harrisburg Library?"

Perri immediately felt guilty. "Yes! Sorry, sorry for that. I just got in the car and was … what can I help you with?"

"I'm calling you about a request for microfilm by interlibrary loan? Have I got the right person?"

"Yes, that was me."

"I got a call from the Springfield library film department this morning letting me know that the roll you requested can't be provided. Evidently, when they tried to fill the request this morning they discovered that it's missing from the catalog. I'm sorry."

"Missing?"

"Yes. It doesn't happen often, but it does happen. It may just be misfiled or misplaced. They'll keep your request active in the system and if they come across it, they'll notify us and send it if you still want it."

"Yes, I definitely do want it if it's found. Thank you for calling. Oh wait!"

"Yes?"

"Can you tell me if the roll had been requested by someone else previously, I mean not too long ago? Is that how it was lost?"

The clacking of a keyboard came through the phone, followed by, "It wasn't requested from here. That doesn't mean it wasn't requested anywhere else in the US though. To find that out, you'd need to call Springfield."

"Right. Thanks, I appreciate you checking."

"You're welcome. Anything else?"

"No, that's all. Let me know if it turns up."

Perri sat with her phone in her lap. As many times as a roll of microfilm may be handled, especially one that makes several journeys out and back for loans, it wasn't inconceivable, or even unlikely, that one would be temporarily misplaced or lost. She couldn't help but feel a little suspicious that it was this roll of film that went missing. It only served to pique her interest in the death of Arminda McCade even more.

Perri saw Pearl peeking through the lace panel curtains, probably wondering why she was still sitting in front of the house. Perri waved at her and held up her phone as explanation. She Googled the library in Springfield and tapped on the number to call.

Less than five minutes later, Perri drove away from the curb, clutching the wheel. According to the Springfield Library, the missing roll of film had been loaned out but they weren't able to tell her the specific patron who had ordered it. All they could say was that the film had been sent out on loan to the library in

Shawneetown, IL and had not been returned. Perri asked how long before lost service copies were replaced with another from the master copy and the librarian told her she wasn't sure how long it would take. She did say if it wasn't found in a couple of weeks, a request for a new one would be created, but the Microfilm lab always had a backlog, so how long it would take she couldn't say.

"Shawneetown. Right in the midst of all the other towns where possible suspects lived. It could have been anyone." Perri drummed her thumbs against the steering wheel while reasoning through the conversation aloud. "Someone either legitimately ordered the microfilm and it was misplaced or the borrower intentionally 'lost' it." She wasn't sure how she'd be able to find out, if she could find out, who had ordered it. She knew that the library in Springfield was the only library listed to have a service copy, so there was no other library to borrow from. What she could do was try to find the information somewhere else, and she knew the first place she would look.

Before Perri arrived at her next patient's house, her phone rang again. Pulling over in the parking lot of a florist, she answered and listened, then said, "Let me grab a pen to write with…hang on, please." Perri had checked her email after her first morning patient. There was a response email from Christy in the Elizabethtown Clerk's office in Hardin County stating they had a couple of later birth records Perri might be interested in. Perri had messaged her back saying she did want the records and asked if she could pay for them by Pay Pal or by phone. She read the second message after her second patient. The bad news was she couldn't pay by a method other than mail or in the office. The good news was that if Perri was coming to Elizabethtown, a woman who was something of a local historian might have information of interest if Perri wanted to contact her. Perri had eagerly sent back an email saying she would and included her phone number. Christy was calling to give her the info.

"Ok, I'm ready."

"Her name is Tabby Ford."

"Tabby?" Perri asked.

"Yes, her name's Tabitha but she goes by Tabby. She lives here in E'town, down by the river, supposed to have belonged to one of the later Masons. That's what made me think of Tabby, when you asked about records for the Masons. Anyway, it's like a museum. She keeps everything and has a head full of history." Christy gave Perri the address and Tabby's phone number to call ahead if she wanted to visit.

"Thank you so much. This is very helpful. I'll try to make it over there this afternoon." Perri called Tabby Ford to see if it would be alright to drop by and chat with her for a while. Her easy-going, agreeable response eased Perri's apprehension about intruding on her. She sounded genuinely happy at the prospect of a visitor who wanted to talk about the local history. Perri promised she and Nick would get there as soon as they could. She hung up and, before continuing to her last patient, made a call to Nick to let him know she'd like to leave for Elizabethtown as soon as she could get home and changed.

Nick was ready to go when she got back to the apartment. He sprawled on the toilet lid and gave her a running narrative about his day while she took a lightning fast shower.

"I got finished by ten o'clock, so I tightened up a couple of loose kitchen cabinet doors. It got a little murky in there with the wood dust from sanding down the rough places on the door frame, so I tried to open the window over the sink but it was painted shut. I scraped around it and finally got it open. I waxed the runners so it opens and closes easily now. It has an old double lock on it, one at each side, and they're still in great shape. And before you ask, yes, I swept the sawdust off the floor. The countertops might still be a bit gritty though."

"I'm glad you did all that." Perri's muffled voice came from inside her bulky sweater as she pulled it on over her head. "I hope Pearl decides to keep the house, but I can understand why she may not want to." Perri recalled all the furnishings that were family heirlooms from many, many decades. "It would be awfully hard to part with so much of her family history though."

"Maybe she won't have to. Did you have any luck with the Historic Register thing?"

"Ugh. That's something else I haven't gotten to yet. Why do I have to work? Why can't I just do the stuff I like, huh?" Her attempt at laughter was half serious and more than a bit frustrated.

Hearing the edge in Perri's voice, the tone that was just this side of tearing up, Nick recognized stress mode. He put one hand on each of her shoulders while she was running the brush through her hair and squeezed the taut muscle, running his thumbs along its path over her shoulder blades.

"Oh my gosh. That feels so good. The muscles are so knotted up, I can feel a pain in my head every time you press down. I'm a little tense, I guess."

"I'll say. We'll work on that later."

Finished dressing, Perri stretched out her too-long shoelaces and looked at Nick questioningly. "Why? Why do they make these things way too long?" She tied them in surgeon's knot bows so they wouldn't untie easily, but still had to double tie the bows to keep the loops from dragging the ground. She jumped up and grabbed her suede jacket, since it was getting chillier by the minute, and said, "Let's go." She raced for the door.

"Whoa, hang on!" Nick reached out and snagged his jacket as he passed the couch. Perri was thundering down the stairs, already well ahead of him. "Slow down, we've got plenty of time. Didn't you say it was about forty-five minutes away? It's only 1:15."

"Yeah, but if we get slowed down anywhere, we might be late."

"You mean if there's a huge backup on the six-lane expressway?"

"Ha-ha. You know what I mean. And I don't want to show up at Mrs. Ford's house right at suppertime."

Once they were on the road, Perri told Nick about her conversation with the two libraries. "The fact that someone took the film which possibly has Arminda's obituary, or a news article about it, tends to convince me that it does. What about that information does that person want to hide? We need to find that out."

"How?" Nick asked.

"When the library called this morning, at first I decided we should go to the research library this afternoon. Then I got the call about the birth records and Tabby Ford, so the research library will have to wait until tomorrow. Someone may have taken the only available microfilm with newspaper information of Arminda's death, but I think there may be somewhere else to find it. We also haven't read the journals up to the time of her death. I would think surely there will be something in them so we need to skip ahead. We can do that tonight after we get home."

The cities of Eldorado and Harrisburg receding behind them, they headed due south on Highway 145. The afternoon sunshine streaming through the windows glowed a warm hue of amber, but the warmth was only in the color. The winds had ushered in a cold, nippy edge to the air which made Perri yearn for a cup of hot cider and a cozy chair in front of a fireplace. She pulled her jacket closer and zipped it.

"You cold?" Nick automatically cranked up the heater as he asked.

"Just a little. All that dashing around warmed me up, but now that I'm sitting, I'm cold."

The journey to Elizabethtown took them through the Shawnee National Forest, the landscape transformed to gently rolling hills. Through an occasional break in the masses of trees flaunting their autumn colors, Perri could see the line of ridges, bluffs, and large rock formations jutting out of the ground. Small rivers and streams snaked around the base of flush limestone cliffs. Then the scenery would break and they'd once again be traveling through plowed over fields with small clumps of remaining forest scattered along the road's edge.

Following a gentle curve to the east, Elizabethtown came into view. They first passed some abandoned buildings — an old gas station, storefronts, and a few houses — then longstanding buildings being put to use as shops, bars, and restaurants. Some two-story brick structures that served in their past life as main level businesses with upper story living quarters for the family were now converted to homes. At the four-way stop, Perri indicated for Nick to turn left. The red brick court building was impressive in its elevated location. Perched on a rise at a three-way junction, its towering presence dominated the diminutive downtown area.

Nick parked the Jeep in a sloping lot next to the building. Perri stopped before entering to take in the view of the Ohio River, plainly visible at the end of Main Street. Even from this distance, it appeared as a wide, slowly advancing band of grayish-brown against the trees on the Kentucky bank, which grew right up to the water line and hung over it like they were being shoved out of a crowded boat.

"It's a smaller town than I expected," Nick remarked.

"Not unusual in Southern Illinois. It isn't always the largest town that has the city hall or clerk's office. Cities and towns can change drastically over time, too. Look at Old Shawneetown, it used to be the hub of Illinois, even more significant than Chicago at the time, and now it's nearly gone." Perri turned back to the building. "Well, let's get this done." Nick pulled open the heavy glass door and held it for her.

Eager to get the birth records and move on to Tabitha Ford's house, Perri was glad it took only a few minutes to get the copies and pay for them. Knowing they were coming, Christy very efficiently had them waiting at the desk.

Perri merely glanced at them while thanking Christy. She and Nick returned to the Jeep.

"Let's see what you've got." Nick said, starting the Jeep to keep the interior warm.

Perri leant toward Nick with the paperwork between them, Nick holding on to the opposite side. "Ok. First one is…Thomas McCade! Bingo, that's one we know. He was born on August 18, 1854 to Hugo Bernard McCade and," Perri paused, re-read the information, then continued, "Arminda Layne *Mason*! Francis's son married a Mason."

"You think Arminda Mason was Alexander's daughter? The age is right if you think about it."

"Right. The 1837 newspaper article said Alexander left behind a wife and two children, Nathaniel and Arminda, ages five and three. If Arminda was three-years-old in 1837, she would have been about nineteen or twenty when Thomas was born. Also, remember the grave stone for the second Arminda McCade in Gold Hill Cemetery? It said 'Wife of H.G. McCade. So, that stone did belong to Arminda Mason McCade. And the fact that the marriage records prior to 1884 for this county were destroyed in the fire, it explains why their marriage wasn't listed in the Index online. Had they married in Gallatin County, it probably would have survived. We don't know their actual marriage date, but at least we do know who married whom. This is valid documentation of it, in the absence of a marriage record."

"Do birth records normally give the mother's maiden name?" Nick asked.

"Many times, as they should, but some are less detailed and don't. I love it when I find one that does. It can be a windfall of information. I've had a couple of brick walls knocked down by a maiden name being included."

"Let's see the second one." Nick set the first sheet on his lap.

"Hello. This one is for Samuel Alexander Mason, born October 16, 1855. Parents were Nathaniel Magnus Mason and Jane Susannah McCade."

"So…sister and brother married brother and sister?"

"Yes. Both couples apparently married in Hardin County rather than Gallatin. It makes me wonder if Francis McCade wasn't sold on the idea of his children marrying into the Mason family, and we probably know why. The question is, did Francis's children know Francis had killed Alexander, and did the Mason family know about it?"

"It could be a Romeo and Juliet type of situation, both families opposed."

"It appears the families knew each other, at least maybe after Alexander died. In the journals, there is no mention of visiting with the Masons before that, although Nathaniel and Arminda would have been very young or infants at the point we have reached in reading. These marriages were likely well after Arminda McCade passed away. Maybe things had died down by that time."

"If nothing else, it's given us quite a few things to look for in the diaries." Perri glanced at her watch. "Let's go on to Mrs. Ford's house and see what we can learn there."

Nick pulled out of the small parking lot and drove south on Main Street. It wasn't far, only taking a couple of minutes to find Tabby's house. Like the McCade home, it was perched high above the river, but here there was no road separating the house from the rocky cliffside. Nick shut off the engine and they both walked toward the craggy edge for a look first.

"Great scenery to wake up to every morning." Nick exclaimed, slipping an arm around Perri's shoulders. "I'd love to have a house with a view like this someday."

Perri responded, "Me too. I like my house, but I'd take this over a view of my street or neighbor's backyard any day." She paused, studying the opposite side of the river. "You know, from up the street, I thought that shoreline was the main bank in Kentucky, but it's Hurricane Island. I didn't realize it was as large as it is. This is the downstream tip of it. You can see the main shore behind it."

"Someone actually farms the island? I can see the corn stubble."

"Looks like it. I guess they ferry the equipment out there when it's time for planting or harvesting."

"That would be a big undertaking. I guess it's worth it though."

They turned away from the river vista and approached the house.

## Chapter 28

October 19, 2016, Late afternoon

The house reminded Perri of some of the coastal homes in the south. A covered porch ran the full length of both stories, rocking chairs were placed along both, empty hooks evidence of the hanging plants that would line the eaves in summer.

Purple, gold, and burgundy mums lined both sides of the walk to the front door, which was opened by a very smartly dressed elderly woman as they reached the stoop. "Good afternoon. I'm Tabby Ford. Come on in."

Nick and Perri stepped into the foyer and introduced themselves. Tabby firmly shook their hands, each in turn, and gestured to a sofa in the large room immediately off the entry. "Please, have a seat. I'm so glad you could visit. Can I get you some coffee? I have a pot ready."

"That would be perfect. It's getting nippy out there." Perri replied gratefully, rubbing her hands together, her cheeks cold from the wind blustering off the water.

"I'll be back in just a moment. Make yourselves comfortable." Tabby smiled warmly and exited the room.

Perri raised her eyebrows in Nick's direction as they settled into the overstuffed, chintz-covered couch. She didn't want to risk being overheard. Tabby was not what she had expected. Given that she knew Mrs. Ford was in her seventies, and perhaps influenced by the name Tabby, Perri had pictured her as plump and powdery, with wandering wisps of gray hair and a jovial, round face.

That isn't at all what they found. Tabby Ford was quite tall, nearly as tall as Nick's six-foot-two frame, and slender as a willow. She must have remained active because her movements were one of an agile person. Her hair was a pleasant mixture of dark and light gray that gave it depth, cut fashionably just above shoulder length and brushed smooth. Her clothing, camel colored wool slacks with a finely knit sweater in rich chocolate brown, flattered a lithe frame and was accented only by a bracelet style watch, earrings that probably were real pearls, and a delicate gold chain with a single, small amber stone in a gold setting.

Tabby returned carrying a tray of three mugs, steam twisting in a spiral above them. She set them down on a nearby table and handed a mug to Perri and Nick before settling into a chair with her own. "Now. What can I help you with? Christina told me you were wanting to talk to me about some local history?"

"Yes, I'm very interested in information on a family that lived in this area in the 1800s, the Masons."

"Oh, yes, the Masons! They have a checkered past, that's for sure."

"If I understood her right, Christy said that this house belonged to one of them?"

"It did, that's true. This house was owned, at one time, by Samuel A. McCade. He lived here with his wife, Leah, until he died in 1925."

"Samuel A.," Perri referred to the birth record they'd just obtained, "would be the son of Jane McCade and Nathaniel Mason, so the grandson of Alexander Mason?"

"Yes, that's correct. You've already done homework on the Masons." It was a statement, not a question.

"I started out by gathering information to write a story about the Francis McCade house, over in Old Shawneetown, and in doing that, it's turning out that the McCades are inextricably wound up with the Masons. I was hoping you could share some family history about them, especially Alexander and his children, both of whom married McCades."

"You just came from the records office, so you got the birth records?"

"That's right." Perri replied. "Of course, there aren't any marriage records for them because of the fires."

"I've done some research on the Mason family, and knowing you were coming, I got out my information." Tabby lifted a leather-bound folio from a lower shelf of the same table where she set the tray. She settled it on her lap and opened it, leafing through a few pages before saying in a studied tone, "I knew the Samuel Mason who had lived here was the grandson of the

Alexander Mason who ran roughshod over this entire region for so many years. I suspected he might be related to the Samuel Mason who terrorized the southern Illinois and northern Kentucky area in the late 1700s. That prospect made it more interesting to me to find out more about the family. Samuel A. was, indeed, the great-grandson of that Samuel Mason. This Samuel was blessed, or cursed, depending on how you look at it, with both his great-grandfather's and his father's first names. He probably felt there was no chance of anyone forgetting about them."

"You say you knew Samuel was the grandson of Alexander Mason when you started researching. How did you know?"

"From local hearsay. When I was looking at the property, I heard all sorts of tales about it and its ties to the family. Both this Samuel and his father Nathaniel were docile creatures compared to their notorious family members. Nathaniel saw enough of it as a child to convince him which side of the law it was best to be on. He and Arminda, his sister, along with their mother, Celie Ann, were in the house when Alexander was dragged from his bed and shot in the hallway. After that, a life of crime didn't appeal to him. He tried to keep his existence as low profile as possible."

"Was it in this house where Alexander was killed?"

"No. That house is long gone. Alexander's wife and children lived in it for several years after his death, according to the tax records, but Celie Ann eventually remarried and moved to Gallatin County. I haven't made the trip over there to find more records for them." Tabby cleared her throat. "There may be a few remnants of it left, of the house I mean, but for the most part it isn't visible anymore, at least not driving by. You'd have to get out and walk through the lot. The only thing marking where the house used to be is a stone well. The tumble-down pieces of it still stand in what was the side yard." Tabby pointed to her left. "It's just up the road a little that way, towards Rosiclare. Which way did you come in?"

Perri described their route and Tabby continued, "You might try driving past it when you go, it wouldn't be out of your way at all," she cast a glance over her shoulder out the window, "although it might be dark and there isn't any lighting around it. You wouldn't want to wander too close to the edge of the property and fall off." Perri cast an uneasy glance to Nick, they nodded to each other.

Tabby continued without referring to her notes, "Samuel wasn't the first person to own this house. It was built by a man named Randolph Jackson who died rather soon after having built it. That's when Samuel bought it and worked the farm. There's evidence that his wife, Leah, was a talent in the kitchen using the produce from their fruit trees and vines for jellies and jams, as well as seasonal wines. I found a permit for selling the wine locally, which they did out of their home, as well as some scattered records for sales of the jarred goods. Their products were evidently quite favored by locals, since they've been mentioned in letters and some grocery inventories owned by other families from the area."

"Did Samuel and Leah have any children?" Perri asked.

"They did, they had four children, but only two survived infancy. The eldest was a boy named Elias and the other was a girl named Elizabeth." Tabby shuffled a couple sheets of paper. "The last record I found for Elias was a mention of him in a letter from his mother to her mother, so Leah's mother. She mentions that Elias had taken a job aboard a riverboat as a deck hand and was leaving for the delta, so, a ship that was headed for New Orleans. I don't know what happened to him. I couldn't find any other records on him, at least not here, and I didn't look beyond here at the time since I was more focused on learning which ancestors still lived in the area. He could have settled and lived a full life somewhere else, but all indications are that it wasn't here. The other child, Elizabeth, married an Arthur Frederick."

Setting aside the paper she was holding, she said, "The other information I have includes a packet from the National Archives in Washington, DC. I sent for Nathaniel's Civil War records, he served in Company A of the 29th Illinois Infantry during the Civil War, which was comprised of many men from Hardin County. Included in the packet are the enlistment and discharge paperwork, the widow's pension that Jane McCade Mason filed for when Nathaniel passed away in," she paused for a moment to consult her file, "1903."

"How far down the family tree did you go?"

Tabby exhaled slowly through puckered lips and rearranged the folio on her lap. "I checked for marriage records for the name Mason beginning in 1884, the earliest records still surviving. That's where I found Elizabeth's marriage to Arthur Frederick in 1894. There is a birth recorded for a son Arthur, Jr. in 1895; a second son, Phillip in 1896; and a daughter, Nettie in 1898. After that, the records for the Mason name taper off, the family having dispersed to other places. The two sons, Arthur and Phillip have no death records here, so they most likely moved away and I didn't pursue them."

Perri had been writing down everything Tabby said. She looked up and asked, "Have you come across any contemporary accounts about the raid on Alexander Mason's home the night he was killed?"

"I did. Here's a copy." Tabby held out a copy of the article from the Western Voice.

Perri didn't take it, saying, "Yes, this is the one I found too. I couldn't find any newspapers in the archive that were printed in Elizabethtown."

"I haven't come across any extant examples of a newspaper from here either. However," more shuffling of papers, "Nathaniel was interviewed in 1892 for a book about Hardin County. He was around fifty-eight years old at the time."

"Would that be one of the Biographicals?"

"Yes, you've seen them before?" Tabby asked. "Sorry, I guess you would since you do this sort of research."

Perri shrugged it away, "No problem. I've seen several of them, but I hadn't gotten my hands on the one for Hardin County yet."

"Since you already have this article," Tabby replaced the copy in the folio, "you already have an understanding of the situation. It appears Alexander was surprised during the middle of the night and dragged from his bed while his family looked on in horror. It wasn't the best way to handle it, probably scared the bejesus out of the children."

"I would think it was like a nightmare. The article said they were only three and five at the time. I'm sure it was a terrible night. About the interview with Nathaniel?"

Tabby took a deep breath, "Right. I can't say I remember it verbatim and I don't seem to have a copy of it here. I thought I did, but it could be stuck somewhere in another file. Essentially,

Nathaniel recalled loud banging on the doors. He heard splintering wood, lots of heavy footsteps in the hallway, and the shouts of his parents. He heard his mother screaming, a gunshot, and then relative quiet, other than his mother crying. He and his sister passed a large spill of blood on the floor as they were shuttled away to a neighbor's house. Their mother was slumped into a rocking chair in the main room, surrounded by the men who had come to the house."

"That had to be extremely traumatic. I'm sure I can find a copy of the book to read the full interview." Perri hesitated a moment, then asked, "Can I ask you a more personal question?"

"Certainly. What would you like to ask?" Tabby smiled a gentle smile.

"Your surname, are you related to the Fords from Kentucky?"

She chuckled quietly, then answered, "I am. Hard to get away from that history in these parts. I'm descended, albeit indirectly, from the illustrious James Ford, a great grand uncle. He also had an unexpected death by firearm, assisted by a lit candle held behind his head to help target him."

Perri replied, "The person holding the candle had a great deal of confidence in the marksmanship of the shooter to calmly stand there, so close, waiting for it."

"Indeed, he did." Tabby sipped from her mug, uncrossed and re-crossed her legs. "I'm a Ford by birth. My name is still Ford since I never married. I chose to continue with college for my Master's degree and then taught in Chicago until I retired. I loved living there, the excitement and opportunities, and never aspired to the married life. I was born outside of Tolu, Kentucky, basically just across the river, not far off the old Ferry Road. A lot of the family still lived in that area then. By the time I decided to retire, they were all gone. I was looking around southern Illinois and northern Kentucky for a place, and this house was for sale. I was thrilled to be able to buy it."

Tabby held up one finger and waggled it in the air, "There's something else. I can't believe I nearly forgot this, but talking about buying the house reminded me. When I moved in, the sellers passed on a collection of things they'd held on to from the owner before them. It was a box of odds and ends, but some dated back to the Masons. I don't think anyone had paid much attention to any of the items other than to have a look through them and put them away again. Probably saw them as junk but hesitated to just toss them out."

"What caught my attention were a couple pieces of decaying leather, a colored-pencil drawing, and a few mother-of-pearl buttons. I'm not an expert at dating things, so I tried doing a little research to see if I could pin down a time period. Those items were definitely from the 19th century, early on I would guess."

"What significance did they have? Or do you think they just happened to be left behind from when the Masons lived here?"

"The leather pieces, if arranged, looked like they were part of a holster at one time. It wasn't all there and the pieces were curling up around the edges, so hard to say exactly what it looked like when it was whole, but the pouch-like piece with some dark staining around the lip of the top certainly looked like it to me. The drawing was of a river, the obvious one being the Ohio, although it wasn't labeled as such. There was no signature, but it didn't look like it had been completed. The outer portions of the drawing were not yet filled in with detail or color. The artist either abandoned it or for some reason couldn't finish it. The paper was wavy too, like it had been wet at some point, but that could have happened at any time during its existence."

Nick asked, "What about the buttons?"

"The buttons were small, delicate, from a ladies' piece of clothing. They weren't new buttons that hadn't been used. They'd been removed from a garment, and rather than the thread being snipped and plucked out, the buttons were cut off, leaving a tiny swatch of the blue fabric still attached. The back side of each button was stained with the same blue coloring, so the fabric wasn't completely color-fast when wet. It probably didn't rub off on the wearer or other objects, but ran just enough if damp or wet to stain the back of the buttons."

"Blue fabric...could you tell anything about it or was it too degraded?" Perri asked.

"Much of it was, but the threads themselves were very fine, not rough-made, more like a satin or silk."

"That would indicate someone well-off, not someone scrounging to eke out a living. Those types of garments weren't just expensive but were high-maintenance too. They couldn't be cleaned like we do today."

"That's right. They were a lot of trouble, mostly trouble not having to be taken by the owner of the garment." Tabby agreed.

"There's a passel of different methods people used to clean silk, some seem outrageous now. I remember one excerpt from a laundress's handbook that I read while I was doing some other research that advised sponging potato water over the pieces of a dress after picking out all the stitching and taking it apart first. After cleaning and drying, it had to be sewn back together. Not something that would be done very often, and obviously more work than we would ever go through. People wore full undergarments meant to protect the clothing from sweat and skin oils and only brushed and aired the item."

Nick commented, "Still…it doesn't seem like they'd stay clean very long, or get very clean like that, especially if they wore them outside. Think about the heat in the summer."

"I know, it's hard to imagine." Perri agreed. "Standards were a little different at the time." She thought about the buttons and their careless method of removal. "I wonder if the dampness was from perspiration or if the dress got wet somehow. Accidents happened, like spilling something or getting caught in a cloudburst. That could ruin the entire piece of clothing. It makes sense, too, that they'd keep the buttons for use on something else. That was common even up into the 20$^{th}$ century. I still have a miniature cedar chest full of buttons my great-grandmother snipped off to re-use."

"Maybe that's what happened to it. It was ruined by getting wet so no special care was taken removing the buttons." Nick said.

Perri asked hopefully, "Do you still have the items?"

Tabby shook her head. "After I looked them over and satisfied my curiosity I donated them."

Perri was disappointed, but tried not to look it. "Where did you donate them?"

"To a woman who was postmaster here at the time, she's retired now, who set up a corner of the post office for a small Elizabethtown museum. The post office isn't huge, and it's just up the Main Street close to the county offices," Tabby nodded her head in a generally north-east direction, "but part of the lobby area wasn't really being used for much. She had the idea because her husband had picked up a couple of display cases from one of the stores that closed and was selling off all their furnishings." She leaned forward and asked, "Would you like more coffee?"

Perri and Nick both said they were fine. Nick asked, "What did she have in the museum?"

"And, are the exhibits still there, since she's retired?" Perri added.

Tabby laughed softly and said, "You know, I go in there every other week or so, but I'm so accustomed to it being there that it's hard to remember what's left in the cases."

"What's left?"

"Yes. That was something unusual. It's been...oh, I don't know how long now, a few weeks or a couple of months. Margie went in to open the office one morning and found the side window and one of the display cases smashed. Several items were taken, and they all happened to be the ones I'd donated. I don't understand some people and their destructive tendencies. In smashing the display case, a little clay pot someone found in their field was broken. Complete disregard."

"They only took the items from the time of the Mason's ownership of the house?"

"That's right."

"Was the thief caught?"

"No, never was."

"The stolen items were never recovered."

"Right. I have to wonder, who went to the trouble of breaking into a federal building for some moldy old leather, used buttons, and an unfinished drawing?"

Perri nodded thoughtfully, "Exactly, who would want those?"

Chapter 29

October 19, 2016, Evening

The sun had set while Nick and Perri talked to Tabby Ford. Driving back through the forest, the rapidly waning light glowed coolly over the tops of the trees, they discussed what Tabby had told them.

"It puts a lot of things in perspective. It has to be someone either tied to or part of the Mason family. Don't you think?"

"It seems very likely, yes." Nick agreed.

"There's a murky sense starting to form out of this. Again, we have to skip ahead in the journals to the point where Arminda McCade died, the one who was Francis's wife. I think we'll find something there. Francis was careful not to say much about the death of Alexander in his personal diaries, but I wonder if he was as sparing with words when Arminda died."

"Why do you think her death will be enlightening about all this other stuff going on?" Nick asked.

"I…can't quite say why. It keeps popping back into my mind as something important. Obviously, the death of a spouse is important no matter what, but I want to know more about it."

"We'll see what we can find."

"I wish I didn't have to work tomorrow. There's too much I want to do. Work gets in the way," Perri sighed. "I wish I could do this type of thing for work, but I know that's crazy."

"This type of thing? You mean research?" Nick asked.

"Yeah. I know that's a dream, but it sure would make getting up and going easier. I think I'm getting the burned-out nursing blues."

Nick turned to look at Perri, then back to the winding road. "You've mentioned this several times just in the last couple of days. You don't want to do nursing anymore?"

"Not anymore as in not ever, but maybe take a break. I'm enjoying this change of pace, the home health assignment, but it will end." She sighed and shook her head in exasperation. "I feel like I'm talking out of both sides of my mouth, but I don't know that I would want to do this on a continual basis either. It's nice to not be inside the same hospital building for 12-plus hours at a time, but I think I'd get weary of all the daily driving around this type of work requires." She shook her head again as if to fend off the feeling. "Sorry."

"You don't have to apologize to me. I totally get it. Sometimes I want to chuck one or the other job. Either work on the sound business, or be a bartender."

"What keeps you from deciding one or the other?"

"The sensible choice would be to develop the sound business, because it is sustainable and can grow. The bartender job is definitely not going to provide a great income and over time it will get harder as I get older, or more accurately, I'll get tired of it if that's all I do." Nick glanced over at Perri momentarily. "You've said that yourself about some of the nursing jobs you've had."

Perri nodded in agreement.

"I've thought about quitting the Rogue and just going with the business. Then I realize I'd miss it, and not only that, I've gotten some of my best paying sound jobs through people I met while bartending. It's like the two jobs have a symbiotic relationship and I can't give up one without affecting the other." He laughed.

"I get that. Well, maybe things will change soon and you'll be able to focus on your own business."

"Maybe. We'll see. What are you planning to do? Any ideas?" He asked Perri.

"No, I haven't thought that far into it. It's just general unrest, you know? Truthfully, I think the scales tipped when my contract at the hospital was suddenly terminated."

"Yeah, I do. And I agree about the contract. You don't want to keep putting up with that type of thing."

"Except...I didn't realize so much until now, but I think I've been putting a lot of expectations in to writing this article, the one about the McCade house."

"You want to do freelance writing?"

"Yeah, I think so. At least just on the side at first and see where it might take me. I would like to put my love of history, genealogy, and discovering information about just this kind of thing to good use, and to make a living at it if I can."

"Sounds like a good idea, especially if it makes you happy." Nick said.

The darkness of the settling countryside was soon illuminated by the lights of Harrisburg. Nick asked, "Do you want to stop and get something to eat or scrounge up something at home?"

Perri started to answer his question, but said, "Wait…what day is it, it's Wednesday, right?"

"Yeah."

"And it's only 6:30 now."

"Yes." Nick said uncertainly.

"Yes! Turn left at the next light."

"Why?" Nick asked.

"This is great. We have two things we wanted to look for. We want to read the interview with Nathaniel Mason and we want to find any record of Arminda McCade's death."

"Right, but I don't see what that has to do with Wednesday night."

"Because this Wednesday night is the third Wednesday of the month. And this is the night the Genealogical Society meets in Harrisburg. Ha-ha!" Perri sat back, smiling and happy at their luck. "And we're already here."

"You want to go there now and look for the information tonight?"

"Why not? Why wait until tomorrow afternoon and hope I'll be able to get away in time? I have more patients on Thursday than any other day. This is the perfect time. And I have my notes with me. It was meant to be. I love synchronicity."

"Me too, it's a great CD." Nick added, casting a sly glance at Perri.

She looked at him blankly for a second, then said, "I get it. That Synchronicity is great too, but you know what I mean."

Walking along a side street, Perri could see her breath on the air as she exhaled. Nick remarked, "It's your time of year, isn't it? You love this."

"I do. I love all the mushy stuff that is associated with Autumn: hot cocoa, roaring fires, snuggly socks, and baking. I even like pumpkin-flavored lattes." She laughed.

"I especially like the baking." Nick said, as he held the door to the research library open for Perri. "That's a hint," he whispered at the back of her neck.

There were half a dozen people milling around the desk area. As the door closed behind Perri and Nick, everyone turned to see who the new arrivals were. Martin stepped forward to greet them. Perri made their introductions to Martin and the other attendees.

"I'm so glad you could come for the meeting. This is the first one you've been to, isn't it?" A thirty-something woman in a tight red turtleneck sweater and tight black slacks asked as she slithered up and took possession of Nick's arm. Nick craned his neck to toss an incredulous look back at Perri who just gaped back in return.

"Yes, it is." Nick answered. "Perri has been to the, well, here before, but it's the first time I've been in Harrisburg at all."

"Well, now. We're glad to have you." She steered Nick away from where Perri stood by the door wearing a look of disbelief. She could just hear the woman's voice over the conversation in the room. "There are some cookies and a pound cake on the table in the store room, and some coffee too."

"That's great, thanks. I'll get Perri." Nick extracted his arm from her grasp and turned back toward Perri.

"Alright, you help yourselves." The woman smiled and glided away as Perri approached.

"They have cake! I'm for that." Nick suggested, his face a little pinked up from embarrassment.

Perri didn't let him off the hook. "Sure you got time for that, Casanova?" she asked, enjoying teasing him for a change.

"Come on, that wasn't my fault."

"I know that." Perri turned toward the storeroom. "Dessert for supper. Why not?"

Balancing their paper plates and cups of coffee, Perri and Nick occupied a couple of available chairs and settled in to enjoy their snacks while listening to the featured speaker. A middle-aged, salt-and-pepper haired gentleman, nattily dressed, gave a well-researched and informative talk about the history of the coal industry in Saline County. He came prepared with a geographical map that illustrated the existing mines beneath the cities of Harrisburg and Eldorado, pointing out the different types of mines: room and pillar, checkerboard, long wall, and auger mines.

Afterward, Nick turned to Perri in astonishment and said, "I had no idea such a network of tunnels and excavated areas still existed under these cities. Good grief."

"I know. The ground is like a huge Swiss cheese. It's almost scary, isn't it, especially considering the New Madrid fault line runs close by?" Perri tossed her plate and cup in the trash can and brushed the crumbs off her hands. "Let's get to work. We only have about half an hour." They hurried into the stacks.

"Why are the books I want always on the bottom shelf, one-sixteenth of an inch off the floor?" Perri asked, of no one in particular, as she crabbed along scanning the titles of the books about Hardin County on the lowest row. She straightened up and said, "And right after I've eaten something isn't the best time to be squishing my innards against these jeans."

In the interest of self-preservation, Nick declined even the most benign comment, not trusting himself to keep his mouth foot free. Instead, he offered to switch places with her and bent down to take a turn. Perri switched to the upper row in the previous bookcase where the Gallatin County books were located.

At the same time that Perri said "Here's the deaths book," Nick stood with a fat book in his hands, "Here's the book on Hardin County." He chuckled a little and said, "There aren't many places, packed with people, where you can call out, 'Here's the deaths book' and no one notices."

"Cross your fingers, our luck's holding. Let's have a look." Perri led the way back toward the front of the room. They crowded together at one end of the table, the other researchers automatically scooting down to accommodate them without so much as breaking their focus or interrupting their reading.

Perri opened the top book, *Early Deaths, Recorded by County Commissioners*. There was no index or table of contents. Both the title page and that following it were produced on a manual typewriter stating the original records had been photocopied by Maryann Dodd and Georgia Lewis. The records began with the year 1821 on the third page. The records for the earliest years were sparse. As the years passed, the number of records for each one grew.

Perri explained to Nick. "Deaths were not initially required to be reported for documentation. Doctors tended to report the deaths they attended, so that's probably what most of these are."

Nick replied, "It looks like it." He reached out and touched the page lightly, "This one is a three-year-old who's cause of death was *'accidental burning.'* That's horrible. Here's another, *'Murphy, Infant. Age 2 hours. Cause of Death: No doctor nor inquest.'* It seems unreal that an infant's death would be recorded yet not list a cause or make any attempt to find one."

"It's sad, so many things that usually can be cured or treated now were a death sentence for both children and adults barely even one hundred years ago." Perri scanned through the listings. "Listen to these causes of death: *congestion of bowels, malnutrition, senility, brain fever,* and this one, a 29-year-old who died of *chill followed by heart failure.*

Perri checked the time, shook her head, and said, "Let's skip ahead to 1843." She paged through until she came to the 1840s, only a few pages away. "Here we go, 1842…1843." There were only a handful of deaths reported in 1843, and Arminda McCade was one of them.

Perri turned to Nick with a huge smile. "We got something," she said quietly, almost under her breath. She read aloud: *Arminda Eloise Grey, Residence: Sandy Ridge, Shawneetown. Place of Birth: Philadelphia, Pennsylvania. Date of Birth: March 21, 1808. Date of Death: August 3, 1843. Age: 35y. Father: Hubert M. Grey of Philadelphia. Mother: Rose Ellis of Philadelphia.*

The final sentence of the record gave Perri a full body chill. *Cause of Death: Drowning. Criminal Misadventure. Place of Death: Saltworks Well.* "She was murdered!" Perri said a little louder than she meant to. Seven heads simultaneously whipped up from their own work and turned toward her. "Sorry," she whispered.

She lowered her head toward Nick, their foreheads nearly touching. "She didn't ride out to the salt well by herself and jump in to drown. She was murdered." It's way too similar not to have some connection with the Duncans' death at the same place. I knew it!" She squeezed Nick's wrist in concentration. "What about revenge killing?"

"It could be. We'd have to figure out who would be interested in revenge? A family member would be logical, but why wait a hundred and fifty years to do it? Even reading about it, or figuring out what happened to an ancestor shouldn't provoke someone to murder. If I read about a great-great grandfather being murdered, I wouldn't be tempted to go out and kill a handful of the murderer's descendants, would you?"

"No, of course not. Some people are a little unhinged though. But, I'll agree that, while it could be a family descendant of the Mason's, revenge for Arminda's murder may not even remotely be the cause."

Perri took a photo of the page and set the book aside. "We don't have much longer." Nick slid the second book in front of her. *The Biographical Review of Johnson, Massac, Pope, and Hardin Counties.* "It's publishing date is 1893, the year after they interviewed Nathaniel." She opened it to the index, "Depending on how long this interview is, we may have to just copy it and read it at home." She turned a couple pages to reach the M's.

Nick leaned over the page, and said, "Jackpot. Mason, Alexander. Mason, Nathaniel."

Perri quickly thumbed to the page for Alexander first. This book was one of the same series as the book about Gallatin County, written in embellished prose and glowing descriptions, but very informative nonetheless. "Oh, this is awesome to find. I'll make copies."

"I'll put the other book back on the returns cart while you do that." Nick retreated to the stacks while Perri sought out Martin Sloat. By the time Nick returned to the desk area, Perri was busily copying pages from the book.

"It looks like there's a good amount of information here, even accounting for the wordiness. I can't wait to read through this."

She finished copying the two sections, handing the book to Nick who returned it to the cart. They put on their jackets, thanked Martin, and said their goodbyes to the people they'd met. Perri promised to come back to the next month's meeting, barring anything coming up to prevent her.

She wanted to sprint back to the Jeep and get home, but suggested picking up some drive-through food. The cake and cookies they'd eaten would soon cause a blood sugar crash-and-burn and she wanted to stay alert.

They drove through the same place Perri had been lured into by the heavenly-smelling char-grilled burgers. "Get the onion rings, they're magnificent."

"How many times have you been through here?"

"Hey, just the once. What are you saying?"

"Nothing, nothing at all. Just joking. I'm just saying that if it were me, I'd probably be here every night. You know me."

"You're right, you would." Nodding in agreement, she added, "I've been tempted, that's for sure, just didn't have time."

## Chapter 30

October 19, 2016

Back in the apartment, they got their plates ready first and sat together on the couch with their food on the coffee table in front of them. Perri squirted a generous helping of Brooks Ketchup, her favorite, into a bowl to dip the onion rings in and set it between them.

"Did you bring your ketchup with you or can you get it here?" Nick asked as he dunked a hot ring in the bowl.

"I always travel with my ketchup. Well, if I'm not flying anyway. I tried packing it in my checked bag once and it wasn't pretty when I opened it." Seeing the knowing grin on Nick's face, she retorted, "I'll have you know, it's the best ketchup there is and yes, I have tried others and I don't like them nearly as well. They're either too sweet or runny" She playfully bumped his hand out of the way to dunk her own onion ring. "And I'll keep my ketchup to myself if you don't agree. Looks to me like you don't hate it," she teased in return.

"I agree, I agree." Nick laughed. "I also agree that the burgers are excellent. Nice choice."

Perri stopped mid bite of her burger, then chewed rapidly and said, "You know what we forgot to do?"

"What?"

"We didn't go by the site of the old Mason house. Tabby was going to tell us where it was. Well, I'm glad we didn't or we would have been late to the meeting or missed it."

"I totally forgot about that. Maybe we can go another day."

"Mm, let's do."

After finishing their meal and clearing the coffee table, Perri started her laptop. While it booted up, she set out the copies of the Mason bios, the journals that would cover the time period of

Arminda's death, and a stack of other notes and copies she'd accumulated in the last couple of weeks.

"What's first?" Nick asked, leaning forward, elbows on knees.

"Let's read the copies we made tonight, then the journal."

It took about ten minutes to read the biographies for Alexander and Nathaniel. Perri sat back on the couch and turned toward Nick, the journal in her lap ready to be read next. "Alexander, obviously, had no input into his bio, having already been dead for longer than some of the people printing the book had been alive."

"Yeah." Nick was thoughtful. "I know Alexander was a thief, but the information seemed to apply some of the residual community hatred for his father to him. By all accounts, Samuel Mason was far and away the worse villain. I almost feel sorry for the guy."

"I know what you mean, but I doubt people who were robbed by him were sympathetic towards him."

"Francis McCade certainly wasn't in the end. Your theory that Alexander's bunch robbing his father-in-law tipped him over the edge and he went after Alexander."

"Very likely. Maybe he made that decision too quickly and then couldn't get out of it. You can't take back spoken words. Francis may have realized after he'd committed to capturing the bandits that Alexander being arrested alive wasn't the best outcome for his own good." Nick mused.

"He went along with the arresting party, even took charge of it, and shot Alexander dead before he could talk." Perri said.

"Sounds plausible. I guess that's why he took charge of it." Nick pointed to the journal. "Let's see what Francis says about Arminda's death."

Perri opened the front of the journal. "This one covers June of 1842 through September of 1843. Arminda died, was murdered rather, on August third." She paged to the first of the month of August. "Here we go, August 1, 1843."

Perri held the worn book between them, cradling it in her hand, supporting its spine without opening the book too flat. They read through the first couple of entries together. Tuesday the first and Wednesday the second were fairly generic entries, mainly covering the steamy weather and ordering provisions for the horses in the stable. "The only indication of anything amiss is on the second of August, Francis says he *Returned from salt works. New foreman difficult. AS may need to be replaced.* "He doesn't appear to have been overly concerned about anything as far as danger to his family goes. I wonder who AS is? An AS was mentioned in the first journal, right? I assume it was a man." Perri stated.

Nick frowned in concentration. Perri continued, "Remember when Francis met with the two men in the dining room of Potts' Inn? It was AS and AM. We know one was Alexander but not who the other man was. Maybe this AS is the same one. If so, he was at least aware of, if not a part of, the business Francis carried on with Alexander. AS is working as a foreman of the salt works in 1843."

"Maybe because the whole gang and robbery business fell apart after Alexander was murdered?"

"Very probably. He was considered the leader of the group. Some of them may have gone on their own or joined up with others, but it seems likely that AS got a respectable job in Francis's employ."

"That may have nothing to do with Arminda," Nick answered.

"Except that he was causing problems for Francis, at the salt works, the day before Arminda was murdered." Perri said. "Let's move on to the big day."

She read the next entry aloud. "This one is dated August 4, so he didn't write in the diary on the day Arminda was killed. *They have waited this long. I thought the danger passed, and perhaps that is why the action is…I cannot comprehend this now. I wish I had not embarked on this path but wishing now is too late to save my beloved Arminda. I am bereft for my greed and anger. I am haunted. He said he didn't know about Hubert but I didn't believe him. What if he didn't? None of this had to happen. I have prayed for absolution for my guilt. In his own home. It was rash. The children don't understand the brutality. I can't tell them. It would have ruined me and maybe others at the bank. I was able to return Hubert's penknife. He was grateful. The only silver lining.* Well, that clears up at least one thing."

Nick nodded. "Right, Francis killed Alexander to keep him from talking but then regretted it. But..." Nick's forehead creased in concentration, "...why would Francis's illicit business harm other people at the bank, unless they were involved in it too, and that doesn't seem plausible."

"I don't know. He says Alexander claimed not to have known about Hubert. I take that to mean Alexander told Francis he didn't know his father-in-law was robbed until after the fact, and he certainly didn't sanction it. It must have been a bad coincidence that whoever was out robbing that night didn't know who they were robbing. Francis says he didn't believe him. Sounds like his temper got the better of him and he outed the Mason gang, then regretted it too late."

"I think so too. They probably had an agreement not to interfere with each other's families. They had done their business, or whatever you want to call it, for eighteen years and never had a major conflict."

"Remember though, there were a few entries at this same time where Francis remarked that his wife was grumbling about his business contacts, who she called 'characters,' coming to the house because she worried about the children being around them. He wrote about suggesting they meet in the carriage house rather than in the house from then on."

"That's true. That was in February of 1836. Wasn't it the same day as the dinner where Francis found out about Hubert Grey being robbed, because we read that section several times, so the dates stuck with me."

"I know this sounds crazy, but I feel bad for Alexander, in a way." Perri glanced up at Nick with a sheepish grin.

"Now you sound like me. He was a thief, though, not an innocent," Nick reminded her.

"I know its romanticizing it, but being shot to death in his house in front of his wife and kids by someone he trusted seems a bit cruel." Perri pushed around her pile of papers, read something from one of them, then said, "I wonder who was responsible for killing Arminda. Alexander's children were too young to have done it. In August of 1843, Nathaniel was only eleven and his sister was not quite nine."

"Yeah, it had to be someone else. My money is on AS or one of the other henchmen left over from Alexander's gang?" Nick suggested. "If they had a really good set-up going, and it was brought down by Francis McCade, there were probably quite a few fellows who had a bone to pick with him."

"Yep. The arrests made in 1836 took in three other men. I doubt those three were all of them, but even at that, the bio account says the men arrested were released between three and six years later. Even the last to be released would have been out by the time Arminda was murdered. As a matter of fact, that seems to make it more likely since she was killed within a year after the last one was released."

Perri rummaged through her pile of documents and pulled out another folder of photocopies and prints of microfilm articles. "Let's see who it was they arrested." She scanned through several articles. "As we were saying, according to historical accounts, the robberies decreased considerably after Alexander's death. As time went on, it became more dangerous to rob people on the road. The population in the area increased and laws were better enforced. Their livelihood was significantly restricted, so if they didn't want to move on to somewhere else, most of them had to get regular jobs or settle down and farm like everyone else."

"Here it is." She scrutinized the small print on the printed copy, moving her head so the light of the lamp shone directly on the paper. "Those arrested were Joshua Rutledge, Abrahm Stegall, and Luke Potts. Stewart Pike was arrested but released. There it is. Abrahm Stegall. He has to be AS."

"Putting Arminda's body in the salt well would be a statement directed at Francis. Since Stegall was out of prison in time to get the foreman job, begin to cause problems, and then kill Arminda, it's even more likely it was revenge. Even Francis thought so. He says 'they' but doesn't name anyone. Let's read on and see if he eventually does name names."

"I wonder if Francis saw giving Stegall the job at the salt works as a form of making amends."

"Good point."

After reading through the rest of the journal, Perri and Nick discussed what they learned by reading between the lines of

Francis's entries. Nick said, "There was something that stood out to me."

Perri asked, "What was that?"

"Francis, when he wrote about his disagreements with Alexander, kept referring to 'them' or 'those' like there was something Alexander wanted from him but he wasn't willing to give him, or sell him."

"Right, he mentioned that he 'gave one back' to Alexander and it was enough for a while, but then he wanted more. Do you think it was something, or several things, they stole from someone and then couldn't agree on how to split them up?"

"Could be. It's really hard to say without more information than he gives."

"I agree. The fact that he said he gave one *back* to Alexander indicates Francis got whatever it was from Alexander to begin with."

They sat in silence for a few minutes. Perri opened her mouth to say something but hesitated. Nick said, "What?"

"I was just wondering."

"About what?"

"Remember Tabby told us about some things left in the house that she believed were from the Mason's time, the things she donated to the museum which were eventually stolen?"

"Yeah."

"We wondered at the time, why go to the trouble of breaking into the post office to steal seemingly worthless items and nothing else? Sure, their age makes them antiques, but not in good shape and not of any obvious value."

"True."

"What if something in that group had value no one else knows about?"

Nick nodded slowly, mulling over what Perri was saying. "Ok. I'll buy that."

"Tabby said there were the remains of a holster, Alexander's maybe? Even so, the most unlikely thing to be valuable since it was so degraded. She didn't mention finding a gun. Any gun Alexander had was probably long gone, kept by another family member, sold off, or taken by one of his cohorts. I doubt the remnants of a holster were anything someone wanted, even though they took it too."

Nick said, "Maybe they took it to cover what they really wanted. There were some mother-of-pearl buttons. I don't know anything about that. Would they be valuable?"

"They could have some intrinsic value, but they're hardly unique or rare enough to go to such lengths for three of them."

"That leaves the unfinished drawing." Nick asked.

"Right. A drawing, unfinished and unsigned. That has much more potential as a possibility. And there's an itch in the back of my brain about this, something I've read that's ringing a bell, but it's so faint, I can't quite drag it up into the light."

"Something you've read about a drawing?"

"Yeah. More than that though." Perri took her laptop from the coffee table and sat it in her lap. Nick turned toward her on the couch and she shifted to lean back against Nick's shoulder so he could see. "Let's see if we can find something."

"Was it about missing artwork, like an art theft?" Nick wondered.

"No, not an art heist." Perri tapped away on the keyboard, at the same time saying, "I think the reason I don't remember all the details about it was that I was reading about something else at the time and it was mentioned in passing." She suddenly looked up, then at Nick.

"What?" He asked.

Perri laughed. "I remember what it was about it that caught my attention. The name of the artist."

"A well-known artist?"

"No, but it was my name although it was spelled differently. It was spelled S-e-y-m-o-u-r. The guy was part of an expedition, yeah, I'm remembering it now. Ok, that is significant."

"You want to tell me about this, or shall I keep saying 'What?'" Nick gave her a lopsided grin.

"Sorry." Perri opened a new tab in her browser while explaining to Nick. "I don't have the book, not a printed copy of it anyway, but I do have it saved in my Google Books library online."

"You can do that?"

"Sure. There are all sorts of free books available. Lots of them are educational, like history or reference. There are so many that I had no idea existed and couldn't find anywhere else." The Google Books web page displayed and Perri clicked on My Library. "Anyway, the reason this is important is that," she opened a saved book, "this expedition went right past Elizabethtown."

"Oh, really? That is significant."

"Even more so because..." Perri paused as she entered Seymour into the search box for the text, "...as I recall, some of Mr. Seymour's artwork went missing."

"Missing? Like someone took them?" Nick asked.

"That's the thing, no one knows why, at least not now. I'm sure he did at the time but there is no record of it, that we know about anyway." The first occurrence of the name was in the introduction where the members of the expedition were introduced. Perri tapped the link. "See, he's listed as 'painter for the expedition.' It explains each person's responsibilities, like a modern job description.

Nick reached around her and pointed to the name below Seymour's. "Wow, this is great. They had a naturalist, a Mr. Peale, and Lieutenant Graham and Cadet Swift were to be Topographers, Mr. Say was the Zoologist. This was quite a production. Here's a talented guy, Edwin James was Botanist, Geologist, and Surgeon. That's some combination."

"It was a production. The land along the Ohio was still wild and mostly uncharted at the time. The group was meant to travel from Pittsburgh to the northern Rockies taking note of everything, as much information as they could gather. They even had a special steamboat built for the trip, it was called the Western Engineer."

"What made it special?"

"It was made to maneuver in much shallower water than most flat-bottomed boats, especially with all the gear they were carrying. It was also equipped with a cannon, howitzers, and the crew had sabers and rifles. Very impressive. The boat itself was made to look like a serpent to scare off would-be Native American attackers. It had some other unique features too," clicking to another page, she said, "there's a whole section here about it."

"I had no idea. That's amazing."

Perri scrolled the book back to the first page, chapter one. "The Western Engineer under the command of the Honorable Secretary of War, Major Long."

Nick read the text for a few moments. "I'd like to read this book."

"Just search for the title and you can put it in your library and come back to it anytime you want." Perri answered. Nick added the name of the book to the Notes in his phone.

Perri talked while typing in a new search term, "It's too bad though, the expedition had a lot of problems, mainly money related, and ended up being abandoned before completion due to going way over budget."

"What happened to some of the artwork this Seymour artist did is a mystery then?"

"Correct." Perri turned toward Nick and set the laptop on his lap. "Here, look at this paragraph, page 32. It describes two sketches of 'the cave' done by Seymour. The cave mentioned is Cave-in-Rock. These sketches have never been found. Actually, none of the artwork he did prior to arriving at the Mississippi has been found. That sketch Tabby told us about was a river scene, but was unfinished." She stood up and paced back and forth in front of the coffee table, getting more excited about the possibility the more she thought about it.

Nick looked up at Perri, "You think that drawing was one of his? One of his lost drawings?"

"It seems like a longshot at first, doesn't it? But the more I think about it, it makes more sense than anything else. But then there's the problem of how would anyone know? Who found out and how? If the world at large doesn't know what happened to Samuel Seymour's artwork, how *did* someone find out."

"We found out, or at least we have an idea. Who's to say someone else didn't find out the same way? And, it's been somewhere all this time, so presumably, someone knew. Maybe it was recorded in a book or private letters that we don't have access to and wouldn't know to look for."

"You mean like family information, stories or whatever, handed down?" Perri asked.

"Yeah, like an off-hand mention in a letter, not really thinking it meant much. We've got Francis's diaries, who's to say someone else doesn't have diaries or papers left behind by a person who knew about it?" Nick said.

"True." Perri sat down, then got right back up. "Let's have a look again at the earliest journals. Wasn't there something about a packet of papers that Francis got?"

"You're right, I think there was." Nick sorted through the journals and located the first one, leafing through the pages until he found what they were looking for.

"Here it is." Perri sat back down next to Nick and placed her finger on the page for an entry at the end of May 1819. We read this before but it didn't have any significance at the time. Now, maybe it does."

"Francis had to rearrange the contents of his travel pack to make room for a packet of papers. Think it might have been the artwork?" Nick asked.

"I want to think so, but that doesn't make it so." Perri grinned. "Let's compare the expedition account." Perri picked up the laptop and cleared the search box. "What was that day in May, the night Francis spent at Potts' Inn when he first met Alexander and AS?"

Nick glanced at the page, then said, "It was…May 29."

Perri typed in May 29. "That brought up the day they reached Cumberland, that's too far, let me scroll back. She worked her way back through the pages. A nearly silent 'Oh' escaped her lips.

"Oh? Oh what? Come on." Nick urged her, impatiently.

"Here it is! They left Shawneetown at noon on May 28. It says they were at the cave on the 29[th.] They left 'Cave Inn,' sometime during the day on May 29 because it says they passed the mouth of the Cumberland and a village called Smithland and those are further downstream. At any rate, they were at the cave the same day that Alexander gave a packet of papers to Francis at Potts' Inn in the evening. Potts' Inn is just a few miles up the ferry road from Cave-in-Rock, and the ferry road was Alexander's main hunting grounds."

Perri looked up, all smiles. "This is way too much of a coincidence, don't you think?"

"It seems like it. You think Samuel Seymour accidently left some of his drawings behind when they left?"

"He must have. Maybe they left in a hurry and he dropped them. Cave-in-Rock was ready-made shelter often used to tie up for the night. That being common knowledge, bandits roamed both sides of the entire river bank around there. If the party spent the night in the cave, and according to this account they very well may have, it would be likely that some things were lost or left behind if they had to leave in a hurry. Elizabethtown isn't far from Cave-in-Rock, so it was prime real estate, not for just any thieves, for Mason and his bunch."

"And remember, the journal said that on the night of the 29th, Francis was accompanied by a group of men on the road."

"Right. Mason's men?"

"Mason *and* his men. They all stayed at Pott's Inn." Perri furiously typed to bring up Google maps and narrow down a location. "Here." She turned the computer toward Nick again and pointed. "That's where Potts' Inn was located. And here's Elizabethtown, Cave-in-Rock, and the original Shawneetown."

Nick nodded. "Centrally located to all those places." Becoming more convinced, Nick nodded vigorously. "I think we're on to something."

"Me too. So...if Mason got possession of some of Seymour's drawings, the one Tabby was given in the box of things from the house may have been one of his. The fact that it wasn't finished and looked like it had gotten wet could mean it had been near, or in, the river."

"Right. Tabby said it was a view of the river, so he could have been sitting along the bank and maybe it fell or blew into the water when he got up." Nick replied.

"That's something we may never be able to find out. If he'd written an account of it, it would either have been in here," she nodded her head toward the pages of the book on the screen, "or published separately."

"Do you think he wrote a book about it himself?" Nick asked.

"No. As a matter of fact, he basically dropped out of sight after this expedition. According to the annotations for this book, the only drawings of his that survived were west of the Mississippi with the exception of two that were along the Ohio River further up toward Pittsburgh. Since the journey began in there, it would mean quite a hoard of paintings and drawings that Francis might have gotten from Alexander.

They both sat, quietly reflecting on the information. Tapping her fingers along the edges of the laptop, Perri said, "And remember, in the journal, Francis said he 'gave one back' to Alexander but it wasn't enough."

"You're right. You think once the expedition was over and became publicized that Alexander or Francis, or both, figured out what they had and Alexander wanted back in on it?"

"That seems plausible. If Alexander started asking for, or making demands for, some of the drawings and Francis gave him the one that wasn't finished, you can see why he may have been upset and wanted a different one."

"Yes, he might have been angry that Francis gave him an unfinished drawing that wasn't worth as much as the finished ones."

"Ok. Here's what I'm wondering." Perri said. Nick leaned forward, one knee bouncing up and down while he waited for her to gather her thoughts. "It's a fact that Seymour's work has been missing all these years." She stopped, lost in thought again.

Nick shifted restlessly on the couch.

"So...assuming it wasn't destroyed, it's been somewhere all this time. What if someone thought, whether right or wrong, that those drawings were in the Duncan house, stashed away with all the other family memories? Wouldn't that be a reason for searching the house?"

Nick blinked a couple times, his expression sobering. "Oh wow, yeah, that would be a reason to go searching for it. I wonder if the person who killed Ruby and George thought they..."

Perri finished his sentence, "...knew where the drawings were and wouldn't tell. Oh my gosh. They may have been killed over something they didn't even know about."

"And, the salt well. That could all tie together, right? A little symbology." Nick asked.

Perri's brows knitted together, "Yeah, it could. If it isn't a huge coincidence, it would have to be someone who knew about Arminda's death and maybe the reason for it. And..." she thought again for a few moments, "...that's why that someone stole the roll of microfilm from the library in Shawneetown!"

"That makes sense, except, how would the person know why Arminda was killed? We didn't put two and two together until we read the journal entry. Wouldn't they have had to read the same journal?"

"Or another source we don't have, but they do. Remember, Alexander's kids may have been too young to comprehend what was going on, but his wife wasn't, and she was still around for a while. Who's to say she didn't write it all down from her point of view and pass that on to her descendants."

"That would make everything fit, wouldn't it?"

"It looks like Ruby Duncan was reading the journals since she was keeping one of them in the kitchen. Could she have mentioned it to someone?"

"That's possible. If that's the case, it'd be someone in the family, or at least a close friend."

Perri caught a glance of the clock in the kitchen. "Ugh. I have to get to bed. We need to find out if there's anyone around here who is descended from the Masons. I'm going to ask Pearl some questions tomorrow when I see her. Maybe she'll think of something that will give us a clue." She pushed herself up from the couch and shut the laptop. "I'm ready for Friday. I don't have anyone to see Friday, at least not yet. They could add someone on, but so far, all my Friday people have healed up or are in the hospital again, and since I'm a temp, they aren't giving me new ones until everyone else's schedules are full."

"Then Friday will be open for investigating, won't it?" Nick smiled.

"You got that right."

## Chapter 31

October 20, 2016, 8:00 a.m.

"It's in the normal range. You're doing really well keeping your glucose regulated." Perri packed the glucometer and supplies in her tote bag.

Pearl beamed a smile back at her. "I'm trying. I'm not cheating." Her smile turned mischievous. "Not as much anyway."

"It's good enough that we can reduce your checks to a couple times a week."

"I have to admit that Stella not staying here as often helps, because she eats a lot of junk food and I can't resist if it's here. I never could understand how she stays stick thin and eats nothing but trash and drinks all the time. I guess it's because she smokes. My mom smoked and said she did it because it kept her thin, but that's how she got lung cancer."

"Different people have different metabolisms. Smoking to keep thin is…well, I'm sure you know firsthand that it isn't a good idea." Perri ached to say more, such as 'Just because Stella weighs a scant hundred pounds doesn't mean she's healthy.' She pushed away the temptation since it would cause Pearl to worry and she already had enough grief from Stella. What she thought to herself was that Stella could keel over at any given time from any number of causes and it wouldn't be a surprise.

Changing topics, Perri said, "Can I ask you a couple questions? It's not necessarily about your family history, but it might tie into it."

"Sure. What do you want to ask me?" Pearl anticipated Perri's questions with a gentle smile.

"Do you, or did you in the past, know any family or person with the surname Mason?"

"Mason. Hmm. Well, I went to high school with a girl named Aggie Mason, but I think they moved here from somewhere out west, I don't remember where."

"Ok. Do you recall anything Ruby or George might have told you about anyone outside of the family wanting to read Francis's diaries?"

Pearl answered right away. "No, never, because I didn't even know they were there."

Perri nodded, disappointed. "Well, I'd better get…"

"Now wait." Pearl pinched her lips together and placed her forefinger over them, thinking. "I do remember someone. She wasn't a Mason, but her mama was. Does that count?"

"Sure."

"I didn't really know her personally, but Stella worked for Cleaning Crew the week they cleared out the old Anderson house, over on Big 4 Street in Eldorado."

Perri was perplexed and tried for a moment to see the relevancy in what Pearl was saying. "Anderson house? I'm sorry, I don't see the connection."

"Of course, you wouldn't know. Well, Nettie Anderson, the lady who died, was Nettie Frederick. My granny knew her back when they were young. The Fredericks used to live in Old Shawneetown too but moved to Eldorado after the flood. Nettie's son, Gerald, lived in the house until he died last year. That's when Stella helped with the cleanout. Gerald never married and didn't have any children." With a snicker, she said, "Not that he claimed anyway." Pearl watched Perri's face, expectantly.

A vague recognition stirred in Perri's mind. "I still don't quite…"

"Nettie's mamma was a Mason. You see?"

"Oh! Ok, I had…I see now." Perri rapidly processed the new information, Nettie was a name she'd just heard. "Do you know if she's from the same Mason family who lived in Elizabethtown?"

"I'm pretty sure they are because I remember my granny telling us stories about that bunch and how crazy some of them were. At first, she wasn't happy with momma running around with a Mason, but I guess the mean streak burned out by the time it got to Nettie."

Perri wasn't so sure the 'crazy' had passed on to anyone after Alexander, but didn't mention it. "You don't happen to know what Nettie's father's first name was, do you?" Perri asked hopefully.

"No, I don't. But you ought to be able to find that out, I would think, as good as you have been looking up other stuff."

"What about Nettie's mother's first name?"

"Her momma's name was Elizabeth."

Perri stared at Pearl. "Elizabeth Mason?"

"Yes, that was it."

"Do you know about how old Nettie was when she died?"

"Oh lawsy…let's see. I don't know exactly, but she had to at least have been nigh on eighty. Gerald was in his early eighties when he passed and Nettie was almost forty when Gerald was born. Nettie died back in the early 70s.

Doing some mental subtraction, Perri thought Nettie fit in the age group to have been a daughter of the Elizabeth Mason who "married a Frederick," as Tabby Ford had told them. "Thanks." Perri turned for the door. "If you think of anything else, I'd really appreciate it if you let me know. I…want to follow up on something."

"I will, honey."

"Pearl. If anyone calls on you again about the old house…"

"Then what?"

"Well, just be cautious, ok?"

"Ok, I will. You worry too much about that house, Perri."

Perri opened the car door and slid into the seat in one motion. She scribbled the information about Nettie Frederick and her mother on the paper package of a 4x4 and slipped it in her pocket. She headed back for Eldorado as quickly as she could go without worrying too much about collecting a speeding ticket.

Stanley Tollander was next on her list and Perri found him waiting on the front step of his home, a blanket draped across his shoulders against the crisp air. Fortunately, he wasn't suffering from the abscessed wounds he had the first time Perri saw him, but rather just needed a check to make sure they were still healing properly.

"Hiya Stanley. How're things today?" Perri called to the elderly man as soon as she stepped out of the car while she took her bag from the back seat and shut the door.

"Things are just grand, I'm tellin' ya. You keepin' outta trouble, girl?" Stanley flashed Perri a Cheshire cat grin and used the mailbox post to pull himself to a standing position then leaned on his cane.

Touched that Stanley had come outside to wait for her, Perri opened the door to the house and watched Stanley as he stepped up into the living room, assessing his mobility with the cane. "You look like you're getting around well. Do you feel better? Any pain?"

"I feel fine and I can't say I've had any pain except for my joints aching from the exercise. I've been doing like you said, keeping the bandages dry and not using any lotion on my feet. I've been gettin' my walks in too. Feels good to have the circulation going a bit even if it isn't great."

"I'm so glad to see you up and about. Let's take a quick look."

After completing her assessment and dressing change, Perri told Stanley, "You know, it won't be long and you won't need any dressings. The left leg is nearly healed up already."

Stanley smiled a wide grin again, pleased with himself. "I can't wait for that."

"Before I take off again, can I ask you something, Stanley?"

"Why sure."

"Being from this area, you probably are familiar with stories about the Mason gang? I know it's been two hundred years, but the tales are still floating around."

Stanley nodded quickly, "You bet. Loved those stories when I was a boy. Adventure, that's what it was. We didn't think about the lawless part, just the idea of ridin' horses and shootin' guns and hangin' around the river banks all day. That seemed like the life to a bunch of kids. Kinda like Tom Sawyer and Huckleberry Finn." His cackly laugh filled the living room and echoed like it was coming from all sides.

"Did you know anyone who was related to that family of Masons?"

Stanley coughed violently, then gasped in a lungful and exhaled a long "Hoo-boy! Well...let's see. I knew a few Masons as a kid, at school, and there were a couple at the mine, but I can't say I know who their kin were."

"I understand. Not something kids talk about too often, is it?"

"No, not unless they're related to Jesse James or Daniel Boone. Had plenty of kids around who boasted they were. Most of 'em probably weren't. Used to play cowboys and outlaws, had shoot-em-ups. Those kids always had to be the Sheriff or the best six-shooter." Stanley laughed again, much softer this time. "Plenty of fights behind the old Lincoln school too. Those were the days. School's gone now too, just like most of those boys."

"It's hard when so many people you grew up with and knew are gone, isn't it? My Great-Aunt said as much. She was almost one hundred years old."

"You got that right, girly. I remember her, they lived right down this road." Stanley visibly shook off the mood. "Isn't exactly an uncommon name, but there was a family of Masons that lived on Womack Street. All those houses on that street were mining company houses put up well before I was born. My grandparents lived in one in 1920, and my dad grew up in one."

Adding another Mason family to the tally, Perri asked, "Did you know them, the Masons on Womack, I mean?"

"They had kids, but they weren't my age. They were older and I didn't run with them, but I remember them because my best friend, Jimmy Norman, lived in the house next door. His older brother was friends with the Mason boys so they were over at the Norman house sometimes, but they didn't talk to us much. They all used to work in the fields detasseling and picking corn during the summer and they'd come in to eat when they were done. There was a whole passel of Masons, so maybe they got more to eat at Jimmy's house than at home."

"I had heard there was another descendant of the Masons, Gerald Anderson, who lived on Big 4 Street. Do you know if he was part of the Masons your friend lived next to?"

"Gerald Anderson? I think they were cousins of some sort."

"Then they *were* related?"

"I'm pretty sure. It's vague, you understand, but I seem to recall some scuffling over a family inheritance. Something to do with somebody's Will. We were about ten years old and that grown-up stuff didn't concern us much. There was some hollerin' and door-slammin' to be heard but no details. If I heard details, I don't remember them."

"You helped me just with what you did remember. Thank you."

"You writing something about the Masons now? Thought you were writing about the old McCade place."

"I am, but the Mason family is wound up in the McCade family." Perri shifted off her chair. "Well, Stanley, you're doing amazingly well. I'm so glad to see you up and around. I'll be back the first part of next week, ok?"

"I look forward to it."

Perri took her leave of Stanley feeling both heartened by his progress and saddened by his memories. She wanted to go back to the apartment for lunch, but knew if she did, she wouldn't want to leave. It would be too tempting to be with Nick and for them both to work on figuring out who was involved in the drawing theft, robbing the Duncans, and most of all, killing the Duncans.

To steer clear of one temptation, she opted for another and decided to go through a drive-thru and take her lunch to Mahoney Park. She could sit in the car or find a table in the sun and eat in the peace and quiet. It would give her a chance to mull over what she knew. As she tossed her bag into the back seat, she tried to avoid, but failed, to run her gaze over the old Douglas Street Market. Once, it had been a thriving neighborhood market. Now it was abandoned, the windows spray painted or covered with plywood, the awnings ripped away, and trash accumulated around the outside. She shook her head, wondering how much longer it would stand before someone pulled it down, leaving another empty lot peppered with stray bricks and chunks of mortar.

After a protracted snarl of wholly unintelligible crackling sounds from the speaker, Perri launched into her order and waited for a response. Trying to decipher the buzzing response that most likely represented her bill total, she swatted at a brush against her ankle. "Damn flies, you'd think they'd die off by now." She decided no further squawks would be forthcoming and pulled forward to the window.

The girl working the window was busy taking another order and speaking Klingon in return. Perri pulled a few bills from her wallet and dug around in the cache of pennies in the change purse, looking for change if she needed it. Glad she put the car in park, her leg automatically jerked forward as the insect crawled around under her scrub pants leg. "Ugh...get away!"

"I'm sorry, what?" The bespectacled, ball-capped girl at the window looked at Perri with a mixture of astonishment and apathy.

"Sorry, just a bug. Here you go." Perri handed her money to the girl who did a less than stellar job of hiding her eyeroll. Within a few seconds, she handed back the change and thrust a large waxed paper cup and a paper bag through the window, already taking the next order over her headset.

Perri took the sack and turned to sit it in the passenger seat. A brief motion in the driver's side floorboard caught her eye. She sat the bag down and leaned sideways, next to the steering wheel to peer down. The car behind her tooted its horn, but she didn't hear it. After a moment of processing time, her brain finally comprehended the triangular-shaped head she was looking at. Once it registered, the screaming began.

The snake was draped over her foot and ankle, just above the tongue of her shoe so it was sliding over her sock. It slithered up toward the center console. Even knowing she shouldn't make quick movements, Perri was completely consumed with panic and all restraint went out the still open window. She flung her car door open which immediately crashed against the brick wall of the building. Nowhere near enough room to get out. Uselessly, she shoved against it again, clearly not registering that she couldn't move the building to get out of the car and away from the snake.

The dark brown color which had blended so well in the darkness of the floorboard area now was visible as it used the gear shift to climb upward. She reached toward the drive-thru window, without taking her eyes off the snake, she struggled to organize her vocal cords enough to croak out, "Cottonmouth!" Then, building up a little more steam, "Cottonmouth!!"

The cashier, who had initially been amused at what she thought was Perri's fear of a bee or wasp, shouted back, "I just gave you your iced tea! Drink some of that. Geez." She smirked and jerked her thumb at the window, calling her co-workers to come see the crazy woman in the drive through.

Not daring to take her eyes off it, Perri pointed frantically at the snake, which was now fluidly wrapping around the gear shift. Having put the car in park, she couldn't shift it into drive to pull away from the building, not with the serpent coiling tighter around the gear shift. With horrifying graceful slowness, it reared up in front of the dashboard and turned its broad head toward the motion of Perri's flailing and went into a defensive pose. It opened its mouth wide, displaying its fangs and the pale white flesh lining its mouth. The elevated position revealed russet bands the length of the snake which were visible on its underbelly but muted on its upper body by the dark brown coloring.

By now, the scornful cashier had spotted the cause of the problem. Realizing a dry mouth from a post recreational drug was not the entertaining problem she had suspected, she plowed her way backwards through her fellow fast food workers just beginning to gather behind her.

Almost not daring to breathe, Perri wrestled her panic under enough control to keep from trying to claw her way through the roof of the Cooper. She held as still as she could. She didn't move her legs, and her only arm movement was from trembling. She was unable to keep her chest from heaving as she breathed rapidly and deeply. The snake held still as well in a standoff.

Perri said, in a near-whisper, "Please call 911 or animal control or both!" No one answered.

She tried to focus on formulating a plan of what to do next. She had grown up near the banks of the Ohio River and knew that, while the aquatic Cottonmouths were a pit viper and were venomous, they weren't unnecessarily aggressive, but would no doubt sink those amazingly long fangs into her flesh if provoked. It was obviously feeling more than a little threatened by all the commotion. Perri knew it would prefer to get away rather than strike. She kept repeating, "Be still, be still," in her head, but it was mighty difficult to think rationally with those slit-pupil eyes staring at her. She obviously couldn't get out through her door, she couldn't shift into gear, or climb out through another window since the Cottonmouth was between her and the rest of the car. She was thinking that maybe she could ask someone to…

The agitated man from the pickup truck behind her chose that moment to pound on the passenger window and grab the door handle, flinging the door open. Perri heard his first few words, "Just what the hell do you…," but they were snipped off in a flash of fear. The snake, surprised and frightened by the sudden sound and movement behind it, lunged sideways toward the new threat.

The snake moved faster than she imagined and was nothing more than a blur. Before she could even gasp in a breath, it soundlessly flowed like a silk scarf across and down the opposite side of the console and vanished beneath the passenger seat.

Perri looked down, examining her arms, turning them over and back again, but saw no marks. She had felt motion against her outer forearm, but no pain. Cottonmouth bites were extremely painful. She looked at her arms again curiously, then her legs, not quite believing she hadn't been bitten.

She looked up and out the now open passenger door. The man from the pickup had backed at least fifteen feet away from the car and was waving off a woman from the car behind him with one hand while talking on his phone with the other. Most of the burger joint employees had vaporized, leaving only one young lady peering out at Perri.

The girl at the drive-up window said, "I called 911. Do you need anything? I mean, can we do anything for you?"

Her voice barely audible, she answered, "Not right now, especially not with it still in the car." Perri listened and rolled her eyes around without moving her head, looking for any sign of the Cottonmouth. Nothing. Knowing she should just sit as still as possible until help arrived, the urge to get out was rapidly overtaking her logic.

Since it was on the other side of the console, or at least she hoped it still was, she decided to very carefully move the car forward enough to bail out. She'd take a concrete scrape from diving out the door any day over a pit viper bite. The odds of having antivenin in stock at the local hospital weren't promising.

With painful slowness, she pressed one foot to the brake so the car wouldn't jolt. She raised her right hand to the gear shift and as quietly as the mechanics allowed, eased it into drive and let up enough pressure on the brake to let the Cooper roll forward a few yards, until the drivers' side door cleared the building. She didn't want the car to roll out into traffic, so she shifted back to park.

She pulled the door handle and launched herself as far out of the car as she could. It was more of a tumble and roll action, but it got her out of the car. She scrambled loosely to her feet, hands scrabbling over the pavement strewn with cigarette butts to keep her balance as she put distance between herself and the car. Once she made it to the grassy verge near the street, she flopped down on her knees, forehead pressed to the cool green blades, her fists closing around white clover flowers. Jagged sobs of relief broke uncontrollably. She didn't care who heard.

The feet of the girl from the drive-up window appeared next to Perri. "You ok?" The girl crouched down.

Perri couldn't answer, she just nodded. Frazzled from the adrenal rush and subsequent let down, she attempted to sit up, but the effort deteriorated into rolling on her side and then flopping onto to her back. She closed her eyes against the glare of the sun, directly overhead.

The girl stood up and looked west. "I hear sirens."

## Chapter 32

October 20, 2016, Afternoon

Perri had declined a trip to the hospital. She didn't have any bite marks. No pain, shortness of breath, blurred vision, or nausea. The paramedics had checked her blood pressure, temperature, and respiratory sounds and reluctantly released her in the absence of any symptoms.

She'd also finished talking to the police, which had been less pleasant since she needed to answer their questions without admitting she could possibly have been asking a lot of questions that some people may not have viewed as her business. She didn't want to point the finger at anyone without knowing and, right now, there were a few people who were vying for the top spot of suspect. She wanted to get back to the apartment, where it was quiet, but she still had another patient to see, and she was more than a little late already.

The animal control officers had captured the snake and taken it away to release it in an appropriate area.

Perri had gone back to sit in the grass while the police officers called in her car to verify she wasn't someone they needed to arrest, then filled out their report. She just needed their signal that she could go. She squeezed her eyes together as she spotted Nick hastening across the adjacent parking lot, where he'd parked the Jeep. "Oh boy," she muttered.

Nick dropped down on his knees in the grass in front of Perri, his face twisted into a mask of worry. "What's going on? I hear from Reuben that your car is sitting at the burger place with both doors open, a police car, and an ambulance. Why didn't you call me? What happened? Are you alright?"

"I'm sorry for not calling you. I should have." She gave a deep sigh, then said, "I guess I just wanted to sit and try to sort it out in my head." Nick's furrowed brow didn't smooth any after that statement, so she continued. "Someone put a snake in my car."

"A snake? In your car? What kind of snake?" Nick fired questions at her.

Perri put up a hand to stem the tide. "Hang on. It was a Cottonmouth." Nick's eyes widened and his mouth opened. "Hang on. I wasn't bitten." She raised both arms as proof, but it went past Nick's notice. "I'm glad, because there's a shortage of antivenin."

"Antivenin?" Nick looked at her in confusion, still reeling over the news.

"Same thing as antivenom, but in nursing school, we learned it as antivenin."

Impatiently, Nick asked, "How did that happen? You always lock your car. It wasn't broken into, was it? Maybe it just crawled up in the car on its own."

"That's what I've been mulling over for the last half hour. I realized that when I left my last patient's house before lunch, I don't recall unlocking the car. I remember opening the door and putting my bag inside, but not unlocking it first. I had to get my keys out of the pocket in my purse after I was sitting in the car, so I couldn't have unlocked it first. Normally, I do always lock it, but today, when I got to that patient's house, he was outside when I arrived. He's a little shaky, so I was concerned he might fall. I had my attention on him and I was talking to him and hurrying to get up to the house. I think I just got my bag and walked off."

"That means your car sat in front of his house unlocked. For how long?"

"Between thirty-five and forty minutes. And, before you ask, I didn't look out the window while I was there, I had my back to it."

Nick ran both hands down his face and breathed through them. He dropped them back to his knees, then steadied himself with the fingertips of one hand. "How do you do it? In a town where most people can't get their mail without everyone knowing, someone puts a venomous snake in your car and no one saw it? How do you find such trouble?" He gave her a wan smile. "I know, I know, you didn't mean for it to happen, but you do have a knack for getting into screwball situations. That being said, I'm relieved you weren't hurt and we need to pay attention to this. Someone is aware you're asking questions and doesn't like it."

"Exactly. Which means we're on the right path." Perri agreed, her eyes lighting up.

"You are…"

One of the policemen was crossing the pavement from the parked cruiser. "Incorrigible, yeah, yeah, I know." Perri pulled her legs beneath her, Nick helped her stand up.

The officer said, "You're free to go. If you get any additional information about this incident, call the station and report it. Otherwise, there isn't much we can do unless a witness turns up."

"I understand that, I didn't expect you could. Thank you."

The officer nodded and returned to the patrol car, taking a seat on the passenger side. The cruiser pulled out of the lot. "Done here?" Nick asked.

"Lordy, yes, and I'm glad. I knew I shouldn't eat another burger, but this was one helluva way to keep me from doing it." Perri looked at her watch. "I've got another patient. I already called the agency to let them know I would be late. I want to get this over with and go home."

"I'll follow you and wait while you are there, is that against the healthcare law for me to see what house you go to?"

"I can't see how it would since I'm not giving you information about who lives there. It isn't like a patient's neighbors don't all see a home health nurse park and walk up to the house anyway. It isn't like we have a secret entrance or go incognito. I hate for you to have to wait, but I'm glad you are. I won't be long."

They walked together back to the Mini, its doors now closed and looking very normal. Perri opened the driver's door and felt her stomach lurch just a little. She hesitated.

"You want me to drive the Cooper and you drive the Jeep?" Nick offered.

"Yes, but no, because I need to get back on this horse now or it'll be too easy to avoid it more and more. I don't want to dread driving my own car. The snake's gone, I saw them tote it off in a bag. And they checked to make sure there weren't any others." She slipped into the seat and shut the door. "I'm ok. Not going to throw up, I don't think. I didn't have lunch, so nothing to regurgitate."

Nick laughed. "That's one thing I like about you, you're so dainty." Perri shrugged wearily. He bent down and kissed her on the forehead through the open window. "I'll follow you there."

## Chapter 33

October 21, 2016, Late morning

"Yesterday is a day I'm glad to see the backside of." Perri was finished showering and dressed, breakfast made, eaten, and cleared away. She'd tried to wash up the few dishes from breakfast, but Nick insisted she relax while he did it. She'd welcomed the chance to do a little more digging on some of the niggling loose threads in her mind.

When Nick walked into the living room, she said, "Thanks for that. I feel much better today. I'm starting to feel guilty leaving you with getting the meals all the time."

"I'll take making scrambled eggs over doing battle with a Cottonmouth any day, thank you very much." Nick lifted Perri's feet and sat down on the couch, settling her legs across his lap. "You know, I'm afraid checking into this mess is getting too dangerous. I know you want to write the article, but can't you do that with what you already have? Surely it's enough for one e-zine article?"

"It is, that's true. But, honestly, I don't want to stop. I want to know who killed the Duncans and why."

"But I don't want you killed in the process."

"I don't want me killed in the process either. Don't you feel like we're almost there? I think we only lack a few pieces of information and we could put this together."

"Ok. What do we need to know to figure this out?"

"We need to find out if someone in this area is a descendant of Nettie Frederick, and thus from the Mason line. If there is, that's who would have the most reason to kill the Duncans if they were hoping to find the lost artwork. It would be worth a fortune if they could find it."

"Do you think you can find that out?" Nick asked.

"I'm going to try. While I've been sitting here, I looked up something I read, oh gosh, last week sometime. It was when I first heard about the vandalism in the cave. I was reading about the past instances of vandalism and the people from long ago that used to bury their valuables, which is why people are digging holes now."

"Were you linking the hole in the cemetery to the ones in the cave?"

"Yeah. People who buried valuables that they knew would be there longer than just overnight often marked the spot by burying them next to a tree that stood out from the others, one that wasn't easy to miss. Marking a tree or a spot wasn't a good practice since it alerted others that there could be something buried there."

"Makes sense."

"Remember, right next to the hole at Gold Hill, there was a sassafras tree growing into the path and was leaning over it?"

"Yeah, I do."

"Well, I think that's why the hole was dug there. It doesn't tell us anything about who may have done it, just makes a tentative sort of link to the vandalism in the cave. Both places were historically locations for buried valuables. And Gold Hill used to be even closer to the McCade property than it is now."

"Alright, I can see that. But how does that help?"

"It just gives us something else to consider when thinking about who could be responsible. It always comes down to someone who had to know family information not readily available to just anyone. I wouldn't know most of this stuff without Pearl's help."

"Why don't you tell me if you have someone in mind?" Nick asked. "I've had the feeling for a couple of days that you suspect someone, but don't want to say, like you're turning it over and over in your mind seeing if it fits the puzzle pieces."

"Ok. I hate to say, because I obviously don't know. We've talked before about Stella and her creep of a boyfriend, Eric. They have a good motive, and would be capable and greedy enough to do it, but we both feel unsure they could get away with it." Nick nodded in agreement. "Then there's ... well, Beth Trammel."

"Beth Trammel?"

"I know, I know. When I first got to town and went to the rental agency for my key, I could overhear this argument she was having on the phone." Perri related the incident to Nick.

"So, when Beth shouted, 'What do they want?' you think she might have meant the Duncans, like she'd been trying to get them to sell their house and they kept refusing?"

"I don't know, but when we were there to pick up Pearl to go to the house, Beth's card was lying on the table right inside the door. And Pearl has admitted she's been approached over selling the house. With Ruby and George gone, Pearl is the new owner."

"As we talked about before, Beth doesn't seem like she'd be able to manage two people, unless she had a gun and/or accomplices." Nick countered. "Is there something new that's changed your mind about that?"

"Nothing concrete, but I do think she could have had help. Remember, the day Stella and I did a round out on the sidewalk?" Nick nodded. "Stella was coming out of Beth's office. Why? Maybe she and Eric are helping Beth."

"I can't see them all working together, but I can't discount it either." Nick thought. "What else?"

"Nothing else. Maybe it's the lack of anything else that keeps me focused on them."

"Alright, where do we start today?" Nick asked.

"I've already started." Perri eagerly scooted up to her open laptop on the coffee table and tapped the space bar. The forest screen saver dissolved to a page on Ancestry. "I found a public family tree with Elizabeth Mason and Arthur Frederick. Their three children are shown here: Nettie, Arthur Jr, and Phillip."

Perri dragged the tree upwards and sideways to reveal the descendants of Nettie Frederick. Here we have two children of Nettie and Luther Anderson, Grace born in 1927 and Gerald born in 1934. Gerald is the one who's house was cleared by the company Stella works for, and she worked on that job. Stella could easily have found something in Gerald Anderson's house that tipped her off to the Seymour drawings."

Nick tilted his head back in realization and said, "Ah, I see. But, do you think she took time while cleaning the place out to notice what she was hauling? I mean, it wouldn't have been a sign saying, 'Read Me. Here Be Treasure.'"

"No, we don't know what it might have been, but Stella is always on the lookout for something that might be worth money. She might have pocketed anything that looked personal or valuable and checked it out later."

"Ok, could be. But if it was that obvious, why didn't Gerald Anderson go looking for the drawings?"

"Maybe he never read it, didn't believe it, or just didn't care."

"Alright. Secondly, would Stella know the Masons had anything to do with her own family? Even Pearl didn't know."

"She may not have had to know. Depending on what she found, if it was spelled out for her, all she'd need to know is something valuable might be at her Aunt's house."

"Again, it is a plausible explanation, but we still don't know." Nick nodded at the screen. "Anyone beyond Gerald? You're getting close."

"The descendants would have to come through Grace Anderson, but this branch ends with these two. The tree owner appears to be descended from another line and this is as far as they went with this one. I have plenty of those stopping points in my own tree. There can be thousands of lines down from a common ancestor. Most genealogists put in their ancestor's siblings, and maybe a few of their children, but don't necessarily go further than that because there's plenty of work to do on their own line. That's probably what happened here."

Perri took a breath and plowed on with her explanation. "I searched Find-a-Grave for a Grace Anderson buried in Gallatin County, got nothing, Tried Saline County and got a hit on a Grace Anderson O'Malley. Fortunately, the person who created her memorial included her maiden name. I searched the obituary archives and came up with an obit that verified this Grace was the daughter of Nettie Frederick and Luther Anderson. She was survived by one son, Liam O'Malley a grandson named Ryan O'Malley and a great-granddaughter named Brenda. I haven't heard mention of the name O'Malley at all. Doesn't mean there isn't someone named that responsible, but it seems unlikely from the description in the obit. They run a family business, a bar and grill in Harrisburg. Looks like a dead end.

"What now?"

"Let's go see if Reuben's home. I've meant to talk with him about his work anyway. Who knows, he crawls all over southern Illinois, maybe he's come across information that would be helpful. It won't hurt to ask."

The echo of Nick's knuckles rapping on Reuben's door resounded through the stairwell. "You think he's home? He might be out working."

Perri took a quick look out the hallway window that overlooked the parking lot. Reuben swung the door open the second the words, "His car is here," left Perri's mouth.

He looked a little disheveled, his hair sticking out over one ear, his clothes rumpled, and his gaze slightly unfocused through repeated blinking.

"Hi, Reuben, hope we aren't interrupting you." Nick said, wishing he hadn't knocked. In the absence of a reply, he took a couple steps backward, "Sorry, we can check back with you later…"

Reuben beckoned them into the apartment. "No, no, you didn't interrupt me." He moved out of the door frame to make room for them and ran both hands through his hair, trying to tame it. "What must I look like? Seriously, I'm glad you knocked."

Perri and Nick stepped into the apartment, the exact floorplan as Perri's but in reverse. "Have a seat, please." Reuben gestured vaguely around the living room and sat down in a recliner just like the one in Perri's living room. "Good lord, is that what time it is? I was up most of the night trying to finish putting together my photos in some semblance of logical order to see if I need to go out for more. Fell asleep in my clothes I'm afraid, as I'm sure you can tell." He gave a wry laugh as he surveyed his wrinkled slacks. "What can I help you with?"

"I wanted to ask you about a couple of different things. I was hoping you might have come across some information during your own research." Reuben nodded to encourage her to continue. "When we first met, didn't you tell me you did some title searches, or deed work, something like that?"

"Yes, I did, I mean I do that, although it isn't my favorite occupation."

"And you mentioned that you'd done some while you were here?"

"That's right." Reuben stood, "Don't mean to be rude, I just want to get something to drink. Can I get you something?"

"No, no thanks. We just had breakfast a little while ago." Nick answered.

"Please, go ahead with what you wanted to say, I'll be able to hear you." Reuben went into the kitchen and reappeared in the pass-through.

"I don't know if this is confidential information or not, but I was wondering about the deed and title work you had done while you were here." Perri paused to gather her thoughts. "I'm trying to find out about a couple of different properties for my own research and thought it might be helpful if you knew anything about them."

"Of course, right. Um, let me think." Reuben returned to the living room with a glass of tomato juice with a sprinkling of pepper over the top. He took a long sip and sat back down. The pulpy juice left a smear down the inside of the glass surrounded by a line of pepper. "I can't think of any reason I can't share some of the generic information."

"You had mentioned that one of the reasons you didn't particularly like doing that type of work was that it often involved land acquisition. Can I ask if the brick house on the river in Old Shawneetown was one of the searches you were hired to do?"

"It was, yes. I won't forget that one so easily because it had such a long deed history."

"The McCades, up until the Duncans lived there, right?" Perri asked.

"Yes, that's right. The couple that were killed, that Carmen and I found. I was surprised to find out who they were."

"Had you been hired to do the title search before or after they were killed?" Nick asked.

Reuben didn't wait to consider before answering. "Definitely before. That's why I was so floored when I heard their identities."

"Do you know if they were going to sell their house, or maybe get a second mortgage or equity loan that would require a title search?"

"I wasn't told the reason. However, I was told to pay particular attention to any liens or unpaid taxes on the property, no matter how small. I thought that odd, because most of the time, that's what a search is done for anyway, to spot money owed by the current owners before it's sold or a new loan taken on it."

"Can I ask who ordered the search?"

Reuben shrugged, "Sure. Beth Trammel ordered it. I had finished and submitted it to her before that Saturday when we found the bodies, so I haven't talked to her since."

"You haven't been asked to do any other searches since then?"

"No. That was the last one."

"Were the other searches from Beth for property in Old Shawneetown, or elsewhere?"

"That was the only one from Old Town. The others were mainly in Eldorado and Harrisburg, one here and there, but they were all for definite property sales."

Nick and Perri stared at each other, each willing the other one to come up with another question. She knew she'd have more questions later, but right now, Perri's thoughts were swirling around in her head like a cyclone with all the pieces of information trying to come together.

"Sorry, that's really all I know about it. I got a list of requests from Beth at one time and that was just one of them. It didn't stand out as something I would question."

"Don't apologize, your information is very interesting."

Perri looked to Nick, who spoke. "There's a lot of strange stuff going on around that house."

"Strange stuff, like what?" Reuben asked.

Perri answered rapidly, "Oh, just things I'm trying to sort out for, you know, the history of the house. I, uh, discovered that it was approved for the National Register years ago, but no one seemed to know. We're just trying to get our information straight and hopefully get the house restored."

"That's great. But, you say no one knew. Didn't the person who submitted the application keep abreast of it?"

"I checked into that. A woman from the local historical society submitted it, but she passed away while it was in process, and it was forgotten. If a notification was sent to the Duncans, they either didn't get it or didn't understand what it was and tossed it out."

Reuben nodded in understanding. "They probably thought it was an advertisement for new windows or something. Well, I'm glad I could help, even if only a small amount. Keep me posted about it, if you can. I do have a photo of the house that I plan to use, and I'll note that it is on the Register in the caption."

Perri and Nick rose from the couch in unison. As they walked toward the door, Nick said, "We'll keep in touch. I'm sorry we barged in on you this morning after a long night of work."

"Oh, no, I'm glad you did. I should have been up already."

"That reminds me," Perri said, "did you get the photos you need of the salt works or is that off the table after Saturday morning?"

Reuben grimaced. "I have some approach shots to the well, but I'm not going to use them since the bodies were in the well at the time. No one would know, they aren't visible, but I know, and the tree branch is visible, so anyone who knew the details would figure it out. I may go back and take photos before I leave. It's a unique relic of the past and I really don't want to leave it out." He sighed, "I hate to admit this, but I also dread going back out there before the murderer is caught. Seems like tempting fate."

Back in Perri's apartment, she scribbled down the title search info. "That's weird, that's just really weird, isn't it?"

"It seems odd, yes." Nick agreed. "Pearl never said anything about doing a search, right?"

"No, she did say she'd been approached about selling it after Ruby's death, but nothing else."

"Think someone had a plan to get the Duncans to sell and they wanted as much time-consuming paperwork to be finished and ready to go as soon as they consented? Or maybe the title search was ordered without the Duncan's knowledge, hoping to find something to leverage with to get them to sell."

"It's possible. The owners don't have to sign for, or even know about a search like that as long as someone pays for it." Perri fidgeted. "I can't sit here. Let's go."

"Where to?" Nick pulled his jacket from the hanger in the closet and handed Perri's to her.

Half an hour later, Perri restlessly waited at the desk in the tiny Shawneetown library. A man materialized from around a corner and asked, "What can I help you with?"

"I am trying to find some information." Perri related her attempt at the interlibrary loan of the missing microfilm. "I was told that it went missing after being loaned to this library. I wonder if you can tell me who ordered the film." She could see the objection forming on the man's lips, but cut him off. "Warren?" Perri asked, glancing at the name plate on the desk behind the counter. He nodded. "I understand that generally this information isn't just handed out to anyone who asks. But, I can't help thinking that, since I'm doing this research for a family concerned with what's on that microfilm, that perhaps we may be able to figure out who took the film if we know who ordered it. Maybe get it back." Warren wavered on his decision on whether to reveal the information or not. Perri chipped away at his resolve. "I'd love to help you find it and be able to return it to Springfield. I know they'd be grateful not to have to replace it. They mentioned how much backlog their microfilm lab has."

Warren bent forward and quietly said, "Alright. Let me check." He glanced around the empty desk area before sliding a one-inch binder from a lap drawer. Perri had to suppress a giggle at Warren's clandestine movements which were more likely to draw attention than if he acted normally. "Let's see." It didn't take long to locate it. "Here it is." Warren lowered his voice to what was likely his perception as an acceptable level for communicating sensitive data. "It was ordered by a Ruby Duncan on September 26. It arrived here on September 30 and she was notified on that day."

Nick stared at Warren in astonishment. Perri jolted at the name and was momentarily dumbstruck. She found her voice, and asked, "Did…did she come in to view it?"

Warren consulted his binder again. "It appears she was here on Saturday, October 1…"

Perri drew breath to ask another question, but Warren continued, "…and again on October 3. We keep the film here for a proscribed amount of time if the patron doesn't finish with it on the first viewing. It appears she came back a couple of days later. After that, the film went missing. And I do mean just the film. The box was replaced in the returns but the film wasn't in it. It took us longer to realize it because of that." Warren's tone of admonishment disappeared instantly as realization swept in. "Oh, my." His face darkened. "Was she...?"

Perri nodded solemnly and quietly said, "Warren, I know this was a few weeks ago, and it wouldn't have seemed important at the time. Were you here either of those days? Do you remember her coming in?"

"I was here, and I'm sure I waited on her." He indicated the log book. "This is my writing."

"Do you remember if there was someone with her or if she was alone?"

"I have no idea. I wish I did. But even if someone was with her, they may not have come to the desk with her." Warren motioned to a small partitioned area tucked in a corner of the room where the lone viewer was located. "I don't make a habit of looking in on people unless they need help." A pained look flickered over his face, obviously struggling with decorum and wanting to find the film. "Do you think you might be able to find it, or at least who took it?"

"I will certainly try, and if I do, I'll personally call and let you know. Warren, thank you so much for your help." Perri smiled warmly.

"Anytime. You're welcome."

Back in the Jeep, Perri and Nick sat in thoughtful silence for a couple of minutes. Perri broke the silence, "I have to say, that's the last name I expected him to give us."

"Me too. Ruby found out something and then someone else found out she knew. The film wasn't just misplaced, since the box was returned empty."

"She had the journal in the kitchen bookcase, so she obviously had been reading it. She may have been through them all. If I remember, it covered June 1836 through March 1837. That's when Francis killed Alexander."

Nick speculated, "Ruby found the journals and read them. She probably had been through Gold Hill numerous times, having lived there all her life, so she would have known who was buried there and when they died. Easy enough to go check. She put two and two together and did what we did. Pearl said they had a computer and the internet. She would have had ample time to browse and search for information. She ordered the microfilm and went to view it when it came in."

"She must have shared her find with someone, someone who either wasn't happy with the information and didn't want anyone else to find out. Unless the film turns up at the house, it seems likely this other person went to the library with her to see the film. I didn't know her, but I can't see Ruby taking the film. Why would she? If she'd wanted a copy of it, it's simple enough to print it out without stealing the film. Besides, I doubt she had a microfilm viewer at home. But a person who planned on using the information for their own purposes and didn't want it to become common knowledge did have a reason for stealing it."

"You mean like if they wanted to kill someone and stick them in the well?"

"That too. It still points to someone who is tied to the Mason family, doesn't it?"

"It would appear to. I need to call Reuben. We might be able to find out."

"What? Why are you calling Reuben?"

"Hang on." Perri pulled her phone from its pocket inside her purse and held it, looking at the contact list.

Nick asked, a barely-there strain in his voice, "You have Reuben's number in your phone?"

"No, I don't." She threw a slightly exasperated look at Nick and said, "Oh, come on, really? I'm thinking if there's another way to get the number besides calling the rental agency. I don't want to have to ask Beth for it and I definitely don't want to drive all the way back to the apartment to talk to Reuben. He may not even be there."

Perri grudgingly accepted the inevitable. "There's nothing for it, I guess." Using her shoulder to press the phone to her ear while it rang, she raked through her purse and produced a pen, turning her file folder over ready to take down the number if she could get it. Drumming her fingers on the console while waiting, she fluttered her hand to signify someone had answered.

With some relief, Perri said, "Hi, Tim, this is Perri Seamore, how are you today? ... Good. What I'm calling about is, I'm wondering if I could get a phone number from you. I know this is an imposition, but I need to call the tenant across the hall from me, Reuben Webb ... Yes, I just want to ask him something and I'm not in town. Is there any possible way I could get his number from you? ...No, there's no problem, it's just about a shared interest." Perri listened, cringed, and said, "Uh-huh, I remember telling you about that when Stella and I had our little go-round. How could I forget, right?" Perri turned toward Nick and made a hopeful face, crossing her fingers. "Yes, I'm ready." She jotted down a number then wrote Reuben's name above it.

"I appreciate it, Tim, it saves us a trip. Oh hey, one other thing. I'm trying to track down as much background info as I can for this history article. While interviewing Pearl about the family history, she mentioned that some of the effects of a descendant of the Masons, a Gerald Anderson, went through the auction barn a few weeks ago." Another pause, then, "Right, that's right. I was wondering if there were any photo albums or family type documents that might have been part of what was up for auction. Do you recall?" Perri tapped the end of the pen on the folder and mm-hmm'd a few times. "Well, thanks anyway, I appreciate it...you too. Bye."

"You got Reuben's number, but what did he say about the Anderson stuff?" Nick asked.

"He said Stella and Eric brought in a truckload of things like old pole lamps, curtains, wall hangings, macramé pot hangers, card tables, stuff like that. He didn't remember any photo albums, but that doesn't mean there weren't any. He said if I was really interested, it might be best to poke through the stuff on the shelves sometime, see what might be lying around."

"Well, at least all hope is not gone."

Perri dialed the number Tim had given her. "Come on Reuben, please know what I need you to ...Hello. Reuben, this is Perri. Sorry to bother you again. I leave you alone for two weeks and then one day I can't stop bugging you." Perri listened and chuckled. "Got a question for you about some property I'm hoping you might have photographed. It's over in Hardin County, and you said you had been over there, it's in Elizabethtown...right. It's the remains of house that used to belong to the one of the Mason bunch. A local historian said there were some remnants left, including a well. I wondered if you knew it..." Perri looked at Nick, nodded affirmatively. "Great! I know you like to give as much history about the places you photograph as possible, so I was hoping you knew who that property belongs to know, or hopefully you might have done a deed history?"

Perri bit her thumbnail in anticipation, willing Reuben to have the information. He told her he hadn't done a deed search on it. Since there was so little left to see, he had planned to note it as the one-time home of Alexander Mason, a notorious Ohio River brigand, and let it go at that. He had a plethora of history on many other locations and wanted to allocate the space to those. Perri thanked him and hung up.

"Were you hoping to find the property is still owned by a descendant?" Nick asked her.

"Yeah, or at least see the progression of ownership. It might have simplified it."

"That's true, do you think if we…"

Perri frowned. Nick's words faded out of her hearing and she didn't respond to him. Her eyes closed, she encouraged the faint tickle, the feathery remembrance of a comment not previously considered, that was trying to surface. Something was said that she might have asked about except there was another discussion, something else was being talked about, and it was forgotten. She opened her eyes but held up one hand to keep the silence. She focused on the brick wall of the building the library shared with City Hall and willed the thought to form. A slow nod became more vehement. She said, "Damn it! Why did I lose track of this?"

"What? What did you lose track of?" Nick's tone had a smidgen of annoyance which brought her back to the present.

"Yes, I'm sorry. I had to coax that from the catacombs of my mind. Now I need to call Tabby Ford. When we were there, we were talking about Alexander being murdered in his house and I asked her if it was the same house she is living in now. She said no, that the house he lived in is now gone."

"Right, I remember that." Nick asked, still seeming a little piqued.

"It was what she said right *after* that, but because we went on talking about the location of the house when she described the ruins and the well, I didn't see the significance at the time and forgot it." Nick drew in a breath, but she forestalled him, "I know, I'm getting there. Tabby said that Alexander's widow, Celie Ann, lived in the house for several more years before she remarried and moved to Gallatin County. That's when I wish I'd asked her if she knew *who* Celie Ann married! My guess is that if Tabby found out Alexander's widow remarried and knows where she moved, surely she has some information about who she married."

Nick understood why Perri was excited about it. "And if you can find that out, you might be able to trace a living descendant from her, not Alexander."

"Right! And, even more importantly, she said they moved to Gallatin County, not within Hardin County, where the courthouse burned. There may be records here that I didn't know to look for. I'm calling her now, and I do have her number in my phone." She smiled at Nick, "I'm sorry I was vague, didn't mean to leave you out of the thought process, but I was struggling with it myself."

"I get it. Don't worry about it. Go ahead and call, I want to find out." Nick prodded her.

Right around five minutes later, Perri ended the call. Tabby still had her notes out from their visit with her on Wednesday, so it had only taken her a minute to find the information. Perri shook her head. "You aren't gonna believe this. In Gallatin County, on April 27, 1842, Celia Ann Mason married Abrahm Stegall."

Nick blurted out, "Holy crap. She married one of Alexander's men, maybe his right-hand man."

"And possibly the man who sought revenge and killed Arminda McCade. Francis killed Celie's husband. Celie's new husband killed Francis's wife, maybe at his bride's urging. Eye for an eye, and they didn't waste much time after Abrahm got out of prison."

"I feel like I ask this a lot, but, what now?" Nick put the Jeep in reverse and sat, foot on the brake, ready to pull out.

"We just happen to be exactly two city blocks away from the Gallatin County Clerk's office. Let's go get as many marriage and birth certificates as they'll let us have."

"Let us have?" Nick asked as he backed the Jeep out onto Lincoln Boulevard, Perri pointing northward up the street.

"Has to be longer ago than seventy years unless you're a family member."

"I see."

Moments later they entered the warm, honey-colored stone building. Twenty minutes later they were back in the Jeep with copies of two different indices for births early enough that no individual certificates were made, and two birth certificates. They drove a few more blocks and went into a bar that served food. They snagged a table by the front windows so they could see in the gloom of the interior and be away from the raucous fun being had by a group of road construction workers on their lunch break.

"What do you want, Perri?" Nick asked as a waitress approached.

"Anything, just anything. If you'll order I'll sort these out." Perri quickly replied.

Nick ordered two tenderloin sandwiches with fries and asked, "Ok, what do we have?"

Perri's pen was already scratching across a pad of paper and her laptop was booting up. Nick pointed to it, asking, "You going to be able to use that in here?"

"There's a *Free Wifi* sign on the door, so I hope so." She wiggled in her seat and sat up straight. Using her finger to keep track of the line for the birth they were interested in, she said, "First, we have Josiah Stegall, born 1843 in Equality, parents Celie Ann and Abrahm. It gives Celie's County of birth as Henderson County, Kentucky and Abrahm as Webster County, Kentucky. That makes me wonder. Henderson and Webster counties adjoin. I wonder if the Hartsaws knew the Stegalls."

"Next down the line is Malcolm Stegall, born 1875 in Equality, Gallatin. His parents were Josiah Stegall and Rose Hanford. I'll leave out the county of birth unless it's different from Gallatin." Perri turned that sheet over and read the first birth certificate. "This one is for Malcom's son, Burton Stegall, born 1898. His mother was…" she bent close to the document copy. "The pen blobbed and was smeared so it's hard to read, but it looks like Victoria Kirke."

"Uhh, the suspense is awful. We don't have any recognizable names yet." Nick's leg was bouncing a mile a minute and jiggling the table. Perri put her hand softly on top of his leg. He stopped.

"Last one. Burton Stegall and Eunice Parmenter had a daughter…here's the break in the name…Allys Stegall. She's going to be the one to find. We need to know who she married, because that's where the name takes a turn."

Their food arrived. Nick waited for Perri before starting to eat, but she urged him on, "Go ahead, don't wait for me. I'm going to have a quick look." Nick bit into the tenderloin. Distracted, while Ancestry loaded, Perri took a big bite of hers too.

Too late, Nick said, "It's hot, right out of the fryer."

Perri gulped down some of her iced tea and gingerly poked at the spot smack in the center of her lower lip that she knew was going to blister.

"You're pulling up Ancestry, can't you use that Statewide Illinois thing to look up the marriage? That looked like it was really easy before."

"I wish, but only marriages up to 1916 are loaded in that database, so Allys's won't be there.

Defining her search to the 'Birth, Marriage, & Death' category, she searched for Allys Stegall with as many particulars as she could. "Damn. Nothing."

"That's a bummer, how will you find it?"

"Give me a minute. These things are often spelled differently or transcribed erroneously so the search doesn't find it without a little creative spelling. For some reason if you type in Smith and it was transcribed as Smyth, I'll get 12,842 results for names that are nothing like Smith, but no Smyth. Then, when I put it in exactly, lo and behold, there's a Smyth. It's like a guardian demon that defies you at every turn. Even with Soundex and sound alikes being included, and telling it to match broadly, sometimes it refuses until you hit it on the head. And then at other times, it works right away."

Perri took another, more tenuous bite after blowing on the sandwich. "Sorry for talking with food in my mouth, but, that's me. We have a list of names: Alice, Alyce, Allyce, and here's an Allyse Stegall." She shook her head. "That 'e' on the end totally threw it off for some reason."

Nick couldn't make out the information on the screen because of the angle with the glare from the window, but he watched Perri's face. Her expression of exuberance faded to confusion, then to dismay, and finally crumbled to consternation.

She choked on the bit of tenderloin she was still chewing on and had to cough and take several sips of tea.

"What now? What is it? *Who* is it?" Nick was just ready to flip the laptop toward him when Perri turned it around and pointed.

"Look! Oh my gosh, I've been so wrong."

## Chapter 34

October 21, 2016

Nick floored the Jeep along highway 13 toward Harrisburg. Perri tossed her phone into the cup holder in agitation and gripped the armrest like she was plunging on a roller coaster, her breath shallow and rapid. "She didn't answer. I can't believe it, but it has to be. Now this all makes more sense. I don't know how all the pieces interlock together, but we've got the overall picture. He was born in 1957, so I'm betting all on Michael Farris being Tim Farris's father. I don't know exactly how old Tim is, but he's in his late twenties, and that's the right age."

Nick had been steadily shaking his head since they dashed out of the tavern after tossing in the neighborhood of thirty dollars on the table to cover their lunch, and Perri racing out the door with her laptop still open and papers crushed between her chest and the laptop.

Her voice was inching up in the register as she talked. "It's my fault. If something happens to Pearl it's my fault. Oh God." The tears broke over her lower lids in a steady drip.

"Hang on, don't get too worked up yet. There may be nothing going on. It hasn't been all that long since you called." Nick didn't sound as convinced as he wanted Perri to believe he was.

"Why didn't she answer then?" Perri's voice was a near squeal as the fear took over. "Nick, I basically told him what we were doing. And to think I was relieved that Beth didn't answer the phone, that I was glad it was Tim, and I spilled it all out. I'm an idiot."

"You aren't. Beth looked really good for being involved in this and Tim didn't. Stella and Eric looked suspicious and they actually *are* guilty of a couple of crimes. Any number of unknown individuals from the internet were likely too. So why would you suspect him? And think about it, evidently Ruby trusted him too, because she had someone with her at the library, someone she was confiding in, and I'll bet it was Tim. She knew him from the auction barn, remember?"

"Yes, but why shouldn't I have caught on to him? Aren't you supposed to suspect everyone until you know who you can eliminate?" Perri sucked in a blubbery gulp of air. She could feel her nose turning red and it started to run. She dug a tissue out of her purse.

"*You* aren't supposed to, the police are. Where the hell have they been with this anyway? Have you heard a single thing other than 'ongoing investigation' since this murder happened, since you've been in town? No. Ok, so you aren't a trained detective, and ok, maybe we shouldn't have been poking around, but no one else was. And to be honest, you had a totally different perspective than they did going into this. Cops aren't genealogists and without good reason to start that line of questioning, why would they?"

Perri clutched at Nick's outstretched right hand. "Thanks. I know, I know, but I still feel terrible. Why is it farther to Harrisburg now that it's ever been?"

The Jeep bounced as they crossed the Middle Fork of the Saline. "We're almost there. Oh please…turn left here, on Poplar, don't take 13 around, this is shorter."

Nick hit the brakes, both of them leaning into the dashboard from the momentum, the tires whining as he took the turn a little too fast.

"Turn left at this light, and keep going until you get to the next light, then turn right."

Nick went as fast as he could, keeping an eye out for police and weaving in and out of traffic. He turned right on Sloan. "We're almost there." Perri directed him the remaining few blocks. "Turn left on Land. There, right there." Perri was perched on the edge of her seat having already removed her seat belt, the warning bell dinging away unheeded.

Rocks skipped into the grass as the Jeep skidded to a halt in front of Pearl's house. Perri slid out of her seat and up the walk without closing her door. She didn't slow down at the porch door, but headed straight for the main entrance to the house and knocked sharply on the glass, first with one hand, then with both hands.

Every second seemed like an eternity, hoping Pearl would open the door, surprised to see them. There was no answer.

Nick leaned around Perri and was pounding on the glass when Perri said, "Let's just go on in if we can, I'd rather explain later than be too late." Nick stepped back, Perri opened the storm door and grasped the doorknob. She immediately jerked her hand away. "The knob is scorching hot!"

"Perri, I smell smoke."

"Oh god, me too." The frilly curtain was drawn over the window in the door but Perri shielded her eyes from the sunlight streaming through the porch and peered through. "I see flashes of orange, Nick, the house is on fire."

"We can't go through here and neither can Pearl, if she's in there."

"She's in there, I know it." Perri tore past Nick and pounded down the steps. "We have to get her out of there!" As she rounded the corner of the yard, the neighbor came out their front door. Perri shouted, "Call 911, the house is on fire and Pearl's inside!"

The neighbor stopped, looking at Perri with a shocked expression. Nick repeated the message in simple terms, "911!! Now! Fire!!" The man turned and ran back into his house.

"I hope he's going in to call, not hide," Perri called over her shoulder as she ran between the houses. "Let's go through the back door. Here, this door goes into a small porch off the kitchen."

The main floor of the house was elevated, including the back door, which was reached by four large steps up from the porch. The flimsy door was secured only with a hook-and-eye latch that gave way easily when Nick jerked it open, but they were met with a second, significantly more substantial door leading into the kitchen. The knob was cool, but there was both a knob and dead bolt lock and the door didn't give a fragment of an inch when Nick rammed his shoulder against it. Nick grabbed a flower pot from the floor of the porch but stopped before sending it through the glass.

"What's wrong? We have to hurry?"

Nick threw the pot down, "Dammit! There's a piece of furniture in front of the door, look!"

Perri stepped up to the door and saw a maker's brand on the back of a large piece of furniture, most likely the huge old china hutch she'd seen in the corner of the kitchen.

Nick grabbed her arm, pulling her out of the small porch. "Let's go through another window, but not the living room because the fire is there."

They ran to the back of the house. The bottom sill of the kitchen windows were at least seven or eight feet off the ground. Perri let out a strangled noise. "And Pearl's bedroom window is over an outdoor stairwell, we can't reach it either."

Nick looked around frantically. "We have to get something to climb up on."

"Wait, I have an idea." Perri spun around and fled back to the side of the house and Nick ran after her. There was a small shelter-like area built around the steps leading to the cellar door. Perri bolted into it and down the cellar steps.

"What are you doing?"

She explained to Nick, "Pearl's house was built at about the same time as my great grandmother's house in Eldorado. The floor plans of the original parts of the houses are almost identical. As long it hasn't been remodeled out of existence, there should be a trap door from the cellar into the central room of the house." She stopped yanking on the door handle which wasn't budging. "Nick, let's get this door open."

Nick began ramming his shoulder into the door. There was no window. Perri continued, "The cellar only runs down the middle of the house, not out to the walls of the main floor, if they'd used a staircase for cellar access, it would have eaten up valuable floor space in the center of a room. They used trap doors instead. My great grandmother always kept the door covered with a rug." Perri could hear wood splintering and Nick continued pummeling away at the door. "Pearl's living room has carpet but I don't remember carpet in the room that is now her dining room, just a rug under the dining table."

The door gave way and Nick stumbled through the opening, catching himself before he fell down the concrete steps. Perri was right behind him as they ran into the cellar. "There! Oh yes, there is one."

Nick climbed the shallow wooden steps, ducking his head under the supports of the floor above. "I hope this thing isn't locked." Perri's heart sank. She hadn't thought about a lock. Her great grandmother's trap door didn't have a lock, just a huge recessed metal ring to pull up on to lift the door.

Nick crouched on the third step from the top, he couldn't manage the second step because of his height. He braced each foot against the outside wooden runner of the ladder-like stairway, squared his back against the underside of the trap door, and set his hands on his knees. He pushed. Dirt crumbled and fell all around the edges of the square opening. He pushed again, as hard as he could manage.

"It's lifting! It's open, it's open. Keep pushing." Perri wildly looked around her for something to prop the door open with, something to give them leverage. She could hear the roar of the fire now and knew they didn't have long. Where was the fire department? She grabbed the nearest thing she could get hold of, the rotating handle from a hand-crank washing machine. It slid from the bracket with a scrape of rust. Handing it to Nick, she said, "I can't get up there by you, put this in the opening and I'll try to find something else."

Nick clutched the handle, pressed up on the door and shoved it into the opening. "This is working. The hinges of the door are rusty and I think there's a chair or table leg on the door."

Climbing up next to Nick, who now could stand more upright, Perri pushed on the door while Nick pushed the handle upward in a prying motion. The door lifted slowly. Nick was able to step up one step and keep pushing. Finally, they heard a thud and the door flew upward. A heavy dining chair was on its side with the edge of the area rug draped over one of the legs. The door banged loudly on the floor as it flipped completely open.

Acrid gray smoke hung thickly from the ten-foot ceiling to within four feet of the floor. "Perri, you stay there, I'll find Pearl." Nick pulled his shirt over his mouth and nose then half walked, half crawled across the room. He glanced around the kitchen, but Pearl wasn't there.

"The bedroom!" Perri rose up through the opening and pointed. "Hurry Nick! The flames are coming through the doorway into the dining room!!"

Seeing her pointing, Nick scurried past the open trap door toward the bedroom. Perri jumped up through the hole and scrambled after him. Pearl was in her bed, not moving. Nick turned and shouted over the increasing roar, "No! Go back, I'll get her."

Perri didn't retreat. Instead, she crawled on her knees to the blanket chest at the foot of Pearl's bed and flung open the lid. She pitched the top quilt to Nick, "Put that around her."

Nick turned and pulled Pearl to slouchy sitting position, throwing the quilt over her back and head. Taking Pearl's right arm, Nick hoisted her up and across his shoulders. He crouched down as much as he could to center her weight. He stepped forward to leave the room but could no longer spot Perri through the obscuring darkness. He panicked for a moment and shouted, "PERRI! Where are you?" as he angled his body to get Pearl through the bedroom door and into the dining room. He crossed the few feet to the open trap door hoping he didn't have to deposit Pearl through the opening and search for Perri.

Walking nearly doubled over and hefting a bundle wrapped in the second quilt from the blanket chest, she appeared suddenly out of the thickening sooty smoke. The eager flames were now traveling across the upper part of the room, their greediness fed by the thick dry wallpaper and desiccated adhesive paste behind it that covered both walls and ceiling. "Let's go!"

Perri slid through the opening first, pulling her bundle behind her. In her haste, the quilt began to unfold and she lost her grip on it, it fell to the cellar floor with a crunch, but she couldn't worry about it now. Nick called down to her, "I can't get through carrying Pearl, I'm going to have to put her down on the edge and…" he coughed several times, "…and you'll have to help ease her down."

Perri braced one foot against one of the narrow steps and the other against the solid rock of the cellar floor. "Ok, ready!"

Nick set Pearl's limp body down at the edge of the trap door, maneuvering her legs through the opening. Perri grasped her ankles. Nick climbed around Pearl and down through the opening until he was on the second step. He slid his arms under Pearl's armpits and inched her forward. Once her rear had cleared the edge of the opening, even though Perri was hugging and hoisting up on both of her legs to try to take part of the dead weight, Pearl's slack limbs bent and her full weight descended on Nick. His knees buckled and he yelled, "Hang on!"

With Pearl draped across his arms and against his chest, he caught the top step with his right hand and leaned against it to steady himself and transfer some of her weight to the stairway. They could hear sirens now. "We're almost there," Nick called down to Perri.

A huge chunk of plastered ceiling dropped onto the dining table and shattered into a thousand shaggy pieces, raining glowing embers down through the open trap door, some landing on Perri's upturned face, tiny pinpoints of heat across her skin. She shook her head to remove them. The impact had hurled a cloud of plaster dust into the air which immediately ignited and lit up like a swarm of tiny, angry fireflies. Glass popped and shattered, shards tinkling to the floor.

Perri reached up higher and wrapped her arms around Pearls knees then pushed up, trying to share the burden. It helped and Nick was able to release his hold on the stair. The remaining steps were much easier and quicker. "Get out!" Nick pushed Perri toward the cellar stairs.

She grabbed the quilt wrapped bundle along with the broken pieces beneath it and ran up the worn steps, bursting out of the shelter door into the blessedly cool air. Nick moved slower but steadily up the stairs behind her. A fire truck was parked in front of the house, the firehose already unrolled and being connected to a hydrant by the curb two doors down. A firefighter pulled her protective helmet and face shield in place and positioned herself in front of the house, waiting for the flow of water to reach the nozzle.

Another firefighter ran toward Nick who dropped shakily to one knee and tried to settle Pearl on the grass as gently as he could. The fireman reached them just before her head could touch the ground and helped ease her down. Perri knelt beside Pearl, still unconscious. Her skin was clammy and damp. She yelled at the fireman over the engine noises, the surge of water through the hose, the hissing when it hit the fire, and the shouts of the other firemen, "She's diabetic. She might be low. I don't know. She wasn't conscious when we found her." The fireman nodded and pointed toward the safety of the neighboring yard. An ambulance was approaching down the street between the parked cars, siren blaring and lights strobing.

Perri dragged her bundle with her into the neighbor's yard. A woman gestured for them to come to the porch. Over the din made by the growl of the engine, the increasing roar of the flames, and the sizzling sound of water spraying onto hot surfaces, another firefighter hollered at Nick while pointing to the Jeep, "Is that yours?" Nick nodded yes. The fireman jogged over to Nick, "I need it out of the way. Give me the keys." Nick gladly placed his keyring in the man's thickly gloved hand and lurched over to the neighbor's porch fighting against the rising urge to vomit from inhaling the oily smoke.

They both sat, heads resting on the back of the wicker chairs, hungrily breathing the clean, cool air, waiting for their singed throats to ease. Perri had propped the quilt-wrapped object against the side of her chair. The woman ran inside the house as a fireman carrying a paramedic kit hustled to the porch with oxygen. He placed the masks and turned the knob on the O2 tanks to 2L/minute and asked them a few yes or no questions, telling them only to nod or shake their heads in answer. Satisfied they were in no imminent danger, he asked them to stay put and returned to the others fighting the now raging fire. The woman had returned and placed a tray with two glasses of water and a pitcher down on the little table between the chairs. She handed one each to Perri and Nick. Her husband stood just off the porch, keeping an eye on the siding of their own house.

Perri opened her mouth to say thank you but instead, tears rolled down her soot-smeared cheek. She hated when she did that, when she wanted to say something but cried instead. There was nothing for it but to wait out the emotion. Nick reached across and grabbed her hand, squeezing it. He didn't say anything. He didn't have to.

Half an hour later, the fire was coming under control. The front half of the home had collapsed inward, burned and blackened. The flames were nearly gone, but the sickening greasy smoke still rose, staining the sky with a chimney of smelly black and gray smoke, marking the site of the fire like a pushpin in a map. The very rear of the house was still standing, but extensive smoke and water damage was visible through the gaping hole where the dining room had crumbled away. The once-white cabinets were now blackened and covered with large deflated bubbles where the enamel paint had erupted from the heat. A couple more vehicles had arrived. Both a small red pickup with a Fire Department Inspector logo on the door and a dark gray sedan were parked blocking the street in front of the Gentry house. A man in a suit stood in the yard talking with the Fire Inspector.

Pearl was tucked under blankets and strapped securely to a gurney. As the two medics worked their way across the lawn toward the waiting ambulance, Pearl waved her hand over her head and tried to look back to the porch where Perri and Nick sat, oxygen now off and sipping the last of their water.

One of the medics jogged over to the porch. "She's insistent on talking to you two before she goes, if you feel able."

"Of course, sure, we'll talk to her," Perri said. She and Nick crossed the yards to where the gurney had stopped at the curbside. Pearl clutched at their hands.

"You two. What would I have done without you two? I'd be dead." She swallowed hard and struggled not to cry. "I want to thank you, so much."

Nick laid a hand on her forearm and said, "We are just thankful we could get to you."

Perri added, "Go to the hospital and get checked out. Get some rest. We'll come see you tomorrow."

"I just can't imagine how it started. I don't even remember. That last thing I remember was that realtor came by and we were talking…"

Perri threw an incredulous look at Nick. She hadn't forgotten about Tim Farris, but he certainly hadn't been uppermost in her mind for the last half hour. She turned back to Pearl. "The realtor was there right before the fire? Was it the same one that always wanted to run that metal detect machine on the property?"

Pearl nodded, wondering how Perri could know that.

"Why did…" Before Perri could get the question out of her mouth, a car pulled up into the driveway of the neighbor's house. The passenger door swung open before the car was in gear. A stooped old man with iron gray hair clambered out and, using two canes, hobbled around the front of the car as fast as he could manage. He called out, "Pearl! Pearl Gentry." The man continued his jerky progress across the yard, heading for the gurney. "Wait. Don't go yet." The driver, a man who looked to be in his early sixties, exited the car and stood watching, his arm leaning on the top of the driver's side door, a slightly bittersweet smile on his face.

Perri's mouth dropped open just a little bit. Nick looked from Pearl, to Perri, to the old man trying to figure out what was happening.

Pearl turned her head and squinted. It took her a few moments, but with a look of utter disbelief, she said, "Stanley?"

## Chapter 35

October 21, 2016

    Stanley Tollander stumped along the sidewalk at a pretty good clip for someone using two canes. He stopped, puffing, at the edge of the gurney. "You ok?" Not being accustomed to sympathetic encounters, he spat the words out like an accusation.

    "Well, I'll be fine, yes, Stanley. Why…how?"

    Stanley turned toward the remains of the house. "Heavens to Betsy, what a mess." He crinkled his nose at the acrid smell of burnt insulation. "I heard the call on my scanner and knew it was your house. Darren here," he indicated his son, still standing by the car, "was at the house and I had him bring me over."

    Pearl focused her astonished gaze to the man standing by the car, who waved at her and shook his head with a smile.

    Stanley brandished one of his canes toward the charred house and said, "You won't be stayin' there again." He pursed his lips and shook his head at her to affirm the truth of his statement.

    "No, I don't suppose I will." Pearl cast a quick glance at Perri as if to ask, 'What is going on?' Perri barely shrugged, but smiled knowingly, her eyes bright. "You have a scanner, Stanley?"

    "Sure do, well, it's not a scanner but I listen to the police band over the computer Darren got for me. I like to know what's going on, and this here's why." His cane arced in a semicircle, nearly colliding with Nick's head. "I want you to know you can stay at my house once you get cut loose from the hospital." Pearl began shaking her head and opened her mouth to speak, but Stanley waggled his head in determination. "Don't refuse and don't complain. I've got plenty of room and there's no use in it going to waste when there's somebody in need of it."

    Pearl gaped at Stanley, completely blindsided by his offer.

    "Besides, I wouldn't mind having someone to jaw around with about the old days." He nodded toward Perri. "This young lady has gotten me to thinkin' about all the good old times and I find that, before I move on, I'd like to talk to somebody else who was there." Stanley cleared his throat in an attempt to conceal his discomfort at voicing such a thing.

"Oh my, Stanley, that's so generous of you. I would so hate to put you to any trouble. My goodness, two old fogies who need help getting around half the time." She laughed. "I guess I could go to the house in Old Town, that's mine now, and not put you out."

Perri interjected, "Pearl, that may not…be a good idea right now. Until all this is settled."

"Why not?"

Other than the fact that Timothy hadn't been captured yet and, Pearl wasn't in any shape to stay on her own just yet, and the chance for companionship while she recovered, Perri didn't have a compelling reason other than wanting to see Pearl and Stanley make up after more than fifty years of being on the outs. It was a grand gesture for Stanley to extend this invitation out of nowhere and Perri realized what that meant. The likelihood of Tim avoiding arrest longer than Pearl would be in the hospital anyway seemed slim since he didn't yet know they were aware of his involvement. Limiting the information, she said to Pearl, "I'm ninety-nine percent sure this fire was set, you've got a walloping big goose egg on your head, and they haven't captured Ruby and George's murderer yet. You probably shouldn't stay in that house, or anywhere, alone until this is cleared up." All that was true.

"That being the case, I don't want to endanger Stanley either."

Stanley loudly objected by hooting, "Horsecrap!" which startled everyone. "You've got to stay somewhere, and unless you plan on staying in the hospital or the police station, you gotta stay with someone, don'tcha? We'll be fine. I got my trusty old Winchester and it stays cleaned and ready. I dare 'em come in my house. I don't have to be able to sprint a mile to shoot somebody. I'll do it, too."

Darren Tollander had strolled over to the clump of people gathered around Pearl's gurney. "Mrs. Gentry, don't worry about imposing or causing a problem. I live on the same block and can be there in a flash if either of you needs something, and I check on Dad every day. It would really do him a lot of good to have the company, if you are up to it." He meaningfully nodded at her from his position behind his father.

Pearl stared at Stanley, her resolve to refuse his hospitality ebbing away with the encouragement. "Well, then. Ok. I guess I will if that's alright."

The medics grabbed their opportunity to load the gurney into the back of the waiting ambulance. Nick and Perri stood on the sidewalk until the ambulance pulled away, threading its way between the cars parked in the street, lights flashing but no siren.

As soon as it reached the end of the block, Perri took off across the yard. Nick followed her, "Where are you going?"

As she got closer to the house, a firefighter threw both arms out wide to block her approach. "Don't get any closer. It isn't safe."

Perri pointed to the Fire Inspector and the suited man. "I'd like to talk to them for a minute. Is that possible? It's about the fire."

"Hang on a minute." The fireman's booted feet created squishing noises as he clomped over the sodden ground, now being churned into mud with grass in it. The heated air from the fire had singed or blown the remaining leaves off the silver maple on the side nearest the house. It looked odd with yellow leaves filling the street side and bare branches on the other. Water was dripping from every angle of the disintegrating house and a steady rivulet of brackish water ran down the front walk to the street, flowing through the gutter toward the corner.

After a brief conversation, the suited man walked to where Nick and Perri stood. "I'm Detective Knox. Can I help you?"

"I hope so. I'm hoping that your presence here means you think this fire may have been arson, because I definitely do. I wanted to let you know that Pearl told us, just now, about a realtor who's been pressuring her to sell the Duncan house in Old Shawneetown. He was here immediately before the fire started, and I believe I know why."

The detective was listening intently. "That's a story I want to hear. Do you know who this realtor is?"

## Chapter 36

October 23, 2016, Early morning

"Let's take a breather over there," Perri nodded toward out a rocky outcropping on the edge of a bluff several yards ahead. Sitting cross-legged atop a weather-worn piece of sandstone, she took her camera from around her neck. The chill from the rock immediately crept through her jeans. She pulled a rolled-up camping blanket from her own backpack and spread it out for them to sit on.

Nick deposited his pack next to hers and settled quietly next to her taking in the marvelous view. "Wow! This is incredible. I had no idea this was here, that it looked like this."

"I know. It's a rugged gem in the midst of otherwise mostly flat farmland." Perri beamed at Nick's reaction.

The panorama of Garden of the Gods, boasting its garment of crayon-box colored leaves scintillating in the cold morning air, was breathtaking. The gray-white of rock formations poked through the quilt of the forest and stood starkly against the vibrant color. Perri pointed to a stony figure to their right. "That's Camel Rock."

Nick responded with a smile. "It does look like a camel. You know, a lot of times it's hard to see the image a rock is named for, but this is obvious."

"There are so many things to see here. We haven't gotten to the Devil's Smokestack or Anvil Rock yet." She stood and took a 360-degree photo, then returned to her spot. "This is exactly what I needed, what we both needed."

"You're right about that. This has been a…strange and trying week."

"That's an understatement. I hoped to find out enough information to write an interesting short essay, but I never expected to end up with so much. I feel like I could write a book."

A heron flew sedately by the bluff where they sat, headed for one of the ponds in the park.

"So many events and details that seemed completely unrelated all end up being part of a bigger picture. Like Beth, for instance. We both thought she was shady and suspected her. I couldn't have imagined the reason she was involved was that she was helping Ruby at one point, and then Pearl after that."

Perri pulled a couple of snacks out of the zipped pocket on the backpack, handing one to Nick. "I know. I had no idea the Vincents, who lived behind the Duncans all those years, were her grandparents. So, of course she knew the Duncans, and the Gentrys too, to an extent."

"When George began selling some of the household belongings, Ruby became worried he might have some debt against the house that she didn't know about. Naturally, she asked Beth to help her find out. It was handy for Beth that Reuben did title searches because having him run it meant she could keep it private and not raise questions in the office about whether the Duncans were wanting to sell the house. They had enough trouble with that as it was."

Perri swallowed and said, "And then when Pearl inherited the house, she needed some help with the property details and Beth was the logical one to ask. Seeing Beth's business card on the table in Pearl's house really put me on the wrong path. The day I was in the rental office and Stella was bellowing at Beth, I thought it might mean they were working together or that Beth wanted Stella to help her, but it turned out to be the other way around. Stella wanted Beth to convince Pearl to deed the house over to her now rather than leave it to her in her will. Beth refused and that's why Stella was bolting out of her office like an angry bull."

"Stella and Eric stealing the Duncan's car and breaking into the house on the first day it was released didn't help their case. I'm glad Wanda was able to put a halt on selling the Hoosier cabinet they stole. She said she'd have her brother haul it back to the house when Pearl was ready."

"I'm glad of that too. The fact that Pearl never mentioned Timothy by name didn't help. I think she just didn't want to talk about it, didn't want to invite questions or discussion, she wanted it all to go away so she only referred to him as 'the realtor,' which we assumed to mean Beth. Pearl may have mistaken Tim's aggressive tack for being new in the business and desperately wanting to get a listing." Nick said.

"Preconceived ideas sometimes get in the way of finding out the truth. It was a blind spot when it came to Stella and Eric too. Stella isn't an innocent, that's for sure, but she wasn't as bad as I painted her. She's sullen and vulgar a lot of the time, but I think she has a lot of problems and deals with them with alcohol. That never solves anything. Eric, her boyfriend, only adds to her problems. Pearl isn't pressing charges, but Orchard Parke isn't the only house they've broken into lately, and they'll both have to deal with those consequences."

"Their involvement at the auction barn added to our suspicions. Eric is the one who got Stella the job at the Cleaning Crew, where he worked, and they both pilfered things that they auctioned themselves. The ironic thing is, Stella is the one who found something significant in Gerald Anderson's house, but she had no interest in it at all. She just turned it over to Tim who was the one working on the evening she took the stuff to the auction barn."

"He was the absolute worst person to have gotten hold of the information in those papers, memoirs, or whatever you want to call them." Perri shook her head for at least the tenth time thinking about the consequences of that one action. "Tim had always known he was related to the Stegall's, it was his grandmother's name, so he didn't have to do any digging to find that out. He knew some of them had been involved with less than respectable characters in the past, but he didn't know about the family business from long ago. His daily struggle trying to get a foothold in real estate plus working at the auction barn probably paled in comparison to the prospect of finding a way to make some easy money, most likely a whole lot of easy money."

Nick stuffed the wrapper from his energy bar in his jeans pocket. "What are the chances too, that a woman in the position of Celie Ann Mason, or rather Stegall, living out in still largely unsettled territory, would turn out to be very literate and prolific as far as keeping records?"

Perri agreed. "It's definitely unusual. She was raised in a wealthy family in Red Banks. Her father, Wilbur Hartsaw, owned a bank there and a branch in Dixon. The Masons traveled up and down the Ohio, stopping overnight in the towns along its banks, which is how she met Alexander. When she married him, her father essentially disowned her for marrying a man he suspected of being a criminal and who was the son of an executed criminal. There were no employment opportunities for Alexander through that avenue so he continued in his own family's livelihood."

"Meeting up with Francis McCade just as he came to Illinois was a real stroke of luck for Alexander, wasn't it?" Nick said, leaning back on his backpack, eyes drooping a little.

"It was a windfall for him. Francis didn't start out to be a criminal, but being new and impressionable, and wanting so badly to do well in life after his parents both died, he was susceptible to Alexander's persuasions." Perri nestled back against the side of the backpack next to Nick, gazing up at the cotton ball clouds.

Nick drawled, "All those rumors about valuables buried on the McCade ground were fantasy, but they did have a basis in truth, didn't they?"

"Celie Ann's copious accounts of their business dealings make that clear. For years, Alexander and Francis oversaw the counterfeiting operation in Cave-in-Rock. In 1835, the thieves were routed out but not without leaving behind some of their silver and gold supply, along with stolen jewelry they were melting down to make coins. That was all confiscated but they did get away with their coining equipment, except for the die that was found years ago, and probably the one George found near the ferry landing. They were probably dropped in their haste to get away."

"For years, Francis had circulated counterfeit coins through both the bank at Old Shawneetown and the branch in Dixon that Celie's father started by replacing the genuine coins with counterfeit substitutes. He and Alexander divided up the legal money, doling out smaller shares to Abrahm Stegall for his help. Stegall's family still lived in Dixon and were his contacts there. No one ever figured out that the money was entering the system at the bank or that Francis was involved, did they?"

"No, he probably seemed above reproach and no one even considered him. But, that's the key to why he ended up killing Alexander. When their counterfeiting arrangement came to an end, Francis still had a business and a job, and Alexander was well-off enough and had other sidelines going that he wasn't hurting, but a lot of the men in his gang weren't the gentleman farmer type and reverted to highway robbery and boarding flatboats on the river to take and sell the goods, like flour, fabrics, and especially gunpowder. But, they got a little too exuberant. They ended up robbing Francis's father-in-law. Francis took great offense to it since their agreement was not to steal from family members. When it was violated by a few of the Mason gang, although unknown to Alexander, Francis lost his cool. He met with Alexander, as his diary says, but Alexander decided the time was ripe to craft a new deal. He wanted a share of the Seymour drawings in exchange for his silence.

Nick pointed out, "Celie mentioned that once the Pittsburgh to the Rockies expedition was over in 1820, the year after he obtained the drawings and sold them to Francis, Alexander discovered the value of the drawings. He wanted at least half of them back, but Francis balked at it saying he'd paid Alexander for them and a deal was a deal. He eventually gave him a couple back, but they weren't the more valuable ones. One of those was the one Tabby Ford found in the box of belongings left at her house."

"Right. Francis wouldn't agree to it, seeing himself as the injured party, and that sealed Alexander's fate. Alexander's refusal to back down stoked Francis's anger and he gave away their identities before he could stop himself and he couldn't undo it." Perri explained.

"Francis realized if he allowed Alexander to be taken alive after ratting him out, he'd probably spill the beans on Francis's activities for the past fifteen years or so and he'd be ruined, he'd lose everything, including his family." Nick added.

"He probably didn't have much of a stomach for killing Alexander, but he didn't want to be discovered, so Alexander had to go without delay. The posse would have had no trouble taking Alexander prisoner since he was sound asleep when they arrived, and he had no reason to suspect impending arrest, but Francis had to silence him, and quick."

"Celie Ann never got over the murder, or the way it was done. What kept her from blabbing about Francis then? Why take so much time writing it all down and then never making it public?" Nick asked.

"My guess would be a couple of things. The lesser reason being that with her having become a woman of less than admirable character, and being someone who was most harmed by Alexander's death, her statement would be taken as sour grapes and wanting revenge than the actual truth, especially since Francis was such an upstanding figure. Or so they thought."

"And the other reason?" Nick wondered.

"She wrote that neither their children, Arminda and Nathaniel, nor Francis's children, Jane and Hugo, ever knew about the crimes Francis had committed. Later in life, her children having married McCade family members, she couldn't bring herself to destroy their happiness, either with each other or in society. However, she always resented that her children had to grow up without their father and understandably never forgave Francis for it. When the issues between Francis and Abrahm at the salt works rose to the top, Celie used the opportunity to deprive his children of their mother. She forever kept it to herself, she and Abrahm anyway. Apparently, it got the point across. The rest of the journals remain silent on Abrahm and Celie."

Nick looked away from the misty depths of the woods, "Has Tim admitted to being the one who broke into the post office?"

"He did, yes. He's not exactly a seasoned criminal, he's spilled his guts about everything. He had been in Elizabethtown, just like we were, doing some genealogy based on the documents Stella gave him. He needed cash for the certified documents so he went to the post office because they have an ATM. It sat right next to the display case with the donated items from Tabby. He went back for them one night and took the leather bits and buttons too to cover what he really was after, but I don't think it mattered until now. I don't believe he began as a cruel or murderous person, but the possibility of getting rich quick can overcome a person sometimes."

Her comment raised Nick's hackles. He retorted, "For someone who wasn't cruel or murderous, he managed to transition into a double murderer smoothly and quickly. It was cold and calculating to take the Duncans out to the salt well to kill them just like he'd read about in Celie's account. And he didn't seem to have trouble putting a venomous snake in your car hoping it bit you. He probably wasn't aiming for just slowing you down, you know? And where did he get it anyway?"

"He lives in Equality. The Saline runs beside the south edge of town. Those things are all along a river like that, so it probably wasn't hard to find one. Catching it and transporting it could be a little iffy, but with the internet, it isn't hard to look up a Do-it-Yourself video on anything these days. And I gave him the perfect opportunity when I didn't lock the car the day I was at Stanley's house."

"He had to be following you around."

"I'm sure he was. You wouldn't want to hang on to an angry snake for any longer than necessary, would you?"

"No, but then I wouldn't be trying to put one into someone's car either." Nick raised his eyebrows meaningfully.

"I hope not anyway." Returning to the previous topic, Perri said, "Tim was convinced there were stores of the remaining counterfeiter's gold and silver, as well as hordes of coins, buried somewhere on the property. He'd asked numerous times if he could metal detect, but George always said no. It probably infuriated him because he felt like he and George knew each other well through the auctions and he thought it would influence George to let him check for buried valuables. He'd also been looking up a lot of the same information I did at the research library. Martin made a comment on my first visit there that the books I was asking for had been popular lately, but I didn't think anything of it."

"Tim was the one who walked into the kitchen when Ruby was alone, wanting her to list the house for sale. He was positive the drawings were hidden there and was convinced he could find them if he could get access to the house with no meddling owners around all the time. He's also the one who half-heartedly poked around in Cave-in-Rock on the off-chance there was something there, and who dug up the area near the sassafras tree in Gold Hill. That wasn't as much of a long shot as it sounds, since Celie Ann did state somewhere in that long, rambling account that the plates and the uncirculated coins were buried by a sassafras tree in the family burying ground. They either never were there or they were dug up long ago...or the ground has shifted enough that they aren't in that exact spot anymore. It's on a hill and I've seen graves in old cemeteries slowly migrate downhill, so I imagine a buried cache would too. They may never surface or a private collector somewhere may have them. Hard to say."

Perri squinted against the cool sunshine and smiled over at Nick. "Celie Ann seemed to delight in starting rumors about the immense wealth the McCades were hiding. She probably enjoyed daydreams of the McCades beleaguered by fortune hunters, and that was a good way to do it, because it worked. The Duncans were murdered over it."

"It's awful. She was so careful to document everything, and it became a handbook for Tim that ended with him killing the Duncans in the same place and manner that Arminda was killed. Without Celie Ann's chapters' worth of notes, Tim never would have known about it. Obviously, he wasn't looking for silver and gold in the house when he turned it over. I guess he lost his temper, his mind, or both when he decided to kill them over it. He thought to the end they knew the location of the precious drawings but just refused to tell him. Ruby's investigations didn't help dispel that idea. She told him about the microfilm story one evening at the auction barn. George was busy unloading and Ruby sat talking to Tim. She was excited about what she was discovering and wanted to share it with someone. He was so interested in her story, it was easy to convince her to take him to the library with her to view the film. He pocketed the film and returned the empty box without Ruby noticing."

"The poor Duncans drowned never knowing what Tim was talking about." Nick shook his head in disgust.

"He thought they'd cave in and tell him where they were if he scared them enough. Didn't work since they didn't know."

Nick groaned painfully, "You practicing your punning techniques?"

She grimaced, "Sorry. It was unintentional. Anyway, Tim used the auction van to haul them out to the salt well. That was probably the slickest thing he did, since the forensics units went over both the Duncan's car and van. No one thought a thing about him using the auction's van since he and the other employees all used it regularly to transport things back to the shop. It would also disguise who might have been responsible, even if it was discovered, since so many people drove it and he had every reason to be one of them."

"Celie Ann realized better than most people at the time what those would be worth to the backers of the expedition. It had been scrapped near the end at enormous expense when it went over budget. The artwork done my Samuel Seymour would have gone a way to recouping at least some money. As it was, only a portion of the work he'd done survived the trip. He disappears from the history books after that. The most prized drawing was the one of the Western Engineer, done on the morning before the expedition launched. Until now, there was only one known extant drawing of the boat built exclusively for that trip. It's a very rare find, and quite a valuable one too, both for history and art."

Nick leaned up on one elbow, looking down at Perri. "I never did completely understand what made you decide to save those framed embroideries on the dining room wall while Pearl's house was going up in a blazing inferno?"

Perri explained. "Yeah, that was pure luck on my part. Well, sort of. That evening I went to talk to Pearl and she made tea and talked about her family?" Nick nodded. "She told me there were still some original furnishings in the house from when it was built, and listed the few things she had brought with her from home when she and her husband married and moved to Harrisburg. She mentioned two framed embroideries that had been done by one of the earliest McCades. While you were rescuing Pearl, I was trying to think of what was handy that I could grab to save from the fire. She'd shown me those quilts and the family Bible before, and they were right there in the blanket chest. When I gave one quilt to you and started to wrap the Bible in the other one, I remembered the old embroideries. I could see them from where I was standing. The fire hadn't gotten to them yet, so I just acted on impulse and snatched them off the wall."

She sat back up and gazed over the cliff into the forest below, the mist not yet burned off from the cold temperatures of night. "I was upset when they slipped out of my grasp in the cellar and the frame broke, but that's how the missing drawings came to light. I don't know that I would have thought to look for them divided up behind the needlework pieces. It was a great hiding place because Tim didn't find them. He probably looked right past them. Hidden in plain sight. Eventually someone would have reframed them because they were getting brittle, or maybe even had them conserved and the drawings would have been found, but they're found now. I'm curious to see if it's determined how old the embroidery is. I like to think it was Arminda who did the embroidery and Francis who hid the drawings behind them when he had them framed for her."

Perri's voice shifted to a more positive tone. "The best thing to come out of all this horrible mess is two people who once had a romance, and who have each been alone for years, are getting another chance! I'm really happy for both Pearl and Stanley. Seeing him show up at Pearl's house during the fire was such a surprise, but it's the best thing that could have happened for them both. Pearl seems very happy and Stanley can only be described as tinkled pink."

Contemplating Pearl and Stanley's new affinity for each other, Perri mused, "I wonder if they'll keep living in Stanley's house in Eldorado or end up at Orchard Parke."

Nick replied, "If they don't feel it's too remote for them, I'd love to see them live in it. It's a big help that the state branch of the historic register has offered to locate businesses willing to donate restoration work or at least do it for a huge discount. Along with the insurance money from her ruined house in Harrisburg, they should be able to get the house up to snuff."

All those years of animosity between the two was basically awkwardness from a lost relationship decades ago and not knowing how to approach a reconciliation after both their spouses had passed. You just never know, do you?"

Nick put his arm around Perri's shoulders. "No, we don't always. One reason it's important to say how you feel about someone and stick with them regardless of what other people say." He gazed intently into Perri's green eyes. It made her feel warm all over despite the frosty nip in the air. He kissed her very gently and said, "You about ready to get back to the trail? I'm ready to see those mushroom rocks."

The End

# Acknowledgements

Thank you very much for reading my book. I truly hope you enjoyed it and will consider leaving a review.

I want to acknowledge the sources for much of the historical information represented in this book, as well as further reading for anyone who would like to learn more about the early days of settlement in the Midwest. Southern Illinois and the areas surrounding the course of the Ohio River are rich with local history, plenty to satisfy anyone who appreciates tales of courage, outlaws, adversity, and exploration.

Otto A. Rothert. *The Outlaws of Cave-in-Rock*. Cleveland, Ohio: A.H. Clark Co., 1924.

Major Stephen H. Long, T. Say, and others, Compiled by Edwin James. *Account of an Expedition from Pittsburgh to the Rocky Mountains*. Philadelphia: H.C. Carey and I. Lea, 1823.

*History of Gallatin, Saline, Hamilton, Franklin, and Williamson Counties, Illinois*. Chicago: Goodspeed Publishing, 1887.

*The Shawnee*. Multiple issues. Compiled and published quarterly by the Saline County Genealogical Society.

"National Register of Historic Places." *National Park Service*, US Department of the Interior. www.nps.gov/Nr/

"Illinois Newspaper Project." *University Library*, University of Illinois at Urbana-Champaign. www.library.illinois.edu/inp/

"Gallatin County Illinois Genealogy." *USGenweb*. http://gallatin.illinoisgenweb.org/

## About the Author

My longstanding interest in Genealogy first reared its head when I was around twelve years old. I started asking the oldest family members questions about the past after seeing some old photos, which included my Great-Great-Grandfather's Civil War portrait. I was fascinated. Being an avid history lover, my fascination with the stories our own pasts have to tell us has continued to grow over the years. I've spent the last couple of decades searching for information, documents, headstones, anything I can find to learn more about who my ancestors were and where they came from. There are so many intriguing stories in our family trees; ferreting them out is just part of the fun. Adventure can be close to home.

Read the Author's Interview at Smashwords:
https://www.smashwords.com/interview/CRaleigh
Webpage: www.cynthiaraleigh.com
Goodreads Author Page:
www.goodreads.com/author/show/15251249.Cynthia_Raleigh

Made in the USA
Columbia, SC
11 October 2017